SO-EIK-610

"Should I trust you?"

"You've already trusted me," he said, "You're in my house. I've been safe so far, haven't I?" *Talk about a wolf in sheep's clothing.* Much as his body might scream in protest, though, she was safe with him. Zack would not let his momentary lust scare her away.

She might be the only person who could help his son. He had offered her the job for the child's sake. Only for Robby, he repeated to himself.

Her eyes searched his. "You don't look safe."

"Looks are deceiving, so they say." *And words, too.*

"I ought to run for cover," she said so softly Zack wondered if she meant for him to hear.

He didn't want her to go anywhere, yet he didn't want her to feel trapped, either. He willed her to look at him. When she did, he offered a steady, reassuring gaze, sending a subliminal message. *Stay, Meg. I want you to stay.* He knew, deep inside, that Robby wasn't the only one who needed her. *He* needed her. . . .

CATCH
A DREAM

Mary Jane Meier

AN ONYX BOOK

ONYX
Published by New American Library, a division of
Penguin Putnam Inc., 375 Hudson Street,
New York, New York 10014, U.S.A.
Penguin Books Ltd, 27 Wrights Lane,
London W8 5TZ, England
Penguin Books Australia Ltd, Ringwood,
Victoria, Australia
Penguin Books Canada Ltd, 10 Alcorn Avenue,
Toronto, Ontario, Canada M4V 3B2
Penguin Books (N.Z.) Ltd, 182–190 Wairau Road,
Auckland 10, New Zealand

Penguin Books Ltd, Registered Offices:
Harmondsworth, Middlesex, England

First published by Onyx, an imprint of New American Library,
a division of Penguin Putnam Inc.

First Printing, March 2001
10 9 8 7 6 5 4 3 2 1

Copyright © Mary Jane Meier, 2001
All rights reserved

 REGISTERED TRADEMARK—MARCA REGISTRADA

Printed in the United States of America

Without limiting the rights under copyright reserved above, no part of
this publication may be reproduced, stored in or introduced into a
retrieval system, or transmitted, in any form, or by any means
(electronic, mechanical, photocopying, recording, or otherwise),
without the prior written permission of both the copyright owner and
the above publisher of this book.

PUBLISHER'S NOTE
This is a work of fiction. Names, characters, places, and incidents either
are the product of the author's imagination or are used fictitiously,
and any resemblance to actual persons, living or dead, business
establishments, events, or locales is entirely coincidental.

BOOKS ARE AVAILABLE AT QUANTITY DISCOUNTS WHEN USED TO PROMOTE
PRODUCTS OR SERVICES. FOR INFORMATION PLEASE WRITE TO PREMIUM
MARKETING DIVISION, PENGUIN PUTNAM INC., 375 HUDSON STREET, NEW YORK,
NEW YORK 10014.

If you purchased this book without a cover you should be aware that
this book is stolen property. It was reported as "unsold and
destroyed" to the publisher and neither the author nor the publisher
has received any payment for this "stripped book."

To Steve,
my soul and inspiration.

To the members of Wasatch Mountain
Fiction Writers,
for years of patient help and advice.

And to Seth, Eric and Tess,
for believing in me before I deserved it.

Chapter One

Meg Delaney heaved a loaded backpack out of Edward's BMW trunk and onto his brand new three-hundred-dollar hiking boots. She wanted to dump the pack's contents on his thick insensitive skull. "Okay, *don't* come with me. If you don't care, why should I?"

As she spoke, a rusty green pickup with home-made wooden stock panels rattled into the grassy area that marked Yellowstone's Slough Creek trailhead. At the end of an isolated dirt road, miles from the route traveled by most tourists, Meg and Edward had been alone until the truck arrived. Solitude hadn't helped them communicate. The way things were going, nothing would help.

Through a haze of dust and a film of her own tears, she saw a bearded man raise a hand from the truck steering wheel in greeting. The engine's rumble moved past and cut off somewhere behind her. Abrupt silence accented the bird songs, the faint buzz of insects. Meg glanced toward the trail leading from the wildflower-strewn meadow into a forest of new-green aspen and darker spruce. She shored up her courage to ask the one question that mattered most. "Do you care, Edward?"

"Of course I do," he announced without hesitation. He loomed closer, blocking out sky and mountains.

"Once I close this deal, I'll *buy* you a piece of national park. We'll take a trip later, after the wedding."

" 'Later' will be too late." She searched for understanding in his contact-enhanced blue eyes, but found only an uncompromising glitter. As a last resort, she tried the logic most likely to appeal to him. "We've already bought camping gear and made arrangements for office backup. You wouldn't want all that effort wasted, would you? Let someone else handle PenUltimate for the next few days."

He flicked at a blue dragonfly that had dared to land on his fresh-off-the-shelf Gore-Tex parka. "The German contract is important, Meg."

She tilted her head, studying him from a new angle, not liking what she saw. "And I'm not important, is that it? We've spent four months apart, and a big-money deal still outweighs time alone with me."

Edward shrugged. "Yellowstone was your plan, not mine. I know you promised your dying grandmother you'd come out here and walk holes in your shoes, gape at a waterfall, sniff moose shit. All in her memory. In a weak moment, I said I'd go along. How was I to predict PenUltimate would have millions at stake?"

"The negotiations could wait," Meg pointed out.

"Maybe," he allowed. "But let's be realistic. What the hell difference will it make? The old lady is dead, princess. Put a few flowers on her grave and leave it at that."

Meg straightened her spine, an attempt to offset the hollow feeling in the region of her heart. All the way from their starting point in Salt Lake City, between his marathons on the cellular, she'd tried to explain. Obviously, he hadn't been listening. "A promise is a promise, Edward. Maybe she'll never know the difference, but I have to be honest with myself."

"Is that a dig at *my* character?" He looked down his long, thin nose with an air of wronged nobility. "The way I see it, you're no role model."

She felt as if he'd knocked the breath out of her. Edward had stood by her when her life caved in. He'd offered her a future. Naturally, she'd assumed he believed in her innocence. She'd loved him for that.

Now it seemed he understood nothing about what she'd done, or why. She gasped a deep, painful breath that blasted her lungs like ice water. A protest froze in her throat.

He ran a hand through his blond hair, ruining the blow-dry styling. "Sorry. I didn't mean . . ."

"Yes, you did," Meg managed to choke out.

"For God's sake, don't dramatize." He kicked her backpack into the dew-laden grass while slamming down the trunk of the silver Beamer. "A fax on the offer will be at Old Faithful Lodge within the hour. I advise you to come along and look it over. If *Athena's Promise* does well stateside, your game might be one of the first PenUltimate titles to go overseas. With me pushing things in the right direction, we can up our percentage of foreign profits considerably."

If Edward had a scrap of insight, he'd know she gave not one flying flip for profits, especially now. But he was a man who scarfed financial gain like chocolate cream pie. The fact that she wanted more out of life seemed to escape him.

A truck door shut somewhere behind her, followed by the sound of boots trudging through grass. The bearded stranger was leaving. She and Edward were isolated again in the mountain quiet, in what should have been peace.

Edward opened the driver's side of the BMW and braced an elbow on top of the door frame. "Let's go,

Meg. We can argue some other time." His gaze strayed to his Rolex.

She shook her head. "I'm staying here."

He grimaced. After drumming his fingernails on the roof a couple of times, he said, "Okay, I give. Take your walk on the wild side. I'll pick you up— when? Tomorrow, about dark?" He came toward her, arms extended, apparently expecting a farewell kiss.

All of a sudden, his fifty-bucks-a-bottle aftershave smelled worse than the nearby chemical toilet. Nausea roiled in Meg's stomach as she dodged his hands and lips. "No need to hang around in a Yellowstone hotel for my sake, Edward. Go home and latch onto a fat bank account before it gets away. When I'm ready, I'll find my own ride."

The average rock was more sensitive than Edward, but at least he recognized sarcasm. He shot her an icy glare. "You're provoking me, princess. That's a serious misjudgment."

Loving him had been the most serious misjudgment of all. Pain bubbled inside Meg. Before she could stop herself, angry words boiled out. "At least now I know how I rate with you. I'm an inconvenience. Probably an embarrassment, too. So do us both a favor and cross our wedding off your day planner. While you're at it, cross me off your list of employees. I quit."

His cheeks puffed like he was about to explode, then collapsed with a sharp exhale. "Fine. Just fucking dandy." He flung himself into the leather-upholstered seat and jammed the key into the ignition.

The heat of Meg's anger evaporated. Her heart sank into the dust. He wasn't going to argue. She'd thought he . . . She'd expected him to . . .

Edward lowered the window halfway and narrowed his frigid blue eyes. "You'll regret this." The window ascended again, tinting him gray. The BMW peeled forward, heading for the main road.

Meg already had regrets. As she watched the car's dust tailings grow smaller, the full implications penetrated. Edward would not be back. She told herself she was glad. If he didn't love her, she was better off solo.

Truly she was.

Ransacking her backpack, which had narrowly escaped being flattened by the BMW's departing tires, she drew out a lavender windbreaker. She zipped the jacket against the June morning's chill and plopped cross-legged in the damp grass. After months of isolation from all that was familiar, Meg needed someone to talk to in the worst way. G. T., her much-loved grandmother, had been her closest confidante for most of her life. But G. T. was gone forever. And Edward, it seemed, had no interest in tuning in to Meg's frequency.

They lived happily ever after. What a crock. She had romanticized Edward beyond all recognition, only to discover her erstwhile Prince Charming preferred the company of a fax machine to her own paltry appeal. She'd offered him her soul, only to find he'd rather have an increase in quarterly profits.

So much for fairy tales.

No, she took that back. She designed computer fantasy games for a living. Myth was her trademark. Illusion was her one skill. As G. T. liked to say, "A girl has to keep on dreaming, Meggie." And she would.

Somewhere, sometime, she'd find a man who could accept her for herself, with all her quirks and flaws. Meanwhile, she'd be more wary of imposters, no matter how promising they appeared. By now, she ought to know enough about reality to expect the unexpected. To accept disappointments without too much surprise.

Leaning back on the heels of her hands, she took a deep breath. The earthy scent of humus blended with the sweet perfume of grass and flowers. Above her, two squirrels scrabbled, chasing each other around a thick evergreen trunk. Birds chirped. Insects whirred. Wind shimmered through aspen leaves and sighed in the boughs of giant spruce.

Across a verdant meadow, Slough Creek's silver ribbon made lazy curves on its journey to the Yellowstone River. The very heartbeat of Earth pulsed in Meg's veins. The dew of life seeped into her pores. She closed her eyes and let herself drift. Dream.

A thumping sound at her back startled her. She turned to see the rusty pickup parked less than twenty feet away. The bearded driver hadn't left after all. He sat on the tailgate securing a sleeping bag onto a huge pack. His hiking boots showed signs of high mileage. His blue jeans had twin holes in the knees, and a T-shirt emblazoned with a grizzly bear stretched across his broad chest.

Keen gray eyes surveyed her. "I heard the fond farewell," he said in a gruff bass. "You're better off without the sonuvabitch."

Her cheeks heated with embarrassment as she scrambled to her feet. "No one invited you to eavesdrop."

He shrugged. "Didn't take much of an effort for anyone this side of Bliss Pass."

A weird combination of pride and misplaced loyalty bristled through Meg, causing her to shore up the miserable truth. "Edward would have stayed, but he had to do some international haggling. Business, you know."

"You're defending that asshole? From what I

heard, I thought you hated him." He arched a dark eyebrow, daring her to admit otherwise.

"I guess I . . . No, I don't hate him." She'd imagined herself in love with Edward. That kind of fantasy didn't poof into nonexistence in the time it took for a car to fade into the distance. "I'm disillusioned, but I'll get over it. Eventually." What choice did she have? She reached down to reorder her pack and prepare it for travel.

"You're not going out there by yourself, are you?" the stranger asked, scowling.

"I . . . haven't decided yet."

His question made her realize that *he* would be "out there", too. Physically powerful, as scruffy as a mountain man, he was a scary-looking dude. For all she knew, he could top the FBI's Most Wanted list. She didn't want him to know where she was going, or not going.

His scathing gaze traveled down her body and back up to her eyes. "New boots, new backpack. Have you ever been in the wilderness before?"

"Of course." She didn't want him to think she was helpless. She'd been down this very trail, although many years ago and never alone. Truth to tell, her wilderness knowledge *was* a bit limited. But if he was going to propose she accompany him, he could forget it. She'd be insane to trudge into the backcountry with a total stranger.

He eased off the tailgate while hitching his muscular arms into backpack straps. "I wouldn't mind you tagging along if you could keep up. But we both know that's not too likely." Tiny lines formed around his eyes as he squinted at the morning sun. "If I were you, I'd wait right here until a ranger comes by and gives you a lift to a telephone. Believe me, you're not ready for a backcountry trip. A greenhorn's no match for the grizzlies." He slammed the pickup tailgate closed. After a slight nod in her direction, he started up the trail at a long-legged pace.

The reminder of bears prickled Meg's scalp, but she was stubborn, as Edward had often accused. She needed a good dose of the great outdoors, minus the grizzlies. And minus rude, insulting, achievement-oriented males. At least she didn't have to worry about the mountain man being a sex-crazed murderer. He gave no indication of being concerned about her one way or the other.

Swinging twenty-something pounds of supplies onto her back, she lifted her face to the sun. Though hiking alone might not be the best choice, she was here. She wasn't going to pass up this opportunity. She needed the time to think things through.

When she returned to civilization, she'd have a few adjustments to make. More than a few, now that she'd quit both Edward and PenUltimate. However, she had survived bad times before. Somehow or other, she'd get by.

A spruce-scented breeze stirred her hair, caressed her skin. High altitude June rays warmed like a microwave, going straight to her marrow. A strange calm welled inside Meg. She was alone for now, and maybe that's how it was meant to be.

Squaring weighted-down shoulders, she started along the path at a rate to rival Buns of Steel, who had already vanished over the first hill.

Zack Burkhart headed up Slough Creek trail like he had a forest fire at his back. He felt sorry for the little woman with the halo of windblown golden hair. An image of her green eyes and slender body stuck in his mind. He couldn't see her paired with the Beamer jockey who'd deserted her, but she had no business alone on a Yellowstone trail, either.

He shook off a vague uneasiness at leaving her

behind. He'd given sound advice. A neophyte in the backcountry was a disaster in the making. He hoped she'd join the tourist crowd and stay out of trouble. Whistling in counterpoint to the bear bells jingling on his pack, he attempted to forget he'd ever seen her. The last thing he needed was to take on someone else's problems. He had plenty enough trouble of his own.

After covering the forested part of the trail in record time, he emerged in a grassy meadow above Slough Creek's first series of falls. He spent an hour fruitlessly searching the brush along the water for Elsa, his lost llama. He'd loaned the animal to a friend, a professional fishing guide who had "misplaced" her. How the hell could a man misplace a two-hundred-fifty-pound llama?

Zack had been inclined to delay the search. Eventually, he figured, a hiker would report Elsa begging for handouts. But Winona, his Sioux mother-in-law, had insisted he needed a "spirit stretch," and the missing pile of mobile wool was a good excuse.

So here he was, although his "spirit" didn't seem any better off than before. A godawful negligence lawsuit in the wake of Sky's death had drained his ability to make peace with Fate. A few days away from his Idaho llama ranch wouldn't help a damn thing.

Even after nearly a year, he thought of Sky all the time, dreamed of her. Sometimes he almost hated her for leaving him so alone. *I'm not good at this, Sky.* Not good at letting go. Not good at putting Band-Aids on a five-year-old son's broken heart. Especially since Zack could use some salve and adhesive tape himself.

He'd hiked eight miles without a sign of Elsa when he reached a campsite near the turnoff to Bliss Pass. After suspending his pack between two lodgepole pines to keep bears and mice out of the Hershey bars, he decided to pitch the tent later. Setting up camp reminded him of Sky. Better to do that chore at the end of a long day, after he'd found the wayward llama.

With a halter and rope looped over his torso like a guerrilla ammunition belt, he backtracked, weaving from one side of the valley to the other. He used binoculars to search rises and hollows.

As he neared one of Slough Creek's deep crescent bends, he found an abandoned blue backpack. Directly across the creek, a faint trail through the grass led to a bluff overlooking the stream's abrupt descent to a lower meadow. The pack's owner must have taken a side trip.

Zack slit his eyes at sun reflecting off sheer granite. Near the top of the cliffs, a spot of pale purple swayed. He glimpsed blond hair and knew it was the woman he'd met at the trailhead. By the time Zack focused his binoculars, she and the splash of color had disappeared behind a boulder.

What the hell was she doing up there? She must be bound and determined to get herself killed. A pebble fell from high on the bluff, ricocheting through a narrow, rock-strewn gorge beneath. He scanned with his binoculars until he spotted her hanging from the uppermost sheet of vertical granite. She wore a lavender jacket swathed around her waist. Legs dangled in midair. Boots groped for purchase. Without benefit of a rope, she was lowering herself to a rock shelf tucked in the side of the cliff. If she didn't land exactly right, she would plunge to unforgiving boulders and vicious current.

Zack had a sinking feeling in his gut. She hadn't seemed distraught earlier, but obviously she was suicidal now. He should have let her tag along with him. He should have talked to her, consoled her, reasoned with her. When a person's life fell apart, death seemed an easy out. He knew that better than most.

From a side view of her pretty face, he saw her mouth open wide. He registered her scream, although no sound reached him over the roar of Slough Creek's whitewater. Tossing the binoculars in the direction of her discarded pack, he started to run with his heart doing tricks that would win a gymnast an Olympic medal.

He splashed across the icy, snow-fed creek. Soaked to the knees, hiking boots heavy with water, he circled the butte and pounded uphill at a point where the climb was relatively easy. Scrambling a hundred vertical feet took less than two minutes.

When he reached the top, she wasn't there. If she'd plummeted into the swift river current, she was beyond anyone's help. His chest ached with a deep sorrow, entwining memories of another accident with this one.

"Hello," he called over the edge, hoping she still clung to the sheer rock face, hoping he could save her.

No answer. No sign of life.

As he dropped to his belly for a closer look, a football-size chunk of granite broke off and crashed to the water far below. Cursing, he inched forward to peer over the rim. He saw part of a ledge, but no blond lady.

Nothing but a distant wink of lavender, churning through rapids and out of sight.

Chapter Two

Meg had settled onto a lovely perch above the falls, a tiny ledge on which to consider what unexpected event to expect next. Green moss covered the surrounding rocks. A whitewater roar shut out all other sounds and filled her with an inner quiet. Strange. The rapids were violence in shape and form, but their tumult made her feel less lonely, more peaceful.

As she'd often done when she was a child, she'd withdrawn from the active world to mend the gouges in her armor, soothe the unrequited love in her heart. It was working. Already she felt stronger.

She could do quite well without Edward. She didn't mind spending a few days alone. In fact, the adventure appealed to her. When she ran out of food in her backpack, she'd buy a bus ticket home, stopping to sightsee on the way. No hurry. Her credit card was maxed, but she had enough cash to . . .

Uh-oh. Until that moment, she hadn't thought about her purse, which was still in the trunk of the silver BMW. She *could* do without Edward. Doing without money and identification would be more difficult.

Once she allowed that piece of reality to permeate, she could no longer deny the rest of her folly. She should not have quit her job. That was indeed a "serious misjudgment." With no work, no Edward to vouch for her, she might end up where she'd spent the last four months, in the middle of a nightmare.

How could she bear it if they locked her away again? The surrounding granite seemed to nudge closer. The ledge was suddenly small and crowded; the air became almost too thick to breathe.

She dug fingernails into sweat-damp palms. The law said she had to be employed to keep her freedom. No problem. She'd find any number of software developers eager to hire a game designer with a criminal record. Really. So what if the sequel rights to her only game already belonged to PenUltimate?

Things could be worse.

She was trying to decide *how* they could be worse when a rock fell from above. Big enough to kill, it smacked in front of her on its journey to the foam below. She pressed against the cliff wall, shielding her eyes from shattered fragments. Pebbles cascaded over the rock face like a granite waterfall.

An animal must be snooping on the ridge. A moose, an elk. Lord help her, a grizzly. The way her day was going, she wouldn't be surprised. To top it off, she'd left her bottle of Nemesis Bear Repellent with Edward, too. She'd never seen a grizzly except in a zoo, but she knew enough to be afraid. Maybe if she stayed extra quiet and still, the creature would go away.

A second rock dropped, this time missing her by a gnat's hind end. She forgot about keeping silent and let out a scream.

"Stay right where you are." Although the words wafting from above were distinctly human, their texture and timbre might have come from a beast.

Scuffed hiking boots and tattered jeans descended over the cliff edge. A smudged grizzly shirt followed. A big, sweaty, hairy, and altogether stunning male specimen lowered himself by a rope. Meg was so astonished she forgot to be scared. Lord in heaven, it was the bearded mountain man!

As he touched down on her ledge, one long, strong arm circled her waist to close the six inches between them. His surprisingly soft, dark beard brushed her cheek. "If you'll hold onto me, I'll get us out of here."

He seemed to think he was rescuing her. She was almost impressed until she recalled he'd left her to the bears a few hours before.

"Leave me alone." She slapped at the man's biceps, which were about as yielding as steel-reinforced concrete.

His smoke-gray eyes became soulful and sad. "I know how you feel, but this is no solution. You're coming with me."

Hot. He was— No, she was hot. Or flustered, or in shock. *Something* was causing the tingles in her lower abdomen. "Who do you think you are? Tarzan?" she demanded. "I'll leave when I'm darn good and ready."

"How?" His patient gaze invited her to examine the situation.

She glanced up the length of rope. Getting here had seemed easy enough, but no way she could return as she'd come without the man and his vine.

Below, continual spray from the seething river coated everything with bright green. Maybe she could work her way lower, but the steep moss-covered granite looked slippery and dangerous.

She dragged her gaze back up her rescuer's daunting chest, taking in his T-shirt and the bear design's claws and teeth. Awareness surged through her. His woodsy male scent, hard body planes, and primitive take-charge power made her feel faint. She'd be in a heck of a fix without him. Maybe she was in a worse fix *with* him.

He was right. She needed help. But accepting it

from him was like surrendering her body as a prize of war. And yet she wasn't afraid, not in the least. How could she be afraid of a man with such beautiful, compassionate eyes?

"Me Tarzan, you Jane." A crooked grin appeared through the beard. "Whenever you're ready, I'll take you for a ride."

While Zack loosened the straps of her backpack and adjusted them to his shoulders, he wondered how he'd gotten into this. He wasn't sure whether, after belated introductions, he'd invited her to hike with him, or whether it was her idea. Either way, he was stuck with Meg Delaney. If only he had a piece of duct tape to slap over her mouth.

She's talked nonstop from the moment he'd hauled her to safety, and she'd continued through the thirty minutes it took her to dawdle down from the cliff. The chatter traversed her limited hiking lore, the mountains, the wildflowers, the inimitable Edward, and somebody named G. T. She leapfrogged from one subject to another as if she had no control over her runaway tongue. She'd still been talking when he piggy-backed her across the creek to the main trail.

"I'm sorry you got all wet saving me," she said, interrupting herself as he deposited her on dry ground. "Not that I needed saving."

He concentrated on coiling his rope. His boots and jeans were soaked for the second time in an hour. His shirt was torn under one arm from rappelling down the sheer rock wall. And he placed all blame squarely on the irritating little woman's fragile shoulders. She should have stayed at the trailhead like he'd told her in the beginning.

"What do you do?" she persisted. "You know, for a living? You look more like Jim Bridger, the mountain man, than Tarzan."

He'd only played along with the Tarzan game to divert her from diving off the cliff. As it turned out she was foolhardy, not suicidal. If anything, her one-sided dialogue would drive *him* to suicide.

He answered succinctly. "I ranch." He hoped that would put an end to her inquisitiveness.

Meg did not seem one bit discouraged. Failing to weasel a life history out of him, she volunteered her own. "I design computer games. The fantasy kind." She paused as if waiting for him to show some interest. When that didn't work, she rushed on. "I've been a gamer since I was a little kid. The adventures, the role-playing, I love all of it. But most games tend to be male-oriented, with a focus on conquering the world and snuffing the opposition. So I've designed a role-playing game with a heroine on a romantic adventure, complete with light humor and fairy-tale mysticism. It's interactive, it's imaginative, it's . . . fun, at least I think it is. I don't suppose you're a gamer?"

"No." Zack thought he should say something more, since she looked so disappointed. "Might as well fill me in on what it means to design one of those things, because I don't have a clue."

She grinned, evidently pleased she'd won that much response from him. "The designer comes up with the characters, the enemies and allies, the levels of play, the puzzles, maps for the special world. I was involved in the artwork, too. I laid out the basics for *Athena* while slaving away at a day job doing graphics for greeting cards. Then, after PenUltimate hired me and took on my game, I worked with a team to add three-D and sound and great animation. The opening scene is *so* cool. Impossible to resist!"

Her enthusiasm made Zack want to smile. He picked up his binoculars, hung them around his neck, and started down the trail, with Meg talking all the while. If he *did* try to silence her, he'd need more than a piece of duct tape. More like an entire roll.

She ran to catch up, talking like she feared he'd cut her off before she could get it all out. Since he'd been thinking exactly along those lines, he was shamed into listening.

The raptures over the game ended abruptly. "Sorry for boring you," she said. "I got carried away and didn't think. Obviously, someone who lives on a ranch prefers the outdoors to computers. Is your home nearby?"

"A couple of hours' drive," he said.

"It's beautiful here. My grandmother Tess—G. T., I called her—brought me to Yellowstone when I was a teenager. She fished for trout on Slough Creek. I explored the paths above the rapids."

"Dumb," he muttered. "Those paths are narrow and slippery."

She sighed. "I know. But I loved the freedom. At home, my stepfather was . . . strict. That's how I got hooked on computer games, because I spent more time grounded in my room than anywhere else. When I was with G. T., we explored the *real* world. Last time I saw her, she made me promise I'd come back here. With . . . Edward, the man I planned to marry."

"I take it you've changed your mind?"

"About Edward? Yes. I was wrong about him," she said. "We were wrong for each other, I see that now."

"Why would your grandmother insist on you dragging Edward out of his fancy car?"

"Because she taught me to love these mountains, and she knew I'd want to share them someday. And because she and her husband, who died before I was born, came here for a honeymoon. G. T. called him

'the heart of her adventure' when she waxed senti-
mental. She hoped my man would be of similar
genus and species."

"She must not have known Edward," Zack com-
mented dryly. In his opinion, any fool could have
predicted Edward and the backcountry wouldn't
mix.

Meg shrugged. "She'd met him. I doubt she knew
how badly he would flunk her little test. Now that
I'm here, though, I'm glad I came. To say good-bye."

Baffled, Zack scratched his beard. "Good-bye? To
the lowlife who dropped you in the parking lot?"

"No. To G. T. She died."

Zack heard the raw pain in Meg's voice and
guessed she'd been closer to her grandmother than
to anyone else on earth. He nodded in sympathy but
didn't offer condolences. To him, death of a loved
one was too personal for words. He hoped Meg felt
the same way.

For a full hundred yards, she was blessedly quiet,
still panting from her soliloquy. Or maybe from the
pace.

Zack sought out some shade. He wasn't pandering
to her, he told himself. He just didn't want an exhausted woman on his hands. Sitting on a fallen tree
trunk, he shed the pack he carried and handed her
a granola bar he found in one of the pockets. When
she offered to split the snack with him, he declined.
She perched on a moss-covered boulder and took a
dainty bite, licking crumbs from a full lower lip.

While she'd been chattering like a defensive squir-
rel, he hadn't noticed the shape of her mouth. He
didn't want to notice it now, either. "How'd you get
tangled up with the boyfriend?" he asked, suddenly
needing her babble to keep his mind off other things.

She perked right up. "He owns PenUltimate, so he

was my boss once I went to work there. He took a personal interest in *Athena*, my role-playing fantasy."

"How long did it take him to get interested in more than the game?"

Meg gazed at the mountains, her green eyes dreamy and misted. "A couple of weeks. I thought God had come down from His cloud." She laughed, but with a twist of irony. "On our first date, we went out for Chinese. I ate egg rolls while he sent E-mail to his distributors. The next evening we went to Luigi's. I ate lasagne while he connected to Paris on his cell phone."

She polished off the granola bar. "I should have seen the handwriting on the fax machine, but I was too busy thinking he was the most important man in the universe to notice he was a jerk. I put on ten pounds; he upped the company's sales by fifty percent."

Zack's gaze wandered down her scrawny frame. If she'd really gained ten pounds, maybe Edward had done her a favor.

Meg smiled, a brilliant full-scale sunbeam that belied any heartache beneath. But sadness tainted her eyes. "To be fair, he wasn't always a jerk. He sent flowers, bought gifts—although now I wonder if he delegated all matters of charm to a secretary, because I doubt he would have thought of them himself. Still, when G. T. was sick and I had to . . . Edward was supportive; I was grateful. We moved in together. He asked me to marry him, and I believed it was true love on both sides. I was wrong, I guess."

Something about her got to Zack. Maybe it was the feisty zest behind her overactive mouth. Maybe it was the way her fluffy yellow hair stuck out in all directions, reminding him of a rumpled Easter chick. Maybe it was his own desperate need to escape the soul-dark cavern where he'd hidden himself for the last year. He wasn't going to respond to her, though. He stood, swinging her pack over his shoulders again.

Meg bolted upright as if terrified he'd leave her. "Forgive me for talking so much. It's like turning on a faucet to clean out the rust. But I can stop. And I will, I promise."

He tamped down the corners of his lips before they had a chance to form an upward curl. If he were a betting man, he'd wager her faucet never stayed shut long enough to develop any rust. At the moment, though, he was feeling magnanimous. Or masochistic.

"You aren't bothering me." He started down the trail, his slower pace cutting her the tiniest bit of slack.

"I'm not?" The granola bar had rejuvenated her. She frisked alongside him. "Do you spend a lot of time alone?"

Why did she have to ask a question like that? He didn't want to talk about loneliness. He had enough trouble living with it. Sky was in his head, but no longer in his life. He compared every woman he met with her, and they all came up lacking. This one, especially. He ought to tell her to back off, go dream about Edward, go jump off a cliff.

No, she'd already tried the cliff.

Increasing his stride, Zack ignored the "Wait up!" she hollered to his backside. Damn it all, she scared him. When he'd put his arms around her on the ledge, an unexpected physical attraction had jolted him. When she'd climbed on his back to cross the creek, her soft warm hands had felt good through the worn fabric of his T-shirt. And he wasn't going to think about what her skinny legs wrapped around his waist had done to him. He hoped to God she hadn't noticed. Since then, the whole time she'd prattled along the trail, he'd been overly aware of the rise and fall of her breasts, and of all her other curves and hollows.

His sex drive boasted a definite yen for Meg Delaney. His higher functions needed her about like a grizzly needed a manicure.

She caught up with him again, talking with characteristic animation. He tried not to listen. When he made the mistake of glancing at her flushed cheeks and agile lips, his ears opened of their own accord, like an uninvited miracle. She was back to Edward, her favorite subject.

"It's funny, I know his routine better than my own. Every morning at 6:05 precisely, he warms up the computer at the same time as his coffeemaker. Compulsive productivity is a virtue, I guess, but it doesn't make for much of a relationship. Getting his one-on-one attention in the morning—or practically any other time of day—is hopeless. Even the cat has to pounce on the keyboard before he remembers to give her some tuna and a scratch behind the ears. Since I'm too big for a keyboard, I . . ."

Zack pictured Meg's trim derriere perched on a desk, with her spine arched and claws out. If he'd been Edward, he'd have fondled more than her ears. "Why do you keep talking about him?" he interrupted. "The man's out of your life, right?"

She blinked. Her eyes got all watery, and Zack figured she was on the brink of a crying jag. He felt like a worse jerk than Edward. Hell, he should have just let her ramble on. It was plain enough she was making an effort to talk the guy out of her system.

His inclination was to take her in his arms, but he held himself back. She was a steamy emotional maelstrom, and he was not nearly as indifferent to her charms as he wanted to be. Physical contact would be a really bad idea.

Looking toward the Absarokas, he sought wisdom from the white-capped peaks. Before he could gain mystical insight, circling vultures caught his attention. He forgot Meg and the set of problems that came with her.

Apprehension bristled at the back of his neck as he recalled why he had come to Yellowstone in the first place. Something was dead or dying, and he thought he knew what it was.

Meg huffed and puffed like a big bad she-wolf with emphysema as she trudged after Zack. He had left her in a hurry, veering off the trail into knee-deep grass and dwarf willows. If he was trying to discourage her from following, he was doing a great job.

Sweat dampened her shirt and stung her legs where she'd lost skin to brambles and thorns. She wouldn't let him give her the slip, not unless keeping up with him killed her, which seemed a distinct possibility. However, she'd be lost—literally—without him.

For some reason she couldn't logically explain, she felt at ease with Zack. True, he said very little. Maybe that was why she'd begun talking, to fill in the empty spaces. She'd kept on talking because he'd listened. His eyes accepted, never judged. And when he did speak, he had a deep calm voice with an appealing gentleness.

Thinking about him in the abstract, she didn't notice he'd stopped. She ran right into him. Off balance, she grabbed him around the waist to keep from falling. As soon as she caught her breath, she would ask him to go slower from now on. Meanwhile, she was in no hurry to move. He felt warm and solid. She smelled his comforting male sweat and . . .

Something else. Something not at all comforting, and definitely not Zack.

She lifted her head. They had reached the top of a hill, and the wind coming over the crest carried an awful odor. The stink of corruption. Of death.

She jerked upright. "What—"

Zack raised a hand in warning.

She moved to his side, holding her breath as the full force of the odor struck hard. They overlooked a wide meadow. Zack had his binoculars trained on the grass below.

About two hundred yards away, a big shaggy creature hunched over a brown-and-white rug. The beast rose on his hind legs, sniffing the air. It looked exactly like the grizzly on Zack's shirt except for a yellow dog collar around its neck and red stuff dripping from its mouth. Meg drew in her breath for a scream.

Zack dropped his binoculars and clamped a hand over her mouth. "Shh," he said into her ear. His arm encircled her ribs and pressed her back flat against his front. She could feel the binoculars imprinting on her spine.

"Let me go," she cried, but his palm caught the sound and silenced it. Panicked by the restraint, she twisted in his grip, scratched at his wrists. She might have had better luck escaping the grizzly. A reverberation began deep in Zack's chest and exploded in a series of low four-letter words. He eased his hold by degrees.

"Keep quiet," he whispered.

"I wasn't going to scream," she lied through his muffling hand. "I'm not completely crazy. Do you happen to have a can of bear repellent on you?"

He shushed in her ear again.

The bear gave forth a horrendous growl before returning his front paws to the rug. On closer examination, Meg realized the rug was a carcass, the source

of the stench that was doing strange things to her
stomach.

"What's it eating?" she whispered over a shoulder.
Zack had released her, but still stood with his body
close against hers.

"My wife's favorite llama."

Meg turned, wondering if she'd heard right. Zack
immediately backed up, leaving a foot of cooling air
between them.

"Wife?" As soon as Meg voiced the word, she
wished she hadn't. It was just that linking Zack to a
woman came as a shock. She'd seen him as a loner.
She'd even felt a kinship with him because now she
was a loner, too.

"My wife's dead." He spoke softly, but the accom-
panying hostile glance stung her.

Meg felt two inches high and wished she could
crawl under the nearest boulder. He was probably
already upset about the llama, without having her
question him about the wife. Worse, her curiosity
could have given the impression she had a personal
interest in his marital state, which was not at all true.
If she weren't heartbroken, destitute, and headed for
a serious legal crisis, she *might* be interested in a man
as appealing as Zack. As things were . . .

He was watching the bear now, ignoring her.

"Sorry," she said. "I didn't mean to—"

"Forget it," he snapped.

To avoid another blunder, she pressed her lips together. Otherwise, something else might have
popped out against her will.

Zack did not wait to hear what indiscretion she'd
come up with next. He was already leaving the way
they'd come, trucking along at a speed exceeded only
by an F-15.

Meg glanced back at the bear, who was on his hind
legs again, testing the air. She suspected neither Zack

nor the grizzly would welcome her company, but at least Zack was semi-civilized and lacked four-inch claws. Taking a deep breath, she hurried down the human side of the hill.

Zack heard her charging after him. She was making so much noise, the grizzly would surely have heard her, too, if he weren't half-deaf from old age. At the moment, Zack wanted to escape Meg more than the bear. The sheer gall of her, prying into his life.

The closer she came, the more he realized he was being unfair. Meg couldn't have known about Sky. She couldn't have known that for him to acknowledge Sky's death, even in monosyllables, was like stabbing icicles into his own heart. And knowing Elsa had just lost a "survival of the fittest" battle made his reaction that much worse.

The pounding in his chest gradually eased. Some of the pain leached out of him. Meg didn't know. It wasn't her fault.

Reluctantly, he slowed his pace. Besides an appalling tongue, she had less outdoor savvy than a cloistered nun. He had to look out for her, even though he was almost certain she could talk an *Ursus horribilis* into a long summer's nap.

"Shouldn't you do something?" she panted from close behind him. "Your llama's over there getting eaten and . . ."

He stopped, gritting his teeth as she stumbled into his back for at least the third time in the last hour. After he'd turned and steadied her, he dropped his hand from her shoulder like she'd burned him. In a way, she had.

It had been a year since he'd shared a bed with Sky, and there had been no one else. With every sway of her hips, Meg made him acutely aware that celibacy was not a natural state. Every word she ut-

tered reminded him of how alone he'd been. "What
do you want me to do?" he snarled. "Arm wrestle
the grizzly for my half of the kill?"

Meg paled, clamping her teeth on her full lower
lip. Zack didn't let that distract him. He tore his gaze
from her mouth and centered his thoughts on the
bear. He knew all about Pegleg, the grizzly bear who
was consuming Elsa. In fact, he'd tagged the bear
himself during his rangering years. A hind foot mangled in a cubhood encounter with a trap had limited
Pegleg's speed. The bear was a notoriously poor
hunter.

Questions circled in Zack's head like the vultures
over the llama corpse. He damn well knew Pegleg
couldn't have caught Elsa unless she were already
injured. So what exactly had happened? *Had* Elsa
been injured? If so, why hadn't Harry, the fishing
guide who'd borrowed her for a pack trip, been able
to locate her before she became lunch for the old,
slow bear?

Meg hooked his left biceps with a dainty hand.
"Why is he wearing a collar?" she asked. "Is that
how park rangers mark the dangerous ones?"

Since Meg was greener than a spring meadow, he
decided he'd better make the bear situation crystal
clear. "*All* grizzlies are dangerous," he stressed. "So
don't get any ideas about snatching the llama hide
to decorate your living room." He stepped back, trying to extricate himself from her without making it
obvious.

"What about reporting this to someone?" she persisted, clinging to his arm like a deer fly. "Shouldn't
we—"

"I'll take care of it. Don't worry your fluffy little
head." Generally speaking, Zack avoided patronizing
sexist remarks. But with Meg touching him, tempting
him, his chauvinism had honed to a fine edge.

Puffed with indignation, she dropped her hold on him as if his skin was contagious. Almost smiling at her reaction, he started down the trail again. She straggled along behind him, pouting in silence for a good ten minutes.

He decided making her mad had been his best move all day.

The wind picked up, dropping the temperature. Zack noted clouds had blown in from the north. He didn't like the look of them. By the time Meg began another spontaneous monologue, he was thinking about the night ahead.

Based on the weight of her pack, which he'd been carrying ever since the cliff rescue, he knew Meg was undersupplied. No tent, he'd guess. She was a typical ignorant tenderfoot, planning to sleep under the stars.

He studied dark clouds obscuring Bliss Pass and sent out a plea. *If you have any influence up there, Sky, I could use a heat wave.*

Scratch that. Meg was enough of a heat wave all by herself. What he really needed was a helicopter that would swoop in and whisk her back to . . . wherever she belonged. Right now. Before dark.

Sure as smoke was a sign of fire, those clouds meant June snow was headed for Yellowstone country. And if it snowed . . .

A night sharing his tent with Meg might lead to madness. Or the fracture of his thus-far inviolate marriage vows.

Or, heaven help him, both.

Chapter Three

Wind lashed Meg's bare legs. Cold anesthetized her face. She was tired, hungry, her mouth was dry. Even her tongue hurt. She'd been babbling like a talk-show host who'd overdosed on caffeine, but she couldn't seem to stop. Although she would have preferred a true conversation, Zack had lapsed into a silence worthy of a Trappist monk working toward sainthood.

When they finally arrived at the circle of stones Zack called home for the night, her head buzzed with problems that had no solution. Thinking and talking about Edward had done no good at all. He would never transform into the Prince Charming of her imaginings.

Edward wasn't coming back. That meant she was in serious trouble with nowhere to turn.

She wished she could ask Zack for help, but he had a dead llama, a dead wife. To judge by his tattered clothes and rusted truck, he also had a cash-flow problem. Besides, he was a stranger. Even though she instinctively trusted him, she had no right to burden him with her past or her future. It was bad enough she'd become his present-tense albatross.

She collapsed under a tree while he started a fire. A light drizzle had turned to sleet. Meg shivered as she dug through her pack. Her shorts and cotton shirt were soaked. Unfortunately, she'd dropped her lavender windbreaker into the rapids, and her sweat-pants were nowhere to be found. All she had available to fend off Arctic gusts was a wool sweater. Hastily pulling it over her head, she huddled beside the crackling flames.

She looked up to see Zack lowering a backpack from where he'd hung it in the trees. He brought the pack near the fire and drew out a small bag from which he magically produced a parka. As he zipped on his coat, white flakes blew out of the graying sky and clung to his beard and thick wavy hair. She looked down at the sleeve of her sweater and found the same white flakes there.

Snow? Could it really snow in mid-June? She glanced from Zack to the items she had jettisoned from her pack. She was ill-equipped, as usual. And, also as usual, she felt the resultant chill.

Zack hunkered beside her. "Do you have everything you need?" he asked, wearing resignation like a martyr.

"Sure, I'm . . ." She hesitated. Admitting a lack of preparedness to a wilderness paragon was only marginally preferable to death from exposure. Nevertheless, he'd discover her true situation sooner or later. She took a deep humiliating breath. "Do you happen to have an extra sleeping bag?"

He frowned at her disordered belongings. "You're kidding, right?"

"I know it's harebrained, but all I have are a flashlight, water bottle, stove, sunscreen, and food packets. I was going to attach a sleeping bag at the last minute. Edward took the tent. He drove away before I could—"

Zack disgorged a litany of curses, halting two letters into a particularly graphic term. "I have a one-man tent and a single sleeping bag. Since neither of us wants to become Yellowstone's version of the Abominable Snowman, I guess we'll have to share."

Meg had a distinct aversion to tiny, crowded enclosures. On the other hand, freezing to death had its disadvantages, too. When she noticed he'd already begun putting up the structure, she rushed to help . . . or at least that was the plan. She tripped on a rock and fell into the mosquito netting just as he was raising the poles. Without a word, Zack picked her up with a sure grip on her arms and set her aside. She should have felt insulted or dismissed, but she had an entirely different reaction. The warmth and strength of his hands sent electric shock therapy to her lower abdomen.

Edward had been quite willing to relieve her pent-up sexual frustration the moment she'd changed from Salt Lake County–issue to street wear. He'd wanted her back in his apartment, back in his bed. But though their sexual relationship had been satisfying once, it seemed the emotional connection had disintegrated somewhere along the way. She'd felt the distance, and maybe that's what had blunted her body's reaction. She'd chosen to sleep alone for the three nights since she'd left her barred residence behind.

Now, in a snowstorm, with an almost-stranger, she felt a jolt of desire. A sense of timing had never been her forte, but this was ridiculous. She wanted to cry for the man she'd thought Edward to be, while her traitorous body demanded a substitute.

She should be afraid—horrified—to sleep beside a man she barely knew. She ought to be claustrophobic, just thinking about crawling into that tent. Instead, she looked forward to the closeness, with only darkness between Zack's hard body and her compliance. Losing out on Prince Charming had made her reckless, willing to risk anything to be loved—physically, if not emotionally.

But Zack showed no interest in Meg's compliance, nor in the state of her heart. He unfurled the only sleeping bag and tossed it into the tent. He must have seen her blowing on icy fingers because he thrust a pair of gloves in her direction. Their hands brushed. She attributed her tingling skin to the frostbite-inducing weather.

In the firelight, Zack's clenched jaw telegraphed annoyance. She responded with a fake, frozen smile.

It was going to be a long night.

The tent was three feet wide, barely enough to accommodate Zack's breadth of shoulder when he lay flat on his back. He'd given Meg his mummy sleeping bag and yielded most of the tent's meager width. He faced away from her, cramped on his side with his down jacket as a blanket. The bumps in her spine and the softness of her well-rounded butt crowded his back. His entire body, every fiber of muscle and tissue, focused on sex.

If he followed his instincts, he'd be on top of her right now, hips nuzzling between her slender thighs, hands threading through her yellow hair, mouth silencing her Edward stories, her protests, or whatever else she'd find to prattle about before he brought her to climax.

Her nearness tempted him more than he wanted to admit, even to himself. Maybe she sensed his lust, because she had been surprisingly subdued since she entered the tent. She seemed unsure of herself all of a sudden. More sweet than sexy. Downright huggable. In spite of his raging testosterone, he wanted to draw her close and protect her from harm—and from him. Which didn't make a whole lot of sense.

She'd been modest, almost Victorian, the way

she'd drawn the sleeping bag to her chin. After all the jabbering earlier in the day, she was now mute, which made her much more appealing.

Zack sensed a yearning in her silence. For Edward, he supposed. Maybe that's what had made her quit talking. She wouldn't expect sympathy from Zack. He'd gone out of his way to make sure she believed he disliked her. It would be better for both of them if she never found out she was wrong.

Snow pelted the tent until an accumulated layer muffled all sound. The wind had stopped blowing, leaving the two of them separated from every other living thing. It was an Adam and Eve kind of feeling. Zack had experienced it with Sky, but never before or since. To feel it now, especially with a woman he didn't know—and didn't want to know—was almost sacrilegious.

I'm lonely without you, Sky. Immediately, he regretted calling her into his head, because he was ashamed of where he was and what he felt.

Sky's voice whispered through his mind, though he couldn't distinguish the words. His chest tightened with familiar anguish— Zack Burkhart's version of hell. He could never be with his wife again, but neither was he detached from her. The strong connection had been a comfort at first. After months and months, it seemed more like a particularly effective form of torture.

He forced his thoughts to Robby, who looked so much like Sky. He dreaded telling his sensitive son about Elsa's death. Robby loved the llamas. Losing another would hurt him, and more psychological pain was the last thing the boy needed.

Another dead llama was the last thing Zack needed, too. If his stock got any more accident-prone, the ranch would soon be history.

He'd lain in one position long enough for his side

to go numb when he heard Meg's sniffles. He listened awhile, telling himself he'd be a fool to offer his shoulder to cry on. If he gave her an opening, she'd start talking again. He wasn't sure how much more blather he could take. Nevertheless, Zack understood how Meg felt. She'd been deserted by the person she'd entrusted with her heart. The same thing had happened to Zack. True, Sky hadn't chosen to die, and Zack held himself at least partly responsible. But she'd deserted him just the same.

Moving awkwardly in the tight space, he turned and propped himself up on a forearm. "Meg, what's wrong?" He touched her hair. "You're not crying for the sonuvabitch in the Beamer, are you?"

She rolled to her back, an elbow colliding with his chest. In the darkness, he imagined her reddened eyes, wet swollen lips. He wanted to see her smile, not cry. She was neurotic and spirited and . . . nice, in an odd sort of way. She deserved better than Edward, the international sleazeball.

Without warning, she launched herself at Zack, knocking him onto his back and almost overturning the tent. "Hey, take it easy," he warned.

She was shaking and shuddering like a leaf in a stampede, and the tent wasn't faring much better. Yielding to the inevitable, he did what came naturally. He wrapped his arms around her, mummy bag and all.

"It's okay," he murmured, the best he could do at consolation. She cried into his shirt, soaking him to the skin. Her lively chatter throughout the day must have been her way of holding back another kind of flood. He should have listened more closely, responded with more care.

Her grief poured forth for a long time. Eventually, the wracking sounds changed to hiccups, then to the gentle, steady breath of sleep. Zack planted a kiss in her feather-soft hair. She felt good, smelled good. And she was just as huggable as he had expected. With her body nestled on top of his, he was intensely aware of his long-denied sexual hunger. He was a man, not a saint. He enjoyed having a woman in his arms again, but the pleasure brought him face to face with guilt. He shifted his rock-hard erection away from the tantalizing pressure of Meg's knee.

Staring at the tent ceiling and beyond, he half-expected to hear Sky wisping through his mind, reproaching him.

Nothing happened.

Relieved, he held Meg a little tighter, savoring the closeness, the human warmth. It was only for one night. Tomorrow he'd escort her to the trailhead—she might get lost on her own—and give her a ride to the nearest telephone. Hell, he'd probably have to give her a few bucks, if she were as organized in the money department as she had been in camping gear.

After that, she'd be out of his life. To his surprise, the thought weighed on him like a truckload of rocks. It took a long time to fall asleep. And when he finally did, he dreamed a yellow Easter chick perched on his shoulder and refused to move.

The sun had climbed over the Beartooth range before Zack unzipped the tent the next morning. He surveyed four inches of snow blanketing the meadow. Mountain peaks glistened. Pure white decorated the branches of spruce and fir.

A moose cow drank from Slough Creek. As she raised her head, water dripped from Roman nose and droopy chin. Vapor jetted from her nostrils. She flopped her ears in Zack's direction before noisily ambling into dwarf willows along the bank.

Zack retrieved the backpacks from where he'd hung them the night before. He took a pad from a side compartment and sketched the moose from memory. Drawing wildlife was an old hobby, one he hadn't had the heart to pursue since Sky's death. Maybe the backcountry had given him a "spirit stretch" after all.

The nylon tent quaked and shifted as if about to give birth. Meg threw back the fly and stuck her head outside. "Zack," she called.

He'd enjoyed the early morning silence. With Meg around, he should have known it wouldn't last. After a pause full of reluctance, he answered, "I'm here."

She withdrew her head. He heard her puttering inside the tent, peeping like the chick she resembled. "I'll fix breakfast for us. I brought dehydrated packets of eggs, the gourmet variety. There's plenty, because Edward insists on good food. He's used to the best, so I . . ."

Her voice, still thickened from midnight tears, caught and faltered. Zack had to fight off the ridiculous urge to go to her and hold her again. He didn't want to remember how good she'd felt in his arms. He wanted to forget everything about last night.

She stepped outside to rummage through her supplies. "What would you like? Take your pick of scrambled eggs with jalapeños and sour cream . . . or scrambled eggs with tomatoes and bacon-flavored bits, or . . ."

In deference to her feelings, Zack refrained from saying he hated anything freeze-dried. If he let her provide breakfast, she'd feel better about borrowing his sleeping bag and crying on his shirt. Later, when she wasn't looking, he would dig summer sausage and bagels from his pack. His appetite would do justice to a dozen meals, since all they'd had the previous evening were two Hershey bars. He hadn't had time to cook anything before the storm drove them into the tent.

As it turned out, they would have starved to death that morning if Meg were their only hope. She set up her brand new, state-of-the-art backpack stove on an incline. Although she referred to the directions frequently, the snow-slick ground and the stove's poor design resulted in two overturned pans, ruining a couple of so-called gourmet meals.

She was on her last packet of eggs when Zack ran out of patience. He rummaged in his backpack until he found what she needed. Moving her aside, he positioned the stove on flat terrain with his special cookstand over it.

"Where did you g-get that?" Meg bent low, wrinkling her nose at the device.

"I made it," he explained. "I overturned a few diners before I came up with the idea."

"T-t-too bad they don't sell these things with the s-s-toves."

He looked up from balancing a pan on his invention. Meg's lips were an awful blue-purple color. Her teeth chattered. He swore under his breath as he surveyed the rest of her. Dressed in shorts and a thin sweater, she had plenty of bare goosebumped skin.

"Get in the tent." When she didn't move, he shouted, *"Now."* He tossed his sweatshirt and extra pants at her. "Put these on, and don't come out until you stop shivering."

Taking the clothes, she quietly complied, much to Zack's surprise. After she'd zipped the nylon flaps, he tried not to think about what she was doing in there, what she was wearing . . . or not wearing. He had eaten a few cautious bites of scrambled eggs, which managed to taste like sawdust in spite of the chunks of jalapeño, when he heard the neigh of a horse. A lanky figure in a green-gray uniform was riding up the trail on a stocky sorrel.

Zack recognized the ranger as his and Sky's old

friend Andrew Houssard. The three of them had been rookies together, before Zack and Sky quit the park service and started ranching almost eight years ago. They had kept in touch. Since Sky's death, Andrew was one of the few people Zack felt comfortable with.

Usually, he looked forward to seeing Andrew, but not today. If Meg poked her feather head out of that tent, Zack would have a hell of a time explaining her. He would feel like a traitor to Sky. He felt like that anyhow, but having Meg in plain sight, especially in Andrew's plain sight, would solidify the longings of the darkness into unforgettable reality.

Suppressing a groan, Zack rose and slogged through the melting snow. In an effort to keep his friend away from the campsite, away from Meg, he intercepted Andrew at a bend in the trail.

Andrew dismounted and hitched his horse to a tree while explaining why he was out in the snow. "Somebody reported a grizzly in the first meadow. I saw an abandoned carcass, but I couldn't tell—" He stopped abruptly, staring over Zack's shoulder. His eyes widened. His lips parted company.

Zack slowly turned. Meg Delaney stood outside the tent, clad in his sweatshirt. He hoped she was wearing shorts beneath, but no trace of them showed. Shapely, naked legs extended from the bulky shirt to a pair of sagging purple socks.

She was tousled and flushed, looking for all the world like she'd just awakened after a mind-blowing night of love.

Chapter Four

Zack lunged in front of his friend in a vain attempt to distract him. "Why don't we take a look at that carcass together?"

"Forget it, Burkhart." Andrew danced past Zack with the agility that had made him first string running back at Mississippi State during his college years. "If you think you can hide a woman from Hound Dog Houssard, you'd better think again. What the hell are you up to, boy?"

Zack wasn't up to a damn thing, but Andrew would never believe that. Muttering an assortment of curses under his breath, Zack followed his friend's overworked nostrils straight to Meg's beckoning smile.

Doffing his ranger hat, Andrew grinned like Sylvester who'd just caught Tweety Bird. "Welcome to Yellowstone, ma'am. I'm pleased to meet the woman who brought a blush to Zack Burkhart's manly cheeks. Much as I've tried to prevent it, he's turned into a recluse since—"

Zack stepped between them, tossing forth curt introductions. "Meg and I hardly know each other," he explained.

Andrew kept right on bantering with Meg, as if finding her there was as pleasing and natural as a red apple in a summer orchard.

Condemnation would have been easier to take. As

a friend of both Zack's and Sky's, Andrew ought to see Meg as an interloper. Andrew, however, was Andrew. He never condemned anyone for anything. For months, he'd been trying to convince Zack to enter the dating scene.

He slapped Zack on the spinal cord with disc-rupturing fervor. "Even a Baptist from Biloxi's heard of love at first sight. I'm pleased as pink lemonade you've got yourself a lady friend."

Zack winced. "That's not the way it is. She was hiking without a tent. When the weather turned bad, we—"

Andrew raised both hands to fend off details. "No need to explain. I'm a married man, you know. I can't wait to tell Callie."

"Shut up, Houssard, before I ram your hound dog nose up your sinuses."

"Right." Andrew made an effort to put on a straight face, but the corners of his mouth quirked.

Meg was tapping an index finger on her lower lip as she glanced from one man to the other, a puzzled expression on her face. The sweatshirt had risen high enough to show the hem of her shorts. For that, Zack was grateful.

"I sure hope you'll pardon all this carrying on, ma'am." Andrew slanted his hat over his heart. "Zack doesn't mean to be offensive. I've tried to teach him good old Southern manners, but he's a mess, plain and simple."

Meg smiled as if she finally understood the two men were friends, which must not have been obvious at first. She stretched lazily, her green eyes sparkling with mischief. "You're so wrong. Zack has been a purr-fect gentleman. He knows how to please." She and Andrew seemed to be on the same field, playing the same ball game.

The ranger grinned appreciatively. "If you could

get the drawl down pat, you'd make a fine Southern gal, Meg. Almost as good as my wife, Callie. She's from Minnesota, not Mississippi, but she makes a mean chicken fried steak. Now that you've met up with Burkhart here, I hope we'll be seeing a lot more of . . ."

"Excuse me." Zack bulldozed through their tête-à-tête and leaned down to rip a six-inch aluminum stake out of the rocky ground. He briefly considered testing its point on Andrew's gray-green uniform, but decided his energy was better spent breaking camp. If Andrew wanted to take on Meg, that was just fine as long as they counted Zack out. He collapsed the tent and stuffed it in its nylon sack with unnecessary violence.

Meanwhile, Andrew pumped Meg for information. She, of course, readily obliged. Before long, she was filling him in on her misbegotten love life. "My dear friend Edward drove off with the tent, my sleeping bag, *and* my money, what little I had."

Zack straightened, staring at her. He hadn't known about the money. He wasn't sure he wanted to know.

"I reckon that means you're stranded out here." Andrew clicked his tongue, glancing slyly at Zack. "You planning to show the lady around Elk Springs?"

Zack rolled his eyes. With friends like Andrew, an enemy would be a welcome switch.

"Elk what?" Meg asked.

"Elk Springs, the one-mule town closest to Zack's ranch. Assuming you don't hit any road construction or slow motor homes, it takes about two hours to get to West Yellowstone. From there, go thirty miles or so to the south end of Henry's Lake, where you'll see a couple of gas stations and a general store. Zack's place is ten miles up a dirt road from town.

He raises llamas, horses, chickens. I keep telling him he ought to get him some pigs."

"Cut the bumpkin act, Houssard." Zack scratched his beard, which had developed a terrible itch. He was probably allergic to Meg or Andrew, or a combination of the two. Either way, he'd had enough well-meaning interference. "Meg's not interested in Elk Springs. I'll lend her some money if that's what it takes. She has a life of her own, and she's going straight back to it."

As soon as the words were out, he began to wonder. She'd been close to her grandmother, but the old lady was dead. Her stepfather, the one who'd restricted her every move, sounded like a male version of the witch who locked Rapunzel in a tower. Then there was Edward, her employer and love interest. Now that she'd split with him, exactly what kind of life did she have?

Andrew draped an arm over Meg's shoulders. "Too bad Zack runs such a tight defense. But don't worry, darlin'. He'll give you a lift to Park Headquarters, at least. He's not *that* much of a scumbag."

He turned to Zack. "Since you're not living up to the rest of my expectations, would you mind telling me what you know about a grizzly roaming these parts?"

"I thought you'd never ask," Zack said with liberal sarcasm. He couldn't get over the way Andrew assumed Meg and Zack were meant for each other. What the hell was Andrew thinking? Couldn't he see Meg was nothing like Sky?

Zack explained that he'd seen Old Pegleg devouring a llama, the one Zack had come here to find. "Take a look at the carcass on your way out, Houssard, once Pegleg's left the neighborhood. If there's any skin or hair for a sample, do me a favor and send it to the Park lab. Have the techs look for anything unusual." Two of Zack's llamas had had fatal accidents in three weeks. After considering the probability, he didn't like the odds. Add in the nasty letter he'd received, and . . . well, it wouldn't hurt to do some checking.

Andrew's brown eyes sharpened, homing in on Zack's suspicions. Before the ranger could get too curious, the radio on his belt began to squawk. He held the speaker to his lips. "Lydia, this is Houssard. What's happening?"

Lydia? Zack thought with disgust. Damn his luck, why did Lydia have to be on duty today? The park's head dispatcher, thrice-divorced daughter of Elk Springs' sheriff, had been chasing Zack none too discreetly for the last six months. Ever since she ditched her last husband. Right after the divorce came through, she'd asked Zack to meet her for a drink. Caught at a weak, lonely moment, he'd agreed. The repercussions had been one continual headache. Zack kept telling her he wasn't ready for a relationship, which was absolutely true. But if she heard about Meg, Lydia would decide he was on the meat market. She'd be parked on his doorstep whenever he turned around. He tried to catch Andrew's attention with a throat-slashing motion, but the ranger never looked his way.

After a series of crackles, Lydia's voice came through the speaker. "The entire staff is sorting out the mother of all wolf jams on Canyon to Norris." She sounded bored. Zack could almost see her sitting at the dispatch desk, buffing her fake fingernails while she talked. "The road's swarming with motor homes and camcorders, so they'll be busy awhile. That leaves you as my main backup, Southern boy. Anything happening out there?"

"You'll never guess who I ran into, sugar plum,"

Andrew replied. "Zack Burkhart. He's here with a lady friend."

The radio waves went still. Lydia's voice, when it finally crackled through, had a brittleness, a false gaiety. "Zack's in Yellowstone?! That son of a gun. With a woman, no less." She coughed, probably to cover a comment unfit for radio waves. After a pause, she embarked on a lengthy harangue about trouble in paradise, ending with Andrew's assigned mission: a search for a couple of missing teenagers.

After Andrew signed off, Zack drew him aside, out of Meg's hearing, and lit into him. "Did you have to mention I was with a woman? Lydia's already hot on my tail. She'll be worse now that she thinks there's competition."

Andrew ran a forefinger around the inside of his collar and looked chagrined. He even mumbled an apology before he counteracted it with unsolicited advice. "Better take the little girl home, Zack." He gestured toward Meg, who was watching them curiously. "You need her for protection. Otherwise, Lydia might just come out to the ranch and swallow you whole." He chuckled. "Me and Callie'll bring the condiments."

So, Andrew had known all along about Lydia's latest nymphomania. Zack should have figured as much.

The ranger leaned closer, his back to Meg. "If you can't—or won't—take Meg with you, give Callie a call. Little Jeremy has the chicken pox, but Callie won't turn anyone away." He sent Zack a look that was half challenge, half palm-rubbing glee.

Turning toward Meg, Andrew bowed with the lady-killer Southern manners that had charmed Callie off her Minnesota feet. "It's been a pleasure, ma'am." With a wink in Zack's direction, he settled his Smoky the Bear headgear into place. He trudged

off to mount his sorrel gelding and ride toward Bliss
Pass, where the missing teenagers were last seen. If
anybody could find them, Andrew could. He wasn't
called Hound Dog Houssard for nothing.

Zack might have helped in the search if he'd been
alone. This time, though, he had a problem child of
his own. What the hell was he going to do about
Meg? Or about Lydia? His defenses against the locust
plague of womankind were rapidly unraveling.

"Is she pretty?" Meg asked as she helped Zack
load their backpacks.

"Who?" What *was* he going to do with Meg? Leave
her at a West Yellowstone phone booth? Give her a
quarter for a call?

"Lydia," Meg chirped. "Wasn't that who you and
Andrew were talking about?"

As Meg handed him his sleeping bag, which she'd
neatly stuffed into its sack, she brushed his arm.
Zack's awareness level shot off the scale at the light
touch. He grabbed the bedding and attached it to his
pack frame, hoping she hadn't noticed the reaction.
Without another word, he shrugged the forty-pound
load onto his back and started down the trail.

Meg jogged behind him. "Well, is she?"

"Is she what?" Zack yelled over his shoulder.
Wasn't Meg ever quiet?

"Pretty. And interested in you." She had reached
his side. Her legs worked overtime to stay there.

"Lydia's interested, all right," Zack said. "But I'm
not. When she came by the ranch a few weeks ago,
my five-year-old son climbed a tree to get away from
her. Robby had the right idea. I'd have been on top of
Mount Nemesis—the mountain behind my house—if
I'd known she was coming."

"Why? Is she that bad?"

Worse, Zack thought. She had two-inch-long
blood-red nails, a body that was a Boise plastic sur-

geon's work of art, and hair sprayed so stiff she could use it for a battering ram. If there was anything real about her, she'd buried it in fake beauty and warped narcissism. The sad thing was, the more desperately she sought love, the less lovable she became.

Zack felt sorry for her. But not sorry enough to sacrifice himself to her man-hungry appetite. "She's bad enough. Lydia's more than capable of tearing a little thing like you to shreds. She gobbles men like me for bedtime snacks."

"I could hire on as your bodyguard," Meg teased. She curled her fingers and held them up as potential weapons. "I'll scratch out her eyes if she takes the first nibble."

Zack snorted his doubt and kept walking, pulling ahead of her. Meg had almost made him laugh, and that bothered him even more than Lydia's blatant sex appeal. Meg had an appeal of her own, much more subtle and alluring.

Hell, what was he thinking? Sky would always be first in his heart, leaving room for no other woman. Meg brought out erotic cravings that muddled his priorities. He'd be glad to get away from her. He'd appreciate the peace and quiet, though it might take him awhile to forget the way she heated his blood and brought his near-forgotten sense of humor to the surface.

Zack stopped dead in the trail, recalling the little secret she'd confided to Andrew. He turned in time to catch her right before she slammed into his chest. Gingerly, he set her at arm's length. "Why didn't you tell *me* about loverboy going off with your money?"

"I didn't want you to feel obligated." She smiled, the same bright, not-quite-happy smile that had beguiled Zack from the moment she'd first sicced it on him.

"You have family, don't you, Meg? Someone you can call? Somewhere you can go from here?"

Meg chewed her lower lip and avoided his gaze. "Everybody has family. Even me. No need to worry." She flashed another smile as she revved up her tireless tongue. "Did I mention G. T. taught botany for thirty-some years? She knew the Latin names for every plant alive. I forget Latin as soon as I hear it, but common names stick with me better. For instance . . ." She pointed out a cluster of snow-kissed wildflowers beside the trail. "These are Springbeauty, aren't they? And—look, a Dogtooth Violet!"

Her blithe babble didn't fool Zack. She was scared, homeless, broke, and she clamped onto his conscience like the teeth of a bear trap. Leaving her to fend for herself just wasn't right. She'd been jilted by the man she loved. She needed . . .

He caught himself right there. Why should he care what she needed? Lydia had nothing on Meg when it came to getting under a man's skin. Come to think of it, Lydia was by far the safer of the two.

"In case I forget later," Meg said as she flitted past him on the narrow trail, "thanks for everything."

Everything? He hadn't done much. He had rescued her from a ledge and a snowstorm. To drop her at a telephone booth, or ranger headquarters, or even on Callie's chicken-pox infested porch, would be like birthing a foal or cria only to let it die for lack of milk. He didn't want the obligation, but he couldn't shirk it, either.

Blast his infernal luck to hell, she needed *someone*. And he was the only damn do-gooder in sight.

Chapter Five

After a three-hour drive through a corner of Montana and into the heart of Idaho, Zack braked in front of a stone house set against the slope of a magnificent mountain.

"This is it," he said, pulling the keys from the ignition and tossing them on the faded dashboard. "Home."

Meg stared through the bug-encrusted windshield. The house seemed to rise from the landscape, fitting exactly into the scene. A dozen llamas grazed on green pasture. A horse whinnied from a paddock shaded with aspen and cottonwood. On first glance, all of it was straight out of fairyland.

She blinked.

Okay, the house was a bit less than perfect. The trim was peeling, and the pillars on the porch were not perpendicular to the ground. In fact, there didn't seem to be a right angle in the entire building. Even the doorframe was awry. The door itself was custom-fitted to a cock-eyed rectangle.

Smiling, she turned to Zack. "It's . . . unusual. Like you."

His smoke-gray eyes had a faraway look as he gazed at the house. "We bought the place from a self-styled architect who worked with a fifth of Jack Daniel's in his coat pocket. I guess it shows." Glancing at Meg, his white teeth flashed through the beard in what almost qualified as a smile. He stepped out of the truck and raised his arms to stretch.

Meg admired the length and strength of him. Unfortunately, he peered in the open door and caught her at it.

"Aren't you going to get out?" he asked.

Meg scrambled across the seat toward the driver's side—she'd already learned that the passenger door was permanently jammed. This time she managed to avoid the exposed spring on the cracked vinyl seat. It had eaten a layer of skin and the hem of her shorts when she'd climbed into the seat at the Slough Creek trailhead.

Once her feet were on the ground, she carefully ignored the muscular chest that met her at nose level. She ducked around him to feast her eyes on a jagged white-tipped peak. It towered over the valley and seemed to touch the sky. "Mount Nemesis, I presume?"

"Right." He attempted another stiff smile. "A towering goddess who oversees everything, good and bad, and doesn't give a damn. Come on, let's find Winona."

"Who?"

Without answering, Zack disappeared around a not-quite-square corner. He hadn't mentioned a "Winona." He hadn't mentioned anyone, but then she hadn't given him much of a chance. Filling in conversational gaps was a bad habit of hers, one Edward had often criticized. But Edward had at least spoken without prompting once in a while, even if his main subject was himself. Zack could hold onto a personal quiet until the devil took an Arctic vacation. But he *was* kind. Since it was Sunday and the banks were closed, he had volunteered to bring her to his ranch.

She crunched across the gravel driveway, jogging to catch up with Zack. As she rounded a blind bend, she ran right into the granite-hewn muscles of his back. He didn't turn around, or grumble, or yell at her. Perhaps he was becoming accustomed to her collisions.

She peeked past him to see a woman leaning over the open engine compartment of a dented, gray van. Both woman and van were parked in a detached garage with a familiar drunken design. The woman wore stained red coveralls. Thick, chin-length black hair hung forward to hide her face.

Glancing up from her work, she slowly turned. She planted a fist clutching a large wrench on one ample hip. "I should have known you'd be back early, Zack. Why didn't you stay gone a while like I . . ." As her gaze shifted to Meg, she dropped the wrench. It hit the vehicle's bumper and clanked onto blackened concrete.

"We have a guest, Win." Zack latched onto Meg's wrist and hauled her to his side. "This is Meg Delaney. I met her in Yellowstone."

Meg fidgeted under Winona's glare.

The woman was an Amazon, as tall as Zack, with an impressive bosom and the posture of a Marine drill sergeant. Her mahogany complexion and broad, high cheekbones distinguished her as Native American. Leathery skin crinkling around hostile black eyes showed signs of both sun and age. She would have done well as a jail inmate, Meg reflected. Not a soul would dare mess with Winona.

Edging closer, Meg offered her hand. "I'm pleased to meet you. Zack hardly talked of anyone else all the way here." Which was true, as far as it went.

Winona squinted, holding up a forearm in a Hollywood cliché of Indian-speak. "How," she greeted. "I don't do handshakes when I'm elbow deep in clutch guts."

A little boy in a cowboy hat jumped out the sliding

side door of the van and made a beeline for Zack, who swooped him into the air. The hat and pint-size cowboy boots fell to the ground. Zack spun the child in a circle until he squealed.

When Zack put him down, the boy's smile faded. He looked up, as sober as if he'd caught Santa Claus and was about to unmask him. "Did you bring Elsa, Daddy?" Since he lisped the "S," Elsa sounded like Eltha.

Zack hunkered beside the child. "No, Robby. Elsa couldn't come home. She's gone to be with Mama."

Robby nodded, registering no surprise. "Gone like Thessa."

At least Meg assumed he meant Thessa, but it was hard to tell, what with the S's and his lisp. He was a stoic little guy, a smaller version of his father. The child's straight black hair and darker skin resembled Winona's, but his set of shoulders and facial expressions were Zack's. His eyes were unique pools of blue and green, like paint swirled in clear water.

"Did Mama send the new lady?" Robby glanced at Meg, then down at his bare toes.

Zack turned pale beneath beard and tan. He seemed to freeze for a second. Meg waited in the tense silence, curious about how he would answer the boy.

Before Zack said anything, a man with the muscle-bound physique of a gorilla emerged from the garage shadows. Meg jumped when she spotted him, taking an involuntary step backward.

With one hand resting on his son's dark hair, Zack introduced the man as Tobias. Meg gathered he was the hired help.

Tobias shuffled into the sun, doffing a green bubba cap labeled *BadAss Café* in silver letters. His sandy blond hair was shorn military close. He wore a grease-smeared, sleeveless undershirt and jeans. As

he shook her hand, Meg noticed one of his beefy
forearms bore a pierced-heart tattoo. She forced a
smile, but the man showed no expression whatsoever. Zack lived with a strange bunch of people, Meg
reflected, as off-kilter as his house.

As if to counteract the generalized lack of emotion,
a big black dog loped in from the pasture and
vaulted on Zack.

"Down, Hoover," Zack ordered. The dog immediately lay on the gravel and rolled to his back. Zack
and his son scratched the exposed belly.

Hoover whined and wiggled in pure contentment.
The dog, at least, had no problem displaying his
feelings.

After a dinner during which Meg, busy eating a
succession of grilled cheese sandwiches, didn't talk,
Zack retreated to the small bedroom he'd converted
to an office. He'd wanted to be alone, but the quiet
seemed oppressive after so many hours of Meg's constant monologue. He glanced out a window and saw
Robby and Meg slipping through the fence to the
north pasture. The child tugged her hand, introducing her to a corral full of female llamas, some with
crias at their sides.

From the moment she had walked in the door,
Meg had done and said exactly the right things, at
least as far as Robby was concerned. First, she'd
taken an interest in Cheeper, Robby's baby wren. A
few days ago, the poor bird had suffered a fall from
its nest and the child had taken it in.

Meg had knelt over the wren's cardboard-box
home, asking questions, making suggestions. When
she'd finished twittering over the bird, she'd moved
on to exclaim over Robby's hamster, and the lizard
he kept in an old aquarium. She was a genuine ani-

mal lover if Zack ever saw one. Robby doted on her immediately.

Maybe Zack and Win should have taken more notice of Robby's pets. Maybe Robby felt neglected. But that didn't stop Zack's surge of jealousy. What right did Meg have to make such quick inroads with his son?

Through the office window, he saw Hoover circling Meg's legs while Robby demonstrated how to greet a llama. The boy leaned forward and blew at a brown female named Hilda. Meg imitated the movement, with her trim rear poked out and her full lips pooched.

Zack gripped the windowsill as a gust of desire buffeted him. His attraction to Meg made him angry. She was like quicksilver, shiny and frivolous and changeable. She was nothing like Sky. Nothing like the woman he would always love.

As far as sex appeal went, though, she was damn hard to beat. She moved closer to the llamas, maintaining her provocative llama-greeting stance. The animals, curious but wary, surrounded her. They made high-pitched humming noises while they arched their long necks and pricked their ears. The hums lowered in pitch as the llamas allowed her to touch them. In minutes, Meg stood between two woolly beasts, scratching them behind the withers. She was shy with neither children nor animals. No surprise. She was shy with no one, as far as Zack could tell.

With the usually aloof llamas conquered and Hoover panting at her feet, Meg resumed prattling. Zack couldn't hear, but he could see her lips moving at near light speed. She paused every now and then to cock her head in Robby's direction. The boy danced around her, smiling, talking.

Robby responding to a stranger, a woman stranger,

was a minor miracle. Other than Winona and now Meg, he had not communicated with any woman since Sky had died. His pre-school teacher had received the silent treatment, which didn't bode well for the kindergarten experience in September. And even Zack's mom, usually great with kids, hadn't been able to get through to Robby on her week-long visit over the Christmas holidays.

Meg, of all people, had drawn him out. Meg, who made Zack feel as if he'd been caught *flagrante delicto*, two-timing Sky. Zack turned from the window and sat heavily in a sagging swivel chair behind his desk. The leather creaked a protest as he rocked back against the wall.

He stared at the yellowed, uneven ceiling. *What should I do, Sky? About Robby? And Meg?* He closed his eyes and sighed. For most of his adult life, he'd shared everything with Sky. But how could he tell her he'd brought another woman home? How did a man tell his wife he wanted permission to be unfaithful?

He sat up, ramrod straight. Where had that thought come from? Unfaithful? With Meg? No, that was what his body wanted—and wasn't going to get. In his mind and spirit, he was still married to Sky. He owed her a lifetime of fidelity. He didn't see how that could ever change.

Leaning forward, he propped his elbows on the desk, in the midst of loose papers and unopened mail. He didn't want to wade through the mess. Not the disaster on his desk, nor the confusion in his life. The visit to Yellowstone had done little to benefit his spirit, but it had renewed deep yearnings for companionship. A desire to make contact with another soul. A hunger for sex.

He should never have brought Meg here.

It wasn't too late. He hadn't promised her anything

but a night's lodging and a lift to Elk Springs in the morning. As soon as she'd contacted her bank and solved her money crisis, she'd be on a bus home. He ignored the mental image of her sunshine fading into the distance and concentrated on ranch business.

An unopened envelope from his lawyer caught his eye. A bill, most likely. The Caldwell litigation had gone before a judge last month. The ruling was in Zack's favor, but the cost had been high. He'd be paying attorney's fees for years.

Frustration grew like a tumor in his chest. He didn't mind the money as much as the continual reminder of the misery oozing from a single day on the river. Two much-loved people had died. He'd give all the money in the world to go back in time and change what had happened, but it wasn't in his power, nor in the Caldwells'. Bringing the damn lawyers into it hadn't eased anyone's grief.

He shoved the attorney's bill to one side, uncovering a newsletter from an environmental organization he and Sky had supported. They'd made some progress in closing down Idaho's most flagrantly polluting mines, but the effort had gained them more enemies than friends. Without Sky he'd lost interest in saving the world. A lot of good environmentalism had done him. He was left behind, his heart torn and bleeding, and the world stayed as screwed up as ever. He tossed the newsletter in the circular file.

As he sorted the bills into piles of those he could put off awhile versus those he couldn't, he came across a plain envelope addressed in heavy block letters. No return address. Local postmark. He knew what he'd find even before he ripped it open. A vein throbbed at his temple as he read the message, handprinted in black ink on a torn-off sheet of yellow paper.

Thou must not Profit on the backs of others. Sacrifice

unto the Lord, lest He Smite you and yours. The Almighty Power knows what thou owest.

An eerie feeling came over Zack, as if someone had looked into his soul and read the secret guilt that had gnawed at him every day for the last year. But no one except Zack—and maybe Win—knew what he'd done, how he'd failed his wife. He shook his head to clear it. This note had to refer to something else.

What did it mean? "Profit"? He hadn't profited from anything recently. Everything he touched turned to shit. In Biblical terms, he felt a lot like Job. All he needed was an outbreak of boils.

Who would write something like this? Why would anyone . . .

A bang on the door startled Zack. From the sheer volume and power, it had to be Winona. He stuffed the hate mail into a drawer on top of the other yellow sheet he'd received after Thessa met an unfortunate demise. This one had different words, but the same ugly tone. Win would be easier to get along with if she didn't know about either note. The "smite" line would put her in a scalp-lifting mood.

"Come in," he yelled.

Red coveralls and Win's solemn face peeked inside. "You busy?"

"Not really." He wished he had an excuse to put her off. It didn't take a rocket scientist to guess what his mother-in-law had on her mind. At least she hadn't blown a cylinder in front of Meg. Not yet, anyway.

Win sat on the sheet-covered loveseat across from his desk. The sheet was there for her because she always seemed to be covered in engine oil. Her black eyes sharpened, lanced him like obsidian arrow points. "Why'd you bring *her* here? She fits in about like a titty-pink Mercedes at a cattle auction. Who is she, anyhow?"

"She comes from Salt Lake City. Says she works with computers. What does it matter, Win? She'll only be here overnight."

"Robby's taken a shine to her. He's liable to get agitated when she goes."

Zack had already figured that out, and it worried him. "Has Robby climbed anything lately?"

"Not since he shimmied up the flagpole the last day of pre-school. The teacher threatened to send him to a special-ed kindergarten next year unless we can straighten him out. This isn't the time to add complications like *her*." Win jabbed a finger in the direction of the window.

The matter-of-fact decree made Zack angry. He didn't like anyone telling him how to live his life, how to raise his own son. Not even Win. "Since when do you decide who I bring home?"

She raised thick.black brows. "That little scrap of woman will cause us all trouble."

"She's already caused *me* trouble, but I . . . She . . ." He took a deep breath. "Hell, I don't know why I brought her here."

Win's enigmatic eyes bored into him. Sky had had the same way of seeing inside a person, and he'd learned to interpret the look. Win questioned his motives, his sanity. She was probably thinking he should have his head examined by a Sioux medicine man.

When he could stand her silent analysis no longer, he made the mistake of glancing outside where Meg and Robby held hands as they wandered through the pasture. They paused to watch a couple of playful young llamas bound around them.

Zack creaked out of his swivel chair and began to pace, even though the room's size allowed only two steps in any direction. "We can't shelter Robby forever. He has to deal with reality, just like the rest of us."

Win's black gaze grew pensive. She picked up a framed wedding photo of Sky and Zack and studied the picture. With a stinging behind his eyelids, Zack envisioned Sky as she had been that day. Long black hair flying in a breeze, almond-colored eyes sparkling with life and love. Her fingers had entwined with his as they spoke heartfelt vows they'd composed themselves.

Ten years ago.

Their nine years together had been good.

Win stroked over the glass, not quite touching. " 'Put a log in the path and the careless will stumble.' That's what Chief Red Hawk used to say."

"What's it mean?" Zack asked impatiently. He didn't have time or inclination to play guessing games with ancestral quotes.

She replaced the photo, turning her full attention to Zack. "Robby's too young to be careful. Your loose-lipped lady will trip him up for sure."

Zack glanced out the window again, watching Robby's lips move as he chattered like . . . like Meg. The kid had changed personality to match her feisty charm. "Robby needs exposure to more women than just you, Win. And Meg is the only one he's allowed within shouting distance in the last year. Like I said, she won't be around here long. Go easy, okay?"

"Have I ever been rude to a guest?" Win asked with all the lethal sweetness of rat poison.

Zack remembered an incident or two. She'd been plenty rude to the single women who'd brought pies and cakes in the months after Sky died. Win had begun sharpening the biggest knife in the house whenever an unmarried female visitor appeared. Once she'd even lugged out a shotgun. Zack was

glad the women had stopped coming, but he suspected Win's conspicuous weapons had been more
discouraging than his own indifference. Then there
was Lydia. After the Yellowstone dispatcher scared
Robby into a tree, Win had threatened to use the
poor woman for tomahawk practice.

As she often did, Win read his mind. "All right,
maybe I was churlish with a few brazen hussies.
You've never complained before."

"No, but Meg's not like the others. She's . . .
different."

Win tilted her head to one side. "Is it Meg? Or is
there something different about you?"

Zack rested a hip on the desk. "Maybe it is me."
While in Yellowstone, he had noted certain changes
in himself. He wasn't sure when they had started,
but the numbness was going away. Time had caught
up with him and he could feel again. The emptiness
hurt worse than ever. He rubbed a hand over his
bearded chin. "I've decided to shave," he announced,
surprising himself. He'd grown the beard after Sky
died, a visible form of mourning, but the damn thing
had started to itch.

"It's the woman," Win said, grunting as she
pushed herself off the sofa. "I don't like her, but I'll
put on my sensitivity act." She shook her head in
disgust. "Just one condition. Keep her away from my
engines, or I swear I'll squash her, flat as recycled
road kill."

He smiled. "No sweat." Win had nothing to worry
about. Dainty Meg, in grease-soaked coveralls, crawling under the hood of an old Chevy van?

Not in this lifetime.

Zack had already tucked Robby into bed and ush-
ered Meg to the spare room when the phone rang.
Through the walls of the study, he could hear Meg

in the shower. She crooned a country love song he recalled hearing on the radio during their drive. Her voice was chock-full of heartbreak and pain, reminding him of what he'd concluded in Yellowstone—that her quirky upbeat chatter was a way of coping with the hurt inside.

His pulse matched the slow, passionate beat of the song. He made a special effort not to picture her swaying to the rhythm as she bathed her slender, naked curves.

He grabbed the insistent telephone and barked a terse "Hello" into the receiver.

"Zack, honey!" Lord help him, Lydia was on his case again. "You sound like you're about to take a bite out of something," she said. "If you've worked up an appetite, come over to my place and I'll take real good care of you." Her voice was low-pitched and husky, spilling over with pornographic promises.

"Why are you calling?" he demanded. "I asked you not to—"

"You *said* you weren't ready for a lover, but from what I hear, you've changed your mind."

"Forget it, Lydia. I wouldn't—" Zack clamped his jaw before he blurted the unvarnished truth. He wouldn't touch Lydia with a vaulting pole, not if she were the last woman west of the Rockies. No need to trample her feelings, though. "Could we take this up some other time? I'm busy right now."

"I understand." Lydia's purring voice had changed, hardened. "One Edward Penrose came into the office this afternoon. His girlfriend is missing. Funny thing is, she was hiking at Slough Creek, right where Andrew saw *you*. Would you happen to know where the elusive lady went from there?"

Zack hissed a lungful of air from between clenched teeth. Damn, Lydia was nosy. But then, a missing person report gave her a reason to ask questions.

Lydia wasn't his problem. Meg was. The pipes groaned as the shower shut off. Zack imagined Meg with water sluicing off all the parts of her he . . . the parts he wouldn't think about. He had to get her out of his house, out of his head. If Edward was still in the area waiting for Lydia's scouting news, Zack could dump Meg in her boyfriend's semi-loving arms. It would be for the best. He opened his mouth to divulge her whereabouts, but he couldn't bring himself to speak.

After an expectant pause, Lydia went on. "The guy's a real stinkbug, pacing the office, calling us Smoky the Bear buffoons, threatening to sue the park service."

Zack snorted. Edward had driven off and left Meg alone, and now he expected the rangers to make it right. From everything Meg had said, and a few things she hadn't, the moronic dandy had treated her like used carpet. That must be why Zack was shielding her. He'd always been a sucker for the underdog.

"We'll organize a search party, unless you know something we don't," Lydia was saying. "Like maybe she's not lost after all."

Zack wanted Edward to sweat a while, but the Forest Service didn't deserve the trouble a lawsuit-happy computer magnate could dish out.

"Let me talk to Andrew." If Zack was going to admit where Meg was, he'd rather give the news to a friend. Maybe Andrew could figure a way to keep Edward off her trail.

"He's still out on patrol," Lydia announced. "Might as well tell me what you know. Or I can put you through to the park superintendent."

The super and Zack had had many heated arguments over grizzly habitat and trail closures and park management in general. All in all, Zack preferred talking to Lydia. "Scratch the super. Just tell Edward his girlfriend's fine." He sighed. "I'd rather keep it quiet, but if he insists on knowing her exact location, she's with me. On the ranch."

"Well, well," Lydia declared. "Has Winona pulled a hatchet on her yet? Or is Win into burning at the stake these days? I'd be more than happy to bring over some kindling."

"Stay right where you are," he said. Shouted, really. Add Lydia to whatever chaos Meg would cause, and Robby might end up on the roof, on the tip of a lighting rod. Besides that, just seeing Lydia would ruin Zack's whole week.

"Unfortunately, I'm on duty. I'll give the obnoxious boyfriend directions to Elk Springs, and Daddy can take it from there." Daddy would, too. Sheriff Larkin, Lydia's father, would do anything for her. He had even covered for her after that little incident during her third marriage when hubby had "accidentally" shot himself twice in the groin while cleaning his gun.

"Don't—" Zack began, hoping to at least keep the sheriff out of it.

Breathy laughter gusted from the receiver. She hung up before he could get out his protest.

He should have been pleased. If Edward came after Meg, Zack would be rid of the human earache who'd afflicted him for two days. But he wasn't pleased at all. He dreaded watching her climb into Edward's BMW and drive away.

The bathroom door opened. He heard Meg pad across the hall to the spare bedroom, crooning the same sad tune she'd sung while she showered. The melody tugged at a loose thread in Zack's heart. Or a loose screw in his brain.

Meg was bad news. For him. In the long run, she was bad news for Robby, too. And her presence in-

vited Win to start up more of her infamous shenanigans. Win, in high gear, would scare the ever-loving
stuffing out of Meg. If it were up to Zack, he might
let her stay on the ranch a few days, but he wasn't
the only person involved. He had to consider what
was best for everyone.

Zack knew exactly what he should do. Tomorrow
morning, he'd vacate the house until Meg's boyfriend
showed up. The two could work things out for themselves. If she still loved Edward—or if she were desperate enough to reclaim the job she'd too
impulsively quit—she'd leave.

Last night, she had cried all over Zack's shirt for
Edward Penrose. The guy must have some re-
deeming qualities. And even if he didn't, why should
Zack concern himself one way or the other? Meg was
nothing to him. They'd shared a tent and trail time,
nothing more.

So why did Zack feel like *he* was the one deserting
her? Why did he feel so damn guilty?

Chapter Six

Meg's bedroom door crashed open, striking the wall.

A hint of dawn shone through gauzy curtains. Shadows drifted in the doorway. Disoriented, her eyes misted from sleep, she sat up in bed and drew a multicolored quilt to her chin. "Who is it?" she rasped in a voice hoarse from a night's disuse. No one answered.

She cleared her throat to try again. A large black beast hurtled toward her, followed by a child in blue-and-white pajamas.

A scream stuck in her larynx. She saw pointed teeth and smelled dog breath as she fell back under the onslaught. A long tongue slurped her like a bowl of soup. Sticky fingers pulled her bare arm from under the covers.

"Up, Meg. Get up." The voice was very young and very loud. "Daddy baked eggs, special for you." The "thpecial" sprayed her cheek and added to Hoover's eager moisture. A whiff of sizzling bacon subdued the anxiety in her stomach.

"Sounds great." And it did. Now that Meg wasn't scared out of her wits, she appreciated the enthusiasm of her welcoming crew. She looped an arm around the boy's neck. He giggled, wiggling an escape. The big black dog circled until he found a place to settle at Meg's side.

A switch clicked. Mellow light bathed the room. One glance at the door had Meg shrinking beneath a sheet until all but her face was hidden.

Zack stood there wearing faded jeans and nothing else. He crossed arms over his chest and leaned a shoulder against the door frame, making no effort to call off either dog or kid. There was something different about him. Even without a shirt, he somehow looked more civilized.

"Hi," she said. And fell awkwardly silent. Under normal circumstances, she never struggled for words. But at the moment, all trace of normal had been pounced right out of her.

He arched a brow. "Now I know how to keep you quiet."

"Send in the special forces?" she guessed.

"Either that, or jump on you and cover your face with slime." When his lips curved in a lazy smile, she pinpointed the change. He'd shaved his beard. The mouth that had emerged was beautifully shaped, making her think of long slow kisses and silken nights. Which was ludicrous. She barely knew the man.

Zack rubbed his newly shaven jaw. "I told Robby to knock first, since ladies like their privacy, but once he'd barged in, I thought I ought to . . . supervise."

Meg wiped Hoover's greeting from her cheek using a corner of blue sheet. The quilt was out of reach, crumpled beneath her uninvited bedmates. When she glanced up again, she found Zack staring at her exposed shoulder. Tugging the sheet around her neck, she was acutely conscious of her lack of dress. After a heavenly shower she'd had nothing clean to wear, so she'd worn nothing at all.

Zack pointed toward the foot of the bed. "I found your clothes in the bathroom and ran them through the wash."

She saw them neatly folded, bra and panties on top. The casual appearance of her underwear heated her face to grilling temperature.

"Lydia called last night," Zack said, jolting her attention back to him. As his eyes traced the shape of her body beneath the thin sheet, she resisted the urge to squirm.

Anxious to transfer Zack's thoughts to something other than what she wasn't wearing, she said the first thing that came to mind. "Should I play Wonder Woman and defend you?" She dared an uncertain smile. Maybe he didn't really want to be saved from the sexpot dispatcher. "Is Lydia coming here? I don't want to be in the way. If you . . ." The sentence faded and died.

It occurred to Meg that she needn't worry about being in the way. Zack had said he would take her to town today, and she was sure he'd keep his word. She had no identification, but there must be some method of wiring money from her bank account. She tried to remember what her balance was. Not much. Maybe enough for bus fare.

She wished she could languish here for a week or two, lie back and enjoy the scenery. Especially the scenery leaning against the door jam. Zack looked like a model for an outdoors magazine, all corded muscle and dark hair, with jeans riding low on his hips. The sight of him made her thighs melt, which had never happened when she looked at Edward.

"Daddy says you're pretty when you're sleeping," Robby said. His damp adhesive fingers pried one of her hands off the sheet and directed her to Hoover's fur.

She patted the dog automatically, but her thoughts remained suspended with Robby's ingenuous comment. How long had Zack watched before she'd known he was there? His eyes gave nothing away.

He straightened, his shoulders spanning the doorway. "Lydia called because she met your boyfriend. He went to Mammoth Ranger Station pitching a fit when you didn't show up at the trailhead, like he'd apparently expected."

"Edward's looking for me?" She almost forgot to maintain a one-handed hold on the sheet. "I thought he'd be back in Utah by now."

"No such luck. I had to admit you're here, or we might have ended up with the F.B.I. on the doorstep."

Her heart clenched at the thought of men with badges coming after her. She shuddered, imagining handcuffs and sirens. She ought to be relieved Edward was still nearby, still cared whether she was alive or dead. Instead, she felt as if an escape hatch had just closed, leaving her chained in a windowless room. She took a deep breath. "Did you get a phone number? If he's willing to meet me in Elk Springs, I guess I could catch a ride with him. It would be . . . the practical thing to do."

Zack moved a step closer. "You don't have to leave right away." He paused as if searching for the right words. "What I mean is, there's no rush."

She raked her teeth over her lower lip and wondered how to explain the situation. Edward had more influence over her than she cared to admit, but she couldn't tell Zack that. Instead, she improvised. "Just because Edward and I had a disagreement is no reason to avoid him forever. I'm almost sure he'll give me my job back. And if he drives me home, I'll be out of your way that much sooner."

Zack scowled. "I wouldn't abandon you on the streets of Elk Springs, if that's what you're thinking."

"I know you wouldn't. You've been wonderful." She met his gaze, smiling her gratitude. "But . . ."

The smile wavered. "I-I need Edward." Unfortunately, it was true.

Zack's eyes narrowed. "Do you *want* to go with him?"

"I . . ." She didn't know what she wanted. And under Zack's concentrated gaze, she forgot the question.

Her lower abdomen felt as if a fast elevator had delivered her to the twentieth floor. Her breasts grew hot and tingly. Her nipples hardened beneath the sheet as his gaze took another lazy tour down her body. The morning sun reflecting in his gray eyes reminded her of a flickering campfire, of licking flames, of wood smoke.

She sniffed. Smoke? The air between them had grown hazy, and not from her erotic imaginings. "Something's burning," she announced.

Zack shook his head like a man coming out of a trance. Whirling, he raced down the hall. Hoover whined and jumped off the bed. Robby covered his ears as a volley of curses echoed from the kitchen.

Almost setting the house on fire brought Zack back to sanity. He couldn't handle a desirable woman sleeping naked in his spare room, not on a regular basis. He hadn't slept at all last night, and not much the night before. If she hung around here for long, he'd end up sharing a bed with her—and he'd already decided that wasn't an option.

Still, the idea of sending Meg off with her former fiancé made him cringe. It was like delivering a naked, defenseless lamb—or Easter chick—into striking range of a greedy coyote. She'd said she *needed* Edward, and he didn't like the sound of that. It was as if the guy had some kind of unholy hold on her. Then again, she was a grown woman, and none of Zack's damn business.

He opened all the windows to clear out the smoke and tossed blackened bacon into the trash can. He'd just gotten down the cereal bowls when he heard a rusty voice call his name. He turned toward the screen door. Tobias stood on the porch holding his crumpled cap in both hands.

Zack put the bowls on the table and walked the couple of steps to the door. He pushed open the screen. "Come on in and have some breakfast," he offered. "I'm running a little late but—"

"We got trouble," Tobias cut in, keeping his voice low. He wore a deep frown on a face battered by weather and innumerable barroom brawls. "The black-and-white llama baby's not in the pasture. His mama's frantic, running all over the place, spitting at anybody who comes near. Figured you'd want to know before I start checking for holes in the fence."

Another missing llama. And Checkers, a three-month-old cria with a stud-quality pedigree, was worth ten thousand dollars if Zack could keep the animal alive long enough to wean.

"Hold on a minute." He left Tobias at the door and grabbed the shirt he'd left on the back of a chair.

Robby was climbing on the counter to reach the cups. Zack paused, took two cups from a cabinet, and swooped the boy to the floor. "Show Meg where we keep the cereal, son. I'll see you later."

Meg had dressed and padded barefoot into the kitchen. She looked at Zack expectantly.

He wished he could think of something to say, but he'd already said more than was wise. He'd as much as offered her sanctuary on his ranch for as long as she wanted it. He hated leaving her to face Edward alone, but she was the one who'd been traveling with the sonuvabitch. She ought to be able to handle him.

Zack turned away from her big green eyes and rushed out the door.

"We'll take horses," he told the hired hand. He jumped off the porch, bypassing the stairs, with Tobias right behind him.

No sooner had Meg poured cereal for her and Robby than Winona, yawning, opened the door of her room and shuffled down the hall. She joined them at the kitchen table. Her lime-green coveralls were a cleaner, brighter version of yesterday's outfit. Meg was thankful they weren't orange, like the ill-fitting garments that had been her own fashion statement for the last few months. For the rest of her life, orange would probably give her a skin rash.

The three of them ate in silence. Meg was too busy thinking to talk. Zack had neglected to give her a number where she could reach Edward, but she supposed it wouldn't matter anyway. Edward was, in all likelihood, already gone. Once he knew she had left Yellowstone with another man, he'd be too furious, too proud, to come looking for her.

Edward was not particularly forgiving.

On the other hand, maybe he was not entirely to blame. Had she ever really loved him for what he was? Perhaps she had a problem with loyalty, too, because when she tried to picture Edward, she saw Zack's wolf-silver eyes instead.

The tapping of a spoon on the table brought Meg out of her reverie. Win glared, spoon in hand. "What's wrong with you, girl?" she demanded. "You having a vision or some such?"

Blushing, Meg jumped up from her chair and began gathering empty cereal bowls. "I'll do the dishes," she volunteered. Anything to turn her mind from the direction it had strayed.

Win rose slowly, a murderous gleam in her eyes. "Don't touch anything." Her voice boomed like the backfire from an eighteen wheeler. "I'll take care of it before supper. I don't want you getting the idea you're needed around here, Little Big Mouth."

"I like being useful." Meg stubbornly ignored the get-lost message and the nickname. She'd been called worse.

Winona's breasts expanded beneath the coveralls. "If you have an eye for Zack, you're wasting your time. I don't want you harassing him."

Meg blinked, wondering what she'd done to earn Winona's contempt. "I'm only trying to help."

"Robby's the one who'll get hurt."

"What do you mean?" Meg asked. "I wouldn't hurt anyone, especially not . . ."

Either Winona wasn't interested in clarification, or she was anxious to get back to clutch guts and axle grease. "I'll be under the van," she announced, slamming through the screen door. "If a guy with a sixty-eight Mustang comes by, send him to the garage."

Robby leaned his upper body on the table as he watched Winona stomp across the yard. His paint-palette eyes rounded. "What's wrong with Gramma Win?"

"I guess she doesn't like me being here." Meg picked up a coffee mug, thinking how good it would feel to hurl it at Win's retreating rump.

"I like you." Robby scooted from his chair to take her hand. "So does Hoover." To emphasize, the big dog lumbered from his place under the table and licked the torn hem of her shorts.

The acceptance meant a lot to Meg, especially now, with her recent mistakes looming much larger than her accomplishments.

She bent down to give the child a hug. At his urging, she planted a kiss on Hoover's black fur. When she wrinkled her nose at Robby, his gap-toothed grin reminded her of Winona's dire prediction.

Hurt Robby? Never. Meg had made her share of

mistakes, but she had never purposefully hurt anyone. She would never hurt a child. Winona was out-
rageous to suggest such a thing.

As Meg saw it, Winona should welcome her help,
at least with the dishes. The kitchen reflected more
than a few days' neglect. The cabinets bore layers of
grease, the stove had dead bugs and blackened noo-
dles in the catch pans. Moldy leftovers crammed the
refrigerator. Obviously, kitchen hygiene was not high
on Winona's list.

Meg wanted to do something to repay Zack's kind-
ness. Saving him from future food poisoning seemed
a reasonable cause. She set to work with Robby
"helping," which meant he was under her bare feet
every time she turned around. Hoover acted as a
vacuum cleaner, inhaling anything she spilled.

After a couple of hours, the kitchen was . . . maybe
not gleaming, but significantly improved. At her sug-
gestion, Robby had taken on the job of stacking
canned goods in the middle of the floor. With one
tower teetering at the upper limits of his reach, he
began groundwork for a neighboring structure. Hoover rested his head on front paws, tail twitching, dark
eyes tracking tins of soup and beans.

Meg glanced out the door. No activity at the barn.
No men on horses returning through the pasture.
Zack must not have found the pesky llama. Since she
had nothing better to do until he came back to drive
her to town, she assigned herself another task. The
huge chest freezer was a mess. She'd sort the good
stuff from what was freezer-burned beyond hope.

As she lifted the lid and poked her head into the
frosty air, she heard tires crunching gravel on the
drive. One car? Two? She assumed Winona's cus-
tomer had brought the Mustang. Meg didn't look
outside, since Win would resent her interference in

the auto repair business even more than in the kitchen.

A sound almost like a donkey's bray came from the back pasture. "That's Heidi," Robby explained, fetching more soup from the pantry. "Daddy's gone to look for her baby. Heidi's like a burglar alarm, Daddy says, 'cept she only works when she wants to." Robby clasped the tip of his tongue in his teeth as he added one more can to the top of his structure.

Meg ducked under the freezer lid again, ignoring the slamming car doors, the outside voices.

When the screen door squeaked, Meg banged her head while exiting the chest freezer with a plastic container of tomatoes in one hand and a sticky carton of ice cream in the other. Hoover made for the door, toenails scrabbling on linoleum.

"Is that you, Meg?"

She squinted at the screen, not quite believing her eyes and ears. Edward. He had come! Had she been wrong about him? Was it possible he'd transmutated from frog to prince after all? A warm spring of hope bubbled inside her. He wouldn't be here unless . . .

A blue-uniformed officer came up behind Edward and filled the rest of the doorway. She shrank from the silver badge before she caught herself and stiffened her spine.

Setting down the frozen goods, she wiped her hands on a faded ink towel. "It's me. Come on in."

Her hope dammed at the source. Edward must have known the policeman would scare her. Was he still trying to manipulate instead of simply saying and showing he cared? Would he use the policeman to force her to return with him? Maybe he'd arrange to have her arrested on some charge or other. Once a person had a conviction on her record, once she'd spent time in jail, she became a likely suspect for anything that resembled a crime. With a sickening lurch in her stomach, she acknowledged that Edward knew her secrets and her greatest fears. And he wasn't above using them to get his way.

The two men eased into the kitchen. Hoover sniffed their shoes before lying at the policeman's feet. Robby stopped his construction to eye the men warily.

"I'm Sheriff Larkin." The officer extended a hand to Meg. He was fiftyish, of medium height and weight. A white cowboy hat shaded his steel-rimmed glasses. She touched her damp palm to his in the briefest possible handshake.

Edward glanced up and down her figure with disdain. Meg did a quick survey of herself and saw what displeased him. She was rumpled and dirty, with a dribble of chocolate ice cream seeping through her untucked blouse. Her feet were bare; grit chafed between her toes.

"I wasn't expecting you, Edward."

"That's obvious," he snapped.

Meg had never seen his face so red. Either he'd been out in the sun too long, or his blood pressure was up. Knowing Edward, it had to be the latter. Wisely, Sheriff Larkin backed out of the line of fire. Robby scooted behind his twin towers.

"What are you doing in this provincial dump?" Edward demanded. "Didn't you know I'd be at the hotel?"

"No." She'd never thought he'd stick around, not after she'd quit both him and the company. "Since you and I are no longer a couple, I assumed—"

"You're enjoying this, aren't you? I spend hours at a low-rent ranger station, trying to figure out where you went. I drive down roads from hell, get spit on by one of those wooly mammoths outside . . ." He indicated a streak of green slime down the front of his beige polo shirt. "Only to find you cleaning some-body's freezer, playing nanny to an Indian brat."

Meg's temper flared. "I happen to like children. And if you don't care for my reception, go interface with a computer screen instead. I'm through trying to please you. No matter what I do, you're never satis—"

The sheriff, still standing behind Edward, knocked on the wall. "Pardon me, but now that you two love-birds have found each other, I'll mosey. I'm behind on my paperwork." He tipped his white hat in Meg's direction. "If you get lost, Penrose, just ask anybody the way to town."

Edward glared after the retreating uniform. "The smart-ass old fart will gloat over our reunion for days. Not that I care what he thinks, but I won't accept you shutting down on me. We're getting out of here right now."

Meg took a deep breath. She would not kowtow to Edward as she had to her stepfather for so long. Obviously, Edward expected her to return to work, and to him. Zack had asked her what *she* wanted, which was a novel consideration, coming from a man. Now she knew the answer. "I'm not going."

The heck with practicality.

Maybe sleeping in a crooked house that negated all the rules of architecture had liberated her to be herself, to act as illogically and impetuously as she wished. "You granted me a vacation, remember? And I intend to make the most of it. I'll get home on my own, hitchhike if I have to."

"What?" he yelled. "Use your head, if you can remember how to boot it up. You need me. I could point out all the ways and whys, but we both know what they are. This Burkhart joker can't take care of you like I can. You need—"

"Don't tell me what I need. I don't give a darn about monetary assets—his or yours."

His thin nostrils flared. "As your future husband *and* your employer, I must insist you exit this . . ." he glanced about scornfully, ". . . this asymmetric agricultural junkyard. You have deplorable taste."

Until recently, that was true. She'd thought Edward was intelligent, persuasive, charming, which certainly demonstrated a lack of discrimination. She backed against the freezer as he moved closer. "I appreciate you standing by me for the last few months, I really do. But now . . . Your priorities are with the latest business deal, and mine are still a little shaky. Give me the freedom to think things through."

He snaked a hand around her waist. "If you want to stay free, you'll get in my car right now."

"Are you threatening me?" she asked, pushing at his arm.

"As I see it, I'm being more than reasonable. I'm willing to disregard the fact that you had a temper tantrum and quit PenUltimate. Remember, you need a job, and I'm your best bet. As you know, I pulled some strings to get you an early release. I *could* tug on the other end of those strings."

"I'll find someone else to tug on my end." She didn't have anyone particularly in mind, but she wouldn't allow Edward to jerk her around any longer.

He blinked. "That won't be necessary. You're annoyed with me right now, princess, but you'll get over—"

She wrenched out of his grasp. "I'm not annoyed," she shouted. "I'm mad as hell. I haven't forgotten what you said about my honesty. You don't trust me, Edward. Without that, there's nothing between us worth talking about. I can survive on my own."

"Who's going to hire an ex-con?" he taunted. "Who'll take on that kind of responsibility? This Burkhart fellow? I heard all about him from the Yellowstone dispatcher. He's a small-time rancher with dirt under his fingernails. A nobody."

Meg saw Zack on a much larger scale, a hero descending a cliff to rescue her. He had exceptionally clean fingernails, and the rest of him was exceptional, too.

"This isn't about Zack, my job, or my parole," she said. "It's about you and me . . . and the relationship we don't have." Her hands clenched into fists at her sides. She backed around the kitchen table, using it as a barrier. Sticky heat collected in her armpits; drops of sweat formed on her inner thighs. She feared a revocation of parole more than anything. But she couldn't let Edward dictate her every move.

"Don't be stubborn, Meg. You know I love you." Those same words had seduced her once. He seemed to think they'd still be effective.

A lead weight settled in her chest. She'd been stupid to believe Edward cared about her. He cared about no one but himself. He'd preyed on her insecurities, and now on her legal dilemma. She shook her head. "You don't love me. I'll never mean more to you than—"

She saw movement to her side. As Robby's towers toppled, cans crashed and rolled across the room. One tin landed on Edward's foot. He yelped and leaped out of the way.

Robby stood where the towers had been, glaring at Edward, sticking out his tongue. Edward cursed viciously and lunged for the child. Hoover planted himself in the way. The dog's fur stood on end. A low growl started in his throat.

Catching the sleeve of Edward's shirt, Meg yanked

until the material ripped. "Don't you dare touch Robby."

Edward changed target in mid stride. He grabbed Meg's hand. "You're coming with me."

"No!" She set her heels while he half-dragged her across the room. Her feet squeaked on the gray linoleum. Passive resistance wasn't working, so she pounded him with her free arm and kicked at his shins. Her bare toes made little impression. He hauled her out the door and down the porch steps. She screamed for help. One of the llamas answered with a braying alarm.

Tools clattered in the garage, but Meg expected no support from that direction. Win would be glad to see her go, willing or not. The silver BMW, sparkling in the sunlight, awaited them. The passenger door was open. All Edward had to do was shove her inside. Meg was beginning to think her struggles were hopeless when she heard a shout from the pasture. Zack, mounted on a powerful bay, was galloping toward the fence. Meg thought man and horse would go right through the rails and hogwire, but the horse leaned back on his haunches at the last minute and skidded to a halt with forelegs locked.

Zack leaped from the horse's back and vaulted a five-foot gate. "Let her go!" he shouted, dashing around the Beamer's taillights.

"Stay out of this," Edward yelled. He hung onto her arm.

"Let go, I said." Fury seethed in Zack's voice as he kept right on coming, hands flexing at his sides.

Meg jerked free, but the ferocious scowl on Zack's face made her think he might lunge at Edward any second. "Wait," she told him. "Edward and I can solve this without violence."

Edward touched her arm, more gently this time. Since type-A physical dominance had failed, he turned up the wattage on his charmer smile. "Please come with me, princess. You're the most important person in my life."

"Sure," she jeered. "I rank just ahead of the cat you only occasionally remember to feed. The one whose name you can never recall. *Her* name is Princess. I'm Meg."

Edward had always tried to control her in any underhanded way he could. Until now, she hadn't recognized what he was doing.

His blue eyes shadowed. He looked worried. "Come back to work, if nothing else. The first sales reports on *Athena* are in, and they're . . . beyond anyone's expectations. The game's worth megabucks. I need you on the sequel team, right away. You know you want to be part of it. Besides, you owe me for . . ." he paused, glanced at Zack.

Meg knew Edward wanted to blurt the details of what and why she owed him, but he hesitated to give away that last ace in front of a stranger. Or maybe he realized she'd never, ever forgive him if he went that far.

She was relieved at what he hadn't said, until what he *had* said sank in. She stared in disbelief, feeling like Pavlov's dog after its first shock treatment. He didn't want her love, only her characters, her game magic, and the money they could bring him. She shuddered; her skin chilled as if she'd been thrust naked into a snowstorm. "Go away," she said hoarsely.

Zack pushed Meg behind him. "She asked you to leave. If I were you, I'd make tracks."

Edward's thin nostrils flared. He tilted his head back and looked down his long nose at Zack. "No hillbilly rancher orders me around."

Grasping his opponent by the neck of the beige Polo, Zack shoved him against the car. "I wouldn't bet on that, hotshot." He drew back his fist for a blow.

"Don't!" Meg said.

Zack froze. A frown drew his brows into a single straight line.

"I'll handle this myself." She pressed his fist downward, meeting considerable resistance. Zack backed off, eyeing Edward with scorn.

"Thank God you've come to your senses, Meg." Edward swiped a shirt sleeve over his sweating forehead. "You can't stay here. This man's a brute, an animal."

"He's not a brute. And I'm not going anywhere with you, Edward. I only stopped him so you'd be conscious while I make one last statement." In a calm and steady voice, she told him exactly where he could store the PenUltimate joystick.

He stiffened at the insult. "If you want to play rough, that's fine with me. You have ten days, Meg, before your leave-time's officially over. If you don't show up at PenUltimate, I'll contact some mutual friends of ours to report you went AWOL. One way or the other, I'll see you soon."

In a choppy gait, he rounded the car, then slid into the gray leather upholstery on the driver's side. The engine purred. The passenger window electronically descended. Edward leaned over to yell across the seat, "If you get enough of your country boy before then, call me. Collect."

He threw her hemp-woven shoulder bag out the window at the same moment he hit the gas. Tires spun, flinging dust and pebbles. He wheeled the car in an about-face and rocketed toward the main road.

Meg drooped like a marionette whose strings had been cut. If she didn't return by the time her travel permit expired, Edward would make sure her parole officer reported her missing. She'd be hunted down and thrown back in jail. Feeling as cornered as a rat on death row, she tried to convince herself that his threats were a sign of desperation, that he really did love her still. But she knew it wasn't true.

She crouched to pick up the shoulder bag, gathering a tube of hand lotion, a comb, a cracked mirror. As she replaced the items, she realized why Edward had said "collect" with such smug satisfaction. Nothing else was inside. No wallet. No money.

Slowly, she stood. Her fingers shook. She had trouble grasping the purse. Zack took it, holding the straps in one hand, slipping his free arm around her shoulders. As he steered her into the house, she couldn't stop shuddering. Not from fear or loss. She shook from anger.

Once she was in a chair, Zack knelt in front of her and nudged up her chin. "Did he hurt you?"

"I'm fine," she hastened to say. "I just wasn't expecting . . . Edward's never been like this before." She knew why. Because she'd almost always done as he demanded. Because he'd been in control.

"What did he mean about going AWOL? Is he holding something over you?"

"Well . . . sort of. I have an employee contract." That was what had swayed the parole board to grant early release. A guarantee of full employment convinced them she'd stay out of trouble.

Zack's hands found their way to her shoulders, where he kneaded gently. "I know a good lawyer. You should get some advice."

"I should have gotten advice a long time ago." She sighed. "Before I sold *Athena* and all associated rights for tiddlywinks."

"How did that happen?" Zack asked. "I thought everyone in the compute business made big money."

"Gaming is different," she said. "Especially for newbies in the field, like me. I was just playing at game design until I heard about PenUltimate looking for talent. I thought I might as well present my prototype. To my shock, Edward made an offer right away."

Zack continued his massage, finding her tightened muscles and easing them. She leaned her head to one side and touched his hand to her cheek. His fingers traced her jaw line before he seemed to realize what he was doing. He abruptly drew back.

Meg pretended not to notice and plunged on with the story. "He gave me a ten thousand dollar advance, a smidgen of royalty, and a chance to get a foot in the door of the gaming business. Working with PenUltimate's heavyweight production team seemed like the gateway to heaven, even if my salary increase over the greeting card job was negligible."

"Edward took you to the cleaners," Zack said grimly.

"He'll reap the benefits, that's for sure. But as combination developer and publisher, he took a big financial risk. It was up to me to insist on better terms. Since I didn't, I can't blame Edward for—"

"You're defending him again," Zack pointed out.

"It's habit, I suppose." She shrugged. "If I'd known better, I would have held onto the copyright, but . . . Well, I thought the guy was a sexy Bill Gates. I put all my effort into proving myself to him. It never occurred to me that he wasn't giving much back. A few months ago he gave me another advance, this time for a sequel storyline. He owns the rights, of course. I thought he was doing me a favor, showing confidence in my abilities, but he must have known *Athena* would do well. He'd seen reviews and had presales orders. He knew . . ."

She banged the flat of her hand on the table. "I trusted him. After all, he'd asked me to be his wife, and . . ." She drooped, sinking lower in the chair.

"Oh, God, that must have been part of it. He proposed marriage to guarantee loyalty to him and the company. To prevent me from looking elsewhere. And it worked so well."

"But Meg," Zack mused, "if he owns sequel rights already, why does he need you?"

She sat up straighter. "*Athena*'s sequel won't have the same feel as the original if someone else designs it. He's afraid players will know the difference right away." Ironically, Edward did need her, although not in the way she'd envisioned.

"Couldn't you just pay back the advance and opt out?" Zack asked.

"Maybe. If I had the money, which I don't." She would receive a royalty check from *Athena* eventually, but that wouldn't help her now. "Meanwhile, if I go to work for another company in the industry, he might sue me." Or cause other disturbances she didn't care to think about.

Zack put his hand over hers on the table. His eyes, dark with compassion, studied her, perhaps expecting a flood of tears. She wasn't going to cry, though. She'd cried over Edward once, which was more than enough.

"I'm okay. Really." She shifted, trying unsuccessfully to retrieve her hand. "I established my independence today, for what it's worth. But he has a right to expect—"

"He has no right to drag you around." Zack caressed the back of her hand with a tenderness that heated her skin.

Meg made a conscious effort to locate her tongue and string logical words together. "From the look on your face when you came to my rescue, I thought you were going to take me by the hair and haul me in the opposite direction." She sounded prim and prissy, which was not at all how she felt. His touch made her want to melt like ice cream on a warm spoon.

"Yeah, I guess for a minute I . . ." A corner of his mouth rose ever so slightly. "Seeing him bully you fired up my protective instincts."

Protective? Yes, that's all it was. His caress was a safeguard, not a seduction. Meg was unaccustomed to such treatment. Edward had coddled PenUltimate; he'd never coddled *her*. Why would Zack, a virtual stranger, go out of his way to protect her? She irritated him, he'd made that plain enough. Yet he'd become her reluctant hero.

She extracted her hand from his. "Thanks for . . ." She wanted to say for caring, but that seemed presumptuous. "For standing up to Edward."

"Any time." Zack rose to his feet and placed her shoulder bag on the table beside her. "At least you have your purse now. That ought to make things easier for you."

Meg nodded. Unfortunately, the contents would not get her very far. She tried to smile.

Zack, however, wasn't looking at her anymore. He glanced around the room, frowning.

"Where's Robby? Wasn't he with you this morning?"

"He was in here when Edward . . ." Meg rose from her chair, forgetting her own troubles. Cans covered the floor, reminding her of toppled towers, of Robby's chivalrous defense. She couldn't remember seeing him after Edward dragged her out of the kitchen.

As Zack rushed down the hall toward the child's room, she peered under the big oak table, expecting to find Hoover. Hoping to find Robby. No dog. No boy. She checked the small living area adjoining the kitchen. No boy there, either. Where could he have gone? Had Edward frightened him into hiding? Or had he retreated to some secret place because he thought Meg had left?

She heard Zack bellowing his son's name as he stalked through the house. Anyone within half a mile must have heard him, but there was no reply.

Robby's the one who'll get hurt. Recalling Win's words, Meg halted in the middle of the kitchen. Her stomach felt queasy all of a sudden. Was Robby hurt? And even if he was fine now, would he still be okay after she was gone?

Somehow, by some accident of fate, she had stirred Robby's longing for a mother's love. She'd sensed what the boy wanted, although she hadn't named it until now. Nor had she considered the significance. He had latched onto her with all the hope in his tender heart.

And she, with her screwed-up life and predetermined future, was doomed to disappoint him.

Chapter Seven

"He's not in the house." Zack ploughed a hand through his hair, wondering where to look next. Dear God, what had he done, bringing Meg and her problems into his confused son's life?

She was flinging bags and brooms from the pantry as if the boy would magically appear behind the clutter. "When I was a kid, I sometimes hid in a closet. My mother and stepfather yelled at each other a lot and I'd get scared. Robby heard me and Edward say awful things. Maybe he—" She stopped her frantic search through the pantry and turned to Zack, as if she expected him to fill in the blank.

He scowled. "Ever since his mother died, Robby climbs when he's upset." And the boy was bound to be upset, after what he'd seen and heard. Zack thought about the most likely places to look while Meg dropped to the floor to check the lazy Susan in a corner cabinet.

One thing about her, she didn't give up easily. "I know Robby misses his mama. He said—"

"Robby *talked* about her?" Zack was dumbfounded. Neither he nor Win nor Robby ever talked about Sky. It hurt too much. Why had the child broken the mold and confided in Meg, an outsider?

"He said she lives in the blue part of the sky, and she never comes down to hug him anymore." Meg closed the cabinet carefully. Her shoulders rose and fell with a sigh. When she got to her feet, her eyes shimmered with moisture. "I promised I wouldn't leave without giving him a hug. Then Edward came. When he pulled me outside, Robby must have thought I was going." Her gaze met Zack's and skittered away.

Robby was upset because he'd lost out on a hug? Considering whom he'd be hugging, Zack could understand the disappointment. He left the house and started for the closest group of trees. Meg trailed behind him.

"Robby's last hiding place was in an aspen," Zack said, thinking aloud. "He shimmied up the trunk and perched on a branch that would have cracked under my weight, so I couldn't go up after him. If it hadn't been for a thunderstorm, he might have stayed there all night."

The wind tearing through delicate leaves had wrenched Zack's heart and sent chills down his spine. That time, Thessa's death had precipitated Robby's climbing spree.

Today, the boy was not in any of the aspen trees, nor in the cottonwoods along the creek. Returning to the house, Zack scaled a trellis to examine the roof, with Meg yelling, "Be careful!" from below.

He vividly recalled the way his heart had pounded and his breath jammed with fear when he'd found four-year-old Robby tottering on a rain spout soon after Sky died. That was another reason he never mentioned Sky in front of his son. The reaction might be dangerous, unpredictable, even fatal.

This time, Robby wasn't on the roof. As Zack eliminated possibilities, his insides grew hollow. He was headed for the barn when Winona appeared at the garage door, waving and shouting, "He's here!"

Zack rushed into the outbuilding where Win was pointing directly above the gray Chevy van.

"How the hell did he get up there?" Zack demanded, straining to see into the dim rafters after the bright sunlight outside.

"He scrambled on top of the van," Win boomed. "I made a swoop for him, but he moved too fast. When I sweet-talked, he covered his ears. I thought it'd be best to shut up and let him hold on with both hands."

The beams crisscrossed like a crooked jungle gym. Robby was perched near the roof's peak, staring downward with eyes as wide and round as an owl's. As Zack's initial panic drained, he wondered if letting Robby sit up there awhile might be the best cure for climbing he could devise.

Maybe the kid sought attention, and their red alerts only reinforced the behavior. Or maybe he was truly unstable, as the experts claimed. Zack's head began to ache. Robby's future depended on him, and he didn't have the slightest idea how to deal with the child.

"The psychiatrist in Pocatello said to keep calm and talk him down." Win sent Meg a glance that put her in the category of a magnified louse. "I guess *she's* what stirred him up."

Hoover had appeared from the shadows and was whining at Meg's feet. Sidestepping the dog, Meg hopped on the van's running board and attempted to boost herself onto the roof. Her legs flailed. Panting, she called, "Don't just stand there, Zack. Help me."

When he saw that she meant to rescue the boy all by herself, he scooped her from the van and deposited her on the ground beside him. "That's all we need, another body poised for disaster," he taunted. "I've already fetched you off a cliff once this week. Give me a break."

Her cheeks stained with a blush. "I'm light and

small enough to get into the rafters. I'm not nearly as clumsy as I look and I could—"

"No." Didn't the woman ever shut up?

"I want to help," she insisted. "Winona's right, it's my fault he's up there."

Zack closed his eyes for a second. It was his fault, not Meg's. If he'd thought ahead, he'd have known Meg would upset Robby. She was a psychological disturbance waiting to happen. But he hadn't thought. Not enough, anyway. He'd brought her here because she made him smile. Because she'd awakened desire he never thought he'd feel again. Simple, selfish, elemental reasons, originating in organs other than his brain.

"You don't understand." He lowered his voice to keep it from carrying to the rafters. "We've taken him to shrinks, counselors, the works. They all have different names for what's wrong with him, but basically, they say Robby's on the edge. This climbing thing's a sign of withdrawal from reality."

Meg shook her head. "I don't buy that. He's just scared. Robby was fine last night. He was happy this morning, right up until Edward . . ."

Win moved in close to Meg. "You have no right to an opinion. You caused this."

"Simmer down, Win." Zack placed a restraining hand on his mother-in-law's shoulder. "Robby's had problems since long before Meg came here. And she may have a point about one thing. I tend to agree that the head docs are off-base."

"Let me go to him," Meg pleaded.

He looked into her earnest eyes and hesitated. She had gained Robby's trust in an incredibly short time, but if she climbed up there and offered a giant hug, things would only be worse when she left for good. "This is out of your territory, Meg. Wait in the house." His harsh tone left no room for argument.

                      *   *   *

Robby returned to earth, but logical persuasion had nothing to do with it. Neither did Zack's increasingly exasperated appeals, punctuated by muffled curses.

The antidote to Robby's anxieties was simple. Meg made chocolate chip cookies and put a plate of them on the van's roof. Robby was off the beam and munching before the cookies cooled.

Zack was furious with Meg's interference. He'd told her to stay out of it. She had no right to . . . But when the boy launched himself, cookie crumbs and all, into her arms, he knew she'd made the correct moves, while his method had been wrong for Robby. Meg looked up at him, eyes begging forgiveness, before she lay her cheek against the boy's black hair and hugged him back.

The lecture he'd planned to give Robby on the dangers of high places could wait, Zack decided. Meg was both good and bad for the boy. Her personal difficulties had triggered a climb into the rafters, yet she was the one he'd come down to see. Zack had no clue what overall effect she would have. For now, though, he felt comfortable leaving Robby in her care.

Since he still had to round up the missing cria, he located the saddled horse he'd abandoned in the pasture earlier. When he'd seen the sheriff's white Bronco and the silver Beamer streaking down the road, all his resolve for letting Meg face Edward alone had blown away like a tumbleweed in a windstorm. He just hoped he wouldn't end up sorry he'd intervened.

He mounted his horse again and rode out to rejoin Tobias. The hired man was still hunting. He'd just spotted tracks crossing the road.

They left their horses and followed the tracks into

the thicket along the creek. As Zack searched, he wondered about Meg. What was there about her that appealed so strongly to Robby? What had she given the child that Zack and Win had failed to supply? If she stayed just a few days longer, maybe Zack could figure it out.

He emerged from chest-deep gooseberry bushes at the muddy bank of the stream. Across the rippling water, he spotted a tuft of white wool on the low-hanging needles of a Lodgepole pine.

"Tobias!" he called. "Over here."

The hired man came running, crashing through the underbrush. Minutes later, they found a trail of blood.

"He'll live," Doc Allen said, after stitching Checkers's wounds. "But tangling with rusty barbed wire did a heck of a job on him. You were lucky to find him before he bled to death."

Lucky wasn't the word Zack would have chosen, but he kept his opinion to himself.

The repair job took several hours. Afterward, Zack stayed to settle Checkers in a stall in the back of Doc's building. He couldn't help thinking about how much Sky would have loved this animal. She'd planned and supervised his mother's breeding, but she hadn't lived to see the result.

The memories hurt, and it took Zack a while to resign himself to them. When he walked through the office on his way out, he found the vet was ready to leave, too.

"Guess I'll skip the co-op meeting," Doc Allen said as he closed the office door behind him. "My back's been acting up, and sitting on folding chairs gives me fits." The vet was seventy-something, white-haired, and fatherly. He looked at Zack over half-glasses. "I know you're not asking my opinion, but you ought to go. You've been holed up long enough."

Zack shifted uneasily. "I'd forgotten the meeting's tonight." On purpose, he'd forgotten.

Doc Allen adjusted his glasses for better viewing and shook out his keys, searching through at least a dozen on the ring. "Where the heck is it?" he mumbled to himself. "I hate fooling with this deadbolt. After the place got robbed last month, though, I had to do something to satisfy the insurance people." He grunted as he found the key and turned the lock. "Crime is a pain in the ass," he muttered. "Now, about the meeting, Zack. It's at Jesse Caldwell's, a good opportunity for the two of you to kiss and make up. Besides, they'll be setting a schedule for the haying season. You need to be there if you want your fields done before first frost."

As Doc and everyone else knew, Zack hadn't been big on group gatherings since Sky died. He especially wasn't big on this one. He hadn't seen Jesse since the lawsuit over the Caldwell boy's death was dismissed in the county court over a month ago. But since Elk Springs was a small community, avoiding anyone for long was impossible. He'd slip into the meeting, keep a low profile, and stay out of Jesse's way.

The plan backfired in phase one. Zack arrived late, attracting unwanted attention. Heads turned to see who had come. All of the faces were familiar; most were friendly.

Gradually, the murmurs died down. Every folding chair in the sprawling oak-paneled living room was occupied, so Zack leaned against the wall nearest the door. The haying plans proceeded with minimal argument, a minor miracle for this group. The chairman made a list and promised to post a schedule, ending the official part of the meeting. Chairs emptied as people stretched, exchanged comments. Others flowed toward the refreshment table, which happened to be next to Zack. He shook a few hands, responded to questions.

Jesse was facing the back of the room, but if he noticed Zack, he showed no sign. He was engaged in his usual shenanigans, sidling up to a woman rancher whose husband was absent. Jesse fancied himself a lady's man. He seemed bent on pleasing all the ladies except the one who should have counted most—his wife.

Zack spotted Ellen up front near the podium. She had endured God knew how many of Jesse's extramarital affairs over the last twenty years. Some marriage, Zack reflected. More like hell in fifth gear. Ironically, if Ellen had left Jesse, if she'd taken her son with her, a lot of things might have turned out differently. For young Mike. For Sky.

Ellen and Sky had been friends. Sky had distracted Ellen from a taste for industrial quantities of gin, her substitute for a decent life and reasonable husband. Mike had never gotten along with his father. To escape home, he'd worked with the llamas on weekends and with Sky on the rafts during the summer breaks until . . . until it was too damn late.

The Caldwell marital problems were worse than ever now. Ellen had gone back to gin.

A familiar emptiness grew in Zack's chest. He'd thought he could face Ellen and all these people he'd seen so many times with Sky, but he couldn't do it. He couldn't take the memories. Conversation buzzed around him like a chain saw slicing him in half. Cigarette fumes burned his eyes and nose. He had to get outside.

When he turned toward the door, he found himself face to face with Jesse, who must have struck out with his chosen lady of the night. From the look in the man's glacial blue eyes, he was after a pound of flesh, and he meant to have some of Zack's.

"You have a hell of a nerve coming here, Burkhart." Jesse's volume would have done credit to a loudspeaker. All conversation stopped. Heads turned.

Zack clenched his teeth. "It's an open meeting, isn't it?"

An eager crowd gathered around, probably hoping for a brawl to liven up an otherwise dull event.

"Yeah, wide open." Jesse lit a cigarette as he glanced at the growing audience. He looked like the original Marlboro man, all tough cowboy and testosterone-driven bravado. "Look here, everybody. Look who has the New York brass to walk straight into my living room. The man who killed my son."

Murmurs rippled in a wave throughout the crowd of onlookers.

Zack knew he shouldn't respond to the goading, but he had limits. He deserved a defense. "Mike drowned, Jesse. Nobody killed him."

"Shut up!" Jesse roared. "You must've paid off the judge in that mock court hearing we had, because you're responsible even more than the redskin slut you married. You were half owner of her slipshod rafting business. You left a woman to do a man's job. Two people died. And *you* killed them." His bellow echoed off the wood beam ceiling.

The crowd gasped.

Zack hadn't been anywhere near the river when Mike died, though his own sense of guilt said he should have been. For Sky's sake, for Mike's, he should have been. Still, he kept his gaze steady. "We went over this at the hearing. I'm not getting into it again." Zack was itching to rearrange Jesse's sneer, but he wouldn't start a fight over accusations that meant nothing. He'd be more likely to battle over the slight to Sky's honor, except he knew she wouldn't have wanted that.

An arrow pierces the heart, but a forked tongue is no worse than a burr on the buttocks. Like Win, Sky had often quoted that infamous old codger Chief Red Hawk. Zack had spent a night in jail once for beating to a bloody pulp a man who had insulted Sky's Sioux heritage. She had been mad as hell. Not at the ignorant redneck who'd maligned her. At Zack.

Jesse, though, wouldn't let up. He was beefy and mean, chafing for a reason to exercise his fists. He sucked on his cigarette and blew the smoke full in Zack's face. "Conscience botherin' you, Burkhart? Is that why you've turned yellower than a summer squash?" He inhaled what was left of his cancer stick before dropping the stub in an empty punch cup.

"I have nothing to say to you." Zack tried to brush past Jesse. The rancher blocked his path.

"I hear you've got yourself a white woman now. It's about time you learned your colors." Loose phlegm rattled in Jesse's throat. He hacked, craned his neck forward, and spat like an enraged llama.

The glob landed on the front of Zack's chest. As warm moisture seeped through the grizzly bear T, his control slipped. He grasped Jesse by the sleeve of an embroidered Western shirt and mashed him up against the wall. "I'd be damn careful if I were you. Sometimes I have trouble seeing gray. Sometimes I accidentally step on a slug like you. And I hate getting slime on my boots."

Releasing Jesse, Zack snagged a can of cold soda from the nearest ice chest. He shoved the can at the rancher's gut with the force of a belly punch. "Maybe this'll put some color in you." A satisfying pouf of air fled Jesse's lungs.

The soda hit the floor and burst open, spraying and foaming. Jesse lunged at Zack, but before he could land a blow, a couple of burly bystanders seized their host by the arms. Zack was a little surprised anyone in this group would prevent a fight, but even beer-loving Idaho cowboys weren't keen on murder. They must have seen the fury in Zack's eyes, and the answering fury in Jesse's.

A neighbor put a hand on Zack's shoulder. "Take it easy," the man said. "No use scrapin' your knuckles."

Zack slammed out the door, ignoring the curses Jesse was still shouting. Zack was as hot as if he'd run a hundred yard dash. His hands were shaking. He tightened them into fists and kept moving, welcoming the cool evening breeze.

He rushed down the porch steps and would have headed straight for his truck, but he saw Harry Kane sitting on a pickup tailgate nursing a bottle of Bud.

"Don't let him get to you," Harry advised. "Everybody knows Jesse's a hothead."

For a moment Zack wondered what Harry was doing at a co-op meeting. The only land he owned was a quarter acre on the outskirts of Elk Springs. He must have come for the beer.

"I went by your place today, but no one was around," Zack said. "I thought you'd want to know I found Elsa."

Harry nodded, bobbing the narrow-brimmed canvas hat he wore indoors and out. "The sheriff told me. I haven't heard of a grizzly eating anybody's stock since the days of the mountain men. If I'd known . . . I wish I'd put her on a picket line. At least that would have discouraged—"

Zack narrowed his eyes. "You mean you let my llama run free?" He could have kicked himself for loaning Harry one of his animals.

"I figured I'd be able to catch her in the morning

with a bucket of grain," Harry explained. "Hey, I'm sorry, man. If you want me to pay for—"

"No need." Zack considered Harry a helluva nice guy, but one who never paid debts. If he accidentally got hold of any money, he spent it on fishing gear. Even now he wore a vest with home-tied flies lined up over one pocket as if he might come across a nice backwater eddy on Jesse's front lawn. He was a dedicated fisherman and a first-class guide. Unfortunately, he was not so good at handling pack animals.

"Did you happen to see or hear anything unusual the night Elsa disappeared?" Zack asked.

Harry pushed up the brim of the canvas hat. "Not to speak of. I had a pack mule, besides Elsa. I remember the damn mule hee-hawed most of the night. A coyote had him upset, I figured. Believe me, Zack, I never guessed a bear would—"

"I know," Zack interrupted to keep excuses to a minimum. "What did you feed Elsa?"

"The rations you gave me." Harry scratched at the peeling sunburn on his nose. "Why? You don't think I poisoned her, do you?"

Something like that had crossed his mind. He scoffed at his own absurdity. He wouldn't put it past Jesse to poison an animal, but Harry wouldn't . . .

"Zack, honey!" The front door squeaked as Lydia rushed out, headed his way. She'd turned into a flaming redhead since last time he'd seen her. Noted for big boobs, big hair, little brain, she owned neither a field nor a blade of grass. Her first ex had done some ranching. After the divorce, she'd stayed active in the local co-op because it was a gathering of mostly men, her favorite sex.

"You off work next weekend, Lydia?" Harry asked. "How about dinner at the BadAss?"

"I have plans, precious." She focused solely on Zack. "Daddy said he brought the tourist lady's boyfriend out to your ranch. I heard she wasn't happy to see him. Can't blame her, after spending two days with *you.*" She batted false eyelashes. "Why not drop by my house tonight, if you're free? We could— "

"No." He started to tell her he'd be free when hell formed its first glacier, but there was something pathetic about Lydia. She put a hell of an effort into looking good. All she'd ever attracted were worthless bums who used her for a while and left her cold.

Zack nudged Harry off the pickup tailgate, sending him forward with a telling look that said *you owe me.* "Harry, give Lydia the low-down on bone-fishing in the Caribbean."

Harry took over from there. He had a penchant for loose women, the looser the better, so it came naturally for him to put an arm around Lydia and murmur indecent proposals as they headed back inside. Over her shoulder, Lydia shot Zack a glare. She recognized the brush-off and resented it.

Judging from the venom in her eyes, Zack had acquired another enemy. Lately, he seemed to collect them like goddamn bottle caps.

He wove through the parked cavalcade of pickups, heading for his familiar stock-paneled Ford. He'd had about all the Elk Springs fellowship he could stand.

Twilight had settled over the valley and Zack was anxious to get home. He wanted to see Robby . . . and Meg. He hadn't thanked her earlier. Without her help, he might still be coaxing his son down from the rafters. He had to let her know . . .

"Zack!"

He'd almost reached his truck when he heard the soft voice call his name. Ellen Caldwell, slender and graceful as a phantom, garbed in a black-and-silver dress, came toward him. She was tall for a woman. She'd lost weight. Zack thought she looked better for it. Rumor had it Ellen had spent a couple of months last winter in rehab, although Jesse had spread word she was visiting a relative in Oregon.

Her pale face, framed in short brown hair, showed the ravages of too much liquor and too much grief. She'd been beautiful once. She'd still be pretty if it weren't for the melancholy she wore like a purple heart. Zack had seen her only a handful of times since Mike's funeral, but he knew how hard the death of her only child had hit her.

In spite of everything, she'd remained a friend. When her husband had filed the lawsuit, she hadn't taken part. She'd even told Zack's defense attorney that she'd testify on his behalf. Zack hoped Jesse hadn't learned about that, because he sure would've taken it poorly. And he might have taken it out, physically, on his wife.

"I'm sorry about Jesse picking a fight," she said. "He's not himself, hasn't been since . . ." Since Mike. She lowered lashes on violet eyes the same color as clouds the sunset had left behind.

"You don't have to apologize for him." In Zack's opinion, Jesse had not changed much. The man had been a rattlesnake in knee-deep grass since long before his son died. Zack wondered how Jesse was treating his wife now. He wondered if she were off the booze, and whether rehab had helped. "How are you, Ellen?"

Her gaze took on a vague, unfocused quality. "Not so good. I'm alone too much. We're both alone, Zack." She reached out blindly, and he took her hand. "It's strange, seeing you without Sky. The two of you were always together."

"Yeah," he said bitterly. "It's different now."

"I heard about your llamas," she ventured. "Thessa and Elsa were two of Sky's favorites. They're with her now. That's good, isn't it?"

Zack looked past Ellen to the twilight clouds. "I hadn't thought about it that way," he said. But maybe there was something to the idea. Maybe the souls of those poor animals would somehow find their way to Sky.

Ellen sighed. "She tried to save my son and ended by losing her chance to be with Robby. She must miss him."

"I'm sure she does." Zack felt helpless talking about what he couldn't change. He took Ellen's hand and held it. "Sky did what she had to do. You know how much she loved Mike. We all loved him."

Ellen squeezed Zack's fingers with surprising strength before letting go, stepping back. "We must never forget Sky and my Mike. Never."

Never forget. It sounded almost like a curse. For a moment, he wondered if secretly Ellen, like her husband, laid some of the blame on Zack. But from the tortured anguish in her eyes, he knew that wasn't so.

She only blamed herself.

Meg sat on the red-and-green Ninja Turtle quilt covering Robby's bed while the child stripped off dirty shorts and shirt and replaced them with blue-striped pajamas.

Win's and Tobias's voices wafted through the open window. The two were sitting on the porch halfway around the house, but sound carried in the night air. Meg guessed Tobias was sweet on Win. However, Win wasn't giving him much encouragement, to judge by the sharp verbal reprimand and resounding slap of a few moments before. Thankfully, Robby had been in the bathroom brushing his teeth and hadn't heard.

"I like your pictures," Meg said, looking around her at the abundance of crayon art taped on the walls of the boy's room.

Robby finished buttoning his pajama top as he frowned at the pictures. Walking up to one at his eye level, he pointed. "This is Elsa. She's gone to be with Mama."

"She looks beautiful," Meg said, although his matter-of-fact tone made her want to cry.

Robby stood on tiptoes to remove a blue circular frame, decorated with feathers, from the top of his dresser. He slowly carried it over to the open window, as if performing a ritual. With a bit of wire already attached to the frame, he hung it from a nail strategically placed on the bottom of the casing. He adjusted the window's opening so only the screen separated the circle from the outside breeze. It twirled slightly back and forth.

Meg left the bed and joined Robby at the window. She touched the soft, fragile threads that crisscrossed the circle. Beads, like drops of dew, adorned the internal structure. "What is it?" she asked.

"A dreamcatcher. Mama made it for me. She weaved the spider's web from llama hair." The boy fidgeted, scratching the back of one leg with his bare foot. "She told me it catched bad dreams."

Meg recalled seeing earrings made in the same design. Only good dreams could pass through the web, or so the story went. The bad ones would be trapped and evaporated by the morning sun. "Your mama must have loved you a lot to make this especially for you, Robby."

"But she's gone away now," the boy said. "She's mad at me."

Meg took his hand and walked with him to the bed, lifting him up on the mattress to sit beside her. "What makes you think such a thing?" It hurt her that Robby was hurting. She wanted so much to make it better.

With legs crossed, hands clasped in his lap, he

looked up at her with extraordinary eyes shadowed by thick dark lashes. "I put the dreamcatcher under my pillow where it couldn't work right. The bad dream came, and that made Mama go away."

Empathy coursed through Meg. "I know just how you feel. My daddy went away when I was your age. He went away on a plane and didn't come back, because something bad happened to him, too. And I wondered if I should have kissed him twice, or hugged him longer, or let him take along the blankie he always teased me about. I thought maybe one of those things would have saved him and brought him home."

"Was he mad at you?" Robby asked.

She brushed a loose strand of hair from the boy's forehead, wishing she could put his childish worries in place as easily. "I was afraid he might be, but then my grandmother made me see that I couldn't have changed what happened. And neither could you. Your mama isn't angry. She loves you. She sees you hang the dreamcatcher every night, and she's glad that she left it here to protect you from bad dreams. She's glad she can still do something to take care of her little boy."

Robby frowned, considering for a long moment. And then he asked, "Do you know my mama?"

Meg flinched at the unexpected question. "No, Robby. Why don't you tell me about her?"

"Can't remember," he murmured. Lunging forward, he clasped her around the waist and buried his face in her blouse.

As Meg's arms encircled him, she kissed his satiny black hair. He smelled of milk and animals, of earth and green grass.

Meg had struggled with fading memories of her father for years, until G. T. had suggested a solution, one which she could offer to this child. "Close your eyes," she whispered. "Close your eyes and open your heart. You'll remember your mother then."

His nod of agreement bumped her chin. He pushed away from her and got to his knees on the bed, arms reaching high in the air. His face tilted toward the ceiling; the skin around his closed eyes squinched tight. "She smelled good," he lisped. "Like you, Meg. Her hands were nice." He paused, wrinkling his nose. "She rocked me sometimes, right before I went to sleep."

His blue-green eyes opened. He looked around the room as if hoping to see his mother there. His hands fell to his sides. His small shoulders drooped. "That's all I know."

"Think of the stories you've heard about her." Meg brushed the boy's hair back from his forehead with her fingers. She wanted to soothe the loss he felt and return the simple acceptance he had offered her.

"Nobody tells me stories about Mama. They think I'll cry." His lower lip trembled, but his gaze stayed solemn and dry.

Meg's eyes filled with tears. Taking his hand, she led him to a cushioned rocker in the corner. They had to step around Hoover, who was already stretched out on the braided rug, asleep. Robby shushed, finger to lips, letting her know they mustn't disturb him.

A well-worn book lay in the rocker seat. She moved it to the side, making room.

"Read, please." Robby climbed into her lap.

She opened the book while he leaned his head back to smile at her. "Mama liked this one," he said, as if he'd just captured another fragment of memory.

Touched by his smile and his simple trust, Meg began.

" 'It was the Moon of Falling Leaves. Little Eagle begged to ride with his brothers to distant snow-tipped mountains, but Father said he was too small. And so it happened that the boy awoke one morning to find both of his brothers gone.' "

Robby settled deeper into Meg's lap. She held him close as she continued the tale of the young Native American who was left behind.

That year, the People suffered a lasting hunger. Little Eagle's mother and sister became pale and thin. Father rode after the buffalo and did not return. Heavy snows came, and dark days. Little Eagle believed he must travel to the Spirit World to seek wisdom that would save the People.

Each day of travel tested his endurance. Deep snow obscured the trail. Each night, he battled bone-deep cold and wintry wind. His strength was nearly gone when he struggled through a dense mist to reach the highest peak of the Shining Mountains.

There, he found his family—father and sister, mother and the two elder brothers.

Meg turned to the last page. A lovely picture showed the sun's rays penetrating a ring of clouds to touch the very top of a mountain. In the light stood one small boy. " 'Father was proud of his youngest son, who led the family back to the People's camp. Upon their return, Earth rejoiced with the first leaves of spring.' "

As soon as she read the final line of the story, Robby yawned and nestled against her breasts. "I miss Mama," he murmured sleepily.

Meg held him close as he wound his fingers in her cotton blouse, twining his sweet innocence into her heart. They rocked, forward and back, sharing solace and warmth. She was happy here, with this child, in this asymmetric house.

She'd give anything to stay another day, a week. Ten days might be enough time to understand Robby's deeper longings and fears, long enough to do some good.

That glimmer of light lasted only a second before it winked away. Zack didn't want her on his ranch. He didn't want her in his life, or in his son's life. He was tolerating her, but only until she found the means to go home—wherever that might be.

She sighed. Tomorrow she'd say good-bye. Tomorrow evening, someone else would read to Robby. Zack or Win, both of whom ached as badly as the child, would read the story of Little Eagle's journey to the clouds.

Meg would trudge down her own path, alone.

Chapter Eight

From outside Robby's bedroom door, Zack watched Meg kiss his sleeping son's forehead. As she tucked a quilt around the child, Zack experienced a painful déjà vu. Meg was only a substitute, but for a moment he imagined she completed the broken family circle and made them whole again. His rational side knew the illusion would shatter under scrutiny, but his heart was deeply moved. His heart wanted to hang onto the picture, if only for a little while.

When Meg headed out of Robby's room, humming to herself, Zack stepped from the hall shadows into her path. She sucked in a quick breath. Splaying a hand over her breast, she exhaled slowly. "He's asleep," she whispered. "Win was on the porch talking to Tobias and you were still gone, so when Robby asked me to tuck him in, I—"

"It's okay. You're good with him." Better than he was himself, he had to admit. He reached around her and pulled Robby's door closed.

She hooked a strand of hair behind her ear. The fluffy lock immediately sprang free again. "You're not going to yell at me about the cookies?"

Zack resisted the urge to smooth her downy-gold hair. "No. He's safely on the ground. That's the important thing."

She nodded. "I'm sorry about your llama. Winona

started grumbling about vet bills as soon as Tobias came by and told us what happened."

"I know," he said. "I passed Tobias outside, headed down the drive to his cabin. He told me Win's on the warpath. I guess she thinks we could have prevented it somehow. Maybe she's right."

"And maybe not." Meg's mouth curved into the sad-sweet Mona Lisa smile that Zack found so beguiling. "It would be nice if we could read the future and change the bad parts, but it's not something Win should expect."

He tucked his hands in his jeans' hip pockets and leaned a shoulder against the wall. "Vet bills aren't the worst of it. I was counting on selling Checkers in a couple of months. He won't be worth much with all the scars he's sure to have."

She touched his arm, ambushing his weary mind and body. "First Elsa in Yellowstone, and now this."

He shifted his weight to escape the warmth in her fingertips. "Accidents happen. It's the frequency that's unusual. Elsa wasn't the first. Last month, a female we called Thessa caught her halter on a gate post. She died of strangulation. It *looked* like an accident and it might have been, but . . ."

She cocked her head to one side. "You think somebody arranged the deaths?"

"It has occurred to me," he said dryly.

"But with Elsa . . ." She tapped a finger on her lips. "How could a person stage a grizzly bear kill?"

Zack tore his gaze from her mouth with difficulty. That lip-tapping maneuver never failed to get his attention. "Someone could have drugged Elsa. It's only a matter of time before scavengers move in when an animal is helpless."

"But it *could* have been an accident," Meg persisted.

"Sure. Probably was." However, Zack's doubts

grew with each mishap and every Bible-flavored note.

"Why llamas, Zack? I've been wondering why you don't raise cows like everyone else around here."

He shrugged. "We—my wife and I—were more interested in recreational activity than hamburger meat. The idea was to raise outstanding pack animals, and llamas fit the bill. Their hoofs are easy to maintain, easy on the trails. They're intelligent, observant, agile. And there seems to be a market for them, when I can keep one alive long enough to sell."

"Who would kill a llama? And why?"

"To get to me, maybe. I have my share of enemies." He could see she was about to cut loose with a million questions, so he headed her off at the pass. He didn't want to hear her speculations, and he was certain she'd have some. "What about you? Where do you go from here?"

She looked startled. "Tobias said he'd give me a lift to town tomorrow if you're too busy. I checked the bus schedule. There's one at nine-something and another about three. I'll have to go to the bank first, so—"

"Why? You have your purse now. Even Elk Springs accepts credit cards." Sarcasm crept into his voice to cover his sharp disappointment. She was leaving. Wasn't that what he'd expected? What he wanted?

When she tapped her lips again, he glanced quickly away.

"My purse is . . . Edward must have taken my wallet out of—"

"That slimy buffalo turd." Zack wished he'd taken a swing at Edward while he'd had the chance.

"Maybe the wallet fell out and he didn't notice," she offered, although her tone said she didn't believe it. "I'm sure I can arrange a transfer of funds."

Zack didn't like the frown lines between her brows. He didn't like Edward pushing her around. "You still have your vacation time, don't you?"

"Yes, but—"

"I think you should stay here. Reconsider where you're going before you rush back to your . . . obligations. This place isn't exactly a travel guide's paradise, but the price is right."

Meg pressed her lips together. "That's just it. I can draw enough for a bus ticket from my account, but that's about all. I can't pay my way to stay here, and I won't impose."

"I have an idea." Zack had arrived at a decision he was certain to regret. He didn't need the headache of a beautiful woman in his house. But maybe his son *did* need her. It had occurred to Zack that he had no right to shelter Robby from happiness in order to protect him from unhappiness down the line.

She eyed him quizzically. "You've been kind, Zack. More than kind. But it'll be better for everyone if I leave tomorrow. I could easily get attached to Robby, and I think he's—"

"Shh." He put two fingers over her lips. Her skin was silky soft, and he wanted . . . He drew his hand away slowly, reluctantly. His chest ached with a terrible, desperate longing for . . . something, someone.

Night seemed to move inside, to enfold them in its mysteries. The earthy scent of grass and pine wafted through an open window. A breeze ruffled her fine hair. Zack imagined them as Adam and Eve again, before he shook off the feeling. An unusual set of circumstances had brought them together; there sure as hell was nothing mystical about it. Meg was at a crossroads in her life. He had a son who needed her.

Zack did not need her. The only woman he wanted was gone forever. But for better or worse, he'd made his decision. "I have something to show you." He led the way to the basement door. As he descended the dark stairwell, the low ceiling brushed the top of his head. At the bottom, the stairs opened into a large musty room.

He pulled a chain, clicking on a single light bulb. The chilled air was full of shadows. Nothing had changed here. In the underworld, captured memories endured forever. Zack strode across the room to a corner where cardboard boxes lay under a pile of old newspapers bundled with string.

"It's a computer and all the fixings," he explained, sweeping the papers to the floor. A string caught on the runner of an old sled, almost overturning it. He repositioned the sled against the cobweb-laden wall.

Meg stood under the light, looking perplexed. That's when Zack realized he hadn't explained his proposal.

"I'm offering you a job. That way you don't have to feel indebted to me. It's easy work, so you'll still have time to relax. And you won't have to go running back to the boyfriend until you decide you want to."

She glanced from the dusty boxes to him, squinting against the bare hundred-watt bulb. "A job doing what?"

"Sorting out grizzly observations."

"Grizzly, as in bear?" Her eyes widened.

"You'd only deal with them on paper." He grinned at her alarm, recalling how much of a greenhorn she was.

"What exactly would I do?"

"Transfer handwritten notes to a computer. We— me and Sky— spent a lot of weekends studying grizzly habitat, monitoring their movements. It's been a hobby since we were rookie rangers together. Even after we quit the Forest Service, we . . ." He'd said enough. Too much. The memories threatened to swallow him whole.

He closed his eyes for a few seconds before opening them to Meg's sympathetic gaze. He gestured to a stack of boxes. "I have hardware, software, printer, the whole works fresh from the factory. Ordered all of it right before . . ." *Before Sky died. When I still had the capacity to dream.*

"Field notes and journals are in there." He pointed to another, more dilapidated box. "I've promised the pertinent info to the Forest Service, so that has to be organized. The rest . . . The journals are my wife's. I think Win would like a copy. I'll save the originals for Robby."

Zack figured if Meg was going to stay, the handwritten pages would keep Sky between them, where she belonged. "If you want the job, it's yours. I'll pay you whatever seems fair, over and above your keep." He couldn't afford to hire Meg, but he felt compelled to make the offer. If she accepted, he'd work out the details.

She ran a finger through thick dust on an unopened cardboard box. When she glanced at him, her eyes were serious, thoughtful, maybe even scared. "Why are you doing this?"

"Because Robby wants you to stay." It seemed obvious enough to Zack.

Her lips flexed in a soft smile. But only briefly. "Win doesn't approve of me."

His gaze lingered on her mouth. "Don't worry about Win."

"But you have no idea what a mess my life has been lately. You wouldn't want any of that to rub off on your son."

"After seeing you two together, I'm convinced any influence will be for the good. I can't say how or why, but you connect with Robby." Zack didn't know why she connected with *him*, either, and he didn't care to examine it too closely.

"I like Robby. As for the job, the word processing's no problem, but . . ." She considered for a moment. A frown creased her forehead as she blurted, "What else do you want from me?"

He met her eyes, ignoring the heaviness in his loins, the sudden tightness of his jeans. "Nothing else."

"Men usually expect . . . something in exchange for a gift. Edward always did."

Zack gritted his teeth. "Not surprising. But that's not the case with me. For one thing, this isn't a gift, it's employment. And don't compare me to *him*. I'd appreciate it if you'd avoid mentioning his name."

She lifted her chin, pride flashing in her green eyes. "You're right. I ought to wipe him out of my mind." Her shoulders rounded; her fervor dimmed. "It's just that he was supposed to be my future, and now I . . ."

"Hell." Zack took a step forward. He hated the wobble in her voice. He hated that she missed anything about Edward. Before he realized what he was doing, he caressed the line of her jaw.

The moment he touched her, blood pooled in a volatile segment of his anatomy. Her startled eyes told him that his touch aroused her, too. When she placed a hand over his pounding heart, a potent chemistry brewed inside him, a witch's cauldron of lust.

The surge of desire battled more tender feelings. More dangerous feelings.

For Meg? He didn't even like her, Zack reminded himself. She annoyed the hell out of him with her wide-eyed trust and sad-sweet smile, with her aura of innocence. If he had to have a woman, he'd be much better off with someone like Lydia. Someone experienced, who knew about meaningless sex and would understand when he walked away and never looked back. Meg showed every emotion, spoke every thought. She was too damn honest. He couldn't risk hurting her.

Or maybe that was a load of crap. Maybe a little meaningless sex was exactly what Meg needed. What they both needed.

He pulled her into his arms until her cheek rested on his chest. Her breath wove through the fibers of his shirt, the pores of his skin. His day's growth of beard stubble caught in her silken hair.

She lifted her head. Her lips parted. As he looked into her luminous green eyes, his breath mingled with hers. They moved closer and closer to a kiss that would change the texture of the moment, perhaps of their very lives.

A slight trembling at the corner of her mouth stopped him. If he were honest with himself, he knew he would hurt her as badly as Edward had. The bastard had given her a distorted view of love, and Zack would only add to it, make it worse. After one betrayal, another would be even tougher for her to bear. His heart belonged, would always belong, to Sky.

Meg needed a man who would love her as she deserved, but sex was all Zack could give any woman. And he had no intention of giving even that. He brushed his fingers along her pale cheek before forcing his arms to his sides.

Her gaze stayed locked with his for a second. Then she whirled to the computer boxes, busily brushing away dust, coughing on the particle-laden air.

She bent over one of the cartons as if examining a label. Zack thought he saw a tear fall from her lashes and plop on the dusty box. He remained where he was, although he wanted to go to her. He wanted to hold her, kiss her long and deep, but he couldn't allow himself the pleasure.

She straightened, a half-smile on her lips as she moved back toward him. "I trusted Edward too much. I've trusted a lot of people too much." Her head tilted to one side as she studied Zack's eyes. "I wonder, should I trust you?"

Her vulnerability tugged at Zack, sucked him in. He wanted to tell her to slam shut the doors to her heart before someone else, someone besides Edward, wreaked havoc there.

"You've already trusted me," he said. "You're in my house. I've been safe so far, haven't I?" Talk about a wolf in sheep's clothing. Much as his body might scream in protest, though, she *was* safe with him. Zack would not allow his momentary lust to scare her away.

She'd forged a link with Robby, and she might be the only person who could help the child. He had offered her the job for Robby's sake. Only for Robby, he repeated to himself.

Her eyes searched his. The single light bulb illuminated her clear skin. "You don't look safe."

"Looks are deceiving, so they say." *And words, too.* He took her hand, holding it lightly.

She jerked as if he'd applied an electric shock. From the lurch in his heart, he was sure the current flowed both ways.

Pulling her hand free, she stared at it as she backed away. "I ought to run for cover," she said, so softly Zack wondered if she meant for him to hear.

He didn't want her to go anywhere, yet he didn't want her to feel trapped, either. He willed her to look at him. When she did, he offered a steady, reassuring gaze, sending a subliminal message. *Stay, Meg. I want you to stay.* He knew, deep inside, that Robby wasn't the only one who needed her. *He* needed her, although he had no idea why, since he'd ruled out sex. They had nothing in common. She talked too much, knew diddly about ranching, couldn't tell a bear from a Bigfoot.

"Why don't you put the journals into the computer yourself?" she asked.

"I can't type." He could hunt and peck at fifty words per minute, but he didn't have the courage to face those notes, most of which were in Sky's handwriting.

Maybe he and Meg had something in common after all. She had a failed love tearing at her heart. He had Sky whispering in his ear. They were two of a kind, like two left gloves, but they'd never make a pair. Regret weighted his chest. Something more potent ached in his groin.

"If I stay, it can't be for long," she said.

"Are you so anxious to get back to your boyfriend?"

"No, but—well, I— When my vacation time is over, in ten days, I'll have to—"

"I understand." Ten days might be a helluva long time to have a woman like Meg around the house. It would have to be long enough for Robby.

"Give me overnight to think about it." Meg put a hand on the stair rail and a foot on the first step, poised for flight. Then she donned a broad, brave smile. "I'm sorry I doubted you, Zack. You're nothing like Edward."

Zack watched her ascend the stairs, heard her footsteps cross the floor above, while he pondered those parting words. He looked up at the ceiling, seeing nothing but shadows and cobwebs. Cold sweat broke out on his forehead.

Edward was an unscrupulous sleaze who'd used her for his own purposes, lied to her, hidden his real motives for keeping her near.

Nothing like Edward?

Wrong, Meg. Zack's reasons were different. Not totally selfish, he hoped. But he had not told her all of the truth. He hadn't admitted that he wanted her to stay for him as well as for Robby. That he wanted her to . . .

That he wanted her.

Chapter Nine

"Add beauty to a contented teepee," Win proclaimed, "and winter wind blows right through the buffalo skins." She felt the chill already, with Meg on the ranch less than forty-eight hours.

Tobias stood beside Win as she inspected the carburetor of a '68 Mustang. He didn't question her out-of-the-blue remark. He simply waited, which was one of his best qualities, in Win's opinion. His patience convinced her he had Sioux blood somewhere in his ancestry.

"That's what Chief Red Hawk said when his fourth wife ran off with a Mexican horse trader," she explained. "He'd say the same about the situation we have here. Trouble, that's what Meg is. Trouble and nothing but. The way she attached herself to Zack on a Yellowstone trail, when I know he went out there for the solitude, is just plain suspicious."

Tobias rubbed a bump on his crooked nose. "You're coming down on her awful hard, Win. She's a likable little thing. And she's out of a job. I've been there, so I can sympathize."

This was the first time Tobias had mentioned his past to Win in the two months she'd known him. "I don't recall where you worked before you came here," she hinted.

"Haven't said."

Win pretended to adjust an intake valve, but her

attention was on Tobias. She knew if she waited, he'd tell her what she wanted to know.

He sighed. "I worked in a silver mine. It went bust."

Win straightened, rubbing her back. "I guess you know Zack and Sky had a big part in nose-diving the mining operations around here."

"Yeah," he said. "Don't go telling Zack where I worked last. He thinks I've been a farmhand all my life."

"I don't blab secrets," she said in a huff. "Where else have you worked?"

"Army. Oil fields. General maintenance for a trucking company. I haven't been what you'd call faithful to any one thing."

"No wife?" Win glanced up at him to see his expression.

Tobias grimaced. "Haven't been faithful to one woman, either. But I've been thinking on it."

"Hmmph." Win had heard that before from men like Tobias. She doubted his "thinking on it" would amount to anything. "Now about Little Big Mouth. She's a weasel-size tramp, and I don't like her taking up with my grandbaby. The two of them have been sitting in a cottonwood tree by the creek for an hour or more. I'd give my liver to know what they're saying. Did you happen to hear anything when you were out there?"

Tobias glanced out the window, frowning. "Everyone's afraid."

Win tightened the clamp on a hose, checked the battery water. Tobias would explain in his own good time.

After a lengthy pause, he rewarded her patience as she'd known he would. "Meg told the boy all critters are afraid sometimes. Rabbits burrow underground, squirrels and birds go for the trees. Llamas run or spit. Robby climbs." Tobias always got to the core of the issue without wasting words, which was another thing Win liked about him.

"What do grown men do?"

He looked at her, and then out the window again. "A lot of us just move on."

Win gave a short laugh. "Damn right. A grown woman, though, might need some prodding. Think I could chase Meg off with a tire tool?"

Tobias's tough, mangled features remained motionless while he thought about his answer. "Zack needs a woman," he said at last.

"That's where you're wrong. Zack still loves my daughter. And he's not the kind of guy who works from the loins up." She shot Tobias a look that implied *he* was indeed that kind.

"Like I said," Tobias continued stubbornly. "A man needs a woman."

Win made a dismissive noise in her throat. "Zack was fine with his memories until Meg came along and divided his spirit."

"Memories don't warm a man's bed," he told her. With one blunt fingertip, he wiped a speck of oil from her wrist with a gentle touch that astounded Win. She wasn't used to being treated like she was delicate.

Something akin to heartburn ignited in her chest. What was his game, anyway? Why was he playing up to her? She slapped his hand. "We're talking about Zack's bed, not yours. And sure as hell not mine. I haven't let a man between my thighs in years. Can't say I've missed it." Sky's white father had left her to raise a baby alone. Win sure didn't miss that son of a longhair. She didn't miss a damn thing about him. There had been others, but none worth keeping.

"You must've had some piss-poor lovers." Tobias slipped an arm around her waist, pressing his body close. He was a good four inches shorter than Win, but he made up for it in muscular width. Having him near wasn't too unpleasant. In fact, it wasn't unpleasant at all.

She tried hard to concentrate on adjusting the fan belt. She felt flushed, like she had a fever coming on. Tobias caught her earlobe in his teeth as his big rough hands explored the ample territory of her breasts. He'd touched her before, but never like this. Great Spirit, her heartburn turned into a torch. She poked an elbow in Tobias's ribs and extracted herself from his arms.

A broad grin transformed his face into something close to handsome. "You're one fine mechanic, Winona."

"If you can't behave, you'll have to get out," she said with her fiercest scowl.

He sobered. "I'll behave. Seems like I've been a wanderer all my life. But now I've found me a good place and good company. Don't see much reason to pick up stakes just yet."

Win eyed him cautiously. Even though he was a horny paleface, she liked him. She liked working with him, talking to him. He was often silent, but when he said something, a woman was wise to listen. What he'd said about Zack made sense, she had to admit.

Right after Sky died, Zack had sworn he'd never love another woman. He'd said the same thing many times since then. Sex, though, might be a different story.

Zack had never told Win he missed a woman in his bed, but then how many men discussed their needs with a mother-in-law? If he had one of those male itches that needed scratching, Meg might be a good choice. She wouldn't last. No computer whiz from the big city would hang around a ranch ten miles out of Elk Springs, Idaho, for long.

When she left, everything could go back to normal. Robby might be disappointed, seeing as how he'd gotten friendly with her, but the boy would get over it. Win would make sure he did. And Zack could go right on loving Sky, the same as always.

"If you gave them half a chance, Meg and Zack'd end up in the hay," Tobias said.

Win shrugged. "Maybe."

"What about you and me, cupcake? A couple of nights in the hay wouldn't hurt us, either." Tobias reached for her.

When he placed a hand on her buttocks, she knocked it away. "*Cupcake*? You've got the wrong woman, buster." But she did like the attention. She liked feeling desirable. Secret thrills did a ritual medicine dance in her loins as his breath stirred the hair at her nape.

He planted a kiss on her coveralled shoulder. The ratchet she was holding clattered onto the battery. It set off sparks, temporarily connecting the terminals before falling through the engine compartment to the concrete floor.

Tobias feathered kisses from her chin to below her ear. His tongue played tether ball with her lobe. His breath panted through her ear canal like a furnace at full steam. She imagined cool grass beneath her thighs and a man—this man—hot and hard above her.

A roll in the meadow tames a fire in the belly. As the words echoed in her overheated brain, Win reflected that Chief Red Hawk, with his five wives and seventy-plus years of experience, must have known a great deal about man and woman and the flames licking seductively between them.

*   *   *

"I'm gonna climb a mountain today," Robby announced to Meg that afternoon.

She was on her knees behind the computer terminal. Earlier, Tobias had carried all the equipment up from the basement at her request. She hadn't decided on Zack's job offer, but getting the computer running gave her something to do. Looking up from her work, she saw Robby outfitted in midget hiking boots instead of his usual cowboy gear. His childish features contracted into premature worry wrinkles as he waited for her reaction.

"Why a mountain?" Meg thought she knew but wanted to hear it from Robby.

"Mama's up there." He pointed to the ceiling. "In heaven. Daddy says mountains are real close to heaven."

Meg left wires dangling. Blowing wisps of hair out of her eyes, she considered what to say. She'd thought about heaven a lot since G. T. died, and Robby's logic seemed reasonable to her. She'd guessed right about why he climbed. Unfortunately, climbing wouldn't do much to remedy the ache in his heart.

"Come here, Robby." She scrambled to her feet and led him to the window. "Look outside. Can't you see the sky from here just as well as from the top of a tree?"

Standing on his tiptoes, he peered through the window. He nodded and turned back to Meg. "It's easier from down here, 'cause there aren't any tree branches to get in the way."

"That's right. It's the same with heaven. As long as nothing's in the way, you have as good a chance of seeing your mother from here as from the top of a mountain. And you can talk to her from anywhere."

Robby thought a moment. "Do people have ears in heaven?"

"I don't know. Maybe in heaven a person doesn't

need ears. But I'm sure your mother is listening to everything you say, and everything you think. 'Spirit people hear the voices they love.' That's what Grandma Tess always said." In truth, the fictitious quote was exactly like something G. T. would have said. Meg hoped a bit of ancestral wisdom would add weight to her armchair psychology. Besides, there had been times in her life, especially in the isolation and despair of the last few months, when she'd talked to G. T. and her father, and both of them seemed to talk back, soothing some of the turmoil inside her. Surely a mother could find a way to do the same for her small son. To send him good dreams. To catch the bad dreams and whisk them away.

After wrinkle-nosed consideration, Robby said, "Mama must've sent you here."

Meg opened her mouth to deny it, but Robby had already moved past that thought to another.

"If I don't climb a mountain today, will you show me how to draw bears like Daddy does? We can use my crayons."

Shaken by Robby's earlier pronouncement, Meg had difficulty making the leap from heaven to bears to crayons. She was not heaven-sent. And as far as she knew, Zack didn't draw bears, he studied them. To top it off, Meg hated crayons. Her biggest childhood rebellion had been an absolute refusal to color within the lines. All through grade school, one whiff of the distinctive waxen scent had made her eyes cross.

"I don't do crayons," she said firmly. G. T. had given Meg her first computer when she was only a little older than Robby. Meg had loved electronic art at first try. She considered it pure self-expression, without the smell. "Why don't you help me set up the computer? Then I'll show you another way to draw."

She got the system going and booted a paint program. Even if she did say so herself, Meg was a genius with mouse and clip art. She had no trouble introducing Robby to the sport. He delighted in changing colors and creating abstract designs. Watching him, Meg decided she had something important to offer Robby after all. She liked being needed, and he appreciated her much more than Edward ever had.

She showed Robby all the tricks: how to rotate a design on the screen, how to stack, flip, increase size. He caught on quickly. It took an entire hour—a long stretch, Meg guessed, for a five-year-old—to wear out his attention span. Then he ran outside to play, clutching a printout in one fist, shouting "Gramma Win, look what I made!"

Meg smiled, warmed clear through. As she returned to the computer, she decided to accept Zack's job offer in spite of her concerns. True, she was attracted to Zack, which was not good. But she could resist temptation for the short while she'd be here. Robby was already fond of her, so staying longer shouldn't increase the chance of causing him emotional harm. With a little time, she would secure the connection between them and seal it with letters after she left. If he wanted to believe his mother had sent Meg, so be it. No matter what universe he thought she was from—the here, or the hereafter—Meg and Robby would remain friends.

She would stay on a temporary basis.

The decision cheered her. While busily installing software, she whistled "The Good, the Bad and the Ugly" theme song, always one of her favorites. Robby was the Good. Edward and Winona were the

Ugly. But Meg couldn't decide where she fit in. Or Zack.

She reached for the top notebook in the stack of field records she'd brought up from the basement. Scrawled in black marker on the cardboard cover was a date nearly three years past. She leafed through the filled pages. The script was in two very different handwritings. The huge, bold letters must be Zack's. She guessed the small, even script had belonged to Sky. It was strange to see the handwritten legacy of someone Meg would never meet. The same whistled melody ran through her head again. Sky would have required her own special category. The Perfect. The woman must have had a *few* faults, but no one here would ever admit them.

Sketches of birds, squirrels, elk, and especially bears decorated the margins of the notebook and occasionally filled an entire page. One of the bear drawings was almost an exact duplicate of a design on a shirt Zack had worn yesterday. Because of Robby's comment earlier, she gathered Zack was the artist. Although she was no expert, anyone could see he was quite good.

And not only at drawing. In Meg's bedroom closet, she'd found a stack of boxes, neatly labeled. When she looked inside the top one, she'd found bottles of Nemesis bear repellent, the same stuff she'd bought in West Yellowstone and left in Edward's car. She read the fine print on a label and discovered the trademark belonged to Zachariah Burkhart, Elk Springs, Idaho.

Curious, she'd sorted through the other boxes. One was packed with his specialized camp stove stands. Another contained T-shirts embellished with what she now knew were his original bear paintings. The last carton held fleece jackets in a variety of sizes and colors. A scrap of paper in the box listed, in Zack's handwriting, the jackets' virtues: rings for clipping on ski passes or keys or mittens, roomy Gore-Tex–lined hoods, lots of pockets with Velcro closures. Meg was impressed.

The jacket Zack had worn in Yellowstone had been made of different material, but the design was basically the same. His backpack, she recollected, had a uniquely shaped frame. And his tent had gone up and come down with exceptional speed.

Zack, a sporting goods designer? Meg closed the notebook she'd been reading and sat back in the kitchen chair she'd purloined for the computer. She speculated on her find. Why were saleable items languishing in a closet? Certainly, from everything she'd seen and heard on this ranch, Zack could use some extra money.

So why hadn't he marketed the contents of those boxes? Meg guessed the answer was all tied up with his wife.

Perhaps Sky had helped him with the designs, as with the bear research. Maybe he'd put the sales project on hold because he missed her so much. A yearning filled Meg as she realized how well-matched Zack and Sky had been. They'd had the kind of love Meg had always wanted. Meg had felt a strong attraction to Zack, maybe from the beginning, and had subconsciously imagined . . . But he was taken, she saw that now. He would always belong to Sky.

How did a woman earn that special kind of love? Would she ever find a man who could love her that way?

Hope is a treasure, G. T. had once said. *Guard it with your life.* And if Meg believed in anything, she believed in hope. In fantasy. Someday she'd find the man who would become the heart of *her* adventure.

For the moment, Meg settled for the next best

thing. She immersed herself in another woman's romance.

Taking up a second notebook, she began to read. Before long, she was sighing over the love story clearly written between the lines. To her, the journals revealed less about animals and Yellowstone trails than about two people who worked together so well. Since Meg knew the sad ending, her eyes kept misting over with tears.

The kitchen door opened. Meg quickly dabbed at her eyes as Zack entered the living room, looking like a man who had fought demons and lost the war. Dust coated his jeans and boots. He wore a white dress shirt, the first she'd seen him in, but the tail hung out of his pants on one side. The token tie— decorated with a grizzly, of course—was loosened and askew. His hair was as rumpled as his clothes. Under one arm, he carried a bulging grocery sack like the spoils of battle.

He kicked at a ratty tennis ball Hoover had left on the wood floor. The ball became airborne, bounced off a wall, and boomeranged to land on the couch. "I saw Robby outside. He says you taught him to draw on the computer."

"He taught himself," she said, turning sideways in her chair. "I just showed him how the program worked."

Zack nodded. His face might as well have been a boulder on Mount Nemesis for all the emotion he revealed.

Meg had been sure Robby's success would please Zack. His lack of comment stung her. "Is there something wrong with that? He wanted me to show him how to draw bears, but I flunked crayons in grade school. With computers, anybody who can push a button can—"

He held up one hand. "I'm glad Robby liked it."

"Then what's wrong?"

"I talked to my banker today. I was hoping he'd give me a break on this quarter's principle payment—or maybe extend some additional credit. But it's a no-go." He ploughed a hand through disheveled hair. "The way things have disintegrated around here, I guess I should've expected it."

Visions of ranch repossession stomped in Meg's head. "There are other banks, right?" She smiled, hoping to lift his spirits. She could almost see the Worry Monster eating holes in him.

"Yeah, sure." He tossed the paper bag he'd been holding onto the floor in front of her. "Brought you some clothes."

She peeked inside. Blue jeans, a pale green, form-fitting knit shirt. She checked the tags. The right size. He must have noted the labels on the clothes he'd washed for her. At the bottom of the sack she found a froth of lacy underwear, silky and wonderful.

Tears burned in her eyes. For months, her skin had chafed under industrial strength cotton, the only material that survived an institutional laundry.

Zack had seen the one pair of panties she'd had with her. He'd guessed her feminine weakness for hidden softness and frills. Edward had never done anything so personal, so thoughtful. But here was Zack, practically a stranger, thinking of her while his world fell apart.

"Th-thank you." She wiped the back of her hand across her eyes. She wouldn't ruin his beautiful gift by blubbering on it.

"Will you stay?" His voice was tense, to match the set of his shoulders.

She met his gaze. An unwise move. His smoke-gray eyes interfered with her ability to think rationally. He had asked his question with ironclad arrogance, but she sensed a vein of near-desperation pulsing beneath the surface.

Living in the same house with him for any length of time would be a "Serious Misjudgment" indeed. But since his presence had already tweaked her brain circuits, she nodded.

He blew out a long breath. His shoulders relaxed. "Good. Next time I go to town you can come along and do your own shopping. We can't have you running around naked while your clothes are in the wash." His lips curved in a slow smile. He had a mouth to die for, incredibly sexy now that the beard no longer hid its outline. "I forgot to buy you a nightgown. You can borrow one of my T-shirts to sleep in." His gaze strayed to her breasts.

Meg's skin heated. She was acutely conscious of her first night in his house, and the way he'd stood over her bed the next morning when she was nude beneath the sheets.

He sprawled on the couch facing her. With a grimace, he dug Hoover's tennis ball from under a hip and tossed it over his shoulder, where it bounced into the kitchen. "How did it go with Robby?" he asked. "Did he stay on the ground today?"

Relieved at the safer choice of subject, she grinned. "Unless you count perching on a low tree branch with me, he was a confirmed earthling. Robby's a great kid. And he's not in any serious emotional crisis, Zack, I'm sure of it. He likes heights because he thinks climbing brings him closer to his mother."

Zack stretched long legs on a rickety coffee table that groaned under the weight. He leaned his head back against the cushions. "You make more sense than the shrinks, from a dumb rancher's point of view. Hell, if I thought altitude would help, I'd head for Everest tomorrow. Sometimes I just want to talk to Sky. Sometimes I think I hear her whispering to me. Even after a year, I . . ." He paused, shrugging his broad shoulders. "Maybe I'm the one who should be seeing the head docs."

"No," she said firmly. "There's nothing crazy about a love that lasts beyond death. I've always hoped I'd be lucky enough to—"

"Don't even say it." He sat forward, clunking his booted feet onto oak floor planks. "Everlasting love sounds good in poetry, Meg, but it's damn hard when you're the one who's left behind."

Meg wanted to ask Zack about Sky, about everlasting love, but she knew the answers would be painful for him.

The room fell silent except for the tick of the hall clock, the drip of the kitchen faucet. He surged to his feet and began to pace. Whipping a notebook from the computer table, he started to open it but didn't. He set it down again, stroking the cover with his hand.

His jaw muscles tensed. His eyes squeezed shut. When he opened them, he met Meg's gaze with what seemed to be resignation. "When I offered you the job, I said I'd pay you a fair wage. But that was when I thought I'd get this loan. As of now, I can't provide much more than room and board. The wages'll be pocket change."

"It's all right. I eat a lot for a short person, so my board's going to cost you plenty," she said in the lightest tone she could muster. "Otherwise, my needs are pretty basic. As you know, I can get by on a limited wardrobe."

His eyes reflected exactly how limited her wardrobe had been that first night under his roof. Meg shivered, feeling as naked as she had then. Every time he looked her way, her insides turned to melted butter. *Snap out of it, girl,* she told herself. *The man's heart belongs to a ghost.*

"This is a good deal for me," she added hurriedly. "People pay big bucks to stay on dude ranches, and this is almost the same thing. I'll finish the typing by next week. And then . . . I'll be on my way."

"In my opinion, you shouldn't go back. I hate for you to knuckle under to your boss, fiancé, lover . . . whatever the hell you want to call the peckerwood who ran out on you." His voice grew louder with each name he assigned to Edward. His anger surprised Meg.

"I won't sleep with him again, if that's what you think." She wished she could explain that she had more to worry about than what to call Edward. Her most pressing obligation was a meeting with a parole officer. However, she was certain Zack's whole attitude toward her would change if he knew about that. He wouldn't want her associating with his son. "Boss. I'll call Edward boss."

Zack's gray eyes showed his doubts. "Even hearing his name makes me sick. But you still feel . . . something for him, don't you? You don't seem to dread going back."

"I want to start work on the sequel," she said truthfully. "My head is full of ideas for it." She *did* dread leaving the ranch, but that was not something she had the power to change.

"Why not work on your own, like you did for the first game? If you don't have another place, you could stay here, and use my computer. Forget the damn typing. Or finish it in your spare time. And if you feel you have to make a labor contribution after that, I'll think of something else."

Meg flushed. Did he realize how suggestive he sounded . . . or how tempted she was to take him up on it?

"Legitimate work." His reddened face convinced her his offer had been strictly on the level. "Accounting. You could put the ranch bookkeeping on computer."

She cleared her throat, which suddenly felt as thick and fuzzy as unbrushed teeth. "Thanks, but—we'll see. I had considered starting some scripting and basic art while I'm here. I'll do it in the evenings, if that's okay."

He jammed his fingers in his back pockets as he leaned a shoulder against the wall. "Whenever you want."

His casual consent came as a relief. With the help of a friend from the office, Meg could download the programs and data she needed on the short term. She'd missed thinking up storylines and puzzles and magical solutions. Computer fantasies provided a much-needed outlet for her imagination.

Zack liked to create things too, she recalled. She fiddled with the mouse, running it over her palm. "I noticed some boxes in my closet, and I looked inside. Are those Burkhart originals?"

"Yes." His gray eyes grew wary.

"I love the jackets and bear shirts. And if I ever go backpacking again, I definitely need a stove stand like yours. I was thinking, since I know a little about marketing . . ." She'd learned a great deal by osmosis, with Edward's work largely overshadowing their personal relationship. "Maybe I could . . ." Noting Zack's scowl, she trailed the sentence into silence.

He pushed away from the wall. "Don't trouble yourself. I'll move that junk out of your room tomorrow."

"Since I don't have much to put in the closet, it's not in the way. And it's not junk."

He frowned. "The bear repellent's for sale in a West Yellowstone store. It's had limited testing, but it might save somebody from a mauling. The rest isn't worth much."

"What if I prove otherwise?"

"Stay out of it, Meg. I have enough problems without becoming a part-time salesman."

Why was he so opposed to selling his "junk"? Was he unwilling to face associated memories of his wife? Or was he afraid of failure? Either way, he needed a push in the forward direction.

"You should at least test the market. I was terrified *Athena's Promise* would be a flop. But Edward . . ." She grimaced. "Uh-oh, I used the nasty E-word. Will you ever forgive me?"

"Probably not." His mouth twitched up at one corner. "I guess there's no point in banning a name. Hell, there's probably somebody named Edward who's worth a damn."

Confusion riffled through her. She kept thinking of Edward, even when she didn't mean to. A link between them existed in her head, if nowhere else. She needed to debug her program code, but it wasn't easy. "It's not that I'm pining for him," she said. "I just can't help knowing what he'd say, how he'd act or . . ."

Zack raised a hand, fending off her excuses. "You don't need to explain. A relationship's like a habit. It takes a while to sever the ties."

She saw the pain in his eyes and knew he understood her problem all too well. His wife had been dead a year. He had yet to loosen the first knot.

After supper that evening, Zack lugged a couple of sawhorses into the sun in front of the barn. "Robby," he called. "I need help."

Eager to participate, the boy came running. Zack smiled at the sight of the short legs churning across the lawn. As a kid, Zack had learned persistence, pleasure in working with his hands, and a love of land and nature from his dad. But he had allowed grief and day-to-day problems to absorb him, while failing to share those important lessons with his own son. He had a niggling suspicion that it was Meg who had clarified his view of Robby, helping him see what was missing between them.

She stood waving from the porch, dressed in her short shorts and a waist-length, body-hugging T. "Do you need another hand?" she called.

"No thanks," he shouted back. "This is man's work."

Robby, grinning from ear-to-ear and out of breath from his run, arrived at Zack's side.

Zack crouched down to the boy's eye level. "Get set, little man. Here's what we're going to do." He explained the work in advance, asking for input every now and then. The child beamed.

He and Robby carried boards from a storage shed, and then spent a couple of hours measuring and sawing and hammering. When they were through, they'd made ladders to attach beside two llama stalls so that Robby could do those feeding chores all by himself.

Meg came out with a plate of cookies just as they were hammering in the last nails. He looked up to smile at her, noticing a line of pale skin showing between shorts and shirt. That distracted him just long enough. Robby, ever enthusiastic, decided to finish Zack's nail. The only problem was, Zack's hand was in the way.

He yelped as a kid-size hammer struck his thumb.

Robby jumped back as if he were the one who'd been hit. "I-I-I didn't m-mean it," he stammered.

Meg put down the cookies and stood behind Robby. "It was an accident," she said defensively.

Zack stopped muttering curses under his breath and frowned at her. Did she think he was going to beat the kid? Or even scold him?

He took a deep breath and ignored the throbbing. "Robby, come here."

The boy dropped the little hammer and came forward with head down and shoulders scrunched.

"I know you didn't mean it, son," Zack said gently. "Know what else? I didn't mean to yell, either." He held up his hand. "Looks like all the fingers are still there. Let's see yours."

Braving a renewed smile, Robby held up his hand.

"Gimme five, partner." As he slapped big hand to little one, Zack felt that he'd accomplished something a lot more lasting than the ladders they'd built.

At Robby's insistence, Meg followed up by kissing Zack's booboo better. Never content with the ordinary, she applied both lips and tongue.

She cured his thumb. The throbbing took up residence in his jeans, instead.

Chapter Ten

Meg checked her E-mail for the third time in an hour. For days, she'd been expecting a reply from Silverstein, her lawyer. All she'd received so far was an automated response that announced he was vacationing in Paris. Too bad he wasn't like Edward, a slave to electronic messages no matter where he was. Silverstein would be back soon, and he *would* answer her. She kept telling herself that.

She'd been on the ranch nearly a week now. She was running out of time. Contacting Silverstein was her one chance to extend her travel permit and put off her next appearance before a parole officer. In addition, she'd asked Silverstein to look at her PenUltimate contract. Could she, or could she not, fulfill that agreement by working here, at least until such time as she had to return for other reasons? And would he talk to Edward and smooth things over somehow?

With luck, she'd have a storyline completed before she saw Edward again. She would simply hand it to him along with a formal resignation. Since *Athena's* sales and reviews were going so well, she had confidence she could land another job.

But, once again, she had no mail.

She clicked off the Internet provider she was charging to Edward's account. Since he had insisted she was his employee whether she liked it or not, using his Internet access to work things out seemed appropriate.

Glancing out the window, she searched for the wren she and Robby had set free that morning. She caught sight of a gray bird flitting through the leaves and smiled. Robby would be delighted if his winged friend stayed near the house.

When she wasn't typing, she and Robby were often together, feeding llamas, collecting eggs from the scraggly chickens that roosted in the barn, walking alongside the creek, playing wild games of Frisbee. Each day she learned things about Meg Delaney she'd never recognized before. For instance, she'd thought herself devoid of maternal instincts, but she discovered she had them in abundance. Or maybe it was her inner child relating to Robby's outer one. In any case, she loved that kid.

Though Zack made time for Robby in the evenings—which pleased both Meg and the boy—the ranch kept him busy during the day. She'd seen Zack shirtless, sweating, flexing his muscles in the sun as he unloaded a dozen hundred-pound sacks of feed. Or gently coaxing a young llama into a halter. Or out in the yard, training, grooming, trimming an animal's hoofs. Or working on a rail fence he was building near the barn.

Some days he rode his horse out to check remote fences, or otherwise worked out of sight. He seemed content to be outside, doing whatever needed to be done. But he was quiet with Meg, even at mealtime. He seemed distracted. Was he worried about his loan situation? Had she offended him with her offer to market his designs? Had she shocked him when she kissed his hammer-injured hand? She *had* taken the "make better" thing beyond the usual limits.

Or was he distancing himself from her because of

Sky, because Meg's nearness served only to remind him of his loss?

Meg had believed, after he'd given her a job, that the attraction she had for Zack might not be all one-sided. But he demonstrated no craving for her company. Quite the opposite, it seemed.

As she reached for one of Sky's journals, Robby barreled into the living room, cowboy boots clumping with the volume of an approaching cavalry. Zack was right behind, making nearly as much noise with his own well-worn boots. He had a black cowboy hat in one hand, a straw hat in the other, and a look on his face that suggested he was about to face a firing squad.

"Robby and I are going up the mountain a ways," Zack muttered. "Robby wants you to ride with us."

Robby's clear blue-green eyes pleaded, catching at her heart. "Daddy said you wouldn't want to come, but *I* . . ." He poked a thumb at his small chest, "said you would."

Zack obviously did not want her along. He shifted his weight from one foot to the other, avoiding her gaze. She wished she hadn't made such a muddle of their relationship. She wished they could at least be friends.

"What about my work?" she said. "Shouldn't I stay and—"

His gaze homed in on hers. "It's Saturday," he cut in. "A morning off will be good for all of us. But if you'd rather spend the time here, don't let Robby pressure you. I know how attached you are to the computer." He lifted one eyebrow. When he looked at her that way, she almost believed he did want her to go along.

"Is this a dare?" She stood, only to find herself nose to chest with him.

His eyes crinkled at the corners. "You might call it

that. You're a city girl, and I'm guessing your saddle-hugging end is real short on calluses."

She rubbed the seat of the jeans covering her shamefully soft bottom. "Saddle? You mean we're going on horses?" She had never been comfortable with horses. In fact, she was deathly afraid of them. Nevertheless, since Zack had made this gesture—even though Robby had been the instigator—she would do her part. She would ride a rhinoceros, if necessary.

"Come see my pony," Robby piped up, taking her hand.

Zack settled the black hat on his head and plopped the straw one on hers. "I haven't seen him so excited in . . . a long time."

The straw hat was only a little too big. Winona's, she guessed, not Sky's. If it were Sky's, Zack would not be dawning a slow smile as he watched her adjust the brim to a jaunty tilt.

His smile enticed her. That, and Robby's high spirits. She reached behind her to click off the computer. "How can I resist? I've always wanted calluses on my backside."

Robby pulled her outside. "I told you, Daddy," he shouted. "I told you she'd ride with us."

Meg's determination wavered when she saw the three animals tied to the porch rail. Her riding experience was limited to a single lesson at age ten, which had ended badly. But she wouldn't think about that now. She'd lose her courage if she thought too much.

"I saddled Lightning for you." Zack pointed to a stocky gray horse who stared at Meg belligerently, switching his tail.

She held out a shaky hand to pat the horse's nose. Lightning snorted, flapping his lips as if he meant to bite her. She whisked her fingers out of range. "Lightning. Does that refer to his quick teeth?"

"Yeah, right." Zack tilted back his black cowboy hat. He looked both bad-guy surly and devilishly handsome. "The name's a joke. Nothing about ol' Lightning is quick. You could attach a hornet's nest to his tail and he'd move no faster than a turtle."

How could she turn down Zack's idea of a green-horn mount without branding herself a wuss? As she saw it, her pride and honor were at stake. She accepted the mount, setting her teeth when Zack boosted her into the saddle and adjusted the stirrups. The first few times Lightning stomped a hoof or twitched an ear, she clutched the saddle horn in panic. Once they were moving, it got easier.

Her horse was pretty much as advertised. He plodded along the trail, steady and reliable. Zack rode circles around her on his prancing bay. He was as at home in the saddle as John Wayne in his prime. Robby rode like he'd been born to it, which was probably the case. Hoover, the canine vacuum cleaner, trotted alongside the boy's brown-and-white splotched pony.

They traveled up the valley to a meadow where grass and wildflowers grew stirrup high. Zack reined in his mount. Lightning stopped, too, dipping his head for a quick bite. The unexpected lurch threw Meg forward, nearly over the horse's head.

Robby leaped off his pony. "Come on, Meg. The creek is creepy-crawly with tadpoles." The boy disappeared through the bushes, headed toward the sound of rippling water.

Zack dismounted and tied his horse and Robby's pony to the trunk of a tall pine. Meg hesitated. Staying on Lightning hadn't proved difficult, but getting off was the tricky part. She glanced at the ground, measuring the distance. It was farther than she'd thought. Too far. Her knuckles turned white from a death-grip on the horn.

Zack took Lightning's reins and stood close, which should have offered a measure of security. "It's easier than it looks, Meg."

Her fear was historical, not rational. She had been pushed into an equestrian lesson by her mother, who'd needed a social entrance to the horsey crowd. Meg's riding performance had been a terrible disappointment. "It's just that I . . . the last time I rode, the only other time, I fell off and the horse stepped on my arm. I wore a cast for three months."

He cursed softly as he placed a gentle hand on the arm she had unconsciously cradled. "Why didn't you say so before? I figured you had a case of greenhorn jitters. If I'd known—" Zack's brows crowded into a straight line under his hat's shadow. "Don't worry. I'm right here."

Meg appreciated his concern. Edward would have advised her to close her eyes and jump. But then Edward would never have taken her riding in the first place.

Zack guided her with his voice as she brought one leg over the saddle. When she began the downward slide, he gripped her waist. The seat of her jeans rasped along the length of his body. Instead of thinking about the horse and the distance to the ground, her senses filled with heated leather, with the feel of Zack so close to her. She didn't want to touch earth again. Not ever. She wanted to hang suspended, his thigh hard and high between her legs, his heartbeat drumming into her back, his warm breath on her neck, his mouth . . .

Her feet touched earth, but her heartbeat continued to soar. Zack turned her in his arms, pinning her against the unmoving horse. Her hat had fallen into the grass, and his was tipped back so the mid-morning sun revealed his eyes.

Hungry eyes. Wolf eyes. He leaned nearer, at the

same time increasing every point of contact between them, sending her pulse zooming into the next galaxy. She had landed in a wide-based stance, and he moved into the opening. She was practically astride his thigh. The pressure he applied to her most sensitive flesh stole the air from her lungs. She grasped handfuls of his shirt with trembling hands, praying he wouldn't move just yet, wishing he wanted her as she wanted him.

He stroked her cheek with the back of his knuckles, touched her lips with a callused thumb. Anticipation shivered through her. She couldn't speak, couldn't breathe. He was going to kiss her. Please, God, he had to kiss her.

At the last moment, when only millimeters separated their lips, he retreated. The hunger had not left his eyes, but he glanced away to hide it.

Meg ached with desire. She tingled all over, while he easily resisted her lips, her kiss. As she let go of his shirt, she was grateful for the horse at her back. Otherwise her knees might have given way and left her in a puddle on the ground. Zack retrieved her hat and offered it to her. She took it without making contact with his hand. She concentrated all her frustration on gripping the straw brim. It cracked under the pressure.

"Robby will wonder what's taking us so long," Zack said in a voice that was unusually thick and harsh.

Meg pushed away from the horse just as the boy came running out of the brush by the creek.

"I caught a frog!" Robby's T-shirt dripped from his adventure. His boots were missing.

With cupped hand outstretched in front of him, he headed straight for Meg. Right before he slammed into her, he tripped. The frog shot out of his fingers and landed on the front pocket of Meg's shirt, where it clung for dear life. She yelped and sprang backward, colliding with Zack. Lighting leaped in the opposite direction, ears pricked like antennas. The frog apparently decided Meg was not such a safe haven after all. It sprang off her and into the tall grass. Meg splayed a hand at her throat, still absorbing the fact that her assailant was harmless.

At Meg's back, a low vibration began in Zack's chest, growing into deep, rich laughter. Robby giggled, then laughed outright. Lightning snorted. The sounds harmonized with her own laughter and were, to Meg's ears, as lovely as the world's finest music. She would gladly have suffered a hundred frog attacks for that one shared moment.

On the way home, Robby ranged ahead, leaving Meg and Zack to ride side by side. She glanced at him. He glanced at her. When their eyes met, she smiled. He didn't smile back. Even though her bottom was already bruised and saddle sore, even though Zack looked sullen and solitary, Meg was pleased. She'd been wrong in thinking there was nothing mutual between them. He still loved Sky, she understood that. But at least he cared something for Meg Delaney.

The trail narrowed and the two horses moved closer together. Her leg brushed Zack's. When the path widened again, he stayed near enough to touch. Sexual electricity crackled between them. Meg thought she'd never felt a more delicious sensation.

Zack felt as if he had a tree trunk in his jeans, and he thought maybe it was on fire. He'd almost kissed Meg. He'd almost done a whole lot more than kiss her. When he'd helped her dismount, she'd been so soft and willing in his arms. Even now . . . Jesus, it was all he could do to keep from dragging her off the horse and having his way with her.

What the hell was wrong with him? Had the stress

of keeping the ranch together gotten to him? Or was it just that he'd been without sex for so long? He was losing his grip. He loved Sky, damn it, and he would keep on loving her. Besides, only the lowest of the low would take advantage of Meg when he knew how vulnerable she was. Zack still had a brain in charge of his body, even if it faded out once in a while.

He reined his horse away from hers, putting a few inches of relief between them. Meg's green eyes fastened on him as he groped for something to say and came up with exactly nothing.

Meg, though, could coax conversation out of a rock. To his surprise, Zack found himself talking about his childhood on a small Ohio farm. About how he'd grown up with respect for the earth, which had led to an interest in forestry and animal husbandry, and to college in Boise. And that had led to Sky.

"What about your father, mother, sisters, brothers?" Meg asked.

"One older sister, married with three teenage sons. One younger brother, still a bachelor and determined to stay that way. My mother teaches third grade in Springfield, Ohio. Dad died the year I finished high school."

"I'm sorry about your father," Meg said. "What does the family think of your ranch? Do they visit often?"

He smiled, recalling his mother's high-pitched shriek when she'd first touched a llama. The animal and Mom had both jumped at least three feet on contact. "We get together once a year or so. My family is supportive, but every one of them prefers city life. Dad, though, he would have loved it here. He would have loved everything about this place."

Zack found Meg surprisingly easy to talk to. After

a while, she didn't have to prompt him with questions. "When we were kids, I was the only one who enjoyed farm chores. Being outside was like a reward for me. Dad knew agriculture and managed to do well enough even in years that were too wet or too dry. At different times, we had chickens, turkeys, hogs. My brother and I raised steers for 4-H every year. Danny was frustrated as hell because my steer would gain weight twice as fast as his. A huge dollop of molasses in the grain was my secret formula."

Meg laughed. "That sounds like you, using sweetener on the sly. I wasn't allowed to have pets, so I envy your experience. Besides the horse that broke my arm, my most memorable animal was a chimpanzee at the zoo, when I was about eight. I reached over a fence railing to touch its hand. It grabbed me and tried to pull me right into the cage. G. T. was there, holding onto my other arm. Fortunately, she won the tug-of-war."

"The chimp must have been a male," Zack said. "Can't blame him for trying."

She went on to tell about G. T. taking her to arboretums and planetariums, art museums and libraries. They'd grown flower gardens. They'd trekked to the mountains to see summer wildflowers.

Her chatter had bothered Zack on that first hike in Yellowstone, but she didn't talk as much now. She was an excellent listener when she wanted to be. She'd grown used to him . . . and he to her. Meg brought zest to everything she did. Her enthusiasm had permeated him and Robby and life on the ranch. He found himself wishing she'd extend her stay.

With a week gone, he knew she would leave soon. Suddenly, it was important to know exactly when. "Meg."

She looked at him with bright, expectant green eyes.

"Do you . . ." Zack cleared his throat. "When are you planning to . . ."

Hoover's persistent bark came from up ahead. Zack noticed both the dog and Robby were out of sight. "I'll be right back," he told Meg as he urged his horse into a gallop.

He raced down the last of the narrow trail and emerged at the dirt lane leading to the house. Fifty yards distant, Tobias's truck was parked along the fence line.

Robby and his trotting pony had almost reached Tobias as the hired man opened the truck door and stepped out. Somewhere ahead of them, Hoover was still barking. Tobias scowled, motioning Robby to stay back.

Something bad must have happened. Zack called the boy, but Robby had already seen whatever was up there. He turned, eyes wide with horror.

"G-gingko." Robby pointed toward the front of the truck, to a point beyond Zack's view. "Gingko's h-hurt, Daddy. We have to help him."

Zack jumped off his horse and sprinted to Robby's side. "It'll be okay, son." The empty reassurance was all Zack could offer. He knew it wasn't worth much. "Go back down the trail and find Meg. Take her home."

Robby protested, but Zack turned the boy's mount to face the direction they'd come. He smacked the spotted rump and sent Robby on his way.

As soon as the pony rounded the bend, Zack rushed to see what had upset his son. Tobias joined him, muttering something Zack was too harried to catch. In the center of the road, a shaggy red-brown llama struggled to rise, but one foreleg was bent at a strange angle. The leg was shattered. A jagged bone struck through the skin.

Gingko whistled a shrill cry of pain. Or maybe it

was a cry for help. Help Zack couldn't give. Turning away, he shouldered past Tobias, stalked to the truck and lifted a gun from the rear window's rifle rack. God knew he hated what he had to do, but the llama was his responsibility. He had no choice.

A single clean shot to the head ended Gingko's misery.

With his ears ringing from the blast, Zack stood over the now motionless animal. He felt a little sick. He'd never been a hunter, never liked spilling blood. He closed his eyes for a moment. Tobias came up beside him, and Zack silently handed him the gun.

"Don't know who unlocked the pasture gate, but it was wide open," Tobias said. "I drove down here looking for Gingko. Found him just as Hoover started barking. Then Robby showed up."

"I wish we could have kept this from him," Zack said.

"Yeah." Tobias ran a hand around the back of his bull neck. "Too late now, though. Somebody must've come down the road going too fast and—"

Zack cursed. "A hit-and-run's pretty damn unlikely this close to the ranch. Hell, how often does anyone drive through here? The road goes nowhere but to the house, or on up the mountain where no one lives. Why would . . ."

The answer could be right in front of him. Tobias had been at the scene. Zack had only the man's word that the damage had been done by someone else. He glanced at the bumper and front fenders of Tobias's truck. Dents and rust spots were everywhere, making it impossible to tell old from new.

Zack met the hired man's gaze.

Tobias looked guilty. He had keys to all the gates and was supposed to keep them locked. Was he guilty of a lack of diligence? Of something more? Or was Zack becoming paranoid after all the trouble he'd had lately?

He shook his head, wishing he could clear it of questions and doubts. Another accident? He wasn't so sure.

The blows were coming too fast and hard for even the darkest side of luck.

Chapter Eleven

Two mornings later, Meg was rinsing the breakfast dishes when Tobias came to the door.

"Winona here?" he called through the screen.

"I think so," Meg said, turning off the water. "I'll go—" She picked up a dish towel and would have started down the hall, but Tobias surprised her by coming in and scooting past. He seemed to know the correct heading. Seconds later, he knocked softly at Winona's closed door and let himself in. Meg went back to the dishes, wondering how Tobias knew Winona's room, and why Win hadn't tossed him out on his ear by now. Could it be that Win liked Tobias? Really liked him, as in romance? Meg didn't think so. They were probably just having a discussion on good quality gaskets, or Snap-on tools versus Craftsman.

Before Meg had put away the last bowl, Win rushed down the hall with semi-clean purple coveralls zipped to her neck.

Tobias followed at a respectful distance. He glanced at Meg and tipped his bubba cap. "Sorry for barging through, Meg. We have some tools that need tendin'."

Meg stared after him, wondering if there could possibly be a double entendre.

"Not in a million years," she said to herself. Shaking her head, she went to the computer. Before starting the day's work, she checked her E-mail.

The message she'd been waiting for was there. Her lawyer, Sam Silverstein, wrote that Meg's next conference was canceled for at least two weeks and he would reschedule. She smiled as she made the translation from Silverstein's cautious E-mail phrasing. Her parole meeting was postponed. He added that he'd spoken to her employer and that situation, too, was under control.

Meg took a deep breath, expanding her lungs with mountain air. Edward's threats had been all bluff, as she'd hoped they might be. She'd been granted a reprieve.

Silverstein ended his message with a request for another medium for communications—to be used for state emergencies, he said. Translation: He wanted a postal mailing address so he could explain himself more freely. He probably needed one to give her parole officer. And he'd have to send her an extended travel permit, as well.

Meg still hoped to keep her legal problems secret, so she didn't want correspondence from the Utah Department of Corrections coming here. She knew from unpleasant experience that people often believed the bad about a person without looking at the evidence. And Zack was a conventional, law-abiding citizen. Learning she'd spent four months in the cooler would shock him to his toes.

She pushed the problem to the back of her mind and rejoiced at the good news. Two weeks! Two glorious weeks to be a part of the ranch, a part of this life she was learning to love. A part of Robby's life. And Zack's.

Jumping up, almost overturning the kitchen chair she used at the computer, she skipped outside shouting, "Yes!" to the treetops. With two weeks, she could do something useful here, something to make a difference.

Robby had cried himself to sleep after he'd seen Gingko lying in the road. The peaceful afternoon ride had been shattered beyond repair. Meg had held the child and offered what comfort she could. Later, Zack patiently explained that the animal had been in pain and couldn't be mended, and he had done the only possible thing.

Poor Robby. He'd nodded solemnly, accepting yet another death. Given time, he *would* laugh again. Meg knew he would. And now she could be here to see it.

She'd be here for Zack, too. He needed her help, whether he knew it or not. Both of them had to overcome the past. By staying on the ranch, she had begun to heal inside. The open landscape eased her dread of crowded rooms and narrow corridors. Her heart had healed, as well. She'd come to accept that Edward had never loved her. He was not a prince. He was—and always would be—a frog.

Zack's heartache ran deeper than hers and might not heal so easily, but she could help in another way. He needed money to keep the land that meant so much to him. She would gladly offer her royalty income, assuming it came in before his loan payments were due, but the timing was iffy. Besides, he wouldn't want to accept money from her. So Meg had thought of another plan. Silverstein's good tidings gave her the opportunity to see it through. All she needed now was an ally.

Win was the only choice. A female Sioux warrior was a strange confidante, but the woman was pragmatic. She'd see the value of Meg's proposal. And Win had Zack's trust; he would listen to his mother-in-law.

Meg passed Robby, who was playing Frisbee with

Hoover in the yard. At least he was outside instead of moping in his room as he had most of yesterday. He was rebounding with the vigor of youth. Meg hoped she could coax a smile from him before bedtime.

The child saw Meg and waved. Since he'd been in the act of tossing the Frisbee, he misfired, sending the orange disc thirty degrees astray. He took off after it like a short-limbed rabbit, racing the bounding dog. The Frisbee landed on top of a gate post. Robby scaled the rails to retrieve it. Meg noted he wore cowboys boots again today. Thank goodness he had given up on mountain climbing.

She entered the garage where a radio blasted rock and roll at decibels that surely exceeded the EPA safe range. The room was dim in spite of the fluorescent lights along the walls. Old oil and other vehicular fluids stained the concrete floor, and the odor hung in the air. A metallic-blue Corvette, Win's latest repair project, was parked with its taillights facing the garage door. The hood was raised and the front end jacked up, but there was no sign of Win.

The radio rollicked into "Margaritaville." Meg hummed along as she ambled around the car. She nearly tripped over two pairs of legs sticking out from beneath the front bumper. The legs wore jeans and coveralls, ending in Tobias's cracked brown boots and Win's oil-stained Shaq-size tennis shoes. Meg heard a clang from under the car.

"Winona?" she called softly. She didn't want to startle the two preoccupied mechanics into dropping something, like maybe the engine. They were obviously doing some serious work.

When she got no reply, Meg was about to leave. Her timing, as usual, was poor. She'd come back later. She had turned toward the door when she heard watery suction noises. Although she didn't know much about cars, she guessed the sound came from a radiator hose.

She estimated where the mechanics' heads would be. Getting on her knees and bending down for a better look, she peered into the dimness beneath the vehicle. The moist noises grew more distinct when the radio paused between tunes. She heard a definite groan. Thinking something must be wrong, she inched under the car. Winona limply held a rachet. Meg reached for her hand.

As Meg's eyes adjusted to the dark, two heads came into focus, and two bodies. Tobias's leg was linked over Win's. Meg inhaled sharply when she realized what was going on. Not a radiator repair. The activities were physical, not mechanical. Tobias and Winona were in deep lip lock. Very likely in breast-to-chest, thigh-to-groin lock, too.

Embarrassed, Meg crawled backward until her head cleared the Corvette's frame. When she stood up to run, she collided with a box of oil filters. White cylinders spilled across the cement floor. One of them rolled under the car.

Tobias sprang out from beneath the opposite side of the Corvette with the speed of a Hollywood stuntman. His pierced-heart forearms bulged muscle; beefy hands contracted into fists. She'd begun to think of him as a big ugly teddy bear, but right now he looked more like King Kong in a bad mood.

He glanced past Meg to survey the rest of the garage. His combat-ready stance relaxed when he saw she was alone. A grin transformed his ill-favored features into overblown puckish charm. Meg's moment of fear vanished as if it had never been. She took a deep breath.

"What is it, Meg? Zack looking for me?"

"No. I came to see Winona. Is she . . . um, available?"

Tobias chuckled, rasping a hand through his close-cropped hair. "Don't go to thinkin' Win's a loose woman just because she'd get down and dirty with a man." He crouched to look under the car. "Come on out, cupcake. Meg won't tell Zack on you."

With a nod in Meg's direction he straightened and snatched his green bubba cap from a hook on the wall. Slapping it into place, he sauntered out the door humming along with "Wild Thing" blaring from the radio. As he passed her, Meg noted the tiny blue letters inside the heart on his forearm read "Come to Jesus."

She suppressed a smile. Tobias was the last person she'd have pegged the religious type. And she still found it hard to believe he and Win were lovers. Win's overbearing size and personality would surely wilt most men's ardor and other necessary appendages. And Tobias was no Don Juan. When she thought about it, maybe they fit together after all.

Meg busied herself gathering scattered oil filters. She'd stacked most of them on a shelf before Win emerged from under the car.

Win straightened to her daunting height, dwarfing the low-slung sports car. A grease handprint decorated the right breast of the purple coveralls she wore. Her furious gaze declared open warfare. "What are you doing here?" she barked. "Spying on me?"

Meg saw right through the bluster. "Even if I were, what are you ashamed of, Win? You like Tobias. He likes you. He's a nice guy, so what's wrong with that?"

"Hmmph." Win crossed her arms over a formidable chest. "I guess you'll be sniffing after *him* next. You've already bewitched my grandson. And you're luring Zack into a black widow's web."

Meg switched off the radio. Didn't black widows

eat their mates? That seemed more Win's style than Meg's. "I'm not luring anyone anywhere. Zack chooses his own poison."

Win rolled her eyes. "Tell me another one, Little Big Mouth. He's a man isn't he? Men *notice* women like you."

Meg wished that were true. "I'm no seductress, and Zack isn't interested anyhow. He's only keeping me around because Robby and I hit it off. We're friends. At least I hope we are. I'd like to help him with—"

"Your cat-green eyes won't help any of us. I know your kind."

"I'm not a 'kind.'" Meg was on the verge of losing her temper, but didn't dare. She mentally braced herself against Win's scowl, fierce enough to send a bulldozer packing. Meg refused to turn tail and run like the rabbit she was in her heart.

After long moments of scathing eye contact, Win snorted. "You're tougher than I thought. If you've got something to say, spit it out."

Meg had given up on Win as an ally. But while she had the woman's attention, she would make the most of it. "I feel like I'm stepping on a land mine every time I mention your daughter's name. Robby's so sensitive. I wouldn't want to say the wrong thing in front of him. I need to know what happened to her, how she died."

Win lowered herself onto a bench that looked like a church pew after an invasion of devils. It was deeply scarred, the varnish long gone. Black grease encrusted the wood grain. She gripped the bench seat on either side of her thighs, head bent, back bowed. "It happened just downstream from the bridge, where the road crosses the river on the way to town. She was rafting with some clients when . . . No one knows if she drowned first or died from bashing against the rocks below the falls.''

"I'm sorry." Careful not to crowd the larger woman, Meg perched on the far end of the wooden bench. "You must miss her terribly.

Win scooted over, providing Meg a fraction of additional space, in what seemed a sort of peace offering.

"She was independent," Win said. "Sometimes Zack had trouble accepting that. Both of them were stubborn. When they argued, the walls rattled.''

"They argued?" Meg repeated dubiously. She'd thought Sky and Zack had had the ideal marriage. Arguing was an unexpected flaw.

"They fought like a hound and a bobcat. Not that it mattered. When the battle was over, they were more in love than ever."

Meg read enough between those last words to zing hot flashes through her. They had ended up in bed, clasped in each others' arms, bound together by the kind of passion Meg had dreamed of all her life.

"She haunts Zack. Not like a ghost," Win hastened to add. "It's the memories that haunt him. He blames himself for letting her go to the river without him. For not being there. For not saving her. Maybe for not dying along with her. If a man can love a woman too much, that's the way it is with him."

Meg flushed, as embarrassed as if she'd peeked in a window and seen the most intimate details of their lives. But that didn't stop her from saying what needed to be said. "I know Zack mourns her every day, like you do. Robby desperately wants to mourn her and can't, because he knows too little about her. If you and Zack would help him to know his mother, he'd feel less cheated. Safer, because he wouldn't always be asking himself why she left him, if it was somehow his fault."

Win fixed her black gaze on Meg. "Does he feel that way?"

"Yes. He's confused. Scared. If you would just go through old photo albums with him. Let him ask questions about Sky," Meg said. "He needs the answers you could give him."

A deep breath lifted Win's shoulders. "Losing her was like having my heart torn from my breast. Talking about her is still hard. It's the same for Zack." She glanced at Meg with glistening obsidian eyes. "We told ourselves Robby would get over her faster if we didn't say much. We took the only path we could bear."

Win rose to look out the garage window. Robby and Hoover had collapsed in the middle of the yard, both of them panting after their Frisbee game.

"Maybe you see Robby better than those of us who've lived through this with him." Win stroked the glass that separated her from her grandson. " 'Clear visions arise through mist,' Chief Red Hawk used to say."

"The chief sounds like a philosopher." Meg was curious about Red Hawk. Was he real? Some of Win's quotes sounded suspiciously modern, as if they'd been created on the spot.

Win drew herself up proudly. "Red Hawk was my great-uncle, a fine leader of my people." She sighed, sitting back on the bench, her head resting against the concrete block wall. She looked tired, older than before. "When he was in the winter of life, a white judge sent him to prison on trumped-up charges. After his death, he became a legend in the tribe."

She turned her head in Meg's direction, her black eyes dry now, cold and barren. "I don't want you here. Ordinarily, I go after intruders with carving knives, but Zack ruled out torture and dismemberment in your case. He's the chief on this ranch." She tsked at Zack's bad judgment before shrugging her shoulders. "What the hell? None of us will be here much longer, the way things are going."

"What do you mean?"

"Hasn't Zack told you? We're barely making ends meet, what with the llama troubles and legal expenses from the lawsuit."

"Lawsuit?" Meg asked. No wonder Zack had a financial crisis.

"My daughter died trying to save Mike Caldwell, a boy who worked with her on the river. The boy's father sued the rafting company she and Zack owned. The suit was thrown out of court after months of legal shilly-shallying, but the attorney's fees cost plenty."

Meg took a deep breath. Unwittingly, Win had given her the opening she needed. "I think I can help with expenses."

Winona hmmphed. "That's funny. Zack told me you're dead broke." She looked Meg up and down as if checking for dollar bills in her orifices.

"I'm not proposing a donation; Zack doesn't need one. He has the means. He's had it all along."

"What the Sam Hill are you talking about, paleface?" Win boomed.

Meg jumped at the volume before hooking her fingers together in her lap and regaining her composure. "I hate to be a disappointment, but you don't scare me, Win."

"That's a damn shame," Win said. "If you had the sense to find your butt with a compass, you'd skedaddle right now. Zack might take you into his bed for awhile, but he won't take you into his heart. He'll always be married to . . ." Win's voice cracked. "To his one and only woman."

Meg swallowed a sharp longing for someone to

love, someone who would return the emotion in kind. "I'd still like to help."

Win arched an ink-black brow. "All right. Tell me what's up your shorts." ·

Meg explained what she'd found in her closet and how she could market the items. "I mentioned the idea to Zack, but he was not very receptive. If you could convince him, I'll work out the details."

Win narrowed her eyes. "You think he could make big money out of that stuff?"

"I'm ninety-nine percent sure. Will you talk to him?"

"If I talked up a blue norther, he still wouldn't agree. He and my daughter worked on those designs together."

Meg sighed. Sky again. Always Sky. "Won't you at least *try*? There must be some way to get his permission. You said yourself he might lose the ranch. Surely if he's in enough financial trouble, he'll agree to . . ."

Win scratched her square jaw, smearing grease on mahogany skin. "If you think there's profit in it, go ahead. Just keep it a secret for now. I doubt Zack'll throw the money away once we put it in his hip pocket."

"But shouldn't we talk to him before—"

"Don't be so damn lily-livered," Win chided. "Some things, a person would rather not know. He'll sing your praises when it's over and done."

Meg tapped a fingertip on pursed lips, considering. She hated to deceive Zack about this, but if it was the only way to help him . . . "I'll need information on how many stove stands and coats and shirts he has stockpiled, what he's done about trademarks, and if he's tried to sell anywhere before now."

"His records are in the office files." Win jerked her

head in the direction of the house. "Sneak yourself a look."

Meg nodded. "I'll get a post office box in town. That way, after I've sent out inquiries, Zack won't catch on to what we're doing before we're ready to tell him. Would you help me mail samples?"

Win agreed.

Meg sauntered away smiling, satisfied she had found the ally she sought.

That night, Meg couldn't sleep. She was restless and impatient, bursting with ideas, eager to begin. When she felt sure everyone else was asleep, she opened her door a crack and looked out. Moonlight from her bedroom window cast light into the hall. Otherwise, the house was dark.

She listened for a moment, shivering in a knee-length bear T-shirt she'd worn to bed. Someone snored like a sputtering chain saw. Since she'd shared a tent with Zack without hearing any such noise, she figured Winona was the snorer.

The racket overpowered the creaking of cold wood floorboards beneath Meg's bare feet as she tiptoed into Zack's office. She turned on a desk lamp, pulled out a drawer of the file cabinet and thumbed through the folders. The pertinent information was not under "T" for trademarks, or "P" for projects, or "E" for entrepreneurial dreams. It was filed under "S"—in the thick folder marked "Sky."

The label was one more sign of how a dead woman still ruled this little kingdom. Sky belonged here, as Meg never would, even if she stayed a hundred years. Pictures of Sky were everywhere in the tiny office. Sky alone, standing tall and dark and proud against a mountain backdrop. Sky and Zack, Sky and Winona, Sky and a younger version of Robby. Sky and a sunburned teenager on a big yellow raft.

Meg sighed, reminding herself that Zack and Sky's past was none of her affair. She'd do best to stick to business here. Though *she* might be stupid enough to fall in love on the rebound, Zack still adored his wife in an eternal way Meg envied.

Before she turned out the light, she checked to see if she'd moved anything on the desk. It was hard to tell. Unopened mail and piles of bills were scattered everywhere. She noticed the desk's center drawer hung slightly open, with a scrap of yellow paper peeking out.

Meg glimpsed neat block letters in thick black ink. Curious, she tugged the paper free and held it close to the lamp.

Behold the Power of the Lord. As He giveth, so shall He taketh away. Eternity awaits thy offering.

No signature. No identification at all. Just a naked omen from a religious zealot. A warning. Or a threat.

She opened the drawer a few inches and found two other notes. Same yellow paper. Same Biblical jargon. She returned the one she'd withdrawn and wiped damp palms on her hips. The notes were an anonymous written testament to the existence of Zack's enemies—of one enemy, at least, which explained why he suspected the llama troubles were not accidents. No wonder he'd seemed preoccupied lately.

But if he had enemies, he also had a friend. Meg intended to help him whether he liked it or not. Leaving the desk more or less as she'd found it, she carried the "S" file to the living room, where she switched on the computer.

As she thought about what to call her project, she studied the file. Inside were sketches and measurements for different sizes of backpacks, tents, jackets, etc. Each page bore Zack's scrawled signature. He'd planned an entire line of sporting goods products.

The designs could be a veritable gold mine if manufactured and distributed properly.

If all went well, they would set up a production line right in the barn. They'd work together . . .

She deleted those thoughts, realizing she was imagining herself as part of the ranch on a long-term basis, which of course would never work out.

And Meg's scheme was not without flaws. The last time she'd come up with what she thought was a perfect plan, it had backfired in a big way. If Zack were unconvinced of her pure motives in this venture, he would have grounds for charging her with theft, unauthorized advertising of a product, and probably a lot of other crimes she didn't know the names for. In a court of law, she'd be guilty.

But she had Win on her side, she reminded herself. Together, they would tell Zack the whys and hows. He might be angry at first, but he'd see that their efforts were well meaning, and in time he'd be grateful. Everything would be fine.

Maybe Meg's ideas were still a bit hazy, but they would clarify. *Clear visions arise through mist*, according to Win's great-uncle. From that, Meg pinpointed an auspicious title for the project: *Red Hawk*, after the old man whose death had made him a Sioux legend. Zack would approve of the name, if nothing else.

Sealing away fear of Zack's wrath, she worked until two o'clock in the morning creating a catchy advertisement aimed at sporting goods chains, and another flyer for smaller outlets. If responses were good, they could progress to Internet sales someday soon.

The ancient refrigerator buzzed. Mice scrabbled in the attic. As the air grew colder, she tucked her legs beneath the bear T-shirt she wore. Her eyes ached from looking at the bright screen in an otherwise dark house. Her back ached from exhaustion. But she couldn't stop when she was so close to finishing. Only a little longer . . .

A light came on in the hall behind her. She hit the SAVE button and turned, gripping the arms of her chair. When the wood groaned beneath her, she froze. Her heartbeat picked up speed. Her lungs pulled hard to gather enough air. Did the screen's glow reach the hallway? Had the chair's creak given her away?

If she was very still, maybe whoever was there would go into the kitchen or bathroom without discovering her presence.

The computer processor was slow. The screen had not yet cleared. She felt for dimmer knobs but couldn't find them. If she switched off the computer now, she'd erase hours of work. Hurriedly, she piled a stack of bear notebooks on top of the file she'd taken from Zack's office, partially shielding the screen.

Heavy footsteps padded on the wood floor. Someone was coming her way. And a renewal of the snore told her it wasn't Winona.

Chapter Twelve

It was Zack, in a half-buttoned pair of ragged jeans, bare feet, disheveled hair.

"What are you doing up so late?" He stood in the doorway to the living room, arms crossed over his naked chest. Dim light from the hall cast him in unfocused shadow, like the silhouette of a bear.

She turned back to the keyboard long enough to see the SAVE process was complete. She hit the escape key. "I was, uh . . . My game design. You said I could work on it at night. I couldn't sleep anyway," she added for good measure as she scooted the chair halfway around, the better to camouflage the screen.

"Neither could I." His gaze traveled down her body, lingering. "You look great in my shirt."

Self consciously, Meg stretched the cotton material over her knees. When Zack wore one of the bear designs, it accented his masculinity, but under his intent gaze, the same cloth made her feel more exquisitely feminine than if she'd been draped in silk.

He retreated to the kitchen. The refrigerator light came on. "How about a beer? It's an old Burkhart cure for troubles of the heart." Zack reappeared in the door frame with a bottle of brew in each hand. "I don't recommend it if you're seeing a cardiologist." His wry smile faded almost as soon as it formed.

Meg fidgeted with the hem of her shirt. "I don't drink. Edward says it makes me—"

"The hell with that. I don't want to hear about *him* tonight. Come on, Meg, let's check out the stars." A certain recklessness about him caused her to wonder if he'd already indulged in a six-pack of bottled cure. He arched a brow, daring her to join him.

She followed Zack through the kitchen to the porch. The air was cool, scented with evergreen and earth. She took the bottle he proffered and settled her bottom on cold wooden planks near the edge of the porch, her legs drawn up beneath the stretched material of her shirt. Zack sat three feet away. He took a long pull of beer. Fascinated with everything about him, Meg watched his Adam's apple rise and fall with each swallow. He lowered the bottle and wiped his mouth on the back of his hand.

Inside, the refrigerator whirred. Outside, wind rustled through aspen leaves. A mosquito landed on Meg's arm, and she brushed it away.

"Tell me something, Meg. Why would a woman consider marrying a man who treated her like muck on his boot soles?" Zack demanded.

Another mosquito lit on her. She smacked it. "I thought you didn't want to hear about Edward."

"Did I say anything about him?" He tilted his bottle again, draining a good half of it.

Meg was weary of circling the subject. She wanted Zack to understand at least part of the truth. "He stood by me through some difficult times, Zack. He said he loved me." She sighed. "I was pathetically easy to convince."

"How long were you . . . with him?"

"Sharing an apartment? A couple of months. I thought I knew him, but I guess I never really did."

He frowned. "The point is, you need to get shed

of him now. There has to be a way out of this obligation you have to him."

She couldn't resist playing devil's advocate. "Maybe I don't want out. Working on the sequel with a great team is a reasonable opportunity, even with PenUltimate reaping the monetary benefits. And Edward has his good points, believe it or not. Women love his looks. He's rich and getting richer."

"At your expense, Meg. Hell, you *can't* still think you're in love with him."

"No. Of course not." Meg watched Zack's growing frustration with a great deal of interest. "Why can't I?"

"Because he doesn't love you. Because he tries to control you. There's no need for you to give in. The hell with the sequel. I'm dead certain you could land a job with another company any time you want. After all, *he* thinks you're pretty good at what you do. He even offered to marry you to keep the talent in the family."

Meg gulped beer, nearly choking on it. The banter wasn't fun anymore. It still hurt, knowing how Edward had used her. And knowing Zack knew. "Am I that physically repulsive? Couldn't he have had other reasons for wanting me?"

Zack reached out to brush a wayward strand of hair from her cheek. "He doesn't appreciate you, Meg. You have a lot to offer any man."

Her ego grasped at Zack's words. "Like what?"

He stared into the darkness beyond her. Seconds ticked by. He didn't say one darn thing, good or bad. Meg's shoulders slumped in defeat. That's what she got for fishing.

He balanced his beer bottle on the porch rail, taking his time about it. Then he looked right into her eyes. "Like making him smile. Making him feel." His voice was deep and low and husky. He leaned toward her.

Abruptly, he straightened as if he'd caught himself on the brink of a precipice. As if he'd said something he hadn't intended. "Do yourself a favor, Meg. Stay far away from that sonuvabitch. See an attorney if you have to. Send out résumés. Find something better. Someone better."

Meg swigged more beer and licked the foam from her lips. She'd already found someone infinitely better. Zack Burkhart. Unfortunately, *he* didn't want *her*. And what would he say if he knew she was an ex-con? Probably that Edward the Rotten was too good for her.

She hadn't told Zack about her two additional weeks of "vacation." She'd saved it for a surprise, certain Zack would welcome the news as she had. Now, she wondered whether her heart could take the stress of being around him day in and day out, when she knew parole limitations would catch up with her eventually. "I'll consider a change," she hedged. "However, PenUltimate's one of the top—"

Zack cursed. She jumped, spilling beer everywhere.

"Sorry if I got a little too vehement. But, damn it, you shouldn't go back there."

She wiped condensation from the smooth surface of her beer bottle onto her shirt. "Edward does know how to sell a product, even if what he knows about love wouldn't fill a Barbie-doll thimble. As I told you before, I won't be going back to *him*. I see Edward objectively now, and I—"

Zack rested a hand on the floor behind her hips. His arm grazed her shoulder. Heat emanated from his skin. "You shouldn't see him at all."

At the moment, Meg saw only Zack. The dark swirls on his bare chest enthralled her. She visually trailed a line of hair down the middle of his taut abdomen, down below his navel where it disappeared into his jeans. As her sexual awareness soared to a new level, she forced her gaze back up.

Swallowing hard, she focused on his chin. "I won't see Edward. Not for a while. I'll keep him satisfied by informing him, in writing, that I'm hard at work on a storyline."

"Are you?"

"More or less. Just being here makes me feel creative. This place is an inspiration for fantasy." Her skin grew hot as she realized the biggest inspiration, and the best fantasy, was the man beside her.

Fortunately, Zack didn't seem to notice her blush.

"The land is good for battered souls like us, Meg. I would have gone crazy after I lost Sky, if it weren't for Robby and this piece of earth." He smoothed her hair with the palm of his hand. "I'm glad if we've passed that on to you."

Meg sensed there was something more he wanted to say, probably something she'd rather not hear. After all, he hadn't suggested she stay on the ranch permanently. He'd encouraged her to go somewhere else and begin again. She took a swig of beer. Maybe he'd really brought up her future employment as a hint that her welcome was wearing thin.

She cleared her throat. "There are other places I can go, Zack. If I'm a burden, now or later, just tell me. I'll start packing." Everything she owned fit in one blue backpack, but she wasn't going to point that out.

His jaw tensed. "You're not a burden. It's not that."

"What is it then?"

"I wish I knew," he said softly.

"Keep thinking." Meg was afraid she'd say or do something stupid unless she removed herself from temptation. So she set her bottle on the wood planks, unfolded her legs, and began to rise. "I'll get you another beer."

"No." He took her hand to draw her down beside him. She landed much closer than before.

"I don't want you to go," he said in a voice both soft and rough. He touched her shoulders, easing her back so she lay full length on the porch.

Her insides fluttered. If he wanted her, there was no way she could resist him. No possible way. Zack Burkhart was undeniably virile. Indisputably male. Extraordinarily attractive. And she was woman enough to appreciate all those things.

He pinned her with his body, using just enough weight to hold her. Not that she wanted to move. She responded to his scent, his breath, his warmth. He traced her lips with one finger, taking his time, as if hesitant to do more than that.

His muscles were as tense as hers. She could feel his need. He was vibrating with it. But even when his mouth drew within a millimeter of hers, she thought he'd change his mind. She held her breath, preparing herself for the disappointment. But this time he did not withdraw.

When he kissed her, the malt taste of beer was on his lips and tongue. She put her arms around his neck, pulling him closer, reveling in his seamless blend of raw physical power and exquisite gentleness.

She melted like heated candle wax, giving to him, molding beneath him. His kiss gradually changed from tender to fierce. As he eased a thigh between her legs, she felt a hard masculine ridge press against her belly through the cotton of her shirt and the denim of his jeans, unmistakable proof that his desire was as intense as her own.

"Don't stop," she whispered when his kisses

drifted from her lips to her throat. "Please don't stop."

He cupped her breast. His callused thumb circled a nipple through the thin T-shirt. He seemed to want her, but she had no idea why. She was rumpled, reckless Meg who talked too much and loved too hard. Maybe it was all a mistake. If so, he'd have to figure it out for himself, because he wouldn't hear it from her.

Arching her back, she gave herself to his caress. She moaned as his mouth followed his hand. His tongue wet the cloth over one taut nipple. The moisture, followed by the heat of his breath, sent ripples along her midline, straight to the juncture of her thighs. She'd had no idea her body could react with such erotic fervor.

Zack's hands spanned her waist, kneaded along her hips, and lower. He rucked the T-shirt to her waist and outlined the top of her bikini panties, the lacy ones he'd chosen for her. His light touch awakened nerve endings she'd never felt before. She quivered as he traced the crease between abdomen and thigh. Her skin was afire, primed for more. With his palm on her womanly mound, his fingers splayed downward. He stroked. She whimpered.

His heart pounded against hers; his hot breath sighed on her skin. The scent of musk and male imprinted on her brain. His taste and texture intoxicated her. Instinctively, she trusted him with body and soul. And because she allowed him to set the pace, it took her a moment to realize his magical caresses had ceased altogether.

Her pulse thudded in her temples as she tried to guess her mistake. Had she made too much noise or responded the wrong way? But how could that be when everything had felt so right?

He rolled onto his back beside her, his chest rising

and falling, a forearm flung over his eyes. "Sorry," he murmured. "Things went beyond . . ."

She took a deep breath, hoping to disguise her disappointment. "It's okay. I—I wasn't exactly resisting." *I want you, Zack. Can't you tell how much I want you?*

Rising on an elbow, he brushed the hair from her damp forehead and placed his hand there as if testing for a fever. She *did* suffer from a passion fever of epidemic proportion. The night breeze cooled her skin. Inside, though, she was still on fire.

"I know how you feel." His voice was hoarse and strained. "Believe me, I know you want someone, anyone, to fill the emptiness. But you'll regret it if we do this. You need to get over . . . Edward."

"I'm already . . ." She faltered and lost her nerve. Zack didn't know a thing about how she felt. He related his own loss to hers, when the comparison was not at all valid.

Planks creaked under Zack's weight as he rose to leave her. The screen door opened and banged shut. Footsteps padded through the kitchen and down the hall. Meg stared at the shadowy porch ceiling for a long time.

When all was quiet, she collected the bottles. Hers had overturned and spilled. His was balanced on the rail. She drank from it. The beer seemed flat and sour. On Zack's lips, it had been infinitely sweet, a flavor she would never forget.

All the mellow beauty had faded from the darkness. The night was hostile now, the sounds alarming. And her mosquito bites were starting to itch.

She went inside, more alone than she'd ever been. She wanted Zack's approval, his . . . love. The admission shocked her. Perhaps that's what her scheme to help him was all about. She wanted to show him she was worthy of love. That she could be as loving and lovable as Sky. But he'd never see Meg that way, no matter how hard she tried. She knew better than to fall for Zack. Unfortunately, she'd done a darn poor job of guarding her heart.

After discarding the beer bottles, she returned to her computer screen. A cursor blinked, on and off, in a stark background as blue as the Idaho sky.

Meg's fingers flew over the keyboard as she transcribed page after page from Sky's neat script. It was after supper, eight days after the midnight beer. Robby was lying on his stomach near her chair, drawing on an artist's pad propped on a slumbering Hoover's side. Win had gone somewhere with Tobias.

Zack had left that morning in his good white shirt and grizzly tie and had not yet returned. Meg hoped he'd found a sympathetic banker. But even if the bank didn't come through, she thought that soon she might be able to tell him his financial troubles had a cure.

With his ingenuity and hard work, he deserved to succeed. For the last few evenings, with Robby's "help," he'd been working on a design for a better llama pack saddle. He loved coming up with new ideas, just as she loved creating her game fantasies.

The Red Hawk project would please him, she assured herself. He'd be reasonable about separating his memories of Sky from his useful creations. Meg had already received requests for samples, and Win—though still unfriendly and cold to the point of frostbite—had assisted with the mailing.

They would have positive responses, Meg was sure of it. Meanwhile, she had the typing to keep her busy. And Robby's constant activities. And her own game design, which was coming along well. Life was good.

Though communication had been awkward between her and Zack the morning after their kiss on the porch, he'd gradually begun talking more. Smiling more. Even laughing once in a while.

Meg loved the ranch, the house, the barn, the animals. She loved being part of a real family who loved each other. She wished . . . No point in thinking about what she wished, since fairy godmothers were in short supply.

But Meg kept recalling G. T.'s advice on men. *Spend a few nights in a tent with him, Meggie. If you're still on speaking terms, he's the right one for you.* Those words of wisdom and a promise to follow them had sent Meg to Yellowstone with her intended. Edward had been winnowed out, and Meg had shared a tent with Zack instead.

G. T. couldn't have known that would happen. Though she'd been almost like a fairy godmother to Meg, she couldn't act from beyond the pale. Or could she?

Meg scoffed at that far-out theory as she continued typing, immersing herself in someone else's life. The journals no longer made Meg sad. She'd learned to admire Sky's sense of mission, her passionate defense of the environment. Her favorite creature had been the eagle, though she had devoted most of her notebooks to observations of Zack's grizzlies. Quite often, a sense of humor laced her tales.

Rereading a section, Meg laughed aloud.

"What's funny, Meg?" Robby looked up from his near-finished drawing of a big and little llama.

"It's something your mother wrote," Meg explained.

Robby rose to peer into the pages of the notebook filled with small, precise handwriting. "I can't read yet," he said solemnly. "Tell me what she says."

With heartbreaking eagerness, he looked from the page to Meg.

She drew the boy into the circle of her arms with the notebook in front of them. She had been pleased to note that Win had spent several hours with Robby and a photo album the day after their talk in the garage. But the boy had an insatiable need to learn about his mother, just like Meg had needed to know about her father after his death. G. T. had filled the gap for Meg. She'd explained the work Meg's father had done as an architect. She'd taken her to a house he'd designed, shown her blueprints he'd drawn, and photos. After Meg knew something of the man, she came to terms with the loss.

Robby deserved the same chance.

Meg wasn't sure how much he knew, so she began at the beginning, trusting her instincts to tell her where to go from there. "A few years before you were born, your father and mother fell in love. They met when they were rangers in Yellowstone."

"Like Ranger Andrew?" he piped.

She smiled. "Yes, just like Andrew. But your daddy was interested in grizzly bears. That was his special work."

"I know," he said proudly. "Daddy told me about how he used a tranquilizer gun so he could put collars on bears and track them with satellites that fly way up high." He lisped the S's, but otherwise his pronunciation was flawless. Obviously, Zack's stories about bears had intrigued the child.

"You know more about that than I do. But maybe you didn't know that your mama sometimes went along when he tracked the bears." Meg paged through the notebook and pointed to a picture in the margin. "This is Betsy, a mother grizzly. She looks almost like the bear on your T-shirt, doesn't she?"

Robby looked down at his shirt. Sure enough, he

was wearing Betsy. He squinted at the notebook. "Tell me the words."

Meg brushed her fingers over the open page. She already knew what was written there. "One spring, your mother and dad went looking for Betsy. All good bears had awakened from hibernation by then and—"

Robby shook his head in a vigorous denial. "Daddy says bears don't really hibernate. Sometimes they wake up and walk around in the snow."

She held up a hand. "No doubt your daddy is right. I'm no expert on bears."

"I want the part about Mama." He lifted the notebook, as if she'd get to the interesting lines faster if the page were closer.

Meg laughed. "Wait a minute, Robby. I'll go cross-eyed if you hold it to my nose."

The screen door slammed. She looked around the notebook to see Zack entering the living room from the kitchen. He still wore a white dress shirt and a loosened tie. Since he didn't look happy, she guessed the trip to the bank hadn't been successful. His gaze met hers, then lowered to Robby and the notebook, and finally locked on Meg again. His jaw muscles clenched. A forbidding scowl shadowed his face more thoroughly than the day's growth of beard.

Meg was not intimidated as she might have been a week before. She knew him better now, and that made it even harder to do what she had to do. "Robby wants to know—he's aching to know about his mother. I was telling him what Sky wrote about Betsy." She hesitated before holding out the notebook to Zack. "You can tell it best. Why don't you?"

Zack stood stock-still in the doorway and stared at her. His legs felt weak all of a sudden. His lungs were paralyzed, as if he'd taken a blow to the solar plexus. Robby sat on Meg's lap the same way he'd cuddled with his mother a year ago, the way he should have been with Sky even now. Emotion crowded Zack's throat, prickled behind his eyes. He rebelled against the memories and yet they surrounded him, pushed in on him with every breath. Meg forced him to face the past. And maybe she was right.

Although Robby's eyes pleaded, it was Meg who pulled Zack forward. Her steady green gaze lured him like a buoy drew a drowning man. He fought a strong tide of his own resistance, but at last he reached her. She nodded encouragement. He accepted the notebook from her hand.

"Go ahead, Robby," Meg urged. "Sit on the couch with your father."

Zack felt trapped. But when Robby took his hand and led him to the cushions, the pounding in his temples slowed as if he'd absorbed a slug from a tranquilizer gun. He collapsed on the couch, lifted the child onto his lap, and set the notebook aside.

"I don't have to read from those pages, son," he said when Robby sent him a worried glance. "I remember every moment I spent with your mother."

He closed his eyes, seeing Sky's long, black silk hair, her dark eyes sparkling with passion and pleasure. His chest tightened with a deep aching sorrow.

He began to talk, describing the day he and Sky had first met. They were assigned to clear a trail together. He'd resented a female partner. She'd had a Native American chip on her shoulder and was an affirmed feminist to boot.

The first morning they'd barely spoken. The second day they'd learned to tolerate each other while they argued the relative virtues of eagles versus grizzlies. By the third night, they were lovers. Of course he didn't tell Robby that. He said they became good friends.

After a while, talking about her grew easier. The words flowed out of him like a mountain stream from a melting glacier.

"I'd tagged Betsy in the fall, and I wanted to see how she'd fared. I asked your mother to hike out to the bear's territory with me. Once in range, transmitter readings would give us a pretty good idea of where she was. We expected she'd have cubs, so we had to be careful. Mama grizzlies sometimes attack foolish humans who get too close."

"Why?" Robby, wide-eyed, wanted all the details.

"To protect their little ones from danger," Zack said.

The boy frowned. "Why do they think people are dangerous?"

"Because we smell bad to them, I guess."

Robby wrinkled his nose. "Gramma Win says I smell bad when I forget my bath. Nobody told me to take a bath last night," he confided, "and I skipped it."

"That's okay, partner. Just stay away from the bears." He tousled Robby's hair. It occurred to Zack that he hadn't talked so freely with his son in a long time. "To get back to the story, Mama and I had taken our baths like good campers. Betsy wasn't supposed to smell us." Bears were sometimes attracted to soap scent, but he kept that fact to himself. No need to give his son ammunition against basic hygiene.

"The transmitter reading from Betsy's collar said she was a mile away, traveling at a brisk pace in the opposite direction from our campground. What Mama and I didn't know was that the collar wasn't on the bear anymore. It was floating down Hellroaring Creek."

"How did it get there?" Robby asked, snuggling into the crook of Zack's arm.

Zack drew the boy closer to his chest. How could he have forgotten how good it was just to hold Robby? "Betsy must have gone fishing, gotten wet, and one of her cubs wrestled the collar off of her," he explained. "She had two babies that spring, as it turned out. She strolled right into our camp one evening. We thought we were following her, but it turned out she'd been trailing us instead. Your mother and I ended up sitting in a prickly spruce tree while Betsy circled beneath us. Her cubs clawed at the base of our tree. They must have thought it smelled interesting."

"Can baby bears climb?"

"They sure can. First one of them would start up the tree, then the other would knock him down and make a run. They were playing, but sooner or later we figured they'd skitter up the trunk. If Betsy decided to follow them, we'd be in bad trouble."

Robby's eyes rounded. "What did you do?"

"We had our packs in the tree with us, so we searched the supplies for something to scare them off. I found pepper to shake on the cubs. They rubbed their eyes and noses with their paws and bumbled away with their mother following them. That's how I got the idea for Nemesis bear repellent."

"It's made of pepper?"

"A special blend of pepper and other things bears don't like."

"What else don't they like?"

Zack had forgotten Robby was such an inquisitive little guy. He'd forgotten too many things. "Your turn. Tell me something bears *like*."

"They like sweets," the boy replied promptly.

"And so do you, right?" Zack searched his own shirt front. "I know I've got a pack of Lifesavers on me somewhere. Want to help me look?"

With a wide grin that deepened the dimples in his

cheeks, Robby frisked Zack. The boy knew as well as Zack did that the candy was in Daddy's shirt pocket, but he looked everywhere else first to make the game more fun.

They ended up in a mutual tickling match. Robby collapsed in giggles. They hadn't played this "search and tickle" game since . . . Zack's melancholy returned. He doubled his arms around his son, holding him tight.

As if sensing a change of mood, Robby patted Zack's shoulder with one small hand. The boy was trying to console his father, but comforting should be Zack's job. He had neglected Robby for too long. His devastation after Sky's death had left little room for the child. It was past time he opened his heart and let Robby inside.

Zack heard retreating footsteps in the hall and realized Meg had gone to her room, giving them privacy to re-discover their roles as father and son, to remember Sky and her legacy to them.

With Robby snuggled in his arms, Zack related one story after another, striving to recall the little details that would make Sky real. "Your mother was good at most anything she tried. Skiing, riding, swimming. She ran track in high school. She even won a roping contest in 4-H."

"I wanna learn to rope somethin'," Robby mumbled sleepily.

"We'll do it, partner. I'm not as good as your mother was, but I can teach you a thing or two about swinging a lasso."

"Tell me more about Mama," the child murmured.

Zack knew plenty more to tell. "She was the worst creek crosser I ever saw. She'd try to tiptoe over on a log, or jump from rock to rock, but she got wet more times than a salamander. Sometimes when we'd cross a creek, she'd grab for my arm and pull me in, too."

He suddenly had an image of her, soaking wet, hands planted on hips, glaring at him and cursing like a truck driver headed for hell. She'd blamed *him* for the dunking. Equally cold and wet, he'd been pretty angry himself. But thinking about it now made him smile.

She'd been stubborn, irascible, and downright bad-tempered at times. She was not always easy to love. Yet it was her stubbornness, her unflinching loyalty and courage, that Zack had admired most.

"She looked like you, Robby, and she loved all animals, same as you do. She loved to see an eagle spread its wings and soar over the earth. 'That's what we're meant to do,' she'd say. 'To soar.' "

Zack kept on talking, unfolding a collage of Sky memories until sleep's steady rhythm claimed his son. For long past then, he sat there, thinking of all the moments he could never put into words. The joy and sorrow and sharing. Lamplight played softly over Robby's high cheekbones and smooth skin, so much like Sky's.

"She watches over us, I know she does," Zack whispered to the boy they'd both loved.

But life was not static. Her voice and image were fading, like an eagle flying ever higher. Like one season turning to the next. A tear slipped down Zack's cheek. The drop fell onto his son's dark hair and reflected there like a crystal of melting snow.

The long, painful winter was drawing to a close.

Chapter Thirteen

Zack carried Robby to bed, covered him with the red and green Ninja Turtle quilt, and kissed him good night. In the long months of mourning, he'd been unable to think of the child as an individual separate from Sky. But now he understood how much Robby needed him. Meg had made him see. Which brought back another of his concerns.

What would Robby do if—*when* she returned to Edward and her game team at PenUltimate? Would the boy regress? No doubt he would miss Meg. Hell, Zack would miss her too. The sound of her chatter, her laughter. The way she looked in the morning, in the evening. The scent of her hair, the taste of . . .

What the hell was he thinking? Ever since he'd kissed Meg on the porch, he'd known he had to be cautious. He'd managed to keep his hands off her, but abstinence hadn't been much of a solution. He wanted her more with every waking moment. Every sleeping moment, too. For the last week, he'd dreamed of her instead of Sky, which bothered him most of all. Sky was still part of him, part of everything he was and would become. He didn't want to give her up for another woman. Not for Meg, not for anyone.

Meg would leave. He promised himself that he and Robby would do just fine once she was gone.

Retreating to his office, Zack sat at his desk. The

open window let in a cool breeze that ruffled Zack's hair and brought the scent of grass and pine. He flipped through a newly arrived copy of *Llamas* magazine, but most of his concentration focused on sounds of Meg preparing for bed. Familiar sounds.

In the shower, she hummed a melody he didn't recognize. Another love song. She possessed a deep yearning for love, a huge capacity to give of herself. Zack was certain she'd never been appreciated as she deserved.

Her footsteps crossed the hall. Drawers opened and shut in her room. Zack blew out a rush of breath. Would she really go back to Edward? There was more than a sequel, more than an employee contract pulling on her. He kept hoping . . . as long as she hadn't set a date for departure, she might change her mind.

He buried his fingers in his hair. As usual, thinking about Meg led to the wrong end of a box canyon and gave him a pulsing headache. He leaned forward on his desk, burying his elbows in bills. Looking down at the scattered mail, he decided he couldn't put off writing checks for the worst of the past-due notices any longer. Reluctantly, he set to work.

When the phone rang five minutes later, he snatched up the receiver in relief. Even talking to a wrong number would be preferable to juggling negative numbers.

Andrew Houssard's boisterous greeting was a welcome sound.

"How's the chicken pox?" Zack asked his friend.

"The kids are okay, but now Callie's smeared with calamine lotion. She cries like a baby whenever she looks in the mirror. Hormones, I guess. Meg still there?"

"She's here. Do you and Callie want to take her off my hands?"

"No thanks. One pretty lady's enough for me. It's you I'm worried about. At least you had the sense to take Meg home. Now what you ought to do is keep her there. You need a woman's touch, boy. And I'm not talking kinky sex here. Not necessarily. But if you're into that sort of—"

"You're talking yourself into a corner, Houssard. The chicken pox must have gone to your brain."

Andrew chuckled. "My brain's no worse off than usual. I called because I have news."

"Good or bad?" Zack asked.

"That's for you to decide. I took samples of the bear-chewed llama remains, like you asked, and sent them for analysis. Al, our lab tech, says he's found something weird."

Zack's headache took a turn for the worse. "Weird? What does that mean?"

"He's doing more tests. I asked for preliminaries, but Al's lips are like a sealed tomb until he files a written report."

Zack began to think he'd have preferred a wrong number to Andrew and his news. They exchanged a few pleasantries. Zack wished Callie well. After hanging up, he propped booted feet on the desk and leaned back in the squeaky chair to consider possibilities. If Elsa's death had a cause—besides the bear attack—the other "accidents" were probably not accidents either.

He glanced at the desk drawer that now contained four letters in bold black print. He'd received one after each llama death and one after Checkers' near-fatal mishap. At first he'd thought they might have come from someone who learned about the animals' casualties through local gossip and had written the notes to embellish Fate and further punish Zack. But now . . .

He would show the notes to Abe Larkin and see

if modern police techniques could find a way to trace them. Zack could handle menacing mail, but if the author was also killing off animals, that was something else again.

Assuming someone was behind the llama disasters, Zack had to consider Jesse Caldwell. The rancher was definitely mean enough, and he hated Zack. But would he go to the trouble to pen religious-sounding notes, or to make the events appear accidental?

Maybe this had nothing to do with Jesse and their long-standing animosity. Maybe it was linked to the Dutch Mountain silver mine. Zack and Sky had started a campaign against the mine's pollution, which had prompted some scathing commentary from the wealthy owners. The mine had finally closed a few months back, and those owners might be seeking revenge. They wouldn't risk going after Zack themselves, but they could have hired someone to do the dirty work.

Like Harry? Zack shook his head. Harry was a bumbler, not a killer, though he *was* always short of money. He had been negligent about taking care of Elsa, at the very least. However, Zack was pretty sure Harry had been guiding a fishing trip in Montana the week Gingko died. It seemed logical that the same person would be responsible for all the losses.

What about Tobias? He'd been new on the ranch when Thessa hung herself. He could have set that up. He also could have sent Elsa on the Yellowstone trip with drugged or poisoned grain, leaving her susceptible to grizzly attack. Likewise, he might have drugged Checkers and wrapped him in barbed wire. He was right there on the road beside Gingko.

Tobias had had opportunity, but he had no motive that Zack knew about. Except money. Tobias, too, might have been bribed.

Zack scraped the heels of his boots on the desk as

he lowered his feet amid a flurry of loose paper. He sat upright and looked out the window into the darkness. A chill crept down his spine.

The evening breeze no longer soothed. It soughed through the branches of shadowed trees with ominous foreboding. The perpetrator—if there was one—had to be someone nearby, someone who had access to the ranch. Someone who hated Zack and transferred that hate to innocent animals—or who acted as a surrogate, for a fee.

Someone who *would* strike again.

Zack stood at the far end of the west pasture and stared at strands of snipped wire in his hands. He'd been expecting something to happen for the last week, ever since Andrew's disturbing phone call.

This was the third opening he'd found along the south fence dividing his property from Forest Service land. If the young llamas in the adjoining pasture had wandered, he'd have a hell of a time finding them—which he supposed was the very reason that particular fence had been chosen. In case any animals remained inside, he temporarily patched the wire. He'd already sent Tobias to count livestock and determine how many were missing.

Zack still had suspicions about the hired man. So far that was *all* he had. He'd considered firing Tobias, but without reasonable cause it wouldn't be fair. Besides, if Tobias were involved, Zack would be better off having the man where he could keep an eye on him.

Right now, he planned to dump the matter in the sheriff's lap and make damn sure Abe Larkin took him seriously. He hopped into his truck, coaxed it to a start, and clattered down the road. Abe hadn't paid much attention to the notes Zack had shown him several days before, but this would be a lot harder to ignore. Now, he had more than innuendoes and speculations. *This* was no accident. Only a human carried wire cutters in a hip pocket. And only an enemy would have used them to make neat, surgical cuts in someone else's fence.

He braked outside his house. Leaving the engine running, he rushed to the back door, nearly colliding with Meg as he barged into the kitchen. She dropped a cluster of blue lupine she'd been arranging. Zack caught the flowers and shoved them stem-first into the cracked pink vase she clasped against her breast.

"Where's Robby?" he demanded.

"In the garage." She set the bouquet on the table. "Win swore she'd watch him carefully, but if you want me to—"

"Never mind." Zack had already spoken to Win about the need to keep Robby in sight, since there might be an enemy prowling around the place. The boy would be all right with his grandmother. He scribbled a quick note and attached the scrap of paper to the refrigerator with a bear claw magnet. "I'm going to town. Don't know when I'll be back," he told Meg.

"Zack . . ."

He walked outside and down the steps, knowing what she would say if he stopped long enough to listen. She'd ask to go with him. He didn't need anything else to fight against right now, and Meg always managed to throw a seductive come-on in his face.

Ever persistent, she followed him outside. "Zack, wait. I want to . . ."

He climbed in the truck and slammed it into first, hoping for a quick getaway. Unfortunately, the worn clutch was slow to engage. Gears grated. The engine coughed and died. Cursing, he began his starting ritual. Pump the accelerator. Fiddle with the key. Adjust the choke. Meanwhile, Meg jerked at the jammed door on the passenger side. As if fate were in her favor, it miraculously opened. Before the finicky eight cylinders sputtered to life, she was beside him, settling her trim rear over the spring he'd finally gotten around to patching with foam and duct tape.

"Damn it, Meg, what do you think you're doing?" he said over the engine's roar. He didn't want her with him, asking questions he couldn't answer. He didn't want the distraction. She was a temptation. A goddamn nuisance. Every time he looked at her, he thought of how she'd taste, how she'd feel beneath him.

"I need a few things," she said. "Woman things. You don't mind company, do you?"

"How many 'woman things' can a lone female require?" he snapped. "You went shopping with Win at least twice last week. You borrowed my truck for a trip to town this past Saturday. I'll bet the 'woman thing' section of Chet's store is running on empty."

"Don't exaggerate. You gave me a paycheck this morning. I thought I'd stock up on underwear. Chet was out of my size, but he expects a shipment any day."

"If I'd known you were going to waste the money, I wouldn't have strained my budget."

"You're the one who insisted on paying me," she said. "Since you did, it's not fair to criticize what I buy."

"Great. I'll pick up a sackful of underwear for you. Now get out of the truck. I have to talk to Sheriff Larkin, and I'd just as soon you weren't trailing behind me."

"The sheriff?" Her voice was sharp, alarmed.

"Somebody took a wire cutter to one of my fences," he explained. "It's Abe Larkin's job to figure out who did it."

She stared at him a moment, taking in the significance of undisguised sabotage. "I don't mind waiting while you talk to him." She strapped on a seatbelt.

He shook his head in disgust. "If I'd known you had mule genes, I'd have left you in Yellowstone."

"I want to check my post office box." She faced straight ahead as if they were already underway.

He eased off the clutch, gassing the engine to keep it from dying. The truck spurted ahead.

The post office box was a sore spot between him and Meg. She claimed to have opened it for a résumé address, but Zack didn't believe her. As far as he knew, she hadn't sent out any résumés. He figured Edward was the real reason for a private letter box. She must expect to hear from him. Maybe she'd heard already.

What did she think? That Zack would stoop to steaming open envelopes? And what did she have to hide, anyway? If the correspondence was about work, surely she wouldn't have a need for secrecy. He concluded that she still hoped for a love letter.

If it was up to him, he'd destroy all correspondence from dear old Edward Penrose. Hell, maybe the post office box was for the best. Maybe Meg needed to hear from the guy so she could see what an asshole he was.

"Andrew called this morning," Meg said. She was cheerful, as always, but louder than usual to overcome the noisy engine. "You didn't give me a chance to tell you before we left. He wants you to call him back."

Zack frowned at the road ahead, swerving to avoid a fallen tree left over from a storm two nights earlier. "Did he say anything about lab results?"

"No. Only that he has information you'll be interested in. He's invited us to his house for dinner on Saturday. Everyone's over the chicken pox, and Callie wants to meet me." Meg seemed extremely pleased to be included. "Do you mind if I go along with you and Robby?"

The uncertainty in her voice broke down all of Zack's defenses. He buckled like a sheet of aluminum under the weight of solid steel. "I'd be honored. Robby would probably refuse to go without you anyway."

She grinned, then quickly looked out the window, as if afraid to flaunt her victory. As Zack allowed himself to think about it, he looked forward to introducing her to Callie. The two women would enjoy each other's company.

He turned his attention back to the road and the unpleasant fact that his ranch was in big trouble, especially if Andrew's news was what he expected.

"I'll call Andrew tonight," he said, thinking aloud.

"Good idea." Meg bubbled with enthusiasm. "Would you ask if I should bring something Saturday? Potato salad, maybe? While I'm in Chet's store, I could pick up some groceries. Tobias asked me to buy him a pair of leather gloves. Win wants brake fluid. Do you need anything?"

"I'll do my own shopping, thanks." He didn't want Meg becoming any more necessary to him than she already was.

"Just asking." She sounded disappointed.

"Have you heard from Edward?" Zack didn't look at her.

"Yes," she admitted. "I received a letter just the other day. He's delighted, of course, that I'm working on the sequel. He even promised an increase in royalties on this one, a sort of unscheduled bonus. He's promised a huge salary raise, if and when I rejoin the team. And he apologized, if you can believe it. *I* still can't." She laughed. "He says he thinks of me every time he feeds Princess the cat. And he claims she's getting fat. I wonder, is he transferring affection

from me to the cat, or is it the other way around?"
She had to shout the last sentence over the noise
of gravel slapping the truck's underbelly. Without
waiting for an answer, she went on chattering like a
magpie on steroids.

She only talked that fast when she was worried,
or fired up about something. Edward's letter. Even
from a distance of several hundred miles, Edward
had her all hot and bothered.

None of his business, Zack reminded himself. She
was leaving the ranch, and that was that. He had no
right to advise her, no reason to expect her to listen.

When Zack realized she'd stopped talking, he
glanced her way. Air currents from the open window
whipped her short gold hair into a whirling sunburst.

Her gaze was fixed on her lap, where she held her
hands tightly clasped. "He's made a generous offer,
Zack. I'll have to consider—"

He couldn't hold back a protest. "Don't let him
sweep you off your feet. The Beamer jock's out to
use you for whatever profit you'll bring."

When she sent him a glance full of pain, Zack
wished he'd kept silent.

"Even if it's for all the wrong reasons, at least he
claims to want me," she said slowly. "That's
something."

Zack wanted her, too, though he couldn't say so.
He dreamed erotic dreams of Meg every night, but
he wasn't in love with her any more than Edward
was. She flitted like a hummingbird, never still. How
could he love a woman so different from his coura-
geous, rock-solid, self-sufficient Sky?

No, he didn't love Meg. Yet thinking of her resum-
ing her old life, with her old boyfriend, made him
mad enough to pick a fight with a grizzly and make
the fur fly. He ought to ask when she was leaving,
but he didn't want to hear the answer. He stomped

on the gas and took a turn at a speed that would give a stock car driver nightmares.

Zack knew he was driving like an escapee from the loony bin. The way the truck jounced over ruts, he'd probably end up with a hole in an oil pan, or with a trashed transmission. Zack was too frustrated to care. He was mad as hell. At Edward, at Meg, at the whole human race.

Especially at whichever segment was responsible for cutting his fence. His stock was probably spread all over the mountain by now. Even under the best of circumstances, rounding up a herd of loose llamas without mishap required plenty of luck.

Luck? What a joke. If Fate looked his way, it was only to spit. Fortune was a fickle bitch, and Zack never relied on Her. He'd kickstart the sheriff's backside into action, then start mending fence.

Without slowing the truck, he rattled across the shaky one-lane wooden bridge. He heard a strangled sound beside him.

"Would you mind driving a little slower?" Meg asked. "Otherwise I'd better get out. I think I might lose my breakfast." From the way she was holding her stomach and looking green, that seemed a likely scenario.

Zack always crossed the bridge in a hurry, without glancing to either side. He hated thinking about the traitorous river underneath that had taken his Sky away from him.

As soon as they were back on solid dirt road, he eased up on the accelerator. "You can relax, Meg. I'll drive the rest of the way like an old lady schoolteacher."

"The one from Pasadena?" she quipped. "Seriously, I ought to be grateful for the stress test. You should offer certificates. 'Survived ride to town. Heart chambers fully functional.' "

Zack stifled the urge to laugh. "That'll teach you not to get in my truck uninvited."

"You were just as reckless when we drove from Yellowstone," she reminded him. "I was invited that time."

"You've got me there." Bringing her home had been especially reckless, but he'd grown used to her. He refused to think about the time when she'd be gone.

She looked good in his truck, like a class act on a cheap set. She'd been more than a decoration around the ranch. On the practical side, she'd computerized his bookkeeping records, making his haphazard finances almost manageable. She kept fresh flowers on the kitchen table in a useless attempt to civilize the household. She'd planted daisies by the front porch and coaxed a half-dead rose bush into bloom. She cleaned, cooked damn good meals. And there had been other, more significant changes.

"You've been great for Robby, Meg. Every evening when I come in, I find him happy. He can't wait to show off his computer art. Then he drags me around to see his menagerie while he recounts the day's adventures. Sometimes I wonder if he's the same kid who climbed into the rafters a few weeks ago. He talks all the time now, to anyone who'll listen."

Meg's eyes glowed, and her smile followed. "I guess I'm contagious."

He smiled back. "You sure as hell are." Even Zack was talking more and seeking solitude less. It was hard to be morose around Meg. She was like spring sun, enticing him to bask in her warmth. He concentrated on the long windy road instead of her generous mouth, full lips, and shining eyes. If he didn't watch out, he'd get heatstroke.

*   *   *

As soon as she exited the truck, Meg rushed to the post office, eager to check her mail. High on Zack's parting smile, she skipped up the steps and through the screen door.

Flies buzzed around the tiny room.

"You're too soon." Portly Earl Jamison, the postmaster, stood behind a waist-high counter observing her over tinted glasses perched on a red-veined nose. "We don't get the day's delivery until after lunch, like I told you last time."

"That's okay," Meg said. "I'll just pick up whatever you have for me."

With a snort that could only be interpreted as disgust, he abandoned the mail he'd been sorting and went behind a petition to retrieve the contents of her box.

She had a key, but she'd yet to use it. Mr. Jamison took pride in attending to customers personally. He returned with a batch of letters. As he handed her the stack, she smiled and thanked him.

His mouth pinched in disapproval. "Sky never needed a private box. The plain old delivery service was good enough for her." Mr. Jamison knew Meg was living at Zack's ranch. Everyone in town seemed to know, and they were quick to gossip. Meg had heard them in the store, on the streets, speculating about her relationship with Zack. She didn't care what they said or thought or imagined. If it were entirely up to her, she'd give them a whole lot more to gossip about.

She retreated through the screen door to the shaded porch and leaned back against the outer wall of the building, one foot braced against the bricks. There, she leafed through the envelopes, panning for gold. She and Win had already sent multiple product samples. Meg was expecting favorable results.

Her pulse raced as she scanned the return addresses. Her heart skipped an entire beat when Silverstein and Smelly, Attorneys at Law, flashed at her. So far, Silverstein had only used the post office box to send an extended travel permit. He'd promised to write again when he had a definite date for her parole meeting. Meg stared at the envelope, unwilling to open it.

What if she had to return to Salt Lake at once? She'd done her best to prepare Zack. She'd even broached the subject with Robby a time or two. But *she* wasn't ready. She wasn't ready to go back to the emptiness she knew awaited her. She fought off a tidal wave of panic as she ripped into the envelope and read the single sheet of paper. Her heart plummeted to below sea level. She quickly re-read the date she must meet her parole officer.

Monday. That meant she had to catch a bus no later than Sunday, only five days away. She'd known the summons would come, but as long as she had no definite date, she'd ignored it. She'd allowed herself to bond with the ranch, with the people on the ranch. Now she'd have to leave everything—and everyone—she'd come to love.

If all went well, she would have the freedom to return here someday, but the ranch would never again be home. Zack had given her temporary work and shelter out of compassion. Their proximity had sparked a bit of mutual interest, but that was as far as it went. Once she left, the dream dust would never re-form, not in the same shape or glory. She folded the single sheet of paper and put it on the bottom of the stack.

The remaining mail was addressed to Red Hawk. One response was from the biggest sports chain store in the West, requesting samples of all Zack's products. The letter represented a whole panful of figurative gold nuggets in one envelope, a major breakthrough. Another contained a check for the very first paid order. Her spirits rose a fraction of a nanometer. Red Hawk would be a success. The profits would be her way of thanking Zack for everything.

She sagged onto the steps with the mail in her lap. It was time to tell him about the project. Since she was leaving in a few days, she couldn't put it off much longer. How would she do it? Hand him the correspondence and wait for a barrage of questions?

No, she had to be more subtle. She'd create an appropriate mood first. Edward always said a client should be courted. Zack was a client . . . sort of. Did she dare try such a thing with him?

She'd talk Tobias into taking Win and Robby to the movies tonight. Then she and Zack would have a candlelight dinner. She'd tell him all about Red Hawk, giving her best sales pitch. She'd never been particularly good at selling her ideas, but she believed in this. She could make Zack believe, too. With all the trouble on the ranch lately, he needed a mood booster, and she meant to provide it.

If she were lucky, he'd appreciate her efforts. If not, she'd give him something else to appreciate. She'd buy an eye-catching outfit and a few basic cosmetics to point up her personal assets. At least she'd make sure he saw her as an intelligent, desirable woman instead of the blabbermouth greenhorn he'd first met.

She rose from the steps, brushed off the seat of her jeans, and hurried across the street. Nodding to Chet as she entered his store, she headed for the corner labeled "Woman Things."

Chapter Fourteen

Zack sat in the swivel chair opposite the sheriff's desk while Lydia circled him like a hungry red-haired wildcat. If he'd known this was Lydia's day off and she was spending the time with her father, he'd have put in a phone call instead of a personal appearance.

Sheriff Abe Larkin scratched through the messy stacks on his desk and finally came up with a form. "You'll have to fill out one of these." He handed over the slightly crumpled paper.

Zack hated bureaucracy. "Why not just drive out to the ranch with me? I could show you the damages in less time than—" He shrugged Lydia's grasping paw off his shoulder. If her father weren't in the room, she'd probably be unbuttoning his sweaty blue cotton shirt about now. Damn, the woman was aggressive.

"Three quarters of police work is paper," Abe insisted. "Goes with the territory." It was hard to see what Abe did with the paper besides stack it on his desk.

Resigned, Zack scribbled his complaint. "If you're interested in theories, I have some on who did this. There's—"

Abe didn't wait for names. "Outsiders," he declared, pouncing on his favorite bandwagon. "Too damn many Yellowstone tourists coming through,

stirring up trouble. Crime's been rising in this county
for years. Summer's always the worst. Just last night
somebody ripped a stereo out of a car parked at the
Pak-a-Sak. And shoplifting's getting so bad over at
Chet's, he's been asking if it's legal to do strip
searches at the door."

"I doubt any of that's related to my fence," Zack
said. "Why would a tourist wander clear out to my
south pasture?"

Lydia gave up groping Zack and sauntered over
to her father. She looped an arm around his neck,
playing daddy's little girl.

Abe patted her hand. "I'm thinking of your hired
man," he told Zack. "Tobias showed up on your
ranch two, three months ago, right?"

Zack nodded. "I didn't check references, but he
said he worked near Great Falls before he came
here."

"Mmm." Abe picked up a pen and doodled on a
scrap of paper. "I'll see if the sheriff's department
over there has heard of him."

Lydia pouted at Zack with sly-sweet lips. "What
about the woman you've been so cozy with the last
couple of weeks? *She's* an outsider, too."

"Hey, that's right." Abe beamed at his daughter.
"You ought to be sheriff, honey. Ever since you were
little bitty, you've had a knack for—"

"Meg has nothing to do with this," Zack said. "Did
you tell the postmaster about my anonymous
letters?"

"Sure thing. Earl promised he'd be on the lookout
for printed addresses with block lettering."

"What about Jesse?" Zack asked. "Did you question him like I asked you to?"

Abe cleared his throat. "I happened to be on his
ranch yesterday. He was out, but I had a talk with
Ellen. I mentioned the trouble you've been having.

She got all agitated. Thought I was accusing Jesse, I guess. She's . . . fragile, since her son died. I sure hate upsetting her."

Zack knew that. The sheriff was Ellen's second cousin, and they'd been close since childhood. Their early relationship had resumed after Abe's wife split the sheets and Ellen lost Mike. She was lucky to have Abe looking out for her, since Jesse showed damn little consideration. Unfortunately, the sheriff's concern for Ellen might slow down any meaningful investigation of her husband.

"Will you at least have a look at the fence?" Zack said.

Lydia swayed her melted-and-poured jean-clad hips to the front window. "Speak of the angel and the devil!" she trilled. "Ellen and Jesse just drove up."

The sheriff rushed to join Lydia at the window, making no attempt to hide his eagerness. Zack doubted Abe had any interest in seeing Jesse. It was Ellen he cared about. From all appearances, the sheriff had hopes Ellen would look on him as more than mere kin.

Within seconds, Jesse barged inside with his wife trailing behind him. As he entered, he made eye contact with Zack. Immediately, he lunged forward. Zack rose from his chair just in time to dodge a flying fist.

"You son of a bitch!" Jesse yelled. "You cut my fence, didn't you?" He circled Zack like a junkyard dog, hackles up, teeth bared.

"*Your* fence," Zack repeated, wondering what Jesse hoped to gain by the lie. "I found a break along *my* Forest Service boundary. I sure didn't touch your fence. *You're* the one—"

Jesse sneered. "Liar! You've been badmouthing me to Abe, trying to put the blame on me because your damn fool llamas keep snuffing themselves out. Since your charges haven't stuck, you settled for doing a piece of work on my barbed wire." Still in fighting stance, fists raised, he wheeled on Abe. "And *you*. You came on my land, nosing around my wife again. I ought to—"

Ellen had frozen near the door like a shy deer in headlights, but now she came to life. She rushed between her husband and the sheriff. "Abe was only doing his job."

Jesse muscled her aside with enough force to send her banging against the desk. Her mouth pinched, but she didn't cry out.

Furious with the way Jesse treated his wife, Zack seized him with an arm around the throat. Jesse wheezed, clawing at the block to his windpipe. Zack tightened his hold. He hated a bully, and that title fit Jesse to a capital B.

"Stop, Zack!" Abe boomed. "Let him go."

Zack reluctantly freed his captive, and Jesse clutched his throat, coughing. Mostly an act, Zack guessed.

Abe moved closer, face blotched with fury. He crooked a finger at Jesse. "You want to beat up on Ellen, you'll have to go through me."

Jesse stopped coughing and blanched. He was a bully, not a fool. He'd pissed off the county sheriff, and that was not smart.

Ellen sank onto the desk, her eyes like two over-bright amethysts in a chalk-white face. Abe glanced in her direction in time to see she was fading. He rushed to catch her before she collapsed like a heap amongst the muddled paperwork.

Lydia appeared from behind the desk, where she'd ducked as soon as fists were raised. She leaned forward to sniff Ellen's breath. "What's wrong with *her*? Has she been drinking again?"

Jesse sent a disgusted glance in his wife's direction. "She's popping Prozac. And diet pills. Don't ask me why. She's about to dry up and blow way as it is."

Ellen roused herself to sit straighter. "I'm not drinking," she said in a thin voice. "Not anymore."

"That's good, Ellen. You're doing real good," Abe said. He probably even believed it.

"I'm here to file a complaint for destruction of property," Jesse crowed. "You want to take a statement, sheriff? And quit fawning over my wife. She gets too much sympathy as it is."

Zack doubted she'd ever had the first sign of sympathy from her loving husband. If Ellen had cast her lot with a good man like Abe, her life—and her son's—might've had a reasonable chance.

While the sheriff went to the water cooler to fetch a cup for Ellen, Lydia rounded up suitable documents and shoved them at Jesse. Too bad Lydia didn't direct her nymphomania to the randy rancher, where it would be appreciated. Curiously, Jesse was the one man Lydia scorned.

The rancher dropped into the chair Zack had vacated. Zack shook his head, realizing he'd been outmaneuvered. Jesse's claim nullified Zack's, and also managed to deflect the weight of suspicion from Jesse with regard to the letters and llama deaths. To make Zack's position worse, the sheriff would give first consideration to the Caldwells'—i.e. Ellen's— problems. That meant Zack was running a distant second.

He reached across the desk to grab the form he'd filled out earlier. After scrawling a signature across the bottom, he left it where it lay. Eventually, Abe might remember to read it. Jesse lolled in the office chair and smirked. He didn't seem to mind giving up Ellen to the sheriff's ministrations, as long as it worked in his favor.

As Zack turned toward the door, he glanced at Abe. The sheriff held a paper cup to Ellen's lips, never looking away from her fever-bright violet eyes.

Tapping an impatient beat on the steering wheel of his truck, Zack glanced up and down the street. Now that his business with the sheriff was finished—albeit unsuccessfully—he was anxious to return to the ranch. No telling what fresh disaster might brew if he stayed gone longer than a few hours.

He was debating whether or not to go looking for Meg, when he saw a woman walk out of Chet's store. It was Meg, but not the Meg he'd been expecting. A skinny yellow tank top stopped short of her waist. A flowing western-style skirt accentuated her tiny middle and ended just above the knees. A gust of wind blew her blond hair in spirals around her face and played with the hem of the colorful skirt. Zack was peripherally aware of male eyes turning toward her from every direction.

A Land Cruiser sped past, skidded to a halt, and reversed direction. Zack recognized the driver as a Boise businessman who had a summer home in the area. The man communicated his appreciation with a long, slow wolf whistle. Zack was tempted to chime in with a whistle of his own. Either that, or run over and wrap Meg in a blanket before anyone else got an eyeful. He'd always known she was a good-looking woman. All primped and primed, she was sexy as hell.

He was about to get out of the truck to greet her when Lydia, in all her radiant, surgically enhanced beauty, filled the frame of his open window. Her scoop-neck blouse showed plenty of cleavage, especially when she rested her elbows on the door and leaned in. A pink French bra overflowed not six inches from his nose.

"Hey, big boy. You were downright unsociable in Daddy's office, so I thought I'd give you another chance." She bared her teeth in what passed for a smile.

Zack craned his neck to see past her, trying to keep Meg in sight. Lydia glanced over her shoulder. When she returned her attention to Zack, her smile was less sweet. Her mascara-laden eyes narrowed. "Trouble comes from taking in strangers. Strange women in particular. Win should do you a favor and hang that one . . ." she pointed a thumb behind her, "from the nearest cottonwood."

He thought about popping open the door and setting Lydia on her well-padded derriere, right in the middle of Main Street. Instead, he tried to be civil. "I'm short on time, Lydia. How about we put off this discussion for a few decades?"

She ignored the hint. Jutting even further into the truck, she cupped a breast. A crucifix on a gold chain swung out of her deep cleavage as she brushed abundant flesh against his shoulder.

He listed as far away as possible, churning his brain for a polite way to get rid of her. "Why don't you go back and help Abe in the office? You could file all that paperwork on his desk."

She laughed. "Good try, but that's not the kind of work I'm best at. How about I treat you to lunch?"

"No thanks."

"Please, Zack. I'll be dessert. It's been so long since we've been alone, my panties are wet just thinking—"

"We've never been alone, Lydia."

Frown wrinkles cut lines in her pancake war paint. "Why'd you have to remind me? We can make up for it, though. I'll rent us a bed at the Sleepy Hollow Motel. You've never had sex as finger-lickin' good as—"

"Would you back up a step? I need elbow room to start the truck."

Lydia and her magnificent knockers stayed right where they were. Zack was out patience. He rolled up the window until her breasts sagged over the glass. When she still didn't move, he gingerly eased her overflowing titties out of a potentially serious bind.

Outside the mud-spattered glass, she began to whine. "Three months, sugar. I've kept myself pure for three months, just for you."

If Lydia was pure—even short-term pure—Zack was goddamn Mother Theresa. He cranked the ignition key, vowing to take up religion if the truck would only cooperate. The engine turned over and caught immediately.

"Thank you, Jesus," Zack muttered under his breath. As he let off the brake and shifted into first gear, he ignored Lydia banging on the glass. By now, she'd given up semi-lucid persuasion and had moved on to shouting more obscenities than a drunken cowhand on payday Friday night.

Zack scanned the street for Meg. She had reversed direction and was strolling away, her nose in the air like she'd scented a dead skunk. She must have seen Lydia shoving her anatomy at him. Leave it to a woman to get upset about something over which a man had no control.

A couple of old-timers stood gaping in front of the feed store as Meg passed. Shielding their eyes from the noonday sun, they ogled her legs. Zack sent the aged voyeurs a black scowl. He drove the truck alongside her and rolled down the passenger window. "You're going the wrong way."

"That depends on my destination." With a plastic shopping bag clasped to her side, she paused to glare at Zack. The sexy little skirt swirled around her thighs. She used her free hand to keep it from flying higher.

He grinned at her show of temper, and especially at the show of thighs. "Get in the truck," he shouted over the engine's rumble.

She gingerly put her hands on the door frame as if loathe to get too close. "That woman with the . . ." Meg sketched a generous curve over her chest. "Is she why you wanted to come to town alone? If you planned to meet her, why didn't you say so to begin with? If I'd known, I—"

"Meg, shut up and listen. That's Lydia. I told you about her, remember? You even offered to protect me."

"I do vaguely . . ."

"Sure you do. So why did you take one look at her blockbuster chest and start running?"

Meg frowned. "I wasn't running. I thought you and she were—"

"Don't think. Just hop in." Zack considered *helping* her in, but he didn't trust himself to touch her. He was liable to reach up under that skirt, giving the leering old-timers the thrill of their lives.

Fortunately, Meg relented before Zack made a move. She jerked on the door, but it resisted. Zack leaned across the seat and rammed a shoulder into it, forcing it open. Without looking at him, Meg climbed in, taking care not to catch her skirt on the spring that was already bulging through the duct-tape patch. Her sandals tangled with his one purchase of the morning, a new lasso he'd bought for Robby. With remarkable poise, Meg sorted out her shoes from the rope and arranged her own package at her feet.

Zack one-eightied the truck and headed toward home. Lydia stood in front of the sheriff's office, smoldering like a pressure cooker. He expected steam to come out of her ears any minute. Zack raised his hand in a neighborly wave. She responded with a universal finger gesture. Her malignant gaze followed his truck out of town.

"I didn't plan on meeting Lydia," he explained. "She did offer to buy me lunch, but I knew better than to accept. Hell, I was afraid she'd eat *me* for lunch."

Meg turned sideways in her seat to study him. "You do look horrified," she said with obvious sarcasm.

"Any man with the sense God gave a blister beetle is scared of a woman like Lydia. I've done my damnedest to keep her off my trail, but she's determined. Now I've gone and given her a temper tantrum. That's bad. As Chief Red Hawk once said, 'A woman scorned in love has eyes hot enough to burn a hole through three buffalo skins.'"

Meg laughed. "The old chief knew human nature."

Pink flushed her cheeks, and her rosy lips were shinier than usual. A touch of makeup, Zack surmised. He'd never seen her with makeup. He checked out the rest of her—small breasts, no bra, nipples straining against the lemon yellow tank top. His gaze lingered there awhile, before lowering to soft folds of material flowing over feminine hips and thighs. "What are you dressed for?" he demanded. "Driving me crazy?"

A smile played at the corner of her lips. Driving him crazy obviously pleased her. She looked like a kitten who'd lapped up a platter of cream.

Zack wished he could snatch back his words. He hadn't meant to offer a compliment, even a backhanded one. He didn't want to give her the wrong impression—or maybe it was the right impression, but for the wrong reason. He admired her, liked her, but he did not love her. If she wanted to go back to Edward, she was welcome to the privilege.

"What did you find in the mail? Another generous offer from your big-hearted employer?" he taunted.

Her self-satisfied smile faltered. "Not this time."

Zack was sure something had come in the mail, and she was hiding it in the plastic sack she'd stuffed at her feet. Had the big "E" advanced from bribes to love notes?

Before he could make a fool of himself by demanding she read Edward's sonnet aloud, she distracted him. "What about Lydia?" she asked.

Zack narrowed his eyes warily. "What about her? I told you I didn't plan—"

"I know. But anyone can see she wants you, Zack. She knows I've been staying on the ranch. Do you think she might have cut your fence out of jealousy?"

He glanced at her, surprised. Sometimes Meg's brain moved too fast for him. After a moment's consideration, he shook his head. "The fence problem has to be related to all the other 'accidents' we've had lately. Lydia doesn't fit. True, right now she'd take pleasure in slicing off my external organs and feeding them to the pigs. Back when the first llama died, though, she had no reason to hate me. She put all her effort into peeling off my jeans."

"Did you . . . peel?"

"Like I said, she's not my kind of woman." He thought for a moment, then rolled his eyes as he saw where Meg was heading. "Okay, I get it. Lydia might have a motive."

"A darn good motive," Meg insisted. "She's wanted you for a long time, and you won't have her. Anyone can see she takes rejection poorly. She's the personification of Red Hawk's 'woman scorned.' Isn't it possible she killed the llamas and ruined the fence, thinking to offer herself as a consolation prize? And since that didn't work, she's *really* perturbed."

Zack raised an eyebrow. "Lydia sure made a bad impression on you."

Blushing, Meg concentrated on straightening her skirt over sexy thighs.

Tearing his gaze away from her legs and back to the road, Zack decided to tell her the rest. "While I was in the sheriff's office, Jesse Caldwell—my nearest neighbor—came in to file a complaint. Seems his fence was cut last night, too. And he thinks *I'm* the one running around with wire cutters."

She frowned. "That's strange. Do you think maybe the bad guy—male or female—didn't know the boundaries? Maybe the neighbor's fence was cut by accident."

Zack chewed on the idea. "That's one possibility."

Meg tapped her lips with a forefinger. "On the other hand, isn't Jesse Caldwell the man who filed a lawsuit against you?"

Zack sat up straight. "How do you know that?" He didn't recall telling her. Though he'd once thought of her as a dumb blonde, he kept revising her I. Q. in an upward direction.

"I've been doing your bookkeeping, Zack. What did you expect me to think about all those payments to a lawyer over the past year, re: the Caldwell case. I've wondered . . . why the lawsuit?"

Zack slanted her a glance. "You know it's connected to Sky, don't you?" He guessed as much from her hesitancy in asking the question.

"Yes," she admitted. "Win mentioned something about . . . But if you don't want to tell me . . ."

He lifted a hand off the steering wheel in an I-give-up gesture. With Meg, talking was easier than keeping quiet. Besides, since she already knew too much, she might as well know the rest. "Mike Cald-

well worked for Sky. He was just a kid. Only seven-
teen. His father—that's Jesse—had ordered him out
of the house a few days before the rafting trip
when . . . The boy hadn't been home since the quarrel
with his dad, although I didn't know that until later.
Not that I blame him for staying away. Ellen, his
mother, is an alcoholic, and I'm pretty sure Jesse beat
up on both of them once in a while. The kid had
plenty of reason for wanting an out."

"An out?" Meg prompted. "You don't think he'd
have gone home eventually?"

Zack shook his head. "I think he had a death wish.
Either that, or he decided to throw out Sky's safety
rules in some kind of teenage rebellion. From what
the other passengers on his raft said, he shed his
helmet and life jacket right before they got to the
rapids. Then they hit something—a submerged rock,
a log. Mike ended up in the water, sucked down in
an undertow. Sky was in another raft, close enough
to see what happened. She ripped off her life jacket
so she could dive below the surface. She couldn't
save him." Emotions weighted Zack's chest. "Couldn't
save herself either."

"She was a heroine," Meg said softly.

"Yeah." Zack sighed. "Not that it's much comfort
to anyone."

"Why would Jesse blame you for the accident,
Zack? You weren't there, were you?"

"No. But I was half owner of the rafting business.
Jesse maintained I *should* have been there instead of
leaving the trip to Sky and a teenager. He's right,
but the courts didn't see it that way."

"Of course not. You aren't—"

"I understand how Jesse feels, Meg. He wants revenge. Maybe absolution. God knows, I'd like a little
of both myself."

Meg looked puzzled, but she didn't ask for an explanation. Instead, she focused on the more immediate mystery. "How recently was this lawsuit dismissed?"

"Almost two months ago." He met her gaze. "And yes, the first llama incident happened after that."

"So maybe Jesse cut his own *and* your fences, then tried to blame it on you. To divert suspicion."

"Could be," Zack agreed. "No way to prove it, though."

They drove in silence for a mile or so, speeding across the narrow wooden bridge that seemed to become shakier with each passage.

"Who sent the notes you keep in your desk drawer?" she asked. "The ones on yellow legal paper."

He almost drove off the road. "How in the *hell* do you know about those notes?"

"I, uhm, happened to be . . . happened to notice . . ." She faltered. "Do you think they're connected to your other problems?"

"The sheriff's looking into it." Zack wished she'd leave it at that, though he knew she wouldn't. Talking about Sky's death had taken more out of him than he'd thought. He just wanted to be quiet a while.

"Does he have any useful ideas?" Meg persisted.

Zack resigned himself to a complete inquisition. "Abe's leaning toward outside forces. He figures nobody native to his precious little community would disturb the peace."

"So who does that leave?"

"Tobias, for one."

"Tobias?" Meg sounded startled.

"It *could* be him, though it doesn't add up. Why would he cut a fence when he'll be the one patching it? Why would he harm the animals he feeds every day?"

"If he were guilty, Winona would be devastated," Meg said.

"What's Win got to do with it?" He turned off the main road that circled around Henry's Lake, onto a rutted lane leading to Mount Nemesis and the ranch.

"She and Tobias spend a lot of time together. I believe they have a relationship outside the garage. Inside the garage, too. Whenever Tobias is around, she glows like a recharged spark plug. Haven't you noticed?"

Zack hadn't, but it was something to think about. "Let's hope Tobias is clean. I asked the sheriff to run a background check on him."

"Looking for what?" Meg asked.

"Hidden motivation, a secret craving to knock off llamas, a hatred for the name Burkhart. Or a record."

"Record?" Meg's voice sounded faint. Zack glanced over and saw her staring out the front windshield.

"Prison," he said. "Just because a person's done time for one crime doesn't mean he's guilty of another, but you'd have to suspect a connection."

Meg pleated her skirt with nervous fingers. Zack was alarmed at how pale and quiet she'd become. "What's the matter? You look guilty as hell."

Her gaze jerked to his. "What do you think I've done?"

He grinned. "I'd bet the ranch you're not an ax murderer, bank robber, or llama killer."

"You've underestimated my life of crime," she said in a playful tone. A slight shakiness in her voice indicated she was not quite as lighthearted as she tried to appear.

"Don't tell me you've exceeded the speed limit." He raised an eyebrow. "Or smoked an illegal substance, maybe?"

She offered a tremulous smile. "I've done both. A ticket cured me of one. I broke out in hives from the other. I have a history of always getting caught."

He reached across the seat to put his hand over hers, where it rested on the peeling duct tape. "The sheriff might come by the ranch asking questions. Since you're an outsider, too, no telling what crazy ideas good old Abe might hatch. If I'm not there, send Win or Tobias after me. You don't have to deal with the law all alone."

She shifted her feet, rearranging her sandals' position between the rope and the plastic bag. "There's no need to protect me."

That's exactly what Zack wanted to do. Protect her, shield her, cherish her. She looked worried and scared. Of the sheriff, he supposed, although Zack had no notion why. Abe couldn't plant the fear of God in a mouse.

Had Edward turned her world topsy-turvy again? Had he sent a threat of legal action in lieu of a love letter? Was she so naive she thought she could be arrested for breaking an employee contract?

Why the hell couldn't she be open with Zack . . . about Edward, or whatever was bothering her? He resented her lack of trust, until he thought about the pain and guilt he held inside and had refused to share with her or anyone else.

Much to his amazement, he realized a truth he'd been hiding from himself. He *wanted* to tell Meg everything. And he was going to do it today, before he changed his mind.

Chapter Fifteen

There's no need to protect me, Meg had said, although she knew it was a terrible lie. She needed protection, but no one could protect her from herself, or from the truth of who she was.

Sweat sheened on her skin, anxiety fluttered in her stomach as she clenched handfuls of skirt in damp palms. What Zack had said about a prison record made her want to disappear into the cracked vinyl upholstery. If he knew about *her* record . . .

He took a sudden turn and wheeled up a steep narrow road Meg had never seen before.

"Where are you going?" she asked. A deep ravine yawned to her right as they zigzagged around a dizzying curve.

"I want to show you something." He spoke in a curt tone that meant she'd get nothing else from him until he was ready.

Her accumulated deceit swirled in her mind and made her light-headed and nauseous. She wished she could confess, but was terrified of the results.

Rejection. Loathing. What else could she expect?

Her own mother had not understood or forgiven her. Even Edward—in the heat of argument— had revealed how he really felt. That she was dishonest. How could Zack, who didn't know any of the circumstances, excuse her actions?

She braced hands against the dashboard and

willed the roiling in her stomach to cease. They jounced across a dry, rocky creekbed and up another incline. A bump jostled her into the broken spring. Her skirt stuck to loosened duct tape. As she jerked the material free, she heard a rip. The pretty new skirt tore at the hem, just as the fabric of her lies was shredding at the seams.

While Meg contemplated her sins, Zack brooded about sins of his own. His guilt over Sky's death had festered inside him long enough. If he would ever find absolution, he sensed it had to come from Meg. No one else would see as far into his heart. No one would understand better how his mistake haunted him.

High on the side of Mount Nemesis, he stopped at the edge of a precipice. Without a word, he shut off the engine and got out of the truck, leaving his door open for Meg to follow, as he knew she would. He'd come to expect Meg beside him. He needed her now.

He strode to a huge, flat, moss-covered boulder. A tall fir tree growing at the cliff's rim dappled the rock in shade. Using the tree's roots as a step, he leaped onto the rock, which stood several feet higher than the road.

In front of him, the world dropped an abrupt thousand feet. The red-brown of the ranch roof, the barn, Win's garage, all huddled far below. Everything was familiar, but the perspective was vastly different. Sky had loved this view. He'd expected to feel her presence here.

Yet he sensed nothing. No trace of Sky.

Since Meg had come into his world, Sky had faded until he no longer held his wife's image foremost in his mind. He rarely heard her voice. He no longer grieved as deeply.

He'd tried to keep Meg in one compartment and Sky in another, but Meg stuck her toe in a crack and refused to retreat. He'd become used to her persistence. As if to prove the point, she scrambled onto the boulder to join him. When she reached his side, she brushed at her knees, reddened beneath the skirt hem. She'd scraped them on the granite rock, but the damage didn't seem to bother her.

She fit her hand into his. "I'm here."

The simple statement gave him strength. Looking out over the valley, he drew a deep breath. "I released Sky's ashes from this spot. One moment I held her—what was left of her. Then the wind came, and she was gone."

He gestured to the wide expanse of green grass, to the ranch buildings, toward the distant mountains. "I like to think I set her free to become part of the land she loved."

Meg squeezed his hand. "You did the right thing. She would have wanted—"

"There's more."

He released a long sigh as he sat on the boulder and tugged Meg down beside him. "We started the rafting business six years ago. At first, I made the runs with Sky. We had plenty of clients and the money was good. That was important, because a profit from the llamas was slow in coming. But each summer, I was busier with the ranch. I couldn't go along every day anymore. I didn't like her making trips in rough weather. Mike was helping her float a second raft by then, but he was just a kid."

Zack felt the familiar ache start deep inside, but he hoped telling it all to Meg would be a step toward salvation. "Last summer, snowmelt kept the river running fast through early July. I was more uneasy than ever. I tried to convince Sky to send her clients elsewhere so we could both concentrate on the ranch, but she insisted we needed the income. She was right. I felt like scum because I hadn't provided enough for her and Robby on my own."

Ploughing a hand through his hair, he struggled to keep his voice steady. "I pinned my hopes on selling the sporting goods designs. I thought if I could do that, Sky would give up the rafting. She wouldn't have to worry about us paying the bills, and she'd have more time with Robby. Since I'd already crashed and burned a couple of times when I'd tried to peddle my stuff, I didn't tell her I'd made an appointment with the manager of a Boise chain. When the day came, it had rained hard; the river was high. I asked Sky to cancel her run because it was too dangerous, especially since I couldn't go with her. She told me I was high-handed and bossy. She and Mike could handle the trip, she insisted.

"Thinking about it afterward, I figured she was angry with me because I never said why I couldn't go with her, or where I *was* going. Maybe if I'd told her . . . maybe if we'd had more time to talk it out . . . but we were both in a hurry. I was too set on my own goals."

He glanced at Meg. "I was like your Edward. Maybe that's why seeing what he did to you makes me so damn mad. It's a replay of—"

Meg shook her head. "No, Zack. It's not the same."

"Yes, it is. I left her when I should have known nothing was more important than being there. I stormed out of the house. At the last minute, she called for me to come back. I didn't. Her pigheadedness made me furious. She wouldn't budge an inch to give me peace of mind.

"As it turned out, I went twenty miles down the road and had to turn back. A tanker had overturned. The highway was closed. By the time I drove back to the ranch, Sky had left, so I saddled a horse and rode fence. I was still angry at myself, angry at Sky. Then I saw helicopters over the river . . ."

Meg held tight to his hand. "It wasn't your fault. You couldn't have known . . ."

"I should have been with her. It *was* my fault. Mine and those damn boxes of junk. Two people died because of my *dream*." He snarled that last word. "And because I was even more stubborn than she was."

Meg felt the weight of his grief on her shoulders. She wanted to shake him and force him to see his actions in a more rational light. "It was Sky's decision to go out that day, Zack. And you're different from Edward because you loved her. Really loved her. You were pursuing your dream for her sake, too. Edward only cares about money. You're not like him at all."

Even as she spoke, she began to interpret the concentric ripples moving outward from what Zack had said to what she'd done. A sick feeling lodged again in the pit of her stomach. His sporting goods designs were linked to his pain over Sky's death and to his guilt. Project Red Hawk wasn't going to sit well with him. Not well at all. "That's why you told me the things stored in the closet are worthless. Because you can't stand to sell them after . . ."

"I'd rather cut out my heart," he said.

Her head spun with the magnitude of her error. He'd never forgive what she'd done. She'd anticipated some resistance, but how could she have guessed he'd feel *this* strongly? Since Win was on her side, she'd assumed . . .

"Does Win . . ." Meg couldn't bring herself to finish the question.

"She knows," Zack said. "I told her, but we've never talked about it since. We talk around Sky, never about her."

No. Oh, no. Win had known all this and still en-

couraged Meg to go ahead. Win resented her; Meg
had known that from the start. She felt like the vil-
lage idiot. She should have guessed . . .

She couldn't tell Zack about Red Hawk now. She'd
write to the companies and retrieve the samples
she'd mailed before the scheme went any farther.
She'd send back the first check and any others that
arrived. Then, even if Zack found out, he'd have to
forgive her.

Right now, he needed her understanding, not her
shame. He needed acceptance, not a confession to
conflict with his. She looked into his eyes, willing
him to see her love and nothing more. "I understand
the guilt, Zack. But think of what would have happened if Sky had lived. She would have forgiven
you, just as you forgave her for *her* stubbornness."

"Sky won't have the chance," he said. "That's
the difference."

Meg was silent. How could she counter that? In
the branches above, fir needles sighed on the summer
wind, and an imagined whisper brought inspiration.
"You say you hear Sky sometimes. Does she seem
angry?"

That jolted him. He sat straighter. "No. I never
hear words, but she doesn't seem angry. I guess I
never thought too much about her mood. What I
sense is a sort of . . . calm."

Meg nodded. "Because she *has* forgiven you. You
loved her more than life itself. You still love her, and
she knows that. She's waiting for you to understand."

He looked at Meg as if seeing beneath the surface
to who she really was. She almost cringed, afraid of
what he'd find. To her relief, a corner of his mouth
lifted in a hint of a smile. He turned to gaze out
across the valley. " 'A strong spirit soars with the

eagles.' Red Hawk said that, and Sky quoted him more than once. She believed him."

"I think she's with the eagles now, Zack. She's with Red Hawk, too. I'll bet she'd love to tell us what the old man *really* said, because sometimes I wonder about Winona's version."

He managed a full smile. "You're an amazing woman. You and Sky are so different, and yet . . . she'd have liked you." The smile lit his eyes and made the silver in them sparkle. "It took me a while to get used to the way you're always on a high. Always soaring. You have dreams and imagination clear up in the stratosphere."

Her mood lightened along with his. "Am I doomed to fall out of the sky like a lead feather?" she teased.

"I don't think so." He gently stroked her cheek.

Meg savored the tenderness even if she knew her fall was inevitable. Just for a little while, she longed to stay in the stratosphere along with her dreams. Her tongue slid over dry lips. Desire burned from her mouth to her chest to the aching emptiness between her legs. She wanted Zack to want her. To love her. Now. Unless he made love to her now, it might never happen. There was so much he didn't know and wouldn't like.

His fingers brushed across her mouth. "God help me, I think I've wanted you from the moment I rescued you from the ledge."

"You didn't rescue me," she corrected. "I could have—"

"Don't argue, Meg."

As she assimilated the rest of what he'd said, the wanting part, she felt as dizzy as if she'd just taken a spin on a tilt-a-whirl. "D-did you say 'want'? As in desire, crave, covet, lust after . . ." She started to add love, but was afraid to go that far.

"For God's sake, don't analyze." He angled her head just right, and his lips descended, brushing back and forth on her lips. When his tongue delved for hers, she put her arms around him and pressed her body close. She caught on fire.

He responded with an answering blaze, lowering her to the sun-warm, moss-covered boulder. As passion shivered through her, she closed her eyes. She didn't want him to see into her soul and guess how deeply she loved him, in case the emotion was not returned in kind. Most of all, she didn't dare read his thoughts, in case he was thinking of Sky.

But Zack was thinking of Meg, only Meg. She had freed him from memories and sadness. New emotions boiled out of him, violent tremors of desire.

Without breaking their kiss, he rolled onto his back to let her control the pace. She was on top of him now. Their mouths fed on each other, hungry for more. He traced her spine from neck to tailbone, loving the feel of her and her woman's curves. God, how he wanted her. He'd forgotten it could be like this. He'd forgotten passion until Meg reminded him. He wanted her not only with his body, but with his heart and soul.

He feathered kisses across her cheek and buried his nose in her hair, which both looked and smelled like sunshine. She was warm, as warm as the earth beneath them. His groin pulsed with a need that hovered on the threshold of pain.

She reached between them to unbutton his blue cotton shirt. He caught her hands to stop her. None of this was supposed to happen. He'd never meant for them to go this far. "We can't . . ." He squeezed his eyes shut against the agonizing need. "I don't have . . . anything to . . ."

"Oh, but I do." She pulled a hand free. Zack's eyelids popped open in time to see her reach into a pocket of her skirt and produce a half-dozen condom packets in assorted colors.

"I bought them from Chet," she said with a laugh. "You can imagine how shocked he was. I'm sure the news was traveling the telephone lines before I'd cleared the door." She dropped the handful of condoms on the moss beside them and settled her body over his, rocking against him suggestively. "Any more excuses?" she whispered. "Because if you can't think of any, I'd like to touch you, please."

Hell, what man could refuse a request like that? The need was too strong. The passion ran hot in his veins. He wanted her hands on him. All over him. He managed a strangled groan in reply and released her to do as she would. And what she did . . . Jesus, it was good. She uncovered his chest, caressing and stroking. Her tongue tested and tasted his throat, his nipples, the midline of hair leading downward. She rimmed his navel and moved lower. Her teeth caught the button of his jeans and tugged it free.

Zack didn't think he could take much more, considering her unbridled approach to lovemaking. "Meg." His voice was a harsh, hoarse whisper.

She fondled his hardened flesh through his jeans.

"God, Meg. Stop." He grasped her shoulders and forced her upward until her face was level with his. She went completely still. The desire drained from her passion-dark eyes and was replaced by hurt and confusion.

"I-I'm sorry," she said. "I thought you'd like—"

He silenced her with a kiss. "I do. Believe me, I do." He had intended to stop her, to end this before it was too late. But she looked devastated. He wanted to make her happy. Maybe he wanted to give, even more than he wanted to take. "It's just that it's been a long time. The way you're going, it'll all be over pretty damn quick."

Her eyes widened. "Oh. I'm sorry if . . . I didn't mean to . . ." Apparently, his predicament had dawned on her at last. Or maybe not, because she straddled his bulging jeans and rubbed over him with an irresistible friction, keeping him on the edge. In one swift moment, he reversed their positions. It was his turn to build her passion.

With hands and mouth, he kindled her. From eyelids to throat. Neck to breasts. Belly to thighs. He paused to lick her scraped knees as he worked all the way to her toes. On that first foray, he didn't remove a stitch of her clothing, though he had to hold down her arms to keep her from doing it herself.

"I want to please you," she whispered with an earnestness that broke his heart and healed it at the same time. Dear sweet Meg.

He gradually kissed a path to her mouth. "You do please me. Every part of you pleases me." He kissed her temple, licked the lobe of her ear. She was like a ripe peach, all juice and flavor ready to spill out for the man who dared to love her as she was meant to be loved.

At a slow burn that made her whimper—and kept an unmistakable part of him as hard as tempered steel—he unveiled her pale skin. Inch by torrid inch, he peeled off her tank top. Her breasts were perfectly shaped, the color of peaches and cream. Beautiful. Delicious. Her nipples firmed and tightened on his tongue. When she rotated her hips and clawed his shoulders, he knew he was making progress. But she had only begun to blaze. He wanted a bonfire.

He ran his hands down her sides, over the curved contours of her hips. Hiking her skirt to the tops of her thighs, he caressed her through the woman things she wore. Through damp lacy underwear. Through lace and silk to the heat of her body.

He drew the panties down her legs and threw them aside. She wore no stockings; she'd kicked off her sandals. Only the skirt remained, flowing over his hands as he memorized the softness beneath. He wanted to see all of her, but not quite yet. For now, he savored the concealment, the fiery unopened gift. He stroked until she was creamy and swollen with longing, as he was hard and ready for her.

Her hips strained upward. "Now, Zack. I want you now."

"Not yet. Just a little longer." He wanted her out of her mind with wanting him. He wanted her panting, breathless, pleading.

Meg was not inclined to wait. She clamped her legs around his waist and began erotically stroking her wet sex against the bare skin above his jeans.

He gritted his teeth and held her hips. "Don't move. I won't last another minute if you move."

He coaxed her legs away from him. With her thighs spread wide, he slipped one finger inside her body. Impaled on pure sensation, she writhed against the push and pull of his caress. He guided the rhythm of her hips until she took over, rocking forward and back, rocking faster and wilder. He penetrated with two fingers, pushing her ever higher.

She whimpered. She begged. Her every muscle tensed as she reached the zenith and trembled at the precipice. With passion's relentless pulse, she tumbled over the edge.

He pressed against that pulse as it went on and on, until it languished to a tremor. He watched as she came down from the high.

She smiled, a dreamy, satisfied smile. "You please *me*," she whispered. "So far. But haven't I missed something? I'd love a ride on your vine, Tarzan. Please?" She lifted her hips to torment him again.

Lord help him, the waiting and wanting were killing him. He'd started this game, and he sure as hell intended to finish it. "Glad to oblige, Lady Jane." His voice came out husky and hoarse. He unfastened the waist of her silk skirt and stripped it off of her. Every fiber of his being wanted to plunge inside her sweet body and find his release, but he forced himself to stop, to really look at what she offered with all her heart and soul. Almost reverently, he touched the flushed breasts, tiny waist, curved hips. She was damp all over, slick with their shared sweat. She was beautiful. He couldn't breathe, he wanted her so badly.

And she seemed to know exactly how to torture him. She licked her lips while reaching between their bodies. With the tips of her fingers, she rimmed the waistband of his jeans, and then slowly tugged the zipper down. He groaned with relief as she increased the opening. He groaned with agonized pleasure as she took him in her hand. He couldn't stand it. The hunger was too great.

Cursing his own clumsiness, he left her just long enough to whip off his shirt, his jeans. Meanwhile, she found one of the scattered condoms. She worked it onto him, taking her time, taking him to the limit of sanity. And then he was on top of her again. He spread the slick womanfolds hidden in a patch of golden hair and thrust inside. His control was gone.

It seemed hers was, too. She moved in harmony with him, panting breathless pleas for more. Deeper. Harder. Faster. His relentless thrusts sent both of them spiraling toward heaven. Together, still in euphoria, they floated back to the rock-strewn mountainside.

He cradled her in his arms, kissing her face and finding it salty and wet. She tried to brush the tears away, but he did it for her with his thumbs. He thought . . . he was *sure* it had been good for her. So why . . .

Her green eyes shimmered with moisture. "I-I didn't know it could be so wonderful."

Zack smiled tenderly as he caught yet another droplet and wiped it from her cheek. He should have known she'd cry when she was happy. She had emotions enough for both of them, and some of it was transferring to him.

"It was . . . incredible," he said. "I almost feel like crying myself, it was so damn good."

Once wasn't enough. Not nearly enough.

He wanted her still, as fiercely as Adam had ever needed Eve, as passionately as every man since time began needed his own special woman. He kissed her again, branding her as his. He wished she'd never leave him, wished he'd never have to let her go.

The breeze was stronger now. It keened down steep ravines like teardrops down a furrowed face. It rippled through the needles of the fir tree and stirred the scent of the mountain. It signaled change, a warning.

He reached for his jeans. "We should go."

Still dreamy-eyed from their loving, Meg raised one scraped knee and turned her head toward him. The wind grew into a gale, buffeting the rock, moaning through the branches of the tree above.

"Why? I don't mind if it rains. I don't mind if it hails or snows."

"If it does any of those things, we could be stuck up here for quite a while." He glanced at her, still bare and beautiful, and thought to himself that there could be a lot worse things than being stuck anywhere with Meg. But he had Win and Robby to consider. They'd worry.

Noticing unopened condoms packets blowing across the moss, he bent to retrieve them. Then he

pulled on his jeans and paused to watch dark clouds
roll across the sky.

Meg sat up, feeling a chill. She wanted to bask in
the afterglow, but Zack was forcing her to face reality. His insistence seemed strange to her, despite the
threat of inclement weather. She looked at the shadowed valley spread out beneath them and remembered why they'd driven to this spot. A wave of
sadness hit her. She'd thought Zack's love was hers
alone, but maybe it hadn't been.

She shivered.

"What's wrong?" he asked, moving near. "You're
shaking."

"This was Sky's place, wasn't it?"

"Yes," he said cautiously. "I already told you . . ."

"Were you thinking of her? When we made love,
was it . . . ?"

Zack flinched. "No." He sat beside her, reached
for her.

She pushed his arm away.

"I'm sorry, Meg. If I'd been thinking straight, I
would have chosen somewhere else for this to happen. But believe me, once we kissed, you were the
only woman on my mind."

She crossed hands over her breasts, shielding her
heart and her body. "I know you think about her all
the time. I know you can't give her up yet. Maybe
not ever." She sighed. "And I have to leave anyway, so . . ."

"When?" He riveted his gaze on her.

"Sunday. I need to be in Salt Lake City the first of
next week." She looked at the valley again to avoid
his bare chest, his smoke-silver eyes. "I guess I
should have told you before, earlier today, but . . . I
didn't want to spoil our time together. And anyway,
you knew I'd be going soon."

"Meg?" He lifted her chin and made her look at him. "I don't want you to go."

She closed her eyes. "I have to, Zack. For a while, at least. I'll be able to work faster there, and I'll present my ideas to the team. After that, I'll try to . . ."

His forehead touched hers. "It's all right. You don't have to make promises." He traced her lips with an index finger, and the touch was like a kiss. A goodbye kiss. "You know how I feel about Edward and the way he treated you. If you're ever in trouble, if I can help, I want you to call me."

Her mouth trembled. "Yes. I will." She wanted to pour forth her troubles and tell him the real reason she had to go. She wanted him to know she'd never leave him by choice, and certainly not for Edward. But she'd kept her secret too long. It seemed foolish to blab it now. Why take a chance of destroying his respect for her? Why take a chance of seeing rejection in his eyes?

Zack saw a tear start down her cheek. Not one of joy, not this time. He could see her need to go back to her old life warring with her need to stay—with her need for him. Though he'd fight any outside force for her, he couldn't intervene in this. She had to make her own decision. It seemed she'd already made it. That sonuvabitch Edward had won—maybe not with personal charms, but with the charms of his game-making company.

Zack tried to memorize Meg's face. Somehow, she'd slipped into his dreams every night, and into his heart and breath and being. God, he was going to miss her.

Sunday. Only five days away. And she'd known all along. He resented that. He felt used, which wasn't fair to Meg. She had warned him weeks ago. He'd known, and he'd wanted her anyway.

Thunder rumbled in the distance. When she shivered again, he handed her the crumpled skirt.

He watched her dress as he ploughed his arms through the sleeves of his blue work shirt and fumbled with the buttons. His hands shook, making the task difficult. A pressure grew in his chest, a brand-new pain to replace the one he'd carried for a year.

Meg had donned the skirt and was slipping into the yellow tank top. The skin of her neck was pink where his callused hands and rough beard stubble had abraded her.

Damn his heart for caring so much. Damn his soul for wanting to hold her so badly. He'd never forget her. But Meg had a team of talented colleagues waiting for her. She had a career, a fantasy game. And her jackass Edward.

Their gazes met.

"Forgive me," she said. "I was wrong not to tell you sooner—about leaving, I mean—but when you said you wanted me . . . I . . . I love you, Zack." Her eyes pooled. Tears spiked her eyelashes. The wind tossed her golden hair.

Zack knew she was waiting for a response. He longed to give it, but he couldn't find the right words.

An articulate, sensitive man would have spouted poetry. A humble man would have knelt before her and offered his heart. A resourceful man would reply with logic and reason. But Zack was none of those men.

He didn't know how to tell her he would miss her every day of his life. Instead, he lowered his mouth to hers and showed her what he felt.

Chapter Sixteen

Distant thunder boomed from high on Mount Nemesis.

Zack was well into his kiss, with Meg leaning into him. One of his hands roved under her slinky yellow top while the other secured her hips against him. He was hard for her again. Already he wanted . . .

A rumble from above penetrated his belabored senses. He separated his mouth from hers and realized dark clouds hung low overhead. They had to leave before the storm hit. If they stayed beneath the tall fir, they were in danger of being struck by lightning. Besides that, rain would turn the dirt road leading home into a quagmire. If it rained hard, the dry creek crossings would flow door-handle high with rocks and mud.

Reluctantly, he lifted her chin, urging her out of a sensual haze into a more pragmatic time zone. "We have to get out of here, Meg." His voice sounded coherent, but his brain felt definitely addled. He wanted more of her. A lot more. With her face flushed pink and her body molded against his, she was the essence of woman. Just touching her stole his breath, quickened his pulse.

Damn, but he wanted her. Right now. On the boulder, in the bed of the truck, against a tree. But a thick streak of lightning above Mount Nemesis reminded him he'd have to wait. He swooped her off the ground and hurried to the truck just as the first rain-drops fell.

Once inside, he reached behind the seat for a quilt he kept there. He doubled it over the half-protruding spring so she could sit right next to him. Pulling her close, he inhaled her spice-and-flower scent, now overlaid with the scent of sex. Good Lord, she smelled good. He kissed her again, forgetting about the rain until a steady tapping reminded him. A drip of cold water leaked through rust on the roof and landed just below his right ear.

He cursed under his breath. "The road will flood for sure."

Meg sat up straighter, as if she'd just noticed there was a world around them. Then she smiled that sad-sweet smile he'd first loved, sometimes resented, and never completely understood. He wanted to ask about it now, but she distracted him by licking the wet spot from the side of his neck.

He nudged her aside so he could reach the ignition. If the truck didn't start, he figured they'd just have to stay awhile. Damn his luck, the engine roared on the first turn of the key, giving him no excuse to delay. A streak of lightning flashed. The aftermath of thunder rumbled the truck's metal frame.

He felt Meg's body grow tense. "You're not scared of a little thunder, are you?" he asked as the truck negotiated the first steep slope along the narrow road.

She shivered, rubbing her goosebumped arms.

"Well, are you?"

She still didn't answer. The rain drummed hard on the roof, so he couldn't have heard her anyway. He squinted to see through the windshield. The worn blades on the wipers did a poor job against the wind-driven onslaught. The truck's nearly bald tires slipped and slid down the mountain road, but Zack guided them safely through the storm. He'd driven through worse. The weather didn't bother him. Meg's silence did.

Meg was aware of Zack's sidelong glance, but fear closed her throat. She'd let herself imagine everything was fine, that his kiss would last forever. But now, she was back to reality. She cringed with every thunderbolt. She felt so closed in, she could barely breathe. The truck cab seemed airless. The tiny space reminded her of a locked door . . . of a cell. When at last Zack drove down the long driveway and came to a stop near the barn, he took her in his arms. She struggled to free herself. Not from him exactly, but from an inescapable past.

He drew back, a question in his eyes. "Tell me, Meg. Tell me why you're afraid."

She didn't know how to begin. The claustrophobia, combined with the storm, set off an inner panic. "I-I can't, Zack. I just can't."

"Whatever you say won't go anywhere, I swear. A three-ton tractor couldn't drag your secrets from me."

Meg believed him, but trusting was another matter. Nevertheless, she decided to begin with her family.

The whole truth would be too much all at once, she reasoned. So she told him the first tiny part. "I spent an entire night in a closet once. I couldn't get out. The door jammed, or maybe my stepfather . . . I was never sure. I was . . . seven."

She shivered through another thunderbolt. The glass in the truck windshield quaked; the metal reverberated. "It was storming outside, and the sound of every raindrop seemed magnified. Dave, my stepfather, was yelling at my mother. That was almost worse than the stale air and the way the floor shook from the thunder. I was afraid he'd . . . hurt her. And hurt me."

Zack's fingers combed through her hair, soothing her. "Sure you were, Meg. You were just a kid. If I ever meet this Dave character, I'll yell a few things at *him*. He'll be cowering in a closet before I'm done."

She would have smiled if she weren't shaking so badly. Zack was on her side, and that made the telling easier. She began to hope that if he knew how it had started, he'd understand the rest. "After my real father died, I never belonged. Especially after Mother remarried, I felt like the Cracker Jack prize nobody wanted. Except for my grandmother, G. T., there was no one who cared about me. Mother was too busy with parties and the social scene and keeping Dave happy. Even after I had a job and moved into my own apartment, even as I worked my way through college, some of that stayed with me. I always felt . . . not good enough. I didn't quite . . . belong."

Zack nodded, never taking his eyes from her face.

"That's why Edward seemed so wonderful at first," she continued. "He loved my work. He said he loved me, and I couldn't believe my good fortune. I forced myself to see his best qualities and become blind to his faults.

"I went about being in love all wrong. I thought if Edward truly wanted me, I'd never be the cheap plastic throwaway again." She paused. The next part, about G. T. and Meg's transgression, might be too much for now. What if Zack couldn't accept the truth? What if *he* threw her away?

"Any idiot can see you're a keeper." His voice was low and gentle as he traced her upper lip with one fingertip. "You have a rare ability to put people at ease, and a zest for life that's catching. You do belong. You belong anywhere you want to be."

She closed her eyes. "That's what G. T. always

said." Could she belong on Zack's ranch? Would he want her there if he knew what she still lacked the courage to tell him?

Lightning flashed. Thunder followed within seconds. She repressed another shudder. "We should make a run for the house."

Zack put a hand on either side of her face. He sipped her lips as if she were a fine wine and he, a connoisseur. "Not until you know," he said between kisses. "Know without a doubt, how much I want you."

She leaned nearer, inviting him. Her fingers threaded in his hair as he trailed lazy kisses across her cheek and then back to the corner of her mouth. The storm faded to mere background noise, no longer important or frightening. Rain streamed across the windshield. The humidity rose, fogging the glass, isolating them from the rest of the world.

Pure undiluted passion, 190 proof, filled her to bursting. She was drunk on his presence, as he seemed to be drunk on hers. She rubbed taut nipples against his chest while he engaged her tongue with his. Her mouth opened hungrily. He no longer savored her. He consumed her, heart and soul and spirit, as she devoured him. Another boom of thunder made her jump. Their teeth collided. He didn't seem to mind. He turned his head to delve deeper. His arms closed more securely around her.

He kissed her breathless. When he ended with a nibble of her bottom lip, she opened her eyes to see him smiling.

"I keep bumping my elbow on the dashboard, catching my jeans on the broken spring, or hanging my shirt on the gear shift. Let's go inside," he said.

"And what will we do when we get there?" She raised her voice to be heard over another onslaught of rain. The storm swallowed all but a whisper.

"Make love in a bed." He spoke into her ear, his voice husky and seductive. "Lust in a pickup'll be the death of me."

Meg held onto his cotton shirt. "Stay a little longer." She couldn't bear to let go. If they left this safe haven, the symmetry and beauty of their time together might slip away. With her most beguiling smile, she reached for the waistband of his jeans. She shifted position and lay back on the seat, pulling him with her.

He responded with a groan, fitting her hips between his legs and holding her there while he plundered her mouth once again. He was hard and hot against her. He'd be riding her soon. Or she'd be riding him, whichever they would manage in the tight confines of the truck.

She was vaguely aware that the rain had slowed. The thunder was distant now, but her heart pounded so loudly, she couldn't think.

The pounding. There was something strange about . . .

Zack's mouth was on her breast. When he stilled, she knew he'd heard it, too. He lifted his head. They listened. The pounding wasn't only in their hearts. The most insistent clamor came from outside the truck door. Along with a voice.

Robby. Robby's voice. Frantic. "Daddy! Daddy, are you in there?"

Conscience poured ice water on desire.

Zack took a deep, shuddering breath and sat up, bringing Meg with him. He opened the window on the driver's side. Both he and Meg peered down at the small bedraggled child standing in the rain with water streaming down his face.

"What's wrong, son?" Zack asked.

"Hoover's sick. He's in the garage and he can't get up," the boy wailed. "Please, Daddy, hurry."

*   *   *

Zack knelt on the garage's oil-streaked concrete beside the dog. A pitiful attempt to wretch interrupted Hoover's ragged breathing. Not good, he thought. Not good at all. He was soaked to the skin, dripping from the downpour still drumming on the roof. The scent of engines and gasoline mingled with earthy odors of mud and animals and human sweat. He sensed Meg beside him and wondered if this was some kind of hellish retribution, as the notes in his desk drawer warned. It was almost as if their pleasure had led to this, to the pain. To his son's pain.

A soggy, shivering Robby crowded between Zack and Meg, who was gently stroking the dog's head.

"How long has Hoover been this way?" Zack asked the child.

Robby shrugged. He couldn't tell time yet, so both he and Zack looked across the dog's shuddering body to Win. She was hunkered next to the dog, looking drier than the rest of them but just as distressed.

"Robby took him out to the barn an hour ago," Win said. "The dog was fine then. When they came back, he still seemed okay. I was adjusting a carburetor." She gestured to the Ford truck parked a few yards away. "Didn't notice anything wrong until Robby brought me over here a couple of minutes ago."

"Can you make him well, Daddy?" Robby's wet shirt clung to his narrow chest, making him look smaller than usual. His blue-green eyes shone with hope, as if Zack had all the answers and the power to work miracles.

He only wished it were true. "I'll do what I can, son." Robby's little-boy shoulders hunched slightly. The poor kid didn't deserve more grief. Zack couldn't fail him, not again. He turned his full atten-

tion to the dog and examined the distended abdomen. Rainwater dripped from his hair onto shiny
black fur. "What has he eaten today?"

"Llama food," Robby said. "I put some in a bucket
for the crias, but I dropped it. Hoover cleaned up."

The dog had a reputation for eating most anything.
Grain had never made him sick before. The llama
food supply must be spoiled. Or maybe, considering
the sabotage that had been going on lately, it had
been poisoned.

"Did you give any of the grain to the crias?" Zack
asked his son. "Or to Hilda in the birthing stall?"

When the boy shook his head, Zack felt a small
measure of reassurance. Hilda was one of his most
valuable llamas. He badly needed her to produce a
healthy offspring.

"It's not your fault, Robby." He gave the boy a
brief hug. "I'm taking Hoover to Doc Allen. I want
you to stay here."

Meg met his gaze over the boy's dark head. She
nodded, accepting the responsibility. As Zack lifted
the dog in his arms, she was there to offer the child
comfort. Robby buried his face in her skirt. His body
shook with silent sobs.

Zack had reached the door when he stopped,
turned. "Seal up that grain, Win. We'll find out
what's wrong with it later. Just make sure Tobias
feeds only hay tonight."

At long last, the phone rang. Robby scraped a
kitchen chair across the linoleum and climbed up to
grab the receiver. "Daddy?" he said.

Poised with a spatula over a sheet of fresh-baked
chocolate chip cookies, Meg breathed a silent prayer,
hoping the news would be good. Since Zack left for
the vet's office with Hoover, she'd done her best to
occupy the child and keep his mind off disaster.

They'd completed household chores, learned a new computer game, taken care of Robby's menagerie— hamster, lizard, a beetle he'd adopted.

Now, at half past five, they'd finally heard from Zack.

Robby listened a moment, nodding his understanding before handing Meg the phone. She dropped the spatula to reach for it.

"How is Hoover?" she whispered into the receiver as Robby clambered out of the chair. She watched the child walk down the hall toward his room, kicking one of the discarded tennis balls in front of him.

"Doc says he'll make it, but he'll have to stay here overnight," Zack said. "Are all the llamas from the pasture accounted for?"

Meg hesitated. She hated to give him more bad news. "Tobias couldn't find the young female you call Esmeralda at first. He tracked her onto Forest Service land and found her . . . dead. It's such a shame, Zack. She was at the base of a cliff. Tobias said the storm must have confused her. She . . . fell."

Zack cursed softly. Meg knew what he was thinking. Although Esmeralda *might* have fallen while wandering around in the rain, it was unlikely. Just as unlikely as the previous "accidents."

"I want Doc Allen to examine what's left of the carcass," he said.

"Tobias already loaded her body in his truck," Meg told him. "I guess he assumed you'd have suspicions."

Zack muttered something that might have been approval overlaid with a generalized disgust. "How's Robby taking it?"

"I didn't tell him about Esmeralda. He's upset enough over his dog." She sighed. "We're keeping busy."

"Stay with him. I'll stop by the sheriff's office to

report the poisoning—the vet says that's probably what it is—and then I'll be home. And Meg . . ."

When he hesitated, her pulse quickened. Their relationship had undergone a cosmic leap since this morning. They'd shared their bodies and a great deal of their souls. She'd revealed more of herself to him than she'd ever revealed to anyone except G. T. But there was so much Zack didn't know.

"Be careful," he said at last. "When I get back, we have a lot to talk about." He was right about that. But his deep, rough voice implied they'd communicate with more than mere words.

Meg's thighs weakened with an echo of remembered pleasure. She clutched the back of the chair Robby had left against the wall. Before she could reply, the receiver clicked softly.

She hung up the phone. For a moment, all she could do was stand there supported by chair and wall. She'd almost forgotten, in all the subsequent turmoil, how wonderful Zack's mouth had felt on hers, how gentle his hands had been as he explored her body. Being with him was paradise. Life just didn't get any better.

Yet the moments were stolen, built of falsehoods and camouflage. She had to tell him everything and trust him to understand. If he really cared for her as much as she thought he did, maybe he could accept her anyway.

Meanwhile, a little boy needed her. She squared her shoulders. No matter what happened later, she would prove her usefulness now.

She hurried down the hall and pushed open the door to Robby's room. "The cookies are ready," she announced. "I'll pour you a glass of . . . Robby?"

He was not in his room. Meg's heart flip-flopped as she dashed through the house calling him.

No answer. She should have known better than to

let him go off alone. One more disaster added to all the rest might be too much for him. He might do something reckless, climb something dangerous. Another thought nagged at her. If the dog had been poisoned, someone had done the deed. Was that malicious person still nearby? What if Robby were hurt? Or kidnapped.

Meg felt as if a grizzly was mauling her chest, until logic emerged through the panic. The boy was upset about his dog, and he climbed when he was upset. She'd find him in the tiptop of a tree or building, teetering on the brink of danger. She'd find him and everything would be okay.

After a short but frenzied search, she located him in the cottonwood they'd sat in before. He perched in the lowest branch, looking solemn and lonely.

Shading her eyes with one hand to shut out the glare of the overcast sky, she called up a "Hi." She wanted to drag him into the safety of a hug, but she knew he would resist coming down. He might climb higher to escape her. His small jaw was set in stubborn silence, a poignant image of Zack.

"I'm worried about Hoover, too, Robby," she said. "Do you mind if I join you up there?"

The boy sniffed, using one shoulder to swipe at the moisture on his cheeks. "Is Hoover going away like Mama? Like Gingko and Elsa and Thessa?" he lisped. Like Esmeralda, too, although he didn't know about that one yet.

Meg shimmied up the trunk, scraping her already battered knees on rough bark. Settling beside Robby on a stout branch, she put an arm around him to seek solace as well as to give it. The tree was an escape for them both, an escape from the pain and loss and inconsistencies of life. "Doc Allen says Hoover will be fine. He might feel pretty sick for a few days, but he'll be home soon. He'll want you to scratch his belly."

Robby gazed at her through wet, black lashes. "Mama's the best belly-scratcher in the family. Daddy said so."

Meg blinked at the thought of Sky and Robby and Zack. She resented the intrusion. She wanted the title of "Best Burkhart Belly-Scratcher," and she wanted Zack and Robby all to herself. But she had to leave. And soon she'd have to break that news to Robby.

The child snuggled closer. She hugged him against her side. They stayed that way, looking out over the pasture, under the clearing sky. Dampness from the rough cottonwood bark penetrated the seat of the jeans Meg now wore in place of the silky skirt. Dampness reminded her of the rain. Of what had happened before the storm. Of a passion that exceeded even the heights of fantasy. Heat flushed her breasts and rose to her hairline.

Robby, oblivious to Meg's errant thoughts, pointed to a bird flitting high in the tree branches. "It's Cheeper!" he exclaimed.

Meg looked up and saw the flash of gray-brown wings. Although all wrens looked alike to her, she pretended recognition. Another set of grayish wings flitted by. "Look, Robby. He's found a friend."

The child craned his neck to see directly above him. He leaned against Meg. She relaxed, and she could feel him doing the same.

Summer bloomed all about them. The clouds were gone now. Late afternoon sun heated grass and flowers, sending a fresh scent into the air. A cria, newly awakened from its nap, frolicked in the pasture, bounding through the wet grass like a furry antelope.

Tobias drove up in his truck. Win came out of the garage to greet him. The two of them went into the building together. A breeze whispered through shimmering leaves, releasing a shower of stockpiled raindrops.

"I'm ready to go in now," Robby announced. "I want a cookie."

Relieved at his rebound to normalcy, Meg scrambled out of the tree and hit the ground with a little too much assistance from gravity.

After helping Robby down, she limped inside, where she and Robby ate and read a story and talked. The sun dipped and sank below the horizon.

Hours passed. Meg became more and more uneasy. Had Hoover taken a turn for the worse? Zack should have returned by now. He had said he'd go by the sheriff's office, and that nagged at her. Once upon a time, she'd looked upon policemen as friends, but no more. Not since her time in jail. She'd given up expecting fairness from the law or its representatives. Fear gripped her chest, making it difficult to breathe. If Zack found out her secret from someone else . . .

She forced herself to inhale and exhale in a regular rhythm. The sheriff had no reason to investigate her. Silverstein had promised no one from the parole office would check on her whereabouts before Monday's meeting. No one here could possibly know. She was safe.

Long after Win and Robby had gone to sleep, Meg sat at the computer. She worked up an asset sheet for Zack to show the bankers next time he looked for a loan. She was about to go cross-eyed when she finally closed the ranch ledgers and turned off the hard drive. It was nearly eleven. She missed Zack. What was taking him so long?

Leaning back in the chair, she closed her eyes, gritty from hours at the computer. She allowed herself to fantasize.

Tonight Zack would come to her room and make love to her. She would be the only woman in his mind and heart. They would spent the whole night in each other's arms. She'd tell him about G. T. and why she'd broken the law, and he wouldn't condemn her. He'd understand. He'd continue to hold her, kiss her, tell her he'd always love her.

She straightened, shaking her head. A *happily ever after* was not meant to be. Even in the best possible scenario, his heart still belonged to another. This afternoon had been sweet carnal bliss, but that was all. Sure, they'd needed each other, but need was not the same as love.

In Zack's memory, Sky was perfection. Nothing would ever mar her image. No woman could ever compete. Certainly not Meg, with her lies and mottled past.

Inwardly, she shrank from that past, but hiding it was pointless. And dishonest, too. Tonight, all the lies had to end.

She was in the kitchen making a fresh pot of coffee when she heard a truck racing down the long gravel drive, screeching to a halt. She glanced out the kitchen window as Zack leaped from the truck. Rounding the hood, he slammed a fist into the rusted metal with a force that rocked the entire frame. His heavy, determined footsteps crossed the yard and forged up the porch steps.

Meg sensed tension coiled in him like a compressed spring in a steel box. She tried to convince herself he was angry about the poisoning, or about yet another llama death. But she knew there was something more. Something more direct and personal.

He knows. Bile rose in Meg's throat, along with dread. *He knows about me. Somehow he's discovered everything I was trying to hide.*

Chapter Seventeen

Zack was furious, almost shaking with wrath as he stepped into the well-lit kitchen. Meg, with her back against the counter, looked as wary as a cornered badger. And, at least to him, twice as dangerous.

She'd lied. Not once, but again and again. Even now that he had all the evidence, he still wanted to believe in her, which showed how badly she'd screwed up his brain.

He ignored the way her big green eyes widened as he stalked nearer. He didn't stop until his hips were inches from hers. Over the aroma of fresh-brewed coffee and chocolate chip cookies, he caught her womanly scent. She smelled like a field of flowers.

He leaned closer, forcing her to bend backward over the counter. Her dilated eyes tempted; her lips parted. "Zack," she whispered. "What is it? What's wrong?"

Everything. Every damn thing, especially the sharp-edged desire he had for her even now. He wanted desperately to touch her feather-soft hair and breathe in her innocence. But she'd cheated and deceived him. He could never touch her again.

A heaviness in his loins, a tremor in his hands made him step back. He pulled a bundle of mail

from his hip pocket and tossed it on the counter beside her. "The afternoon delivery," he said.

As she looked at the contents of her post office
box—her instrument of deceit—horror filled her eyes.
Horror and something else. Relief? That was it. She
thought the letters were all he knew.

"I was going to tell you," she said.

He was fresh out of sympathy. "Yeah? When? I
opened a few envelopes, in case you're wondering.
The Red Hawk address was so strange, curiosity got
the best of me. And, yes, there's money. You made
quite a haul. A slick scheme, I'll give you that. Did
you plan to send a good-bye note after you'd deposited the checks? After you'd run off and left me to
fill the orders?"

Meg paled. "You don't understand. I did it for
you. A surprise. I wanted to tell you today, but after
what you said up on the mountain . . . about Sky
and your dreams . . . I was afraid—"

"Afraid I'd come to the right conclusion? That
you're a liar and a thief?" The bitterness came
straight from his heart. His voice roared through the
small room and reverberated off the window glass.

She flinched but denied nothing. His pain etched
a little deeper. Although the whole crazy scheme
wore her fingerprints, he had hoped she would convince him otherwise.

He pointed to the stack of mail. "Maybe you'd like
to add up the checks, just to see how close you are
to whatever goal you've set for yourself." His voice
was hard and tight as he clung to the pretense that
he cared about the money, when in fact it was her
betrayal that ripped him to shreds.

"I would never steal from you," she said quietly,
looking at him with the spring-green eyes he'd
thought were guileless.

He did want to believe her. But he knew too much.

He knew all her dirty secrets. "Why didn't you tell me about your criminal record?"

She looked stunned, shocked, overwhelmed. That response, he was sure, was honest. She hadn't expected him to find out any of this. She'd expected to get away clean.

"I went by the sheriff's office," he said. "Utah Department of Corrections sent a fax to Abe Larkin this morning, wanting a confirmation that you're in the area. Abe made a few calls to see what you'd done." Zack banged an open hand on the counter, rattling the coffee pot on the stove. "Right before you came here, you did four months for emptying the bank account of that wicked stepfather you told me about."

She held his gaze. "I have been in jail, but I can explain why—"

"Did you take the money?" he shouted.

"Yes, but—"

"Spare me the details. How can you expect me to believe anything you say now?" He'd wanted her to deny the whole thing. He'd hoped she would explain it away as one of those mix-ups with names and social security numbers, some government error. Her simple admission left him ice cold, inside and out.

Tears flooded her eyes. Her lower lip quivered and she clasped it in her teeth. She turned away, pressing the heels of her hands to her eyes. "You're right, Zack. I can't expect you to believe me. That's why I never told you."

He felt himself warming to her. God help him, he wanted to draw her into his arms and hold her until she seduced his bitterness away. Because he feared she'd succeed, he didn't give her the chance. "Good thing I found out about the Red Hawk scheme *after* I talked to the sheriff. If I'd told Abe about that, he'd have you in the slammer before you could blink."

She whirled around. "W-will you tell him?" The panic in her eyes warred against Zack's disillusioned heart.

He stared at her for a long moment. He wanted to hurt her for hurting him. He owed her nothing, less than nothing. And he should tell Abe, if only to keep her from pulling a fast one on some other poor schmuck. Sighing, he looked up at the cold fluorescent light in the ceiling. He couldn't do it. "No, I won't tell the sheriff anything."

"Please don't hate me." She placed a hand on his arm, an appeal to the chemistry between them. "Don't think the worst, like everyone else. Please . . ." Her eyes pooled with heartbreaking earnestness, which Zack knew to be false.

He pushed her hand away. "You're damn right, everyone will think the worst. The sheriff already has a notion you're the llama killer. I told him it couldn't be you, but—"

"I didn't hurt your llamas, Zack. I wouldn't—"

"That much, I believe. You'd never be *physically* cruel. You're only out for the money, right? You screwed me, literally, while you picked my threadbare pocket."

Tears seeped from under eyelids she squeezed tightly closed. For some damn stupid reason, Zack could taste the salt of those tears.

"You are good, Meg. Really talented at what you do. The show was *almost* worth the money."

She bit down on her lower lip, drawing a tiny bead of blood. "How did you get into my post office box?"

"Thought I'd do you a favor, since you're always so eager for the mail."

"Y-you don't have a key," she stammered. "The postman's not supposed to release the contents to anyone but—"

"You're a fine one to talk about proper procedure.

Is it legal for you to sell my property? Most people would call that out-and-out theft."

"I only wanted to help." Her eyes opened wide, pleading.

He snorted in disbelief. "Hell, Meg, I gave you everything I had to give. If you wanted to 'help,' why weren't you honest with me?"

"The Red Hawk plan was meant to be a surprise. And the other . . . I was afraid you'd hate me," she whispered.

And he did. Almost. He hated her almost as much as he wanted to carry her to his bed and love away all the lies.

"Now I know why you planned on leaving this Sunday," he accused. "By then, you'd have plenty of time to gather the checks. Take the money and run, right? Before the big dumb rancher figures out he's been had."

"That's not true." Her voice had no force or fire. Nothing but resignation.

The pain hardened Zack's heart and made him spew the cruelest words he could think of. "I fell for you, Meg. How could I have been so stupid, when I know what real love is? Sky never lied to me. She never stole or cheated or—"

"Yes, I know." Meg sighed. "Sky the Perfect."

"Sky the Honest, at least. I could *trust* her. More than I can say for you." He knew he'd hit a bull's-eye. Shame spread over her face in a blotch of hot pink.

Meg skimmed past him, the tears flowing freely. He started to let her go, then changed his mind. Grabbing her wrist, he held on while she pushed at his arm. "You're not flitting away from this."

He seized her around the waist and sat her on the kitchen table. Leaning his palms on the smooth wood on either side of her hips, he leaned closer, until his nose almost touched hers, until he could feel her warm breath on his lips. "Exactly how did your scheme work? Was Edward in on it?" And to think he'd sympathized with her heartache, worried about her not letting go. The whole jilting scene was probably a deception.

"Do you really believe I'd cheat you?" she asked. Quietly. With dignity. Her chin was up now. She'd donned pride like an armor.

He ran a hand through his hair, agonizing over the facts, wishing he could change them. "What else can I think?"

"I wouldn't have taken a penny for myself, I swear. I wanted to help you keep the ranch. I wanted—"

"I'm the one who's wanting, Meg. You've driven me to the brink of insanity with wanting you. Even after what you've done."

A powerful force drew him to her. He crushed her body against his, sealed her lips with his own, spread her knees so he could move between her thighs. He tasted the salt of her tears, felt her moisture on his own face. Was she crying because of regret? Because maybe something about their passion had been real? He ached to possess her right then and there. He wanted to plunder and despoil her, lay claim to what should have been his. The probing kiss went on too long. His need became raw and hot.

He didn't intend to let her go until he was damn good and ready, no matter how much she fought. Except she didn't fight, or struggle, or even fail to respond. Instead, she kissed him back. Sweet Jesus, she felt good, tasted good.

He tore his mouth from hers, releasing her too-willing flesh. She'd taken his good judgment from him once, and she was doing it again. He grasped the edge of the table. With a violent shove that rocked the heavy oak trestle, he pushed away from her. He used the back of his wrist to wipe his mouth clean. She tasted like wild honey, but she was as much a poison as whatever was in the llama feed. No, it wasn't Meg that was poison, but the way he wanted her. The poison was in his own soul, in the terrible rampaging lust he felt in spite of everything.

"You have to believe in me," she whispered through lips puffy from his bruising assault.

He turned away. He couldn't look at her. To look at her was to want her. And he couldn't bear to hear more lies, not with her sweet taste still on his tongue. "It's no use, Meg. First thing tomorrow, I want you out of here. Go back to Edward. You and he would both slit your own mother's throat for twenty bucks. You belong with him."

"I don't belong with Edward. I never have." Her voice keened with longing.

Longing for what?

Zack proceeded out the door, down the steps. His mingled lust and anger raged so near the surface, he didn't dare ask, didn't dare look back.

Chapter Eighteen

Meg stood in the middle of the kitchen, hoping she'd wake up from the nightmare, hoping Zack would suddenly understand and come back to her. Drifting to the window, she looked out into the darkness. Lights came on in the barn. She imagined him peering into Hilda's stall, tossing the pregnant llama an extra flake of alfalfa from the bale by the door.

The barn lights went off. She saw him leave the building and get into his truck. After a few engine revs, the tires crunched gravel and sped down the long drive.

Red taillights grew smaller and smaller. The last mechanical sounds faded into the muted voice of darkness. Meg took a deep breath, closed her eyes, and centered her energy on mending the hurt inside her, at least enough to allow her mind to function. Zack had cast her out after giving her the closest thing to true acceptance she'd ever experienced.

She should have told him sooner, though the cynic deep inside her wondered if it would have made any difference. He might have despised her no matter how or where he had learned her unsavory history. She had imagined living in a fairy-tale castle with Zack, but her never-relenting past—and his—had slammed the gates and locked her out forever.

She would not wait for morning. How could she

face Zack again? How could she bear the awful distrust and disappointment in his eyes? She'd leave the letters and checks behind, of course. When he saw them, he'd know she'd told the truth about Red Hawk. But she'd be gone by then.

Searching the bottom-most drawer beside the sink, under the dishtowels, she located the rest of the Red Hawk mail and stacked all of it on the kitchen table. As she stared at the pristine white against time-polished oak, she tried not to remember the punishing-sweet kiss Zack had delivered at this very table, only a few moments before.

After bundling the mail in a rubber band, she took it to Zack's office. In the dark room, she fumbled with a lamp. She scrounged for a pen and scratched the PenUltimate address on the uppermost envelope. The address would serve as a point of contact, since she had no place of her own. She didn't really expect Zack to communicate, but she would feel better knowing the possibility existed.

She kissed the envelope he would touch in a few hours, wishing some of what she felt for him might bleed through like an overflow of ink. Then she placed the stack of correspondence beside the telephone receiver on the desk. Red Hawk had been a cataclysmic success. She'd done her best for Zack, but he didn't want her help. Didn't want *her*.

The worst would be leaving Robby. He was a pawn in this, as all children were pawns, subject to adult emotions and hazards that altered young lives on a whim. She went to the boy's room, tiptoeing across the braided rug to kiss him once, quietly, stealthily.

His cheek was soft and cool, and his breath smelled like toothpaste. Light from the hall highlighted his small nose and parted lips. She smoothed his soft, thick hair one last time.

She was turning to leave when she noticed the dreamcatcher swaying in the open window. She stood in front of it for a moment, tracing a finger over the llama-wool web, touching the cool beads nested there.

"Do your work well," she whispered. "Send him only the sweetest of dreams."

She'd wanted to be his dreamcatcher, both day and night, but her time had run out.

At least he'd grown closer to Zack since she'd been on the ranch. And Zack was beginning to open up to the boy. The two of them would be all right.

In her own room, she gathered her few possessions and laced on sturdy hiking boots. With the old blue backpack thrown over one shoulder, she walked down the hall and out through the kitchen door, into the night. Town was ten miles distant, the closest place to catch a bus.

A crescent moon silvered the meadow. Dew from the high grass seeped into her socks. The air smelled sweet, full of moonbeams and mountain summer, in sharp contrast to the winter in her heart. When she reached the road, she turned and glanced back. The house was silent, listing to the east, endearingly familiar.

She had been happy there.

Robby was restless and hot, even with the covers kicked to the floor. He awoke with pieces of a dream scrambled in his mind.

His mother had come to him. She'd come down from the misty mountaintop to fluff his pillow and snug the sheets around him like she used to do. But when she leaned close for a good-night kiss, Robby heard Meg's voice in his ear. She said, "Good-bye."

It seemed real. Too real for a dream. Real enough

so he got out of bed, yawning, and wobbled across the hall to Meg's room.

He knocked, like Daddy had said he must do, because all grown-up ladies liked their privates. Robby didn't understand why that made any difference. He liked his privates, too, but he didn't care if people knocked before they came in his room.

When Meg didn't answer, he opened the door and went inside. The quilt was smoothed over her bed, too flat for anyone to be underneath.

Suddenly wide awake, Robby knelt to look beneath the bed, where he knew she kept her blue backpack. It was gone.

He dragged a chair to the bureau and pulled out the top drawer. She kept shorts and shirts and lacy stuff in there, but her clothes were gone, too. Even the picture of the llamas he'd drawn special for her was not taped to the mirror anymore.

His heart bumped too hard, like it belonged in Cheeper when the tiny bird fell from its nest. Meg had made Robby feel special. With her, he was safe in his own little nest. He didn't want her to be gone. He wanted to tear the quilt off the bed and dig in the mattress until he found her. He wanted to climb to the highest limb of the cottonwood tree. He wanted to cry.

He ran to Daddy's bedroom. Daddy could find Meg, couldn't he? Robby hoped so, but he wasn't as sure as he wanted to be. Daddy hadn't brought Mama back, even though both of them had wanted her to come home real bad.

Robby felt a little better since Daddy's bed was empty, too. Maybe Meg was with him somewhere. Grandma Win said sometimes grown-ups wanted to be alone, like when Grandma and Tobias locked the door on the garage and it took them a real long time to open it.

He thought about getting Grandma out of bed, but when she snored loud, like right now, she'd be grumpy as a grizzly if he woke her. So he'd look for Meg and Daddy by himself. Maybe Hilda had had her baby, and both of them were petting the new cria. That made sense. That must be where they'd gone. He didn't know why Meg had brought all her clothes with her, but Daddy would figure it out and explain. Robby wished Hoover were with him. He missed having a friend, especially when it was dark and scary out. Maybe he could go visit the dog at the vet's office tomorrow. Maybe he could bring Hoover home by then.

As he entered the barn, he heard Hilda in a stall, rustling the straw. He couldn't reach the light, and he didn't want to wake up the baby if Hilda had already birthed it. He climbed on the ladder rungs that he and Daddy had built beside the stall door, so he could see inside. Hilda's belly was still big. There was no sign of a cria nestled in the bedding.

Robby decided to stay with Hilda until Tobias came to start morning chores. Tobias would find Daddy and Meg.

He climbed onto the stall gate, shimmied up the beam, and pulled himself into the rafters above the stall. He felt better there. Safer. Closer to Meg and Mama.

The crickets chirruped over and over like a lullaby. The darkness made him want to sleep. The rafters' triangles cocooned him, keeping him safe. He wrapped his arms around a beam so he wouldn't fall and leaned his head against the splintery wood. He'd rest for a while, until Tobias came. His heavy eyelids drifted lower and closed altogether.

Hilda brayed a high-pitched alarm, almost startling Robby off his perch. He opened his eyes and peered down. Below him, someone murmured words he couldn't understand. Starlight filtered through the loft window like a flashlight when the batteries ran down. A shadowy figure, all in black, loomed just inside Hilda's stall. It looked like a ninja doll Grandma Win had given him on his birthday, except bigger.

Robby held tight to the beam. His stomach felt all fluttery, like a moth had gotten inside. He knew he ought to do something, but he didn't know what.

Boots rustled through the bedding.

Hilda squealed, ears laid flat against her neck. She backed into a corner. With legs splayed, she was ready to spit. The ninja reached out toward the panicky llama. In the dim light Robby saw an object in the gloved hand. It was a huge syringe with a long sharp needle on the end, a really big needle. No wonder Hilda was afraid. The llama wasn't sick, and this wasn't Doc Allen, the vet. Why would someone give her a shot in the middle of the night, without even turning on the lights? Maybe this person was going to hurt Hilda, or hurt the baby she carried in her belly.

Robby knew he had to do something. He whooped a Sioux war cry he'd learned from Grandma Win and jumped down into the thick straw. He hoped the ninja would be scared and run away before finding out how small Robby was.

The black figure *did* run, but Robby had landed right by the stall gate and he was in the way. The ninja struck out, spinning Robby and knocking him face first into the straw.

A sharp pain stabbed the top of his leg like he'd fallen on a nail. He heard footsteps thumping out the barn door. He thought maybe he should chase the bad person, but his stomach hurt, and he couldn't breathe. The tumble had knocked all the air out of him. His throat made funny gasping noises. He lifted his face from the straw for a moment, then gave up the effort.

Hilda nuzzled him, her nose warm and wet on his neck. He smelled the alfalfa she'd been eating. After a while, when he could breathe better, he scrambled to his feet. By then, Hilda had wandered out the stall door. Uh-oh. Daddy never let the llamas roam free in the barn. Robby would have to catch her.

His leg hurt and he wondered why something sharp was in Hilda's stall. The bedding should be smooth and soft for the new baby. He'd have to dig in the straw to find what had pricked him, before the cria got hurt, too. When he bent down to have a look, he saw a needle stuck through his pajama shorts, right into the skin of his thigh where he'd gotten a tetanus shot last spring.

Except this was bigger. A lot bigger. He plucked out the needle and stared at it. He was afraid, and not just because of a shot, even if it was huge. He didn't like bad people sneaking around the barn. Maybe the same person had poisoned the grain Hoover ate. Maybe the shot would do something bad to a llama. Or to a boy.

He dropped the syringe just outside the gate so he could show it to Daddy later. Right now, he had to get Hilda back in her stall. He called into the darkened corridor, but Hilda did not come. Robby thought she must be hiding. When he finally saw her, she was watching him from a shadowy corner. The white part of her eyes made circles around the dark brown centers. He moved slowly toward her, talking softly like Daddy had taught him to do. Finally, he was close enough. Hilda seemed a little calmer. He reached up to take hold of her halter, but she darted around him.

Hilda made for the sliding barn door and tried to squeeze through. It was not open wide enough for a llama with a swollen belly. Giving up, she backed away from the door and snorted at Robby. He chased her around the barn twice more before herding her into the stall. Just as he was about to close her in, she pushed past him and trotted down the corridor once more.

Robby's head felt funny, kind of light and whirling. He couldn't concentrate on catching Hilda because the walls were turning circles around him. He stumbled inside the stall where the straw was clean and deep. He was so sleepy.

He sank into the soft bedding.

It would be morning soon. Tobias would open the barn door and feed the animals. He'd find Daddy. He'd look for Meg. Everything would be all right when morning came.

Robby heard Meg's soft soothing voice, a whisper in his clouded thoughts. Had she really said, "Good-bye"?

His eyes closed, and he was dreaming once again.

Chapter Nineteen

Zack drove up a series of rutted dirt roads to a mountain pass above the ranch. After parking the truck on the edge of a precipice, he stayed in his seat and stared into the night.

A full hundred yards below, he distinguished the silhouette of the huge fir tree beneath which he and Meg had made love. Another thousand feet down, a speck of dark-on-dark identified the ranch. A crescent moon hung low over the bank of mountains to the west, leeching color from the valley, veiling the world in gray and black.

He dropped his forehead to the steering wheel and wished he could shut out betrayal as easily as he closed his eyes to the night. Meg had been planning this fleece job for weeks, and he'd never once guessed. He'd believed in her, maybe even loved her. He cursed under his breath. Denial would do no good now. He *had* loved her. Definitely past tense. He'd never expected to let a woman into his life again. Meg had caught him off guard. He'd allowed himself to cherish her, want her, need her.

He leaned back, using the seat's lumpy headrest for a pillow, and thought it through one more time. He kept seeing the anguish in Meg's eyes. If she were guilty of what she seemed to be, why the Oscar-winning performance tonight? She'd probably already collected God knew how much money at his expense. He'd promised not to inform the sheriff. What more could she want?

She'd claimed the Red Hawk scheme was an innocent attempt to help, and he could almost believe that. But compounded with a criminal record, also a secret, it was just too much to swallow.

Her crimes bothered him less than the deceit. He'd trusted Meg. He'd told her how he felt about his life, his land, his family. She'd pretended to listen and care. Even as he'd opened his soul to her, she had plotted to steal his meager possessions as well as his heart. How could she be that cold and unfeeling?

Hell, she'd robbed her own family, according to the police report. If she could do that, he wouldn't put anything past her.

If. Why did he doubt? She'd been convicted. And when he'd confronted her, she as much as admitted everything. But the doubt was still there.

He argued and contradicted and reasoned with himself until he felt like vomiting his guts over the cliff. In the end, he was right back where he started. Angry and hollow and overwhelmingly sad.

The milk-white crescent sank below the horizon. He wasn't solving anything by sitting in the dark. The clock on the dash said 3 A.M. He had to go back. He still had the same responsibilities that had kept him going for the past year. From experience, he knew duty would hold him together and keep the worst of the emptiness at bay.

He would sleep the rest of the night in the barn, well away from Meg. Hilda was near her time, which gave him an excuse. Most crias were born in the morning, but he often spent at least one night with an expectant mother. He liked to be nearby in case of a problem. With someone intent on sabotaging the ranch, vigilance seemed an especially good idea.

On the way down the wet mountain road, he

drove too fast, hitting rocks and ruts, skidding on the muddy turns. In the morning, he decided, he'd talk to Meg again.

You have to believe in me, she'd said. He'd make her explain that. All he needed was one good reason why he *should* believe.

The pickup rattled more than usual as it crunched to a halt in the driveway. The suspension had had a helluva workout on the mountain roads. Zack felt as if he'd taken a worse beating than the truck. As he got out and approached the barn, he noted someone had left the door partly open. He thought he remembered sliding it shut earlier. His scalp prickled.

A prowler—*the* prowler—might be within.

Zack listened for footsteps, watched for shadows, before moving silently through the door. When Hilda's high-pitched, anxious hum originated from the wrong side of the building, Zack knew for certain that something was wrong. The salty scents of uterine fluid and blood blended with the sharp-sweet tang of alfalfa. Hilda must have delivered the cria, but why was she outside her stall?

He flicked on the lights. At the end of the long corridor between stalls, Hilda craned her neck, nostrils flared.

"Easy, girl," Zack said softly.

Once she'd seen Zack, her humming pitch lowered to one of crooning contentment. She lowered her nose to the small bedraggled bundle in front of her. Zack kept his distance, waiting to see if the cria would nurse on its own.

The newborn rolled and attempted to rise, spindly legs splayed out in four directions. He bucked and wrestled to keep those legs in order, until finally he balanced himself. Shakily, he wobbled toward his mother, butting her woolly sides as he sought breakfast. When at last he found the udder, he latched on and sucked greedily. Hilda made soft cooing noises, the sounds of contentment. She'd done a good job, even if she'd delivered on the hard-packed dirt of the corridor instead of on straw.

Which reminded Zack . . . Why was she out of her stall? He thought about trying to urge her and the baby back where they belonged, but decided against it. He wouldn't disturb them tonight. Instead, he'd block off that side of the barn to give them privacy.

Outside, an engine roared down the drive. A truck door slammed. Tobias must have arrived early for feeding. Or maybe he, like Zack, was making a pre-dawn check on Hilda's progress.

Once again, Zack wondered about Tobias, but he shoved aside the suspicion. The man was good with the animals, with Robby, and—if Meg had told the truth for once—with Win. If Zack was any judge of character, Tobias could no more kill a llama than Meg could.

Meg. He'd never really looked at Meg as a serious suspect, even though she'd been on the ranch during most of the trouble. He didn't know anything about her, when he came right down to it. Could she be involved somehow? He shook his head and refused to consider the possibility. Refused to consider any aspect of her betrayal. He'd done enough thinking about Meg for one night. His head was starting to pound.

To take his mind off her, he crossed the dirt corridor to examine the bolt on Hilda's open stall door. Llamas were intelligent creatures. He'd known a few who could unlatch gates, although Hilda had never done it before. His gaze fell on something at the edge of the stall's thick bedding. He bent down for a closer look and found a syringe half full of liquid.

Sabotage again? Sabotage of what? He glanced back toward Hilda. The cria still had its head under

Mama's belly, enjoying a noisy breakfast, while Hilda nuzzled its scrawny haunches. Everything except the open stall door seemed normal. But the syringe meant someone had been here. Maybe he'd arrived in time to scare off the intruder before any damage was done.

Hoping the syringe had fingerprints on it, he picked it up with his handkerchief. After unscrewing the needle and tossing it in a trash bin outside the stall, he stuffed the syringe in his back pocket. He'd give it to the sheriff and make sure Abe had the prints and contents analyzed.

As he glanced inside the stall, something half-covered in straw caught his eye. With a start, he realized he was looking at Robby's pale blue pajamas. The boy was curled up on his side. Cold fear curdled in Zack's chest as he knelt beside his son. Robby was so small, so terribly defenseless. And he'd been out here alone. With a syringe-toting maniac.

Zack thought the boy was sleeping at first, until he turned him over. Blue-green eyes stared trance-like at the rafters. Horror gripped Zack like the fist of an invisible giant. Desperately, he fumbled for a neck pulse while putting his face close to the boy's mouth. He felt the warm exhale of air on his cheek as his fingers sensed the rush of blood through veins. Robby was alive. But the gaping eyes were eerie, terrifying, with the still look of death.

Zack gathered Robby's limp body in his arms.

The barn door grated as it slid open a few extra inches to admit Tobias's broad girth. Carrying Robby, Zack strode toward the hired hand.

"Zack?" Tobias blinked at the light and at the child in Zack's arms. "What's Robby doing here?"

"I found him in Hilda's stall, along with a half-empty syringe." Zack brushed past Tobias and out the door.

Tobias hurried after them. "What the hell?"

Zack nodded. "That about sums it up. See to Hilda and the new cria, would you? I'll call Win from the hospital."

"Daddy."

Zack's eyes felt gritty, his brain befogged, as he raised his head. He was in a chair with his lower body resting on the bed where Robby lay. The child was wide awake. His small face and dark hair were surrounded by white instead of the colorful animal-design sheets he had on his bed at home. Zack's gaze took in flowery yellow wallpaper, a waxed terrazzo floor. Pale morning light percolated through beige curtains.

The hospital, Zack remembered. Every detail of the night before came howling back. Meg's betrayal. Robby's coma. The awful waiting while the doctor examined the child. The profound relief when the boy slept normally at last.

"Where's Meg, Daddy?" Robby squinted as if he had a hard time focusing. "I want to see her."

Zack reached under the sheet to find the boy's hand and envelop it in his own much larger one. He hadn't thought of Robby during last night's confrontation with Meg. He'd forgotten how good she had been with his son, how quickly Robby had learned to love her.

"I'll bring her to you, Robby, I promise." He'd drag her feet first if he had to. After what she'd done, she owed Robby that much. "Can you tell me what happened last night?"

Robby nodded solemnly. "I was looking for you and Meg. She wasn't in her bed. When I couldn't find you, either, I was scared."

Zack wondered where Meg was and hoped she hadn't been upset enough to take off alone in the middle of the night. No matter what she'd done, he didn't want her in danger. But he'd worry about that later.

Since Robby hadn't found Meg, and since Win had the capacity to sleep through a volcanic eruption, it wasn't surprising the boy had ended up wandering around by himself.

"What happened in the barn?" Zack urged.

Robby told, in detail, about the all-in-black ninja, and the syringe. "Is Hilda okay?" he asked, puckering his brow anxiously.

It was like Robby to worry about an animal before himself. Paternal love and pride burgeoned. Zack almost smiled. "Hilda was nursing a healthy-looking baby when I saw her, son. You did a fine job protecting her." According to the doctor, Robby had been injected with some kind of tranquilizer. Hilda must have escaped the syringe, since she'd shown no aftereffects. Instead, the boy had taken the brunt of it.

Robby yawned. "Meg's not really gone, is she? In my dream, she told me good-bye."

Zack's heart snagged in the middle of a beat before kicking back into rhythm. She couldn't be gone already. He needed to talk to her . . . about Robby. To ask what she'd seen and heard last night. To ask a dozen questions he'd neglected before. "Don't worry, partner." He spoke to calm himself as much as the boy. Smoothing dark hair from Robby's forehead, he noted the heavy-lidded eyes. "Rest awhile longer. I'll have Meg here by the time you wake up."

When Robby slept again, Zack crept down the hall to the deserted waiting room where he could phone the ranch without disturbing the boy. Win answered on the first ring.

"Robby's okay," he assured her, "but we'll be here a few hours." After he'd explained the child's condition, Win cursed fluently, alternating Lakota Sioux with gutter English. It took a full minute for her to wind down.

"Wake Meg and bring her to the phone," he said when Win calmed enough to listen. "And don't let her refuse to talk to me, because it's important." He'd convinced himself she would be in her bed now. She had to be.

Win clanked down the phone. Zack tuned his senses for Meg's light, sweet pitch. He was sorely disappointed when Win's harsher voice came on the line again.

"She's not in her room." Win sounded out of breath. "All her things are gone."

Zack felt like a black hole, all weight and no visible light. He felt utterly abandoned, although he was the one who'd ordered her to leave.

"Meet me at the clinic," he told Win. "Keep an eye out for Meg along the way. Robby's asked for her, and we have to find her for him. If she's on foot, she can't have gone far." He should have passed her when he brought Robby to the hospital, although there were a lot of shortcuts across fields she might have taken. And since she wouldn't be eager to see him again, she might well have ducked all headlights.

He severed the connection with Win and immediately dialed the sheriff's office.

"Figured I'd be hearing from you, Zack. I was going to ring you up in a minute." Abe Larkin paused, having said just enough to tantalize.

Intuition made Zack grip the phone with both hands. "What is it? Have you seen Meg?"

"How'd you know?" Abe sounded disappointed that Zack had guessed the secret with so little fanfare.

Zack started to breathe again. She was in town. He couldn't guess why she had gone to see the sheriff, but it didn't matter as long as he knew where she was. He collapsed into the waiting room's vinyl love seat.

His heart was beating way too fast. Only now did he realize how afraid he'd been. Never mind that there hadn't been a violent crime in the county in his memory. Robby's assailant was still wandering around. "Keep her there, Abe. I'll be right—"

"She's not in the office. I saw her limping along Main Street half an hour ago when I drove by. Since she was carrying a pack and looking lower than whale dung, I figured the two of you'd had a falling out. Wasn't too surprised after what we learned about her. Innocent and sweet as she looks, who'd've guessed?"

The love seat creaked as Zack shifted his weight. He felt something under his thigh and pulled out a worn stuffed rabbit, apparently left there by a forgetful child. The well-loved, nearly colorless fur stuck out in some places and was absent in others. Black button eyes seemed to accuse him.

"Not me, that's for sure," Zack said wearily. "The main thing is finding her. We had a problem at the ranch last night, and—"

"More llama trouble?"

"Somebody was prowling around the barn. Robby got in the middle of it," Zack explained.

"I sure hate to hear that. Nothing serious, I hope?"

"Not too bad. Looks like the prowler meant to stick my pregnant llama with a potent tranquilizer. The needle ended up in Robby's leg. Fortunately, he didn't get a full dose."

"You still have that syringe?" Abe asked.

"I brought it here to the hospital. Thought the doctor might want it, but he got what he needed from a blood analysis on Robby. You can come by and pick it up. Might be some fingerprints." On a hunch, Zack added, "Robby's eyes were open when I found him, and his muscles seemed paralyzed. The vet uses something for short surgeries that acts the same way. Wasn't there a robbery at Doc Allen's awhile back?"

"About six weeks ago, I think." Papers rustled. "I have the report here somewhere." More rustling.

"Find it," Zack said. "See what was missing. Seems to me there's probably a connection."

"How's your Meg involved?" Abe asked. "Think she's in on it?"

"Not on this," Zack said. At least he hoped not. He shook his head to clear it. Of course Meg hadn't hurt his llamas. And never Robby. "I just want you to find her." Zack lifted a hand and realized he still held the rabbit. He dropped it on the couch, narrowing his eyes at the stuffed toy as if it were somehow responsible for the disaster this day had become.

"When is the next bus due?" He had to reach Meg before she left town.

"Think I have time to keep up with the Greyhound schedule? I'm a busy man. But I do have an 800 number . . . somewhere." A long pause, with sounds of drawers opening and sliding shut. "Dawgone it, I was sure I'd put it . . ."

Zack gripped the love seat cushion. If he were near enough, he'd have decked the sheriff and searched the desk himself.

"We're in luck!" Abe said with the marvel of a caveman who'd just discovered the wheel. "I opened the front blinds and there she blows. The little lady, not the bus. She's right across the street at Max's gas station, sitting on the bench out front."

"Hallelujah." Zack exhaled the breath he'd been holding. He'd forgotten the bus loaded passengers in front of Max's since the old Roundhouse Café had gone out of business.

"Strange," Abe mused. "Ellen just came out of the

station. What's she doing in town so early, I wonder?"

"Maybe you should ask her. *After* you've talked to Meg. Don't let her get on a bus."

Abe grunted. "No problem. With her record, and with her running off right after the trouble with your boy, I'll have to question her."

Zack considered re-declaring her innocence—at least her innocence of hurting Robby—but he didn't see the point. Abe would maintain his view of the matter anyway. The sheriff had a damn thick skull.

"Do me one favor, Abe, and I'd be forever obliged. Tell Meg Robby's in the hospital. Then make sure she stays put until I get there."

"I'll keep her around, all right," Abe said.

"As soon as Win takes my place with Robby, I'll be on the road to your office."

"Take it easy," Abe soothed. "I'll see to Miss Delaney. Then I'll mosey on out to your ranch and have a look at the barn."

As Zack replaced the phone on the metal end table, he noticed the scruffy rabbit lying with one ear bent, face smashed into the cushions. Gently, he straightened the ear and sat the furry toy in a corner of the love seat. The creature reminded him of Meg the Easter Chick, soft and huggable.

Just because she *looked* innocent didn't mean anything. But Zack was angry with himself for breaking his own code of justice. No matter how much evidence he had against her, he should have heard her out.

As he trudged down the hall to Robby's hospital room, he hoped she had some kind of reasonable explanation for everything she'd done, something more than he'd already heard. Even if she didn't, even if she was as crooked as a crippled dog's hind leg, he'd make sure she stayed to help Robby through this recent trauma. In his heart, he knew he wouldn't have to make her. She loved Robby. Nothing could force her into leaving the child when he needed her.

Zack's blind faith in that part of her character started him wondering. If he believed in her where his son was concerned, maybe he was less convinced of her guilt than he'd thought.

When Meg saw the wraithlike woman headed her way, she nearly groaned in frustration. Several people had stopped to talk since she'd been sitting on the bench in front of Max's gas station. First Max himself, then the boy who swept the concrete each morning to keep it tidy, then Chet from the general store. Everyone wanted to know where Zack was, and what she was doing in town alone. They nodded sagely when she said she was leaving.

Of course, they'd all expected as much. She could see it in their eyes. Right now, Meg was past the point of caring. Her feet hurt. She was hot and sweaty and bone tired. She wasn't looking forward to more socializing, not with anyone. Unfortunately, she had nowhere to hide.

The thin woman sat down on the opposite end of the six-foot bench. "Are you leaving town?" she asked.

Meg sighed. "I'm waiting for a bus. Why else would I—" She stopped herself and bit back the sarcasm. "Yes, I'm leaving. Why do you want to know?"

The woman fumbled in the pocket of her gray fleece jacket and found a pill bottle. With trembling fingers, she extracted a tablet. She popped it in her mouth before stuffing the bottle out of sight. "I'm Ellen Caldwell. I live on the ranch next to Zack's."

Meg took a closer look. Zack had mentioned her.

So had a couple of town gossips Meg had overheard. Fragile, alcoholic Ellen, mother of the boy who died. Her face was gray, the same color as her jacket. In spite of her unhealthy skin tones, she had remarkable Liz Taylor eyes. Sad, beautiful eyes.

Ellen scraped limp brown hair back from sallow cheeks. "Sky was my friend. She still is."

Meg lifted her backpack from the ground to her lap. Her emotions were in no shape to deal with Sky memories. Meg had to escape. She shifted forward, but as weight came down on her blistered feet, she decided not to stand just yet. It had been a long ten miles to town.

"Zack and Sky were very close, you know."

Meg didn't want to hear this. She'd heard the story too many times.

"Not like me and my husband," Ellen added tonelessly. "Jesse loves no one but himself. He never cared much about Mike when he was alive. Now that our son's dead, he still doesn't care, except as an excuse to make trouble for Zack. The two of them never got along, but now Jesse's out for blood."

Meg wondered if this was an admission that Jesse was responsible for the llama deaths. If so, what should she do about it? *Nothing,* she told herself. *Zack doesn't want to hear anything from me. He wouldn't believe me anyway.* "Zack has suffered enough," Meg said in defense of the man she still loved. The same man who had judged her so harshly. "Sky's death devastated him, just as the loss of your son did to you. I hope it'll be easier for you and your husband, in time. Zack is . . . that is, I hope he's beginning to accept . . ."

"No!" Ellen's harsh protest made Meg jump. "He won't forget her. *You* almost ruined everything, but he's a good man. He'll make the sacrifice."

"Sacrifice?"

Ellen didn't answer, and Meg assumed the woman meant Zack would forego any other relationship to remain close to Sky. With the exception of yesterday afternoon, Ellen had guessed right.

There was something disturbing about Ellen's violet eyes. The pupils were grossly dilated. Maybe it was the pills. Meg knew the woman was caught up in a terrible depression. Unfortunately, Meg had no idea what to do about it. She had no idea what to do about her own heartache, either.

She glanced over her shoulder at the clock inside the gas station. The bus was late.

Meg wanted to escape Elk Springs. She didn't want to hear about Ellen or her malicious husband. She didn't want to think or talk about Zack, or worry about his problems. He'd barred her from his life, and she had to separate herself from everything about him. She peered down the road and caught a glint of silver at a corner stop sign. The bus.

She leaped off the bench, hastily slipping her arms into the pack straps. Her blisters made themselves known and felt as she hobbled toward the curb. Meg didn't mind. The pain in her feet made it easier to forget the pain in her heart.

"Destiny," Ellen said in a whispery voice. "No one escapes destiny."

Meg shook off what sounded like a prophecy and focused on the street. She pulled a ticket from her jeans pocket.

A Greyhound turned the corner onto the main street. Air brakes expelled gaseous exhaust as the vehicle hissed to a stop. Meg waited, shoulders tense beneath the pack straps, her knees locked against collapse.

The bus doors whooshed open. The driver, a petite grandmotherly woman seated on five inches of extra cushion, barked out a greeting. Meg nodded. She lacked the strength for a vocal response. She mounted dirty silver steps leading to the bus's cavernous, crowded interior. The too-warm air reeked of a nauseating cross between stale popcorn and ammonia. A child wailed from somewhere in the back. A woman in front complained to her neighbor that she hadn't had anything to eat except a Snickers bar since the evening before.

Before Meg could give the driver her ticket, someone grasped her arm from behind. "Step back down here, Miss Delaney. We need to talk." It was Abe Larkin, the sheriff.

She frowned at him, then glanced into the bus. "Could you wait a minute?" she asked the driver.

The gray-haired woman on the seat cushion rolled her eyes and shrugged.

Meg descended the tarnished stairs to the curb. "What is it, Sheriff?"

He tilted his white cowboy hat to scratch his forehead. His eyes seemed overlarge behind steel-rimmed glasses. "I hate interfering with your plans, miss, but you'll have to stay in town a while."

"This is the only bus until three this afternoon." She just *had* to make her getaway before Zack found out she was gone. She couldn't face his revulsion again. Tears built behind her eyelids. "Why can't I leave now?"

"Because . . ." The sheriff looked back toward the gas station bench. "Where's Ellen?"

"What?" she asked, confused by the change in subject.

"Ellen Caldwell." His eyes sharpened like knife blades. "I saw you sitting with her. You didn't start in on her, did you? You didn't bother her about Sky and her boy?"

"No, I—" She scanned the immediate area, but Ellen was nowhere in sight.

The sheriff grunted. "Never mind. You're coming with me for questioning."

Her heart pumped faster. "About Ellen?"

"No. All about you."

"Has something happened?" Meg knew the sheriff wouldn't bring her into his office to discuss past crimes. Was he going to question her about the llamas? Or could Zack have filed a complaint about Red Hawk already? He wouldn't, she was almost certain. No matter what she'd done, or what he believed she'd done, he wouldn't turn her over to the law. She was on parole. Surely he knew any legal complaint might land her back in jail.

"Seems Zack had a little trouble at his place last night," the sheriff said.

She masked a surge of heartache with a careless toss of her head. He *had* talked to the sheriff after he'd promised he wouldn't. "Is he going to press charges against me?"

The sheriff gave her a funny look, part surprise, part skepticism. "Can't say yet. Not until he gets here."

Pure panic set in. If she had to confront Zack and his accusations again, she'd fall apart, cry, scream. She wouldn't wait for more pain and suspicion to gather over her head like a thundercloud and pour its darkness upon her. "I won't stay. You have no right to—"

An impatient high-pitched voice screeched from inside the bus. "Hey, łady, you comin' or ain't you?"

"She ain't," the sheriff answered, holding onto Meg when she tried to wrench free.

"Let me go! You can't make . . ." The revving diesel engine drowned out the rest of Meg's protest.

Silver doors closed. Exhaust plumes wafted as the Greyhound rumbled down the street.

The sheriff shook his head. "Sorry, miss. You'll have to come with me."

After an initial flinch, Meg controlled her indignation and allowed him to guide her across the street to his office.

She half-expected floodlights and police brutality. She was so tired, staying awake was torture enough. Her blisters burned. Her spine felt as if she'd been standing all night. Which she had, come to think of it. She thought about demanding a lawyer, but she didn't have the energy. Besides, what good had legal advice done her the last time she'd faced charges? Let Sheriff Larkin question her to his hard heart's content. She would simply refuse to open her mouth. That way she couldn't incriminate herself.

"Have a seat." The sheriff pointed at a wooden chair in front of his desk. "I won't keep you long, Miss Delaney."

She'd heard those very same words right before her last arrest, which resulted in four months behind bars. "Call Zack," she blurted, jettisoning her pride. She couldn't stand being locked in a cell again, and Zack was her only hope. "This is a misunderstanding. He *wants* me to leave town."

"Maybe so, but he told *me* something different. He said to keep you right here. He'll be coming in, pronto, to file a complaint."

What kind of complaint? "I haven't done anything," she insisted desperately. Unless loving Zack was a crime. She'd heard somewhere that Idaho had a law on the books against fornication, but this was the new millennium, for heaven's sake.

The sheriff grunted. "We'll see. You might have Zack's silverware squirreled away in your knapsack."

"Zack doesn't *have* any silverware." She removed one strap and began to lower the backpack to prove she had nothing inside but cheap clothes, her camp stove, a pair of sandals, and a liter bottle of water.

The sheriff pointed toward the scuffed wooden chair again. "Sit. You're trying my patience."

"And you're trying mine." The pack was heavier than she'd thought. The strap slipped as she swung it in front of her.

The abrupt motion caught Sheriff Larkin by surprise. The backpack smacked him below his belt buckle, right in the groin. His face turned bright red as he struggled for breath and clutched his injury. "Damn it, that's enough," he panted. "I've by God had enough!"

"Sorry, Sheriff. I didn't intend . . ."

He wasn't listening. "If Zack thinks I'll risk my private parts over his run-in with a woman, he can think again. A man has to protect himself, and you are a goddamn hazard. I'm locking you up for assaulting an officer."

Dazed, Meg didn't resist as he pushed her firmly to the back of the office, into a narrow hall leading to a pair of cells. The reek of antiseptic, urine, sweat, and stomach acid issued from concrete walls painted a vile shade of green. Larkin forced her through the nearest barred door, reciting *Miranda* as he did so.

"Wait," Meg interrupted. Reality was setting in, and she didn't like where it was taking her. "This is all a mistake. You have to listen to—"

Too late. The clash of metal and jingle of keys seemed to arise from a cavity in Meg's brain. The sounds echoed down the many long nights she'd spent locked away from beauty and clean air, away from life, from love, from everything worth caring about.

The sheriff stalked away. Moments later, he reopened the hall door to toss her backpack on the floor outside her bars, just out of her reach. Without so much as glancing at her he vanished again, slamming the door behind him. Meg was alone with the zebra stripes shadowing her cell. Alone in the half-light. Alone.

The canvas flap of her backpack gaped wide. She glimpsed the rumpled contents, lace panties spilling onto a yellow stain on the concrete floor. The sheriff must have searched her belongings for weapons. She wondered what he'd thought about the underwear, what he'd think if he knew Zack had chosen them for her.

She paced the six-foot length of the cell once, twice. Her knees buckled. She sat heavily on the single cot. Hugging herself, she tried to still the shivering. She leaned her head back against the institution-green wall.

If she were unjustly condemned again, she wasn't sure she could survive. And if Zack were part of her destruction, the blow would shatter her into a million pieces. Zack, whom she loved—had loved.

Despair nibbled at her like a rat's incisors. She might have forgiven him for mistrusting her, for denying her a defense, for ordering her off his land. But if he'd really insisted the sheriff keep her against her will . . . if he'd had anything to do with having her locked in a cell, even for a few hours . . .

That, she could never forgive.

Chapter Twenty

Zack stormed through the front door of the sheriff's office. He'd expected to find Meg pacing the floor, anxiously awaiting him, eager to go to Robby, but she was nowhere in sight. Abe Larkin wasn't around either.

Maybe she'd left town before the sheriff could stop her. A terrible sense of loss assailed him. What if she'd boarded a bus and was halfway to Salt Lake City or wherever she'd decided to go? He glanced around the empty room. Where the hell was Abe?

He took two long steps to the sheriff's desk and inspected the surface. Reports were strewn helter-skelter, with squares of pink sticky paper covering most of the files. Nothing stood out as a message for Zack. He eyed the phone, wondering how he could contact the sheriff in a hurry.

Strange sounds came from behind the door leading to the cells. The creak of a mattress. A dry, wracking sob. Suspicion crawled down the back of his neck. God, not that. Not Meg in one of Abe's putrid cells.

He felt as if he'd taken a kick in the gut as he realized what the sheriff had done. Zack recalled Meg's terror of being closed in during the storm. She'd been locked in a closet as a child, and in a cell as a woman. The reality that she had spent time in jail hit him full force.

His Meg, locked away. He broke out in a cold

sweat at the idea of her surrounded by drug addicts and gangsters, people without conscience or morals or respect, for her or for themselves. She'd survived all that with no telling how many hidden scars, and he'd sent her back for more.

Zack grabbed the keys from a ring and barged through the door to the rear room. Security was non-existent, which didn't seem to bother the sheriff or the county citizens. If a serious crime were committed, the suspect would be shipped to a better-guarded facility pretty damn quick. Zack had no compunction about letting Meg out. She was not supposed to be there in the first place.

In the hall, a blue backpack's contents spilled over bare concrete. The inside of the cell was worse than a stall in Zack's barn, with no windows and no fresh air. The only light came from a dim panel along the floor. On the single cot, Meg sat with her legs folded beneath her, the back of her head resting against the wall, hands in her lap. Bars cast vertical shadows over her slender frame. Her eyes were closed, but Zack knew she wasn't sleeping. Her body was too rigid. And he'd heard her sobs just moments before.

As he clinked the keys, she opened her eyes and peeled her body away from the wall. "Zack?" She sounded tentative, disoriented. In the dim cell, she looked small and lonely.

He unlocked the door. "It's me."

She slumped against the wall. "What took you so long?" she said in a monotone that didn't sound like her at all. "The sheriff said you'd be here to file a complaint. You'll have to wait now. I guess he's out chasing jaywalkers."

Zack opened the cell door and stepped inside.

As if she feared him, Meg leaped to her feet and moved to the farthest corner. If she'd had something to throw, Zack figured he'd be the target. He would have welcomed a couple of darts to his chest, if that would make her feel better. He doubted anything could make *him* feel worse. Damn, he'd never meant for this to happen.

But she had reason to believe otherwise. Her body's stiff outline sent signals for him to keep his distance.

"Meg . . ."

"Why did you come here? To gloat? How could you do this to me after—" Her voice caught. She stepped forward into light coming from the door behind Zack. Hurt and anger pooled in her green eyes.

"It's all a mistake. I asked Abe to keep you in the office, not lock you up." Zack rasped a hand across twenty-four hour's worth of beard, feeling guilty as hell because he'd let the sheriff jump to conclusions without correcting him. He swung the door open wide. "Come on. I'll explain everything while we—"

"If coming out means talking to you, maybe I'd rather stay in jail. I never thought you'd sic the sheriff on me." She shivered, her gaze fixed on the dirty floor at her feet.

"Abe made his own assumptions. I didn't tell him anything." Zack had to talk her into a forgiving mood. For Robby's sake. The boy needed her. "Come with me, Meg. We'll sort it out. I don't want you here any more than you want to stay."

She shook her head. "I admit I'm a sniveling coward when it comes to being locked behind bars. But not so much of a coward that I'll allow *you* to save me."

"I never meant for this to happen. Or haven't you been listening?"

She raised a brow. "Sure I have. The same way you listened to me last night."

"You're right, I should have listened. And I will, I promise, if you'll come with me now." He hated seeing her this way, bitter and nearly broken, with all her bouncy optimism gone to ground.

She had dark shadows beneath her eyes, a scratch on her chin, a streak of dirt on her cheek. With an expression of mixed horror and loathing, she peered around the cell. "On second thought, maybe I *am* that much of a coward." With her head held high, she brushed past Zack. She reached for her backpack, stuffed the loose clothes back inside, and lifted one strap to her shoulder.

He looked around at the puke-green walls, thin cot, and harsh vertical shadows. It was bad, all right. Just thinking of her in there was enough to make him want to smash someone—and Abe Larkin came to mind. He followed her down the smelly hallway, resting a hand on the curve of her hip, urging her forward. She flinched but kept moving.

When they reached the main office, she whirled. "Don't touch me. Talking's okay, but not touching." She pressed her lips together, avoiding his eyes. "When I was a prisoner, I talked to the other inmates, to myself, to the four bare walls. I talked to remind myself I was still human. So I'm good at that. I can talk to anyone, anytime. I'll talk your socks off, if you want to hear it. But if you touch me, Zack, I'll come apart."

He held up his hands in surrender. "Fine, Meg. No touching. Just don't run away like you did last night. We need to—"

"You ordered me out of the house, remember? I don't stay where I'm not wanted."

She marched through the front door, onto the sidewalk. Zack trailed her, careful not to make the slightest physical contact.

The street was deserted at just past ten in the morning. She lifted her head so the sun shone full on her face. Since Zack had known her, she'd always glowed with life. Now, her vitality was at a low ebb, and he wondered if it would ever come back.

When she headed directly away from his truck, he stepped in front of her to block her path. She dodged. He moved with her. Without thinking, he reached out to stop her, but she flinched away.

He dropped his hands. "I forgot. No touching. Would it do any good to get on my knees and beg you to come with me now?" He badly wanted to take her hand, to lend his strength, but he knew she'd bolt. "We'll work things out, Meg. I won't let the sheriff put you back in . . . there. I'm sorry any of this happened."

She looked up at him with red-rimmed eyes, the lashes long and dark. "Are you?" There was something akin to hope in her eyes. He wondered why she hadn't asked about Robby, but reminded himself she'd been through a lot. She was probably too drained to think past her next breath of air.

When Zack motioned toward the truck, parked crooked and on the wrong side of the street, she sighed. He started toward it, and she limped along beside him. The ten miles to town had taken a toll. His sleepless night, his worry about her and Robby, had taken a toll on him, too. He'd have to look in a mirror to prove it, but he could swear he'd sprouted gray hairs.

The tension inside him loosened a bit. Meg was okay. Robby was okay. Everything else was negotiable. They'd go by the hospital first and stay until Robby was discharged. Seeing her would ease Robby's mind. Later, at home, Meg could rest. Then they'd talk. Zack might be grasping at straws, but he still hoped she had logical answers for all his questions.

He'd left the driver's side open with the door scraping the curb. She climbed behind the wheel and scooted to the middle, pushing the backpack to the floor on top of the mound of rope he'd yet to unload. He got in beside her.

Zack sat there, both hands gripping the steering wheel. He couldn't think of one damn soothing thing to say. Strangely enough, she didn't say anything, either.

After a few heartbeats, she tilted her head until it rested on his shoulder. "It's all right," she whispered, "if I do the touching."

Her hand slowly rose to his chest and took refuge there. It occurred to him that she would bewitch him again, but her touch felt too good to resist.

He started the truck with his left hand on the key to avoid shifting her position. The engine backfired, a protest against recent mistreatment. Zack wondered if something had misfired inside his brain, too. As he eased the truck into first gear, he tried to set things straight. "I'm bringing you back for Robby, Meg, not for me. Later, you can give me the facts. All of them. I'll listen 'til doomsday if you'll just be honest with—"

When Meg's hand dropped from his chest to his thigh, heat rushed to his groin. He almost drove into the sheriff's office, only to make the disappointing discovery that providing pleasurable stimuli was not on her agenda. She used his leg for leverage to push away from him while he wrestled the truck back onto the road. Adding injury to insult, she planted an elbow in his stomach and dug in. He slammed on the brakes. Before he could re-inhale the air she'd forced from his lungs, she had lurched out of reach.

"Damn," he wheezed, "if you want to declare war, do it when I'm not driving."

Her eyes flashed green fury. "Don't use Robby to manipulate me. It's not fair."

"I thought you'd want to see him."

"I do. But I don't understand," she said. "Why would you allow me near your son? I'm a criminal motivated by greed, remember? I'm not supposed to care about a kid. No kid is supposed to care about me."

"Nobody told Robby that, I guess. Do you want to fill him in?"

"No." She lifted her chin. "I'll leave that to you."

"Fine, then. I'll take care of it." He met her steady gaze, looking for the woman he knew, the woman he thought he knew. "I just want to know why, Meg. You must have been pretty desperate, or you wouldn't have . . ." He was making a botch of it again. If there had been extenuating circumstances, though, he wanted her to know he would consider them. "If you need money, I'll . . ."

"I don't need *your* money," she snapped. "I wouldn't take money from someone who thinks I'm no better than a prostitute." She bolted across the seat to the passenger side, gouging her jeans on the spring that popped out from under foam and duct tape. She grasped the door handle and pushed on the door. It didn't open. She kicked and still it didn't open. Finally she gave up wrestling with the jammed door and turned to glare at Zack.

"I was in a rage last night," he said. "Finding out about you from the sheriff made me feel like a damn fool. The Red Hawk fiasco put a match to a tinder-dry haystack. But now that the fire's out, I regret a lot of what I said and did. I wish you'd calm down and talk to me."

She set her mouth in a thin line. His ready ear had come too late, apparently.

"I know you care for Robby," he persisted. "Maybe a little for me, too."

"You're wrong!" she cried. "I *don't* care. Don't want to care. Not about someone who can't . . . won't believe in me." Her lips quivered. She pressed them together again. The way she looked at him, trying her best to be tough and strong, made him think of a china cup under a sledgehammer.

He grasped the steering wheel with both hands to keep from reaching for her. He wanted to hold her and force her to admit . . . But he knew his touch was particularly unwelcome at the moment. "Which one?" he said tightly. "Don't care, or don't want to?"

"Both." She snatched her backpack off the floorboard, and threw all her meager weight into the door. To both of their surprise, it opened. Meg and the backpack bailed out of the truck and into the road.

"You can't leave!" he yelled.

"Watch me." She swung the pack over one shoulder and backed away.

"Robby's counting on you," Zack said, using the only leverage he had. "When he woke up in the hospital, he asked for you first."

She stopped dead, staring wide-eyed at Zack. All color drained from her face. Obviously, the sheriff hadn't told her about Robby's brush with danger. Zack felt a little guilty for not qualifying his statement about the hospital. For letting her believe the child was seriously hurt.

Looking shell-shocked, she stared at him through the truck's open door. "Robby? What happened? How bad is it?"

"Our llama killer came back. Robby got stuck with a tranquilizer shot meant for Hilda."

"Will he—is he okay?"

"The doctor thinks so. But Robby's pretty shook up. He went looking for you last night. That's why he was in the barn. If you don't come back, it'll be a lot harder on him."

From her stricken expression, Zack knew he was gaining ground.

"Please, Meg. For Robby."

She threw her backpack at him. It struck his shoulder before crumpling onto the seat.

Zack raised both brows. "What was that for?"

Tears filled her big green eyes. "You're blackmailing me. You know I'd do anything for Robby." She climbed in and buckled her seatbelt, sitting sideways to avoid the pesky spring. With her stubborn chin tilted high, Meg glared straight ahead.

Him? Blackmailing her? *She* was the one at fault here. She'd tromped on his heart while stealing from right under his nose. Hell, how dare she accuse him of blackmail? Maybe he was twisting her arm a little, but she deserved it. He'd never expected her to complain about helping Robby.

He cursed as he realized he'd just proven her case. He *had* blackmailed her. He'd used the child, the one incentive he knew she couldn't refuse.

Grinding the gears, he shifted into first and hit the gas, leaving twin black streaks for half a block behind them.

Chapter Twenty-one

"Where were you at three a.m., Miss Delaney?" The sheriff's sharp voice pounced at Meg like a hooded executioner with a polished ax. He'd been rotating the same series of questions for over an hour. He paced back and forth, making her increasingly dizzy.

With elbows planted on Zack's kitchen table, she shrugged in response. Hoover pressed against her legs, whining for attention. Win had picked up the dog from the vet while Meg and Zack waited for the doctor to discharge Robby from the hospital. Meg reached down to scratch the silky black ears and wondered if Sheriff Larkin would find some hidden malice in the act.

As soon as they'd returned to the ranch, the sheriff had herded her into the house for an inquisition. She'd already told him she didn't have a watch, then or now, so of course she didn't know where she'd been at any given time. She wished she could sock the man with her backpack again. Although that mishap had contributed to landing her behind bars, she thought of it now with a certain satisfaction.

"You're not cooperating, young lady. Unless you give me some answers, I'll bounce you right back into one of my cells." Sheriff Larkin leaned over her, posturing like a melodramatic TV attorney. The glasses sliding down his sweat-slick nose spoiled the effect.

Meg was fed up. "I haven't done anything wrong. As I've told you at least five times, you should talk to the Caldwells. Ellen said her husband wants to destroy Zack."

"I'll check on Jesse, don't you worry."

"Ellen seems a little weird herself," Meg went on.

"Don't you go mouthing off about Ellen. She's been through hell."

"She has," Meg agreed. "She's still there. She needs a really good head shrink. Besides the Caldwells, you should have a word with your daughter. She's eaten up with jealousy because Zack won't notice her. Does *she* have an alibi?"

His face turned the color of a red brick wall. "Are you accusing Lydia of—"

"No. But someone hurt Robby last night, sheriff. It wasn't me. You're wasting time you should spend hunting the real—"

She stopped when she saw Robby enter the kitchen. He'd changed from pajamas to a shirt and shorts. His hair was wet from a bath. Fortunately, the drug had worn off with no ill effects. He looked alert and no more solemn than usual.

Zack followed close behind his son, as if he couldn't bear to let the boy out of sight. Zack must have heard at least part of her final statement. "She's right, Abe," he said. "She had nothing to do with the attack on Robby. Give her a rest."

Robby left his father and strode forward with his small chest inflated to the max, his head at an arrogant angle that reminded Meg strongly of Zack.

"She didn't hurt anyone." The boy scowled at Abe Larkin. "I *told* you it was a ninja, not Meg."

Robby stood by her chair, a miniature gallant knight ready to joust for her virtue. At least she'd gained Robby's loyalty, she thought. She put an arm around him and drew him close.

"You have it from an eye witness." Zack stepped up and rested a hand lightly on the child's head. "No more questions today, Abe. We've all been through too much." He looked formidable standing there, like a grizzly who'd claw the life out of anyone who dared to bother his offspring.

The sheriff knew when he was beat. He used a forefinger to hitch up his glasses before snagging his white cowboy hat from the center of the table. "All right if I have a word with Tobias, Zack? You're welcome to come along."

Zack muttered approval. As the two men proceeded onto the porch, the sheriff leaned close to Zack's ear. Meg couldn't begin to guess Abe Larkin's mind-set, but from the way he glanced back inside, she guessed he was whispering about her. Maybe he was warning Zack against an act of violence with the malignant backpack.

What different did it make what the sheriff said? Zack already thought the worst. True, he had rescued her from jail, but only so she'd help out with Robby. He still believed she'd meant to steal from him.

The voices on the porch grew louder. ". . . at the Dutch Mountain mine? Tobias?" she heard Zack say. Meg peered through the kitchen window and saw astonishment on his face.

The sheriff answered in a lower volume. "A guy from Great Falls left a message for me. The operator just got around to . . ."

The two men descended the steps and hurried down the drive toward Tobias's log cabin. Meg could no longer hear them, but she guessed what the news meant. Tobias had reason to dislike Zack—a possible motive—and he'd been keeping it a secret. Another suspect would take the pressure off of Meg, but she hated to think Tobias might be . . .

"Are you sick, Meg?" Robby asked, tugging on her hand.

She turned from the window. "No. Do I look it?"

"You're acting funny." He twitched his nose.

"Funny how?"

"You're not saying anything," he pointed out. And even Meg had to admit that was unusual.

"Chief Red Hawk once said silence is food for the spirit," Win remarked as she entered the kitchen from the direction of her room.

Meg was in no mood for Sioux philosophy. "If he said that, he sure didn't live by it. Since I've been here, I've heard enough of his quotes to fill a dictionary."

Red Hawk's name reminded Meg of her bold sales scheme now whittled to the size and importance of a cornflake. And thinking of the scheme underscored what Win had done to subvert it. Meg had plenty to say on that subject. However, with Robby glancing curiously from one woman to the other, she kept quiet.

The boy extracted an unwrapped lollipop out of his front shorts pocket. He frowned at the bits of lint sticking to it before offering it to Meg. "I only licked a little at the edge. The nurse at the hospital said it would cheer me up, but I think you need it more than me."

Her eyes filled with moisture she'd managed to contain through the sheriff's badgering. Robby's generosity made her see she'd gained a child's love, and that was something well worth having. She tucked the lollipop in the breast pocket of her shirt. "Thank you, Robby." She sniffed. "It does make me feel better."

"Daddy said you have to leave," he said. "Are you really going away?"

Meg nodded. "Soon." She wanted to explain, but emotion choked her. Besides, she wasn't sure if anything she said would make her departure easier for Robby—or for her.

"Why are you going? Because the sheriff thinks you're bad?"

No, because your father thinks so. And the Utah justice department. "I have work of my own to do, Robby. I can't stay here."

"Why not?" His blue-green eyes seemed determined to solve the mystery. "Don't you want to stay?"

How could she explain to the boy about jail and parole and consequences she could no longer avoid? How could she describe her fear of facing the inside of yet another cell? Her mouth opened like a landed fish gulping air, but no words came out.

Win came to the rescue. "Don't pester her, Robby. Meg wouldn't leave if she didn't have to."

Bitterness surged through Meg. Win had wanted her out of the way, and the older woman would get her wish.

Meg offered Robby a wavery smile. "When I finish my new computer game, I'll send it straight here. You can be the first to try it."

Robby frowned. "Who'll teach me how to play? I need *you* to teach me."

She bit her lower lip, willing her eyes to stay dry. If she allowed the tears to fall, Robby would only ask more questions she didn't know how to answer. She crouched to Robby's level and hugged him hard. "We can talk on the telephone. I'll guide you through, step by step."

Win drummed grease-encrusted fingernails on the table top. "I think I'll order new shocks for Zack's truck. The rear end's starting to sag." She rose with exaggerated dignity and sauntered out the door. As always, Win seemed uncomfortable with emotion.

Meg wanted to hate the older woman. Her immediate thought was uncharitable—that Win's backside suspension could also use a shock or two.

Shock. Win had had her share of that. She'd had a no-good husband who'd abandoned her and a small child. After devoting years to raising Sky, she'd lost her daughter, too. Sky had been her life. No wonder she didn't want Meg taking Sky's place. Maybe she feared Meg would steal Robby's love, and Zack's, leaving Win with nothing.

Meg's resentment diluted with pity. Win would have another shock when she learned the incriminating information the sheriff had on Tobias. Meg had no doubt Win cared deeply for the hired hand, just as she cared for Robby and Zack and her daughter's memory. Tobias had teased her with a long past-due romance, and Win had had a few weeks of joy. Even if Tobias was not guilty, he would more than likely move on, after the sheriff finished a round of harassment. And if . . .

Sympathy engulfed Meg and left no room for bitterness. If Win's lover turned out to be the villain who had hurt her grandson, the truth would crack Win's impassive features and split her stubborn heart in two.

Zack expected the sheriff to walk straight to Tobias's cabin. Instead, Abe stopped at the white Bronco marked with the county sheriff's emblem.

"Earl Jamison caught me on the way out of the office this morning. He found another letter when he was sorting the mail. The black block writing looks just like what was on the first three notes you showed me."

"Where is it?" Zack demanded.

"In here." Abe opened the Bronco door, then donned a pair of rubber gloves he'd stowed in his pocket. He gingerly pick up the envelope from the seat. "The county's sending me a detective today, but I figured, considering what happened to Robby, we should go ahead and open this."

Zack agreed.

While the sheriff slit the envelope with a penknife, Zack asked, "Does Earl have any idea where this letter came from? Did he see someone drop it by the post office? Or did a carrier bring it in?"

"We know where it came from." Abe's face turned as red as a politician caught on camera with his fly down. "It was in a bundle of outgoing mail from my office."

"It was where?" Zack roared.

The sheriff winced. "Half the town comes by the office at least once a week. And I leave the place open even when I'm not there, as I guess you know from the way you waltzed in and snatched Meg right out of a locked cell." He glared at Zack. "Nobody takes the law seriously around here."

"You know why I did it, Abe. If you'd been there, you'd have let her go with me to see Robby."

"At least she didn't leave the county." He squinted at the envelope, tore it open, and pulled out the single sheet of yellow paper.

Helpless rage gripped Zack as the sheriff unfolded it. He knew what to expect. More cryptic threats. More Bible mis-quotes.

Zack read the note over Abe's shoulder as the sheriff recited it aloud. "Beware. The Lord hath marked the Offering and shall take account. The innocent shall pay."

The innocent shall pay. Robby? Jesus, don't let it mean Robby. Zack put his hands on the Bronco's metal roof and drove his fingernails into the white paint. The ante had escalated. Robby was involved now. Zack's fury was replaced by cold fear.

"Any idea what it means?" Abe asked.

Zack had a hunch, but nothing he dared put into words. "It means we have to find out who's doing this."

"Right. As soon as the detective gets here, we'll dust everything for fingerprints and—"

"How long does the office mail accumulate before you send it out?" Zack asked.

"A day or two. I take it across the street myself."

"Happen to remember if Tobias was in the office recently?"

Abe scratched under the front rim of his hat. "I don't recall."

"Jesse was there yesterday," Zack reminded him. "Was that before or after you took out the mail?"

"Think I punch a time clock every time I come or go?" the sheriff demanded irritably.

"No, I guess not." Zack sighed. "If we don't get anything out of Tobias, will you talk to Jesse again?"

"I doubt he's our man. Jesse wouldn't hesitate to bust another man's jaw, or screw another man's wife. Writing letters, though? It's not his style."

"That doesn't rule him out," Zack insisted.

The sheriff grimaced. "I'll talk to him. He was in a brawl over at the BadAss last night. Fighting over a woman, I hear. I ought to clap him in irons for catting around on Ellen like that. Can't understand why she stays with him."

Abe refused to see the obvious, but Zack saw it clearly. Ellen would never leave her husband. Not now. She was punishing herself for Mike's death. It was illogical, but grief had a mind of its own.

Zack pushed away from the Bronco and started walking toward Tobias's cabin. *If only.* That's what

had tortured him after Sky's death. He had to make
sure there were no more *if onlys* in his life. With this
most recent threat, it seemed Robby was the one in
danger. Zack had to find whoever had written the
note and invaded his barn last night. Before it was
too late. Before he had nothing but another handful
of regrets.

Zack understood Ellen better now. After seeing
Robby lying in the straw, struck down by another's
malice, he knew he'd only scratched the surface of
agony. If anything happened to Robby . . .

Ellen's son had died, and she'd never get him back.
She had failed her child.

Zack began to comprehend the depth of her guilt
and sorrow.

The sheriff paced the only room of Tobias's log
house while Zack watched from a straight chair in
the corner. Tobias sprawled on a dilapidated recliner.
He slapped a well-worn mechanics manual against
his thigh before dropping the book on a nearby table.
"Why don't you have a seat, Sheriff? All your high-
stepping makes me jittery."

That was the general idea, Zack figured. Abe continued to pace, fingers hooked in his belt. He
stopped, pivoted, and leaned slightly forward, a
staged attempt at intimidation. "Tobias, did you ever
work for the mines?"

Tobias's shoulders stiffened. His worried gaze shifted
from the sheriff to Zack. He must have seen Zack's
unspoken accusation, because he dropped chin to chest
in surrender. "I did." His battle-flattened nose made
his face appear deceptively childlike. "I know it looks
bad, my keeping quiet about it."

He paused before meeting Zack's eyes again. "I
took this job because I needed work, that's the gospel
truth. Didn't even hear about your part in closing

down the silver mine on Dutch Mountain until I'd been here a few weeks. You've treated me fair, so I have no call to complain. I hate seeing Robby hurt as much as anybody else around here."

"I'd like to believe you." Zack was weary to the bone, too tired to tell truth from a lie. Until he had time to think everything through, he couldn't assume anyone was innocent. Not with Robby's safety on the line. "The thing is, Tobias, you can't work here while the sheriff's investigating. Once we clear this up, assuming you're not involved in any way, I'll welcome you back."

The sheriff fixed dour eyes on Tobias. "Meanwhile, don't leave the area. Come by my office tomorrow to fill out forms and sign a statement."

More forms, Zack thought. Piles of paper could mount to the ceiling without solving a damn thing. Zack hated the uncertainty. And he hated what he'd have to tell Win—that Tobias, the first man she'd allowed herself to have feelings for in many a year, was one of the sheriff's prime suspects.

Tobias shuffled to his feet, swaying like a punch-drunk boxer. He seemed stunned. "Won't take me long to gather my gear. I'll bring my truck around and load up."

Before he reached the door, Winona barged into the room. Her chin led the way, a sure sign she was steamed for a fight.

"What's going on, boys? An all-male powwow? Seems like I should be—" She stopped, taking in the three men, their positions, their expressions. The situation must have been plain enough to a discerning woman like Win. She glared at the sheriff. "If you were going to question Tobias, why invite Zack along, and not me?"

Tobias moved toward her, his battered face illuminating like a 200-watt flood lamp. "The sheriff did what he thought best. Don't get yourself all worked up, cupcake."

Cupcake? Zack would have laughed at the absurdity, except for the way Win's expression softened as she looked at Tobias. She had it bad, all right. And Tobias played his part very well.

Was he using Win? Had he cozied up to her, thinking she'd divert suspicion while he did his evil deeds? Or was he truly an honest man?

The blinding smile Tobias had donned for his "cupcake" flickered and went out. "I'm moving into town for now, Win, but I'll be in touch." After a wink in her direction, an effort to reassure, he planted his hat on his head and shambled out the door.

The sheriff stood in the middle of the floor, nervously twisting his Stetson in his hands. Win's scowl discouraged him from further comment. With a nod, he opted for a quick exit, leaving Zack to field his mother-in-law's wrath.

Putting off an explanation, Zack parted the incongruously feminine lace curtains that adorned the cabin's raw wood walls. Through the window, he watched Tobias unload ranch equipment from the back of his truck while the sheriff stood by, presumably looking for evidence.

Win spoke first. "You found out about the mining job, didn't you?"

Zack whirled around, caught completely by surprise. "You knew?"

She nodded.

"And you didn't see fit to mention it?"

"I didn't think it was important," Win said.

"Jesus, woman, with all that's been happening around here, how could you keep that from me?"

"Because I knew Tobias held no grudge. He worked for me, too, you know. You had no right to fire him without talking to me."

Zack was angry now. "I had every goddamn right. Somebody almost killed my son. Your grandson. We can't have Tobias living on the ranch when—"

"It wasn't Tobias," she insisted.

"How's that? Did you see something, hear something last night?"

"No. But Tobias likes his job. He likes all of us. He just wouldn't . . ."

"Okay, if it wasn't Tobias, who was it?"

She blew out a breath. "I don't know."

Zack sighed. "Give me your best guess."

"Jesse?"

"That's what I thought at first. But if he planned all this, he's a lot smarter and more subtle than I've given him credit for," Zack said.

"How much smarts does it take to kill an unsuspecting animal?"

"Not just kill, but make the deaths look accidental. I'm guessing all the llamas were drugged first, since that seemed to be the plan for Hilda. A humane form of murder. Does that sound like Jesse? If he's guilty, cutting his own fence to throw off me and the sheriff was damn cagey. And all those letters. Can you see Jesse—"

"What letters?"

Zack had forgotten Win didn't know about the letters. "I'll show you later. Threats couched in religion, mostly. When was the last time you went to church?"

She looked at Zack suspiciously. "I went with Tobias last Sunday. I asked him to go, so don't get the idea—"

"Relax, Win. I'm not trying to trap you or Tobias. Just think a minute. There's only the one church in town, and most everyone goes there. Our llama assassin might have been praying in the pew next to yours. Who did you see?"

"Jesse and Ellen were in the front row. They've

never been regular churchgoers, but I figured they were there because it was a year since Mike and Sky died. Same reason I went."

Zack nodded. He felt the need to make peace with God, too, and he probably would, just as soon as this crisis was over.

"Lydia was there. With Harry. From the looks of it, she's sucking him in for husband number four. If she can't get you, she'll scheme 'til she gets somebody in her bed."

Zack considered Harry. He'd taken a fishing client to Wyoming this week. As far as Zack knew, he was still out of town.

What about Lydia? Zack would never have pegged her as someone who studied the Bible in her spare time, but who could tell? She did wear a crucifix between her breasts. And she had been in the sheriff's office yesterday. She could have slipped a letter into the outgoing mail.

"What do you think about Lydia?" he said aloud.

Win's eyes lit. "I've never liked that bitch. Lydia the Llama Killer has a ring to it," she said eagerly. "Her or Harry or Jesse. Even Ellen's more likely than Tobias. I tell you, it's not him."

"How can you be sure? He did arrive about the time all the problems started."

Win pounded a fist against her upper chest. "The truth is in my heart, the same way Meg's innocence is in yours." It looked as if Win's melodramatic side, long dormant, had detonated like an A-bomb. The mushroom cloud was obscuring her good sense.

"If I'm carrying Meg's so-called innocence inside here," he tapped his own chest, "I'm overdue for a heart attack. Ever since I met her, Meg's been telling whoppers as full of holes as a buckshot rabbit."

"You think *she* hurt Robby last night?" Win asked.

"No, not that." Still, she was guilty as warmed-over sin. Guilty of exploiting his love. Guilty of betraying everything he'd believed about her. "She's eyebrow deep in a crazy scheme to sell my sporting goods." He couldn't quite bring himself to say Meg had plotted to rip him off.

Win ambled to the chair Tobias had occupied earlier. She picked up the worn mechanics manual from the lamp table and thumbed through it, staring vacantly at the pages. "Did she say I was involved?"

"No. She wouldn't lie about . . ." He stopped, regrouped. What was Win getting at? Why would she think Meg had implicated her? Zack was no mind reader, but he made an educated guess. "You mean you knew what she was up to all along?"

Win put down the book and faced Zack like a warrior before a firing squad. "It was her idea, but I encouraged her to go ahead without telling you."

"She asked your advice?"

Win nodded. "She thought I'd steer her in the right direction."

Zack felt sick to his stomach, recalling the accusations he'd flung at Meg last night. If none of them were true . . . "You set her up," he accused. "Hell, you set me up, too."

But Win had not forced him to make the assumptions he'd made. Zack had to take credit for that.

Win bowed her head. "I didn't want Meg here. I figured you'd send her away when you found out what she'd done."

Zack's anger heated up again. "I ought to send *you* away. Did you think I'd condone your part in—"

"No. I was betting she'd be too honorable to snitch on me. And I was right." She looked into Zack's eyes. "It never occurred to me you'd accuse her of theft until I overheard you yelling at her last night. And that bit about the criminal record . . . I flat out don't believe it. She's no criminal."

He recalled the pain he'd seen in Meg's eyes, and he wished he could erase everything he'd said. Guilt weighed on him. "Why tell me now, Win? Now, when it's too late."

"Because it's not too late. She'll forgive you. Go ahead and heap the blame on me. I'm tough enough to handle the consequences." Win thrust her pugnacious jaw forward to prove the point. "Meg's a flimsy wimp."

"Maybe she's the tough one," Zack said slowly. "She's impulsive and rash, but she has courage. She took all the blame on herself. God, Win, why'd you do it? What has Meg ever done to you?"

"Nothing but good, I have to admit. She's been good to all of us. The house runs smooth as a Mercedes carburetor since she's been here. And yesterday—or maybe it was the day before—she practically stood on her head inside an engine compartment to hold a wrench for me. She doesn't mind getting her hands dirty. That's something I admire."

There was a lot to admire about Meg, now that he thought about it. She'd found the patience and compassion to communicate with Robby. She'd listened to Zack when he'd badly needed a listener. She had enriched all of them with her high-octane energy.

Win was still singing Meg's praises. "Last week, when I needed a rebuilt alternator, she dug through catalogs and called junkyards until she found a hell of a deal. Even I was impressed. She learns the ropes quicker than an Indy racer goes zero to sixty. If brainpower could compensate for no mechanical ability, I'd be worried about my job."

The last of the heat drained out of him. Meg had come a long way in his mother-in-law's estimation. He tamped down a smile.

"I'm ashamed of what I've done, Zack."

He was ashamed, too. But he forced his brows together and scowled for Win's benefit. "You ought to be. I can't believe you'd . . ." He thought back on his mother-in-law's methods of discouraging any woman who'd shown an interest in him over the past year—the sharpened knives, the loaded peashooter. "Never mind. I believe it. And I respect you for telling me the truth, even if it came a little late."

She cocked her head. "It's ironic that Little Big Mouth needed me to plead her cause." Her expression turned wistful. "About Tobias . . . I'll plead for him 'til I turn blue. He's as innocent as Meg, I'd bet my life on it."

"I wish I were that sure."

"You'll see. I don't know who's plaguing us, but it's not Tobias. As soon as everything's straightened out on the ranch, the two of us are going to open a garage in town."

"I hope so, Win. I really do hope you're right about him."

She banged her chest again. "The heart knows. It's been a long time since I've listened, but Tobias made me hear. Meg can do the same for you. Tell her your doubts and let her convince you she's as pure as an Idaho whiteout. Listen to her, Zack. Better yet, listen to your heart."

That essential organ pounded in Zack's chest, demanding to be heard. He wasn't quite ready to tune in. "Meg is leaving. It really is too late."

Win snorted. "You couldn't drive her away with whips and chains. I thought getting rid of her would protect you and the boy. I thought Sky's spirit would stay with us longer if she were gone. But I was wrong as pedal power in an Oldsmobile. We can't hang onto the past, be it good or bad. Tobias has taught me that all of us have to move forward. Meg's here, and you've gone and fallen in lust with her, so there's only one thing for you to do."

"What?" When Win offered counsel, Zack usually heard her out before making up his mind. This time, especially, he could use some decent advice.

Her black eyes glistened with a rare show of emotion. "Make love and break the arrow."

He wondered if he'd heard right. "Is that a Red Hawk quote?"

Win patted Zack on the shoulder. "If he didn't say it, he should have."

"You're giving me your blessing?" Zack couldn't decide whether to be shocked or amused.

She nodded, her steady dark gaze full of the wisdom she usually attributed to her ancestor. "My blessing. Sky's, too. Like I said, I've learned a few things in the last couple of weeks. Given the opportunity, you and Meg'll fire up one helluva peace pipe."

Later that night, Zack heard Meg's voice, a sweet soprano, lilting a mellow folk song. Drawn to it like Adam to the apple tree, he went to Robby's bedroom door and watched as she wove a web of warmth and security around his son. He longed to talk to her, but he'd wait until Robby was asleep.

Zack wandered into the office. The first thing he noticed was the neat stack of mail from Meg's post office box. The Red Hawk correspondence. She must have put it there for him to find.

She hadn't taken his money. Zack knew—a part of him had known all along—that she'd never intended to steal from him. And if she'd told the truth about Red Hawk, wasn't it likely that her arrest and conviction had an explanation, too? As Win had said, Meg was no criminal.

Zack picked up the stack of mail and saw something scribbled on the top envelope in Meg's feminine hand. The PenUltimate address burned his eyeballs. She meant to return to Edward's company, maybe even to the sonuvabitch's inept arms. She would throw her life away on a man who didn't appreciate her one-of-a-kind effervescence, her spirit.

But then, what reason had Zack given her to think *he* appreciated her?

He brought the envelope with those few scribbled lines to his nose. Meg's flower scent hit him like a concussion. Damn it to hell, he was going to miss her. He already missed her.

Attempting to put Meg out of his mind, he walked around his desk and sat in the chair. With all that had happened in the last twenty-four hours, he had plenty of other things to brood over. He had to protect his son. Maybe he should send the boy away, but Robby had had enough adjustment problems since Sky died. It didn't seem right to exile him from the only home he'd ever known.

His temples throbbed. He leaned on the desk and propped his head with both hands. Somehow, he had to make sense of this. Robby hadn't been the primary target in the barn last night, but he had been hurt, nevertheless. Next time, the consequences could be worse.

Zack set his jaw. There wouldn't be a next time. He'd ask questions all over the county, get a handwriting analysis of the notes, hire a private investigator, do whatever it took to find the person responsible. If he couldn't beat the guilty party to a bloody pulp—his first preference—he'd settle for seeing the dirty scheming SOB buried in the state pen for the next twenty or thirty years.

All Zack wanted was safety for Robby.

And he wanted . . . Meg. He wanted understanding between them. He wanted to believe in her again. He wanted her to believe in him.

Restless, he left his desk and paced the hall. She was still with Robby, talking softly. He didn't stop to eavesdrop. Instead, he escaped Meg's downy-soft voice that wisped across his nerve endings and drove him crazy with wanting her. He continued through the house and out to the barn, stopping at Hilda's stall. From outside the gate, he watched the cria nurse. Hilda made a soft humming noise as she nuzzled her baby fondly.

A good mother had loving instincts. Instincts Zack saw in Meg whenever she was with his son. Instincts Robby had recognized right away.

Zack strolled outside until the lazy summer twilight passed through all the shades of pink and purple. Until dark.

When he returned to the house, he went straight to Robby's room. The boy slept clutching a bright-yellow stuffed toy Zack had purchased in the hospital gift shop.

Zack paused to listen to Robby's even breathing. He bent low and kissed the baby-soft cheek that smelled of milk and dog and boy. His chest tightened with love. He'd almost lost Robby today; he'd take better care from now on. As he rearranged the Ninja Turtle quilt, Hoover came into the room and lay on the rug beside the bed. He nested his head on his paws, looking up at Zack with liquid-brown eyes.

"Help me protect him," Zack said. The dog slapped his tail on the floor as if he understood. No prowler would approach the room without Hoover sounding the alarm.

Leaving the door slightly open, Zack continued down the hall to Meg's room. He listened at her closed door, but heard no sounds of movement. No light came through the cracks. She was probably asleep, worn out by heartache and a very long day.

Zack put a hand on the doorknob. He didn't want

to wait until morning. He couldn't take the chance that she'd slip away in the night again, this time to disappear forever.

He'd been mulling over what to say for hours, and still he lacked the words. He turned and stalked back down the hall, peeling off his shirt and tossing it at the couch as he went through the living room on the way to the kitchen.

Opening the refrigerator, he armed himself with a bottle of beer. Before he took the first swallow, he recalled that night on the porch when he and Meg had first sipped from each others' lips, first tasted the brew of their mutual desire.

Eyes closed, he imagined the ripple of her breath on his neck, the ghost of her voice in his ear. If he reminded her of that night, maybe he could recreate the mood. Maybe he could salve her damaged pride and get through to the woman he hoped still loved him. She'd been keeping secrets all along, just as he had. Now, for the first time, they'd have no barriers, no pretense, nothing to separate their thoughts and feelings and all the love he was sure both of them wanted to share.

Lifting his bottle of beer, he frowned at the amber glass. Wine was better for romancing, but there was none on hand. Besides, he wasn't a wine and roses kind of guy.

Meg would have to accept him as he was, heart and beer in hand.

Chapter Twenty-two

Meg dreamed of Zack Burkhart. The dream was so real, she imagined she tasted his lips, explored their soft, firm texture. The scent of soap and virility penetrated her defenses as he kissed her.

"Mmm," she murmured.

He deepened the kiss, and she responded with all her heart. When his lips left hers, she whimpered. Why did good dreams have to end so quickly?

The bed creaked. The world shifted. She felt his big body's heat through a layer of sheeting.

She inched open an eyelid. The night was dark; she couldn't see. Strong, capable hands cradled either side of her face. She knew those hands.

Was she awake? Zack's solid warmth and scent seemed real enough. But his tenderness was pure fantasy. As was his voice, deep, rough-textured, unforgettable. "Don't send me away, Meg. Let me stay with you."

She sighed. It was a dream. Zack would never say that. He would never willingly spend another moment with her. He hated her now.

Squeezing her eyes shut, she determined to enjoy this figment of her imagination as long as she possibly could. His breath fanned her lips as she arched for another kiss. Her dream Zack stroked down the side of her cotton T-shirt, awakening every millimeter of nerve cell in the skin beneath. When he inched the hem of her shirt above the lace of her panties, sensation blazed.

Her eyes flew open. Both his touch and her reaction were entirely too real for a dream.

"Pinch me," she whispered.

"What!?" Zack lifted his head, brows drawn together in confusion.

"I just want to be sure you're real."

"I'm real enough." His lips swooped in for another kiss. He began stroking her again.

Meg shivered with the rise in body temperature. Her fingers drifted over the planes of his face and found genuine flesh and bone. He didn't disappear. She could see his eyes now. She imagined he looked at her with love.

It was a cruel trick. He didn't love her. His pretense made him the most sadistic of Prince Charmings. As soon as he realized she was fully awake, he'd cast another hundred-year hex on the enchanted castle.

"What are you doing here?" she demanded crossly.

"Kissing you." He ran a thumb across her lips. "Do you mind?"

"Yes!" She pushed him away and sat up, jerking her rumpled shirt down to cover her underwear. "Of course I mind. Get out of here right now," she said in a stage whisper. She wanted to shriek, but Robby might hear if she gave full vent to her emotions.

He clicked on the bedside lamp. A dusting of hair on his broad, bare chest shone golden-brown in the muted light. Shadows hid his expression. "Your room is closer to Robby's than mine is. I thought . . . he might have a nightmare or something."

She was in the midst of a waking nightmare right this minute. He couldn't sleep here. How would she keep from begging him to hold her, to truly love her?

"If you want this bed, I'll take the couch." She started to get up, but he grasped her shoulders and forced her back onto the mattress again.

"No. We'll both stay. We need to talk, Meg." He stretched out on his side, facing her. His long jean-clad legs extended over mussed sheets and quilt.

She rebounded to a sitting position, poised for escape. "What is there to talk about?" She wanted to blurt her innocence and plead with him to believe her. But what if he didn't? She had to hang on to the fragments of her dignity and avoid groveling. She twisted a wad of bear T-shirt in nervous fingers.

He sat up, too, and gently squeezed her hand. "Relax. I'm not here to find fault with you."

When she tried to disengage her hand from the shirt and his touch, he laced their fingers together. The slow stroking of his sun-browned thumb over her pale skin enthralled her. Any minute, he'd admit it was all a trick. She knew it was a trick, because he had no reason to be nice to her.

"I should have listened last night." The regret in his voice sounded sincere. "I'd convinced myself I knew all the facts, but—"

"You know all you're going to know." She tugged her hand in another unsuccessful attempt to detach herself. "Why should I say anything more when—"

"Let me finish. I've been trying to sort out what I really know from the conclusions I jumped to. I think I'm making progress."

"Really?" She pretended the whole subject bored her. Secretly, she wanted to hear what progress he'd made. Secretly, she wanted to hope.

"I understand why you didn't tell me about the Red Hawk project yesterday afternoon. Once you knew the reason I'd boxed up everything in the first place, you must have been afraid to admit what you'd done."

"I wasn't afrai—"

"I'm not saying you were afraid for yourself. Maybe you were afraid you'd hurt me by talking about it. Maybe you planned to send back the checks and cancel all deals. That would have worked okay if I hadn't stumbled onto the evidence."

"Congratulations. You finally figured it out." She hoped she looked indifferent, though her heart jack-hammered so violently she feared he'd see the vibration of her chest, or feel the tremor in her hand. He must still care for her a little. He was here, wasn't he?

"I don't claim to be a deep thinker," he said. "I'm not nearly as smart as you are. Last night I saw nothing but your lies—or half-truths, or whatever you want to call them. I saw you'd maintained a distance between us, even when we made love. And because you were trying to sell the designs I'd declared off-limits, you burned me twice—with your sin, and with my own. You brought back all the old pain. I couldn't forgive you for that."

She felt like cringing. "Did something change your mind?"

"Win set me straight."

"Win?" She held her breath. Nothing Win said was likely to be in Meg's favor.

"Yes, Win. She told me her part in your scheme. That you'd asked for advice."

Meg merely nodded, her mouth so dry she couldn't speak.

"I was mad as hell that Win encouraged you to go ahead. But I forgave her because she admitted she was wrong. She appreciates what you've done here— for Robby and . . . for all of us."

Meg was dumbfounded. From now on, she would definitely believe in miracles. "Is this the same Wi-nona I know? The one who's snoring as we speak?"

Sure enough, a sound reminiscent of a distant freight engine reached them through the closed door.

Zack grinned. "The very same. I know it's out of character, but I swear she's coming around."

"Coming around to what?" Meg reminded herself to be cautious. Earning Win's favor was too good to be true, even for a person with renewed faith in miracles.

"To liking you. She told me I should let you explain. She told me to listen to . . ." He glanced down at their joined hands. "Your Red Hawk scheme makes sense to me now, even the secrecy. It's the criminal conviction that makes no sense at all. Last night, when you *said* you were guilty, I was too damn furious to analyze. Later, when I'd . . ." He shrugged. "I don't believe you'd steal anything."

"You don't?" Her hopes buoyed like a helium balloon. She wrenched herself back to earth.

"A little late to have faith in my honesty, isn't it?" She wanted to believe he was sincere, but the trust and love she saw in his eyes might vanish if she began to count on him. "What is it about me? Do I *look* like a crook?"

He smiled. "No one has ever looked less crookish. That's why I'm here now, doing my damnedest to humble myself. In my saner moments, I know you're a good person, hardworking, as generous as they come. Every instinct tells me you're honest. That's why I brought you home. Why I trusted you with Robby."

"Thank you for that. He's meant more to me than . . ." Emotion lumped in her throat and burned in her eyes.

"I know. He's special." He raised her hand to his lips and kissed the tip of her little finger. "You're special, too. I wanted absolution from you yesterday, and you gave me that without question. But when you needed something from me, I didn't come through." Letting go of her hand, he shoved a pillow behind his back. "I'm listening. You don't have to keep anything from me anymore." He crossed his arms over his chest as if prepared to be there a while.

She stared at him. Did he really want to hear it all? Did she really want to tell him? Nevertheless, this was no time to be gutless. He deserved to know the truth.

"I was accused of theft," she confessed, clasping and unclasping her hands in her lap. "Technically, I was guilty, like I said last night. But you see . . ."

She was afraid to go on. She'd be on trial all over again. She wasn't sure she could stand another conviction. Not from Zack.

"I can be patient, Meg. I'll wait all day, or all week, but I'm bound and determined to hear this story, start to finish. I won't let you carry the burden alone anymore."

Warmth trickled into her fingers and toes as his gaze settled on her. His gray eyes neither accused nor threatened. They held neither wariness nor suspicion. He would not condemn her.

As long as he looked at her that way, she'd turn herself inside out and let him examine the frayed lining. "I've told you about my grandmother, G. T.," she began again.

He nodded. "She gave you the love you didn't get at home. You cared for her more than anyone else in your life."

He'd described the relationship perfectly. Meg was glad he understood. The helium balloon began to inch up again.

"She had a stroke about two years ago and moved into a nursing home. When I offered to share my one-room apartment with her, she smiled—even with the stroke paralyzing half her face, she had the dearest smile—and said she'd be fine. Her doctor had recommended a place only a half-hour's drive from where I lived. It was expensive, but that was no problem. Her husband had set up a generous trust fund for her before he died. Dave, my stepfather, was the trustee. He's an attorney and handles a lot of trusts."

Meg looked into the dark interior of the room, wishing she could see G. T. one more time. "She'd been there a year when I started working for PenUlti-mate. Edward asked me to go to Europe with him for a two-week game developer's convention. I felt comfortable about leaving her. The home had a won-derful physical therapist who had helped her regain some strength on her left side. I was pleased with the progress. But when I came back, she'd been trans-ferred to a different place." Meg's hands balled into fists. Dave's heartless subterfuge still made her furious.

Zack relaxed his crossed-arm listening pose to gen-tly knead the tense muscles at the nape of her neck. "I'm afraid I see where this is leading. Your stepfa-ther moved her, right?"

She nodded. "As soon as I found out what had happened, I went to him. He said she'd have to stay in the cheaper facility because her money was gone. I didn't see how that was possible. He screamed at me, claimed he had complete control over G. T.'s account and I had no right to question him.

"The new place was awful, really awful. The odor of urine and feces slapped me in the face as soon as I entered the door. The nursing care was haphazard, at best. The physical therapist who came once a week didn't seem interested in rehabilitating anyone. G. T. had given up, I could tell. She was going to die un-less I got her out of there.

"So I did. I used the advance on my game, and

every spare dime of my salary, but the best care is expensive. My resources went fast. Since I was still making payments on a college loan, I couldn't borrow from a bank. After a couple of months, I was broke. And then she was diagnosed with cancer. She needed specialized care, around the clock, and I just didn't have the funds.

"As a last resort, I did some research in Dave's office files. G. T.'s money *was* gone, but it had disappeared at a much faster rate than her expenses could explain. I knew her expenses, because I'd been paying them myself. There were bills for services not provided. Money paid out to people I'd never heard of. I knew from what I saw that Dave had ripped off the trust big time."

Zack interjected an unflattering description of her stepfather's ancestry.

Meg wanted to add a few expletives of her own. "I should have hired an attorney, but I knew a legal probe could take years. G. T. didn't have that kind of time. She needed help right away. So . . ." She drew a deep breath and let it out slowly. *Please, Zack. Please understand.* "I found a four-digit number scrawled on Dave's bank file, and I knew it had to be a PIN. That made it easy to transfer funds I needed for G. T. from his account to one I opened in my name."

"I should have guessed a fractured good deed was your downfall." Zack's wry smile was not disparaging, but proud. He really seemed to be proud of her.

When he eased an arm around her, Meg leaned into his chest. "Unfortunately, Dave and my mother discovered what I'd done almost right away. Mother called me at work and accused me of stealing from them. I explained. I begged her to examine the trust fund for herself, but she didn't care. She didn't want to know. G. T. was my father's mother. I'd always thought my mother loved her as much as I did. Apparently, I was wrong."

Zack kissed the top of her head. "Now I see why you never said much about maternal influences. I guess what you had wasn't too noteworthy."

"At least she didn't turn me in. Dave called the cops. Since I spilled my guilt to the first detective who asked, I really had no defense. I never thought it would come down to criminal charges, but of course it did. The lawyer I hired did his best. He tried to convince the judge that my motives were altruistic, but it didn't fly. I couldn't prove Dave had mishandled funds. Dave wasn't the accused. He presented some records out of 'good faith,' bless him, but he must have had a creative accountant working overtime. Everything looked impeccable when it reached the judge's eyes. I had no choice but to plea-bargain."

"There must be some way to investigate that trust," Zack said.

"There is, now. I was the sole beneficiary in G. T.'s will, as it turned out. Silverstein, my attorney, has demanded an official accounting. He's been telling me he's onto something for months, though I know better than to get excited. Dave has friends in high places."

"Damn the sick bastard," Zack exploded. "He let you go to jail because of what he'd done. I wish I'd been there. I'd have pinned his ears to a barbed wire fence and set a grizzly on him." Zack's arm circling Meg had tightened with his anger. She squirmed, and he eased his hold.

"Sorry. I didn't mean to hurt you." He rubbed his big warm hand up and down her arm. "What happened to your grandmother?"

Remembering was difficult, but she took a deep breath and forced herself to speak. "Even before the preliminary hearing, G. T. was pretty far gone. I went to Edward begging for help, and he came through with the sequel advance. Right after, we moved in together, and he asked me to marry him, and I was so grateful for the support that . . ."

"Sure, honey," Zack soothed. "Sure you were."

"It was his advance that allowed G. T. to spend her last days with the best possible care. I couldn't save her. Couldn't defend myself. And I was so darn scared of going to jail."

Tears dripped down Meg's face and made wet circles on her T-shirt. All the desperation blew through her again, like a nasty winter storm that chilled the bones and frostbit the skin.

"Just hearing about it scares me," Zack said. "If I ever get my hands on your stepfather, I swear I'll commit a felony. Did anyone . . . the other inmates . . ."

"No, they didn't hurt me." She tried to laugh, but it sounded more like an out-of-control hiccup. "I thought—well, I'd heard stories about lesbian sex and all sorts of bodily violations. Nothing like that happened, thank God. I was in the county lockup, and that's far safer than prison. Physically, the worst thing was the strip search by the guards. Emotionally, I guess it was the language. I heard some choice vocabulary, believe me."

"I've noticed you don't swear."

"It's reactionary." Meg managed a small smile. "Do you really want to hear all this?"

"Yes," he said. "I want to know."

She heaved a sigh. "In the daytime, we were let out of the four-woman cells and into a big room. The first day, I took a book off a library cart and tried to hide out in a plastic chair in a corner. As soon as I sat down, a huge woman loomed over me, her face right up to mine. I slumped lower and lower, but her face followed me down while she screamed,

'What you doin', motherfuckin' bitch? What you doin' in my chair?' It took me maybe one second to dart under her meaty arm and race across the room."

"What was so special about the chair?"

Meg shook her head and laughed softly. "It had a tiny Spiderman figure pasted on the back. Lila had a thing for Spiderman."

"Did she bother you again?"

"No. I soon found out Lila called everyone a 'motherfuckin' bitch.' She paid no attention to me once I'd steered clear of that chair."

"Tell me the rest, Meg. It'll be easier all at once."

"There's not much else to say. After a while, I closed ranks right along with the others. Us against the world. We made conversation about legal technicalities and appeals. We complained of the tasteless food and the boredom. I sat on my butt—definitely not in Lila's chair—and played cards, read books, watched TV, or otherwise wiled away the hours. I missed my computer, but I did plan out puzzles and animations and antagonists for games in my head. When I was drawing characters or writing snips of dialogue, the others would notice and ask questions. Eventually, a lot of them knew abut *Athena*. I devised a paper version of the game because it entertained me and them."

"I'm not surprised you made friends, even there."

Meg looked thoughtful. "I tried. I listened to a lot of sad life stories. Most of them moved on before I did. Prostitutes didn't stay long, but they made repeat appearances. Dope pushers were transferred to the state pen after trial. One woman was in for shooting her boyfriend. She walked when the boyfriend dropped charges."

"I wish I could have cleared you out of there, sweetheart." Zack drew her head to his chest and gently finger-combed her hair.

She heard his heartbeat, steady and strong. He'd called her "sweetheart." Her internal helium balloon went right through the ceiling.

Pulling away from him, she rooted for a crumpled tissue under her pillow. She blew her nose. "I have to meet with my parole officer on Monday."

"So you're not going back because of Edward or the sequel?"

"Not directly. I am required to maintain a job. Since I've taken Edward's advance, I pretty much have to work for PenUltimate until I finish the storyline. If I don't go back, he could kick up trouble. Silverstein has reassured me that it wouldn't mean more jail time, but—"

"I'll put a muzzle on Edward if he says anything to hurt you." Zack felt light-headed with relief. So that was why she needed Edward. That was why she insisted on going back. Not because she still cared for the boss man. Not because she still felt some unreasonable emotional tie. Not because she didn't want to stay on the ranch.

"We're going to be all right, Meg." He took the beer off the bedside table where he'd left it. After wiping the condensation on his bare chest, he offered her the amber bottle.

"Good for troubles of the heart." He intentionally repeated the same phrase he'd used weeks before.

She looked at the bottle, then at him. The warmth in her eyes told him she was thinking of that night, of the first time he'd kissed her. She tipped the beer and took one dainty sip. He appropriated the bottle and set it aside. His gaze fastened on her moist lips.

He wanted to offer her something much more important and lasting than a beer. He wanted to show how sorry he was that he'd prejudged her. When Meg looked at him with those big trusting eyes, he had an inspiration. He knew the one thing that would please her most.

He paused a moment, waiting for an inner voice of protest, but he heard nothing. He could move forward now, in the direction Meg had led him. He'd redeem himself by allowing her to be his savior. "I've been thinking about your Red Hawk plan. Maybe it's not such a bad idea."

When a broad smile radiated across her face, he decided the plan really *was* good. He felt as if a hundred-pound weight had been lifted from his chest. Meg had done that. She'd relieved him of guilt.

"Every store I contacted wants to buy, Zack," she said with a renewal of her old enthusiasm. "If you decide to follow up, you'll do fine, I'm certain. Before you know it, you'll have the bills paid and the bankers satisfied."

He pursed his lips, pretending to consider. Truthfully, though, he was already convinced. "You have a knack for business I never suspected. How did you come up with this scheme?"

"Practicality," she chirped. Her smile had grown so wide, it threatened to take over her face. Her eyes smiled, too. "Like Edward always said, practicality is the key to—"

He lay a finger across her lips. "Don't talk about him." He heard the edge in his own voice, the jealousy. When he saw alarm in her eyes, he forced a lighter tone. "If you bring him up one more time, I'll have to kiss you."

"Edward," she breathed.

Zack grinned. "You really know how to tempt a guy." He pushed her to the mattress, holding her wrists on either side of her head, and kissed her until she whimpered. When he freed her hands, she made no attempt to escape. He stood to take off his jeans, watching Meg the whole time. Her tongue darted out to moisten her lips. She looked as hungry as he felt, and he groaned in anticipation. He left the jeans in a heap on the floor. He stood before her, as naked as Adam before Eve.

Meg took a slow survey and liked what she saw. Hard and firm and . . . ready. But she wasn't ready yet. Before he could reach for her, she slipped from the opposite side of the bed and did a striptease of her own. While he watched, she slithered out of the T-shirt and wiggled the panties off her hips. Smiling what she hoped was an erotic smile, she crawled back onto the bed. They met on hands and knees in the middle of the mattress. Their lips touched.

"Not good enough," he murmured into her mouth.

"Make it better," she urged. Before she knew what had happened, he'd flipped her over and positioned her under him. Nothing was between them now. Skin to skin felt exactly right.

"You're one beautiful lady," he whispered.

She purred. "You're one big, strong man." She blinked her eyes in an attempt to be flirtatious, a skill she was learning at a rapid rate. "And I'm not talking arm muscles here."

His chest vibrated with laughter as he nuzzled her neck. The heat of his breath tickled her skin.

"Good thing I still have some of those condoms that ruined my Elk Springs reputation," she said.

He reached to one side and grabbed his jeans. Three packets fell onto the bed. "I salvaged some from the first time around. Thought I'd bring them along, since I've turned into a Meg-caliber optimist."

She laughed. She was still laughing when he began kissing and nipping and licking his way down her neck. She managed a smile, even as he reached her breast.

By the time he finished with her navel and kept right on inching down, all she could do was moan. He was

slow and careful and deliciously devious, until he finally allowed her a mind-and body-pulsing climax.

"Now," he said, "we can try those condoms."

"Whoa, Tarzan. Jane's not that easy." And she
forced him to endure some of the same treatment
he'd given her. Equally slow, and twice as devious.
She breathed his scent, tasted the salt on his skin.
She enjoyed every move she made, almost as much
as he did.

By the time she'd finished tormenting him, both of
them were slick with sweat and frantic to finish what
they'd started. The bed creaked rhythmically. Meg's
whole body hurt with tension before she reached a
nirvana that would have ended in screams, had Zack
not thought of Robby at the last minute and covered
her mouth.

Seconds later, Zack climaxed. Meg held him, absorbing his thrusts and muffling his ecstasy. When
he was still, she absorbed his peace. She felt loved
as fully as a woman could possibly be loved.

He had ended on top of her, but he rolled both of
them over. With bodies still connected, she settled
on top of him as if they were truly one and could
remain so.

"Meg," he whispered. "God, Meg, that was good."

"Mmm," she said, afraid more words would spoil
their idyllic symmetry.

He held her until his breathing evened, until she
knew he was asleep. She didn't move. She didn't
ever want to move. She felt safe. Cherished. Glorious.
As if she'd truly entered the enchanted castle and
was living her dream.

Everything would be fairy-tale perfect, if she could
just stay with him forever.

But the magic would end on Sunday. And after
that, when she was able to return, she couldn't be
certain if the splendor would come back.

She lay with her head on his chest, listening. Outside, insects scraped a shrill tune. A horse nickered in the pasture. In the far distance, the river rushed along its relentless path.

Zack stirred and began to kiss her again.

Soon, she heard only the beat of their hearts.

Chapter Twenty-three

Zack banged the telephone receiver back onto his desk. It had been a long morning. After calling every number and extension in the Yellowstone Park Service, he still hadn't located Andrew. The ranger was "out of pocket." Al from the lab was on vacation. Even Callie didn't answer. No one he talked to knew anything about a chemical analysis on Elsa's remains.

A check on the dispatcher schedule for the last week had been easier. According to a secretary, Lydia was on duty the night the new cria was born. So she couldn't have been sneaking around Zack's barn. And Harry had really been in Wyoming all week, according to the fly shop that scheduled his guided fishing tours. Now all Zack had to do was investigate the *rest* of Elk Springs' population.

Swiveling in his squeaky chair, he glanced toward the window. Robby seemed fine this morning, although a little disappointed Hoover wasn't well enough to play. He was outside now, rambling through the pasture with Meg. As Zack watched, Meg leaned down to kiss the child on the top of the head. She was right for Robby, just as she was right for him. He felt warmed all over, recalling just how loving and tender she could be. The last thing Zack wanted was for her to go anywhere without him.

A feeling of urgency had propelled him to his desk

at first light and kept him there, making phone calls back to back while he thought and planned and worried. If he could find the llama killer before Sunday, Meg wouldn't have to leave alone. Zack would accompany her to the meeting with the parole officer. He'd have a talk with Edward and make damn sure the sonuvabitch listened carefully. Meg could do plenty enough work from Idaho to fulfill any obligation she might have. One way or another, Zack was determined to arrange things so she could return home with him.

If. If he could safeguard his ranch and Robby first, then he could go with her. And he *would* bring her back.

The sun was high now, shining on grass aglitter with the remnants of the rain shower that had fallen just before dawn. The entire world looked new and washed clean. But the view was deceptive.

Evil lurked.

Something was terribly wrong in Eden.

He *had* to have information. Otherwise, how could he fend off the unknown and unseen?

He stared at the phone. He'd left messages with at least a dozen voice mails, pleading for someone, anyone, to get hold of Andrew and tell him to call. When the phone did ring, he snatched it off the hook.

"Andrew?"

"No, it's Abe. With bad news."

"Am I supposed to be surprised?" Zack said. "*Good* news, now that would be surprising. Spit it out."

"There weren't any fingerprints on the note. The detective says the perp wore gloves."

Zack had expected as much. "What about the syringe?"

"No prints there either, except Robby's. I sent the contents to a lab in Boise. We might know something later today."

Everything was in a holding pattern. No clues, and somebody out there was hovering, waiting for an opening to commit the next crime. Maybe watching from a hiding place right this minute. *The innocent shall pay.* The words had left an indelible imprint on Zack's brain. "Anything else?" he asked.

"I found paperwork on the break-in at the vet's. Tranquilizers were missing. I haven't been able to get Doc Allen on the phone to find out the effects of the stolen drugs, just in case they turn out to be what's in the syringe."

Zack had been trying to reach the vet, too. He wanted to know if Doc had found anything unusual about Esmeralda's corpse. It bothered him that the fence cutting was the first enemy move that hadn't been made to appear an accident. Either the bad guy was getting cocky, or reckless. But not reckless enough to be caught. Even if the stolen tranquilizers were the same stuff used in Robby's injection, he doubted the thief had left more clues in the vet's office than they'd found on the ranch.

"I talked to Tobias earlier," Abe went on. "He still claims he knows nothing. Then I went out to see Jesse. He and Ellen were in the middle of a knock-down, drag-out. I overheard some of it while I was waiting at the door. Finally, Jesse answered the bell. Ellen stormed out the back. Looks like she quit him."

"I hope, for her sake, it's permanent," Zack said. He knew Abe hoped so, too. "Did you talk to Jesse? Did he have an alibi for last night?"

"Yeah. That's what started their argument, I think. He swears he was with a woman he picked up at the BadAss until 4 A.M. If she'll back him up, he's clean. But, Zack, I'm worried about Ellen. She's been acting strange."

"Leaving Jesse isn't strange. It's the first sensible thing she's done in years."

"I'd have to agree, but she must've seen my Bronco parked in front of their house. I would've thought she'd stay to talk to me, maybe ride to town with me. Instead, she took off in Jesse's new Jeep 4X4. She's never been much good with a stick shift, but she didn't kill the engine once. Jesse says she's been driving the Jeep around at night, sneaking back in the wee hours. Has to be the wee hours for him to be home from his carousing before she gets there."

Zack sat forward slowly. "She's been drinking?"

"Jesse says no, but she is taking a lot of pills. For depression, I guess. Since she got back from rehab, she's been more obsessed than ever with Mike and Sky's death. In the last couple of weeks, every time I've talked to her she's mentioned suicide. She seems to think it's what the Lord would want. I've told her that's crazy. She even agreed with me, and I thought she'd be all right, but now . . . If you should see her—"

Zack stood and went to the window. *Ellen.* She always seemed so meek and cowed, he hadn't considered . . . "What makes you think *I'*ll see her?"

"Just a hunch. You know better than anyone what she's gone through in the last year. She might want to talk it out."

What the Lord would want. What else might Ellen do in the name of the Lord? She'd never blamed Zack for Mike's death, as Jesse had, but maybe this wasn't about anger or revenge.

He stared through the window glass.

Never forget, Ellen had said weeks ago, when he'd seen her at the co-op meeting. *We must never forget Sky and my Mike.* He hadn't understood then, but now he thought he might. If so, God help them both. Ellen had said Sky would be comforted to have the llamas with her. Maybe Ellen had sent the animals to heaven by her own hand. The next step in the same progression would be to make an offering of Robby, too. Jesus. Not that. She wouldn't go that far. Would she?

Zack scanned the pasture. Meg was about twenty yards inside the far fence, bending down to examine something. He didn't see Robby at first, and that sent fear skittering down his spine. Then he saw the child, outside the fence, near the main road.

Ellen had truly loved both Mike and Sky. Her agony of self-blame, combined with too many mood-warping pills, might have distorted love into a dangerous, all-consuming monster that demanded more than she could give. The only way to redeem herself was to offer more. More than her life. More than her death. Sacrifice. The notes demanded a sacrifice. She wanted to give Sky and Mike what they had loved in life. And if that meant another creature had to die, so be it.

As he followed the tortuous logic Ellen might have embraced, he even saw the reason for the tranquilizers. She wouldn't want the animals to feel pain when she killed them. She would maintain some level of compassion, however twisted it might be. But was she capable of . . .

Zack focused on the road that passed in front of the ranch. A roostertail of mud grew larger and closer by the second. A vehicle was coming down the road, traveling fast.

"Zack, you there?" the sheriff asked.

The roostertail reached the top of the long drive to the ranch house. It made an abrupt, skidding turn, and Zack got a good look at the vehicle for the first time. "What color is Ellen's Jeep?"

"Red," Abe answered. "She'll be—"

"Christ almighty, it's Ellen. Ellen's the one!" Zack dropped the receiver. There was no outside door to the room, and going down the hall would take too long. He began tearing at the window latch.

His heart thumped wildly as the mud-spattered red vehicle came to a stop. Robby was right there, within spitting distance of the Jeep. Zack flung the window sash open as wide as it would go. The entire frame shook from the force. Knocking out the screen, he jumped through, onto the grass.

"Robby! Meg!" Wind blew in his face, throwing the words back at him. He ran for his truck, the fastest way to reach them.

The innocent shall pay. Oh, God.

"NOOOO!"

When Meg looked up and saw the red Jeep approaching, she was alarmed. Robby was on the other side of the fence, and the vehicle was coming fast. If it swerved, even slightly, he'd be in its path. Robby had never been around traffic. He didn't understand the danger He just stood there, watching it come.

"Robby!" The wind blew against Meg. He didn't seem to hear. She sprinted toward the boy with the blue forget-me-nots she'd been gathering clutched in one fist. Her skin grew clammy with fear.

The red Jeep slowed. Meg stopped running, thinking Robby was safe. The driver must have seen the boy and . . . She started jogging again, forget-me-nots fluttering from her hand. Robby was no longer in danger of being mowed down, but there were other dangers. Sabotage and syringes. Dead animals and ominous notes.

A woman smiled and waved out the open Jeep window. Robby returned the wave as if he knew her. Was it—Yes, it was Ellen, her skin the color of flour paste against the black turtleneck she wore. The clothing, a strange choice in the July heat, confirmed Ellen's eccentricity. Meg had guessed that much from yesterday's meeting. Strange, but not dangerous. Not a killer.

Meg slowed again, panting. Nevertheless, she couldn't let go of her anxiety, her feeling of impending disaster. Maybe it was the fixed expression on Ellen's face. Maybe it was something else. Something Ellen had said yesterday.

The woman must have beckoned, because Robby went right up to the Jeep's door. She tossed a small, shiny object—a quarter?—out the window. As Robby bent to retrieve it, something dark fluttered through the air. A blanket covered him completely.

Meg rocketed for the fence, screaming. With blood pounding in her throat, she scraped between two strands of wire, leaving bits of shirt and skin on the barbs.

Ellen had leaped out of the Jeep and was pushing a squirming, blanket-wrapped bundle onto the passenger side floorboard. Meg lunged for a black shirtsleeve. Ellen turned, her mouth contorted in a teeth-baring snarl. Something long and solid swept in Meg's direction. She dodged, but not soon enough. It whacked her on the side of the head. The impact knocked her to her knees.

The red door slammed shut. Wheels spun in the wet road, spraying mud everywhere.

Blinded by flying sludge, Meg staggered in the general direction of the bumper. She lunged for something to latch onto and missed, landing face-first in the mud. The back end of the Jeep fishtailed down the road, leaving a brown liquid wake streaming behind.

Meg lurched upright, her heart sinking along with her boots. "Robby," she whispered. She pivoted toward the house. "Help! Someone help!"

A voice shouted back to her. Zack. She didn't understand what he said, but it didn't matter. He was running across the yard toward his truck. Within seconds, he'd started the engine and was speeding toward her. He must have seen everything from his office window. He would know what to do. He'd get Robby back safely if anyone could.

Meg thought he would pass her by, but he screeched to a halt beside her.

"Get in!" he yelled.

Meg didn't have to be told twice. She tried to open the door, but it wouldn't budge. With a running-board boost, she nose-dived through the open window. She was still on her head when Zack shifted gears and rammed the accelerator to the floor.

"It's Ellen," Zack shouted over the lashing of mud and pebbles against metal. "I think she plans to kill him."

Meg scuttled her legs through the window and rolled to a sitting position. The engine whined, straining. She wiped mud from her face with a corner of her shirt and peered through the dirty windshield. *Why would Ellen* . . . But it didn't matter why. Meg only wanted Robby back.

"Where?" she yelled over the ear-splitting road noise. "Where is she taking him?"

"To the bridge." Up to that moment, Zack hadn't known where they were going. But if Ellen meant to kill herself—and, as Zack feared, take Robby with her—she'd do it from the bridge, above the falls where Mike and Sky had died.

The red Jeep made a turn down another rutted lane, gaining ground. Zack wheeled after them. Ellen's vehicle was much newer, equipped with a better engine. He'd never catch them in time, unless . . .

The innocent shall pay. Not if Zack could help it.

If he'd guessed right about the destination, there was a chance. He'd just passed a logging cut through the woods when he screeched to a stop, reversed, and bolted into the turn. The lane, no more than parallel wheel tracks, was a shortcut to the bridge. He knew he was gambling with Robby's life, but he had no choice. He'd never catch up any other way. The bottom of the truck crashed over rocks buried in grass, rattling teeth and metal. Zack hoped the truck's essential parts would hang on long enough to take him to Robby.

Gut-wrenching moments later, he came to where the shortcut intersected the road to town—right at the river. Ellen was already there, parked on the rickety one-car bridge. Zack hadn't lost them, but his tension increased when he saw the blanket-wrapped bundle Ellen was lugging through the Jeep door.

Zack hit the brakes with a force that locked his bald tires and sent the truck skidding sideways.

He left the engine running while he boiled out, towing Meg along with him. "Distract her," he told Meg as he ducked behind the truck door, out of Ellen's line of sight. "I'll circle around. If we're lucky, I can get close enough to grab Robby before she . . ."

Meg nodded, already moving past Zack to the front of the truck. During the chase, she'd puzzled it out. She knew what Ellen had in mind, and it twisted her stomach into knots. She should have guessed from Ellen's weird prophecy at the bus stop yesterday. *Destiny. Sacrifice.* This was what she meant.

But Meg wouldn't let it happen. She mustered all her skills from a long-ago Acting 101 class. If Ellen sensed Meg's panic, it might drive her over the edge—literally, taking Robby along with her. Only by remaining dispassionate could Meg hope to sway her.

"Ellen!" Meg called. She was relieved to find that the lump in her throat held back the hysteria, but not the name she shouted.

Face ruddy from wind and exertion, Ellen looked

up from the wiggling blanket-wrapped prisoner she held in her arms. She panned the area. "Where's Zack? He's supposed to be here." Her gaze locked on Meg and narrowed. "Why aren't you gone?"

"I missed the bus," Meg yelled over the roar of the seething current. She slipped and slid down the bank to the river's edge, so she was below the bridge, looking up into those strange dilated eyes. "Robby's scared, Ellen. Please don't hurt him. This isn't *his* destiny."

"Stay away!" With Robby in her arms, she clambered onto the first of five guardrails separating her from the river.

Meg's heart thumped in her chest. Blood pounded in her temples. Every muscle tensed. Trying to position herself closer, she stepped into the water. The breath-stopping cold made her flinch. The river ran swift and deep, muddy from last night's rain. A small tree washed past, not far from Meg's ankle-deep stance.

She stared above her, where Robby squirmed within the blanket folds, bound with what appeared to be a bungie cord. Tiny boots stuck out one end of the blanket. The boots scissored and kicked until one of them fell. It plunged twenty or so feet to the rain-swollen river and disappeared into the foam. On the bridge, Robby's small bare foot continued the struggle.

Ellen climbed another rail, awkwardly keeping Robby in front of her. "Zack is supposed to come with us," she shouted. "Sky wants *him*, too."

Meg's heart banged against her chest wall. Her stomach felt as if she'd swallowed a gravel pit. She didn't know what to do. Just then, she saw a figure glide between the two vehicles, headed for the far side of the Jeep. Zack. Only a little longer, and he would be close enough.

She forced herself to talk, though the words kept sticking in her throat. "That's right, Ellen. Wait for Zack. He'll be here soon. You shouldn't do this alone. Zack can help you. He *wants* to help you. You have to . . ." Meg kept the syllables rolling out of her mouth. Anything to distract. Anything to delay. If Ellen spotted Zack before he was within rescue range, she might take Robby right over the rail, assuming Zack would follow. Meg had to keep the woman's attention focused on her, giving Zack an opportunity for stealth.

Ellen's eyes were white-rimmed, her hair blowing dark and frenzied around her head. She looked like a maniacal avenging angel.

The rushing current thundered in Meg's ears. Her nostrils filled with scents of rainwater and river moss and damp soil. The smell of life. Of death. Either or both.

In the distance, a siren whined.

Ellen glanced over her shoulder. For a moment, Meg thought the woman had seen Zack, but she quickly looked toward Meg again.

"Abe is coming." With jerky, uncoordinated movements, Ellen climbed two more rails. "He'll stop me. I can't let him stop me. Sky wants Robby. Mike wants me."

Zack had had time to reach the front of the Jeep, Meg judged. He'd be there, waiting for the chance to sneak up and reclaim his son. Meg waved her arms. "Listen, Ellen. Sky doesn't want you to do this. Mike doesn't want it either. And it's not Robby's time."

"This is the only way," Ellen screamed. She swung a leg over the top rail and perched there, lifting Robby like an offering to the heavens. "It's the only way to cleanse our souls."

For a moment, Meg thought her heart had stopped. The scene in front of her blacked out. She blinked, and everything became vivid again. Horribly, chill-ingly vivid. Both Ellen and Robby perched on a sin-gle wood rail with nothing but twenty feet of air between them and the water.

Zack emerged from behind the Jeep. Ellen turned. She swayed as she saw him.

Cautiously, he inched forward. "We'll do this to-gether, Ellen. Give me Robby, and I'll help you."

Wild-eyed and shaking, she glanced in the direc-tion of the siren that wailed ever closer. A flash of red and blue lights showed through the trees.

"You're lying! You called Abe. He wants to stop me." She leaned forward, releasing the bundle in her arms. As Robby fell, his legs flailed beneath the blan-ket and tangled with Ellen. She joined him in a bi-zarre, airborne duet. Slowly, almost gracefully, they fell.

"No!" Meg screamed. A dark head surfaced, awash in the flow, not three feet from where she stood. A bit of blanket floated for a millisecond, then disappeared.

Without another thought, Meg took a deep breath and dove into the swiftly flowing river. Icy, opaque water closed over her head. The intense cold para-lyzed her muscles. She sank toward the bottom, un-able to fight the undertow. She tried to move, but no part of her responded. Even if she'd had air to breathe, she couldn't have expanded her lungs. It was over. The water dragged her down, and she was unable to fight.

This is it, she thought. *This is how death feels.* Her numbed brain knew only a vague regret.

From a distant part of the body that she no longer claimed as hers, she felt a twinge. A prickle.

Pain.

Her skin began to sting. The barbed wire cuts she'd inflicted on herself—it seemed like hours ago when she'd watched Robby being kidnapped—bit into her consciousness. The pain reminded her of why she was immersed in freezing water in the first place. Robby needed her. She wouldn't let him down.

I won't die. I can't die! She had to keep trying, keep hoping, keep moving. She spurred her arms and legs through the water until she was aware of pain in each and every cell.

Her lungs were about to burst. When she broke the surface, she gasped for air. Half-blinded by glare and murky water, she frantically groped with arms outstretched. The current swept her downstream, but it swept Robby, too. He had to be close.

Robby, where are you? She shouted the words in her head, cutting into the surrounding roar of swirl and torrent. She dove again, plunging toward the center of the river. Nothing. When she rose for another breath, she glanced around in panic. Still nothing. That's when she heard a voice. Over the deafening rush of the falls, a soft, calming whisper prevailed. Was this the haunting presence Zack had spoken of? Sky's voice? Desperate for guidance, Meg reached toward the sound.

Her fingers brushed something. The blanket. She groped the heavy folds, but Robby wasn't inside. She was about to dive again when small hands splashed to the surface.

Robby. She caught his shirt and jerked upward until his head was above water. He immediately began to gasp and cough. He clutched Meg, nearly dragging them both under. Meg swam. Using her free arm and both feet, beneath the surface most of the time, she angled for shore.

He body was so cold, she couldn't feel pain any longer. She couldn't feel herself move. A steadily increasing roar and vibration charged her with fear. They were near the falls. Too near. Thrusting Robby high enough to inhale another lungful of air, she glanced toward land. It didn't seem any closer.

White froth and dark water formed a barrier she somehow had to cross. If she wanted to live. If she wanted Robby to live.

Meg sucked in a breath. She kicked harder.

From the bridge, Zack had seen Meg dive into the river. The whitewater devoured her, as it had already consumed Robby. Zack vaulted to the top of the railing. Fifteen yards or more downstream, a head bobbed. A dark head. Robby or Ellen, he couldn't tell which. The swift current was carrying them away. No swimmer could possibly overtake the ten-mile-an-hour current. Not Zack, not anyone.

His only chance was to reach them by land, before they were swept over the falls.

He leaped back onto the bridge. In passing, he glanced inside the Jeep. No keys in the ignition. But his truck was still running, turned sideways in the road, facing downstream. He raced toward it. He didn't have a plan at first, other than using the truck to catch up.

The moment he jumped behind the wheel and glimpsed the rope on the floorboard, he knew what he would do. He mashed the accelerator as far as it would go and ploughed the battered truck into the brush alongside the river. Bent saplings scraped the undercarriage. Wheels jolted over fallen timber. The force of the collisions sent Zack airborne, but he held onto the steering wheel and kept the pedal on the floor, always watching the river, always looking for a head, a hand, a face.

He almost flew into the windshield as the truck plunged through a ravine. As soon as he regained his seat and could focus, he searched the foaming water again. Debris, whitewater, jagged rocks. No

Meg. No Robby. A horrifying déjà vu invaded his mind and threatened to break him apart, but he kept driving, skidding around a bend to follow the river's path. He wouldn't give up. He wouldn't allow this river to take anyone else he loved.

Where were they? He had to find them soon, or . . .

A speck of gold glimmered amongst the churning rapids. Meg. Meg's gold hair caught the light. Once Zack knew where to look, he saw Robby's dark head beside her. The river tossed them at will. Meg was working toward shore, Robby in tow, but they would never make it in time.

They were almost to the falls. And before they went over, they'd almost certainly crash into one of the huge boulders in their path. The impact alone would pulverize them. Zack sprang out of the truck, rope in hand. He had a chance for one throw. He swung the lariat overhead and pitched the looped end out over the water.

He missed.

The rope was slightly ahead and to one side of Meg. She could still reach it, if she wasn't too cold and exhausted to maneuver in the right direction.

He screamed at her, though the roar of the waterfall stole his words away. *Don't let it happen*, he prayed. *Don't let them die.* He willed her to turn her head, to change direction, just a few inches to the left.

As if she'd heard him speak, her feet scissored, breaking the surface. She made a slight adjustment, ever so slight. Enough, he thought. She seemed to see the rope. Her free arm lashed out. And then both she and Robby sank out of sight.

Had she grasped the rope? Or were her fingers too numb to grip? Did he dare pull, or should he give her more time?

But there was no time.

As the river propelled them toward a boulder and

the falls, Zack felt weight at the end of the rope. He leaned back, the hemp tearing skin from his palms. The force of the water was more than he could overcome. But if he could just hang on, the current would work for him, arcing them toward the downstream bank. He strained so hard, he couldn't breathe. He closed his eyes and pulled for his life. For their lives. He wanted them more than Death did. The river had to let them go.

He pulled with every ounce of strength he possessed. His lungs were exploding for lack of oxygen. Sweat ran down his forehead and stung his eyes. Slowly, he brought them back. Back to him. Back to life. His precious burden swung from the main current into the slower water near shore. He could see them now. Free of foam and whitewater fury, Meg and Robby still clung to the rope.

Zack dared to fill his lungs again. Gulping air as he ran downstream, he splashed in the shallows until he reached them. He took Meg's hand and grabbed Robby by the shirt. When he had both of them on dry land, he enfolded them, wet and cold and soggy in his arms. They were coughing and hacking and frozen. But alive. Alive!

A muffled wail arose from the river. Disembodied. Heart-wrenching. Meg must have heard it, too, because she pushed away from Zack's chest and looked toward the sound. Both of them went still. After a few jolting heartbeats, her eyes met his, and he saw that she knew. Ellen had gone over the falls. If Zack had been ten seconds later, Meg and Robby would be . . .

"No!" he bellowed into the wind. He hauled the two soggy survivors a few feet farther from the bank.

He held them again, defying anyone or anything that would take them away. Meg's teeth chattered and her whole body was one big shiver. She had to be exhausted. Robby was sandwiched between them, partially shielded from the wind, wheezing and coughing water out of his lungs.

They're safe. Thank God, they're safe was the repeating rhythm in Zack's brain. But unless he did something more, they were going to freeze to death. He urged them to the truck and lifted them inside the cab, out of the wind. He joined them inside after fetching a quilt from behind the seat. Painstakingly, he draped it around Meg and Robby's shoulders.

The boy sat in her lap, arms glued to her neck as if he were still in the water and she were his only lifeline. Zack wanted to hang onto her, too. He wanted to hang onto both of them, now and forever.

Instead, he helped Meg pull off the boy's wet clothes. He was rubbing Robby all over when Abe arrived, panting after a charge through the woods. For a second, Zack wondered why he was there. But then he knew. After the abrupt end of their phone call, Abe must have headed for the ranch. The bridge was on his way.

Abe peered into the open window at the three of them, assessing damages. He looked beyond them, around them. "Where's Ellen?"

Zack didn't want to say, but there was nothing else to do. He pointed to the falls. Abe plodded to the water's edge and stood there, looking into the spray. Zack shuddered. He might have been standing shoulder to shoulder with Abe, knowing there was no hope whatsoever, no hope at all. He'd been there once before.

He wrapped his arms around Robby and Meg, offering the heat of his body, showing them his love. Meg was no longer shivering. When she looked at him, her eyes held all the clover-sweet promise of an Idaho spring.

Yes, she belonged with them. Why had he ever doubted that?

Robby took one of his arms from Meg's neck and fastened it around his father.

Zack hugged him. "It's okay now, son. You don't have to be scared."

"I'm not scared." Linking the three of them, Robby drew their heads together. "I saw Mama in the water." His blue-green eyes glanced from Meg to Zack. His voice was clear and sure, softened by the baby lisp. "She said not to worry, 'cause she sent Meg to help us."

And Zack wondered, just for a moment, if it were true.

Chapter Twenty-four

Yellowstone National Park
Two months later

Out of breath from the climb to Bliss Pass, Meg turned to look back at Slough Creek winding through an autumn valley gilded in aspen. The view would have taken her breath away if the altitude hadn't already done the job. Zack, scouting ahead as usual, had stopped at the high point. Since she wasn't looking where she was going, she ran right into him.

He didn't seem to mind. He turned, smiling. "I was waiting for you to do that."

"Why?" Meg panted.

"So I could do this." He swept her into his arms and kissed the tiny remainder of her breath into nonexistence.

Being with him, here, now, felt exactly right. They had made so many treks between Elk Springs and Salt Lake in the past several weeks, Meg was dizzy thinking about it. She was glad all the traveling was finally over.

Zack had accompanied her everywhere, except the day she'd gone to PenUltimate. She'd insisted Zack let her meet Edward alone, since she wanted to act as negotiator instead of referee. The powwow had gone well. PenUltimate's chief executive had been more than willing to compromise.

Good old Edward. Anything to keep the game rolling and the bottom line on the rise. When she refused to work for him directly, he pleaded with her to continue the freelancing. In fact, he wanted her to sign on for another sequel. She said she'd keep him in mind. They both knew she'd receive a considerable chunk of money from *Athena* soon. After that, she could start her own development company, if she so chose.

She'd met with the parole board. She and Zack had attended several reviews before she obtained permission to work in Idaho with only periodic check-ins. Since the district attorney was bringing charges against Dave for a multitude of trust violations, Meg's sentence would soon be reconsidered, and then the long nightmare would be over for good.

Her last act in Salt Lake had been to call her mother. The conversation hadn't gone well, but Zack had been there when it was over. "Don't let her drag you down, Meg," he said. "If she won't see you, it's her loss, not yours."

And for the first time in her life, Meg believed that was true.

Upon their return, Win had insisted Meg and Zack needed a "spirit stretch." She'd volunteered to take care of her grandson so they could be alone.

Robby had adjusted nicely to kindergarten. He'd made friends. He'd joined a soccer team. He never climbed anything unusual. There was no need to worry about him while they were gone.

And so, they had come here. On the way, they'd stopped for a long-promised barbecue at Andrew and Callie's house, where Meg was welcomed as one of the clan.

Now, deep in Yellowstone's backcountry, she

shared the harmony with nature that came so easily to Zack. Her spirit stretched beyond normal limits. Beyond time.

They left the trail holding hands. Far, far below, Zack pointed out the campground where they had once shared a one-man tent. He took off his backpack and searched inside until he produced a small green bottle. "Champagne," he said, holding it up to sparkle in the sun. "We're going to celebrate." He dug deeper and, with a flourish, produced one crumpled red rose. "For you, Meg."

She held the blossom to her nose and inhaled the sweetness while Zack searched further into the bottomless pack. This time, he came up with two tin cups. He popped the champagne cork and poured. Bubbles rose over the rims.

Drink in hand, Meg waited. So much good had happened lately, she couldn't be certain what Zack meant to celebrate. They hadn't yet broached the subject of their future together beyond the fact that, for now, Meg would do her computer work from the ranch. In her spare time, she'd continue to mastermind Red Hawk.

Of course, she hoped for more. She wanted the whole enchanted castle, but life wasn't a fairy tale, after all.

"You first," Zack urged. "Make a toast."

"To Tobias and Win," she said.

They each took a liberal swallow in honor of the happy couple. Win and Tobias were looking forward to their November wedding almost as much as to the opening of their new garage, *Elk Springs Lube It or Lose It*, conveniently located next door to the Bad-Ass Café.

With bubbles going straight to her brain, Meg leaned forward and demanded a kiss. Zack tried to draw back after a light joining of lips, but Meg wouldn't let him. The kiss deepened. She licked champagne from his mouth.

Zack finally managed to extricate himself. He steadied the cup sloshing in her hand. "We aren't finished with the appetizer yet."

Meg sighed. If Zack wouldn't kiss her to paradise, maybe she could at least find out the real reason for this celebration. "It's your turn. Toast away."

He nodded but remained silent, jaw muscles working. He seemed to be thinking about what to say. Or how to say it.

Meg gulped champagne. The bubbles made her sneeze. "Better hurry, Zack. If you wait too long, I'll drink it all, and you'll have to fetch another bottle."

He smiled. His tin cup glowed as he lifted it. "To Meg Delaney, who's changed my life."

It was true, she admitted to herself. Everything *had* changed because of her. She wondered now if what she'd done was entirely good. "Red Hawk will make you rich," she said with diminished enthusiasm. Would he care more for his bank account than for her?

Zack must have seen her expression and guessed what she was thinking. "I know what's important. You. Robby. Our time together."

Her whole body warmed with pleasure. "It's been good, Zack. The best."

He reached down for the red rose that had fallen into the grass between them. He tickled the soft, slightly crumpled petals across her lips. "I love you."

She nearly dropped her cup. "Love?"

"Yes," he announced solemnly. "I do."

She held her breath for a moment, then let her joy burst forth. "Oh, Zack, I want to be perfect for you. I'm going to try really hard to be—"

He lifted her chin and looked into her eyes with a mix of tenderness and passion. "You don't have to be anyone but yourself. It's the not-quite-perfect Meg

that I love." He took her hand and kissed the under-
side where palm met wrist. "It's the not-quite-perfect
Meg I want to marry."

"Really?" Meg wondered if she'd heard right. She
wanted nothing more than to live with him forever,
but she'd thought it would take years to convince him.

"I dare you to take me on full time." His solemnity
became a grin. "I promise I'll be a challenge."

"Yes!" She threw herself into his arms. "Definitely
yes." Champagne went flying and showered them
with tiny bubbles, but neither cared.

This time they didn't stop with kisses.

A long while later, they lay sated on the grass. Meg
turned her face to the autumn sun. She felt peaceful,
happier than she'd ever been. The wind blew gently,
whispering secrets to the trees on the mountainside.

She kissed the fangs on Zack's bear T-shirt. Half-
asleep, he mumbled something incoherent and didn't
move. She sat, drew up her legs, and rested her chin
on her knees, as she looked out over the wild beauty
of Yellowstone's backcountry. Far, far below, Slough
Creek made lazy turns through its valley. Sunlight
bathed the aspens, turned gold by crisp autumn
nights. The whole world shone like a vast treasure.

If this was a dream, Meg never wanted to wake up.

And then she felt something. She looked behind
her, hand raised to swat the bug she expected to find
attacking her bottom.

It wasn't a bug. It was a pinch. She caught sight
of Zack's retreating hand and knew what he'd been
up to. Even though his eyes were closed, his bad-
boy smile gave him away.

She leaped on him and pinched him back. Which
led to laughter, and tickling, and then to touching of
a more sensual variety.

He was real enough, Meg decided.

Much better than a dream.

Signet Onyx   (0-451-)

The compelling romance of lost love and redemption

❑ **TWELVE DAYS** *Teresa Hill*   201450 / $5.99

*In a season of hope, she discovered the greatest gift of all....*As snow falls
on the picture-perfect town of Baxter, Ohio, Rachel McRae longs
for a time when Christmases were full of joy. With her husband
preparing to say good-bye forever, Rachel must discover the
courage to forgive the past and embrace the future, and to trust in
the most precious gift of all.

❑ **THE PASSAGE** *Alex Lawrence*   409442 / $5.99

*A beautiful adventure of the heart....*For David Thomas, a white-water
rafting trip was the perfect antidote to his troubled marriage. For
Sierra Stone, owner of the Elkhorn Lodge and wilderness guide,
David is just another guest. But when disaster strikes, Sierra and
David are forced to rely on each other for survival, and they soon
discover that the only way to live is to risk losing it all.

❑ **THE PERFECT WIFE** *Jane Goodger*   20130-2 / $5.99

*It takes a perfect love to break an imperfect heart....*In a world where
beauty defines society, the perfect wife has devised the perfect
revenge: become a jewel among her peers, draw her errant husband back to her arms—and break his heart. Yet nothing is as
simple as it seems....

Prices slightly higher in Canada

Payable by Visa, MC or AMEX only ($10.00 min.), No cash, checks or COD.
Shipping & handling: US/Can. $2.75 for one book, $1.00 for each add'l book; Int'l
$5.00 for one book, $1.00 for each add'l. Call (800) 788-6262 or (201) 933-
9292, fax (201) 896-8569 or mail your orders to:

Penguin Putnam Inc. P.O. Box 12289, Dept. B Newark, NJ 07101-5289 <small>Please allow 4-6 weeks for delivery.</small> <small>Foreign and Canadian delivery 6-8 weeks.</small>	Bill my: ❑ Visa ❑ MasterCard ❑ Amex_____(expires) Card# _____ Signature _____

Bill to:

Name _____

Address _____ City _____

State/ZIP _____ Daytime Phone # _____

Ship to:

Name _____ Book Total $_____

Address _____ Applicable Sales Tax $_____

City _____ Postage & Handling $_____

State/ZIP _____ Total Amount Due $_____

This offer subject to change without notice.   Ad # D112 (11/00)

ONYX

New York Times bestselling author

Heather Graham

"Graham knows what readers want."—*Publishers Weekly*

☐ **Dying to Have Her**   0-451-40988-4/$6.99
☐ **Long, Lean, and Lethal**   0-451-40915-9/$6.99
☐ **Drop Dead Gorgeous**   0-451-40846-2/$6.99
☐ **Tall, Dark, and Deadly**   0-451-40847-0/$6.99

*Heather Graham's acclaimed Civil War saga has
captured readers' hearts with an epic family drama
as bold and passionate as America itself.*

"Breathtaking...hurrah for Ms. Graham for bringing many
fascinating historical events to life."—*Romantic Times*

☐ **Captive**   0-451-40687-7/$6.99
☐ **Rebel**   0-451-40689-3/$6.99
☐ **Surrender**   0-451-40690-7/$6.99
☐ **Glory**   0-451-40848-9/$6.99
☐ **Triumph**   0-451-40849-7/$6.99

Prices slightly higher in Canada

Payable by Visa, MC or AMEX only ($10.00 min.), No cash, checks or COD.
Shipping & handling: US/Can. $2.75 for one book, $1.00 for each add'l book; Int'l
$5.00 for one book, $1.00 for each add'l. Call (800) 788-6262 or (201) 933-
9292, fax (201) 896-8569 or mail your orders to:

Penguin Putnam Inc.	Bill my: ☐ Visa ☐ MasterCard ☐ Amex_____(expires)
P.O. Box 12289, Dept. B	Card# _____
Newark, NJ 07101-5289	
Please allow 4-6 weeks for delivery.	
Foreign and Canadian delivery 6-8 weeks.	Signature _____

Bill to:

Name _____

Address_____ City _____

State/ZIP _____ Daytime Phone # _____

Ship to:

Name _____ Book Total $_____

Address _____ Applicable Sales Tax $_____

City _____ Postage & Handling $_____

State/ZIP _____ Total Amount Due $_____

This offer subject to change without notice.   Ad # GrahamLst (9/00)

Ⓢ SIGNET   (0451)

Family drama and intrigue from
New York Times bestselling author

EILEEN GOUDGE

"Double-dipped passion...in a glamorous, cut-throat world...
satisfying...irresistible."—*San Francisco Chronicle*

"Love and deceit in a tainted world of glamour and money...
will find a devoted audience!"—*Chicago Sun-Times*

☐ BLESSING IN DISGUISE   (184041 / $7.50)

☐ GARDEN OF LIES   (162919 / $7.99)

☐ ONE LAST DANCE   (199480 / $7.50)

☐ SUCH DEVOTED SISTERS   (173376 / $7.50)

☐ THORNS OF TRUTH   (185277 / $7.50)

☐ TRAIL OF SECRETS   (187741 / $7.50)

Prices slightly higher in Canada

Payable by Visa, MC or AMEX only ($10.00 min.), No cash, checks or COD.
Shipping & handling: US/Can. $2.75 for one book, $1.00 for each add'l book;
Int'l $5.00 for one book, $1.00 for each add'l. Call (800) 788-6262
or (201) 933-9292, fax (201) 896-8569 or mail your orders to:

Penguin Putnam Inc.   Bill my: ☐ Visa ☐ MasterCard ☐ Amex_____(expires)
P.O. Box 12289, Dept. B
Newark, NJ 07101-5289   Card# _____
Please allow 4-6 weeks for delivery.
Foreign and Canadian delivery 6-8 weeks.   Signature _____

Bill to:
Name _____
Address_____   City _____
State/ZIP _____   Daytime Phone # _____
Ship to:
Name_____   Book Total $ _____
Address _____   Applicable Sales Tax $_____
City _____   Postage & Handling $_____
State/ZIP _____   Total Amount Due $_____
This offer subject to change without notice.   Ad # N121 (11/00)

ONYX (0-451)

"*Lovelace has made a name for herself delivering tightly drawn, exciting tales of romantic suspense.*"—Romantic Times

"*Fascinating, behind-the-scenes details...and the serious consequences of falling into forbidden relationships.*"—Publishers Weekly

MERLINE LOVELACE

☐ CALL OF DUTY — 40673-7 / $6.99

☐ DARK SIDE OF DAWN — 40966-3 / $5.99

☐ DUTY AND DISHONOR — 40672-9 / $5.99

☐ RIVER RISING — 40850-0 / $5.99

Prices slightly higher in Canada

Payable by Visa, MC or AMEX only ($10.00 min.), No cash, checks or COD. Shipping & handling: US/Can. $2.75 for one book, $1.00 for each add'l book; Int'l $5.00 for one book, $1.00 for each add'l. Call (800) 788-6262 or (201) 933-9292, fax (201) 896-8569 or mail your orders to:

Penguin Putnam Inc.
P.O. Box 12289, Dept. B
Newark, NJ 07101-5289
Please allow 4-6 weeks for delivery.
Foreign and Canadian delivery 6-8 weeks.

Bill my: ☐ Visa ☐ MasterCard ☐ Amex_____(expires)
Card# _____
Signature _____

Bill to:
Name _____
Address_____ City _____
State/ZIP _____ Daytime Phone # _____

Ship to:
Name_____ Book Total $ _____
Address _____ Applicable Sales Tax $ ___
City _____ Postage & Handling $ ____
State/ZIP _____ Total Amount Due $ _____

This offer subject to change without notice. Ad # N149 (10/00)